D1334780

This omnibus edition first published in Great Britain in 2008
by Orion Children's Books
a division of the Orion Publishing Group Ltd
Orion House
5 Upper St Martin's Lane
London WC2H 9EA
An Hachette Livre UK Company

3 5 7 9 10 8 6 4 2

Originally published as three separate volumes:
Shadow of the Minotaur
First published in Great Britain 2000
Vampyr Legion
First published in Great Britain 2000
Warriors of the Raven
First published in Great Britain 2001
All by Orion Children's Books

A catalogue record for this is available
from the British Library

The Orion Publishing Group's policy is to use papers that are natural,
renewable and recyclable products and made from wood grown is
sustainable forests. The logging and manufacturing processses are expected
to conform to the environmental regulations of the country of origin.

ISBN 978 1 84255 624 5

Printed in Great Britain by Clays Ltd, St Ives plc.

www.orionbooks.co.uk

CONTENTS

SHADOW OF THE MINOTAUR

Like flies to wanton boys are we to the gods. Aeschylus

What fools we are to live in a generation in which war is a computer game for our children. Tony Benn, MP.

BOOK ONE

The Book of Phoenix

1

The first of the beast's roars almost tore the flesh from his bones. The second, a nerve-splitting bellow that crashed inside his brain, very nearly made him give in before he'd even begun his challenge. He glanced back at the hatch in the door through which he'd just walked and saw the reassuring smile of the dark-eyed girl on the other side. Mustering his own thin smile, he knelt down and picked up the things he'd dropped, a sword with a finely-wrought handle and a ball of strong, thick string.

'You can do this,' he told himself. 'You really can do this.'

But he hadn't convinced his body he could do it. His first attempt at tying the string to the door failed. He was so nervous his fingers just wouldn't work. It was like wearing mittens and trying to knot raw sausages. Taking a deep, shuddering breath he finally managed to pass the string through the hatch and secure it to one of the little bars in the opening. Weighing the sword uncertainly in his hand and letting the string play out behind him, he took his first faltering steps down the dark passageway. The blackness clung to him, trying to crawl inside his skin. The maze of tunnels was everything he'd been expecting – and more. They had the mystery of night, the terror of loneliness. They lay deep beneath the earth, where the sun never shone and the fresh wind never blew, and the silence there was heavy. The air was clogged with a choking animal musk. The walls of the tunnel by the entrance were smooth and regular, built from huge blocks of stone. But as he penetrated deeper into the gloom, he noticed a change. The walls were worn and they were slippery with something thick and slimy. Blood maybe. He flinched then walked on, his feet thudding dully in the cold, still air. Those echoing footsteps shook the close, uncomfortable blackness that clutched at him like a hand. No more than fifty paces from the door the tunnel branched in half a dozen different directions.

He moved forward, unrolling the ball of thread as he went, and stopped. He was still considering his options when he heard the beast again. This time the sound was a low, throaty growl. It was closer, and moving purposefully towards him.

'It's stalking me.'

In the darkness he stumbled and reached out to steady himself. The moment his hand came into contact with the cold stone surface, he recoiled in horror. It was blood all right. There was no mistaking its greasy slide. The walls were slippery with the stuff. The stone floor too. That wasn't all; there were splintered bones, matted hair, gobbets of torn flesh. The tunnels were a slaughterhouse.

'Ugh!'

He immediately wished he hadn't given in so readily to his feeling of disgust. His voice resounded loudly through the tunnels, inviting the beast to attack.

'Now it knows,' he murmured. 'It knows where I am.'

As if to confirm the fact, the beast bellowed through the passageways, mad with rage and hunger. This time the noise was so loud and so shattering that everything around him seemed on the verge of coming apart. The dust began to fall in fine spirals from the ceiling. It was out there in the darkness, snorting and panting, preparing to charge.

'What are you waiting for? Why don't you just do it?'

His breath was coming in troubled gasps. He gripped the sword tightly and edged forward. That's when he noticed a change in the lighting of the tunnel. A shaft of hazy light slanted onto him from above. He looked up and saw a face gazing down at him, the sympathetic face of the girl who had handed him the sword and the ball of string.

'The beast is coming,' she said.

'I know.'

He felt the urge to crouch down, his arms wrapped round himself in a feeble attempt at protection. Now the blackness had a voice.

'Keep down,' it was saying. 'Be small, boy.'

He needed little encouragement. He would have crawled inside himself if that was possible.

But forward he went. And still he played out the thread, marking his route back to the door. Whatever else, he knew he had to hold on to the ball of string. It was his lifeline.

'Where are you?' he whispered under his breath, but there was no answer. The beast wasn't about to give itself away that easily.

Several minutes passed and in that time the beast didn't so much as take a heavy breath. It knew its game, and the game was cat and mouse.

He passed on glancing first ahead, then behind, unsure from which direction the onslaught would come. And the deeper he went into the tunnels the more confused he became. The blackness was tickling his skin, teasing him. Or was that just fear? Where was he? Had he started his approach from the left or the right? Was he moving towards the entrance or away from it? Every one of the passages had the same stone construction and every one of them was worn. Perhaps by the beast, rubbing its horns, or its brawny shoulders against the slippery walls. On he went, bits of bone occasionally crunching under his feet. Once he even kicked a skull, sending it rolling ahead of him. He imagined the bleached, gaping grin and the eye sockets looking up at him, staring their darkness into his soul and sending a rush of fright down his spine.

'Come on,' he hissed. 'Show yourself, for goodness' sake.'

But the sound just hung in the heavy black void, then died away. Savage and untamed as it was, the beast was no dumb animal. It was part-human, and its thinking half was proving both wily and calculating.

It was a dangerous thing, this monster that thought.

'Where are you?'

Leaving the stinking closeness of one of the smaller tunnels, he found himself at a junction in the maze. Then, as he looked around, his heart lurched. He had just tripped over the thread that marked his own path. The string lay criss-crossed over itself.

'I'm going round in circles,' he said in dismay, and his voice rebounded in the chill tunnels. He peered into each of the passageways that led off from the junction. Ignoring the one where the thread lay accusingly on the floor, he made his way down a second tunnel. This one sloped gradually downward.

It was getting colder and the stone floor was oily with puddles of foul water. Dimly shining globs of something unspeakable floated on their dull surfaces. Touching the walls earlier had turned his stomach. He had no intention of making the same mistake with the floor.

Something stirred. A rat? He had never dreamed that he would ever wish for a rat, but just then he would have taken a hundred of the things, rather than the lumbering form waiting for him in the darkness. Hooves scraped on the floor. The sound was made by something big and powerful. This was no rat.

Then he heard the breathing. Slow and steady, calculated and unhurried, a predator's breathing. It had hunted before, yes, and killed too. The thought made his legs weak and rubbery. He turned a corner and found himself at yet another junction, from which more passageways spread like the spokes of a wheel.

'This could go on forever.'

Perhaps the beast shared his feeling that the pursuit had gone on long enough, because it chose that moment to make its move. There was a scraping sound in the gloom, the loudest yet.

He spun round. Framed in the half-light of one opening, the beast was pawing the ground.

'I'm not scared.'

It wasn't true. What's more, the beast knew. His quavering voice settled on the air, painting a picture of his mounting fear. He was clutching the sword's hilt the way a drowning man clings to a piece of driftwood. For comfort. For survival. And, for the first time, he felt its weight. It made his arm shake. His strength was draining away. He tried to grip the hilt with both hands, steadying his weapon.

'Come on then, what are you waiting for?'

But still the beast stood in the archway, pawing at the floor. It was bigger than a man. It stood almost three metres tall and was massively built with slabs of muscle on its chest and shoulders. Below the waist it was bull-like. It had a swinging tail and mud-splattered hooves. Or was it mud? Above the waist it was a man except, that is, for the head. And what a head! The muzzle was huge and when it opened it revealed the sharp, curved teeth, not of a bull but of a big cat. They were the fangs of a lion or tiger, made for ripping flesh. Its eyes were yellow and blazed unflinchingly through the murk. Then there were the great horns, glinting and sharp, curving from its monstrous brow. Thick and muscular as the neck was, it seemed barely able to support such a fearsome head, and strained visibly under the impossible weight.

'Oh my—'

The beast stepped out from the tunnel, and the boy actually took a few steps back. It was as if his soul had crept out of his body and was tugging at him, begging him to get away. In the sparse light shed from the gratings in the ceiling, the beast looked even more hideous. There was the sweat for a start, standing out in gleaming beads on that enormous neck and shoulders.

But that wasn't all. The creature was smeared from head to foot with filth and dried blood. It was every inch a killer. The beast began to stamp forward, its hooves clashing on the stone floor. It raised its head, the horns scraping on the ceiling, and gave a bellow that seemed to crush the air.

'I can't do this . . .'

He fell back, scrambling over obstacles on the floor, and fled. That's when he realized he'd dropped the ball of string. His lifeline had gone.

'Oh no!'

The beast was charging head down.

Got to get out of here!

In his mind's eye, he could see himself impaled on the points of those evil-looking horns, his legs pedalling feebly in the air, his head snapped back, his eyes growing pale and lifeless.

Suddenly, he was running for his life, skidding on the slimy floor.

'Help me!'

He saw the startled brown eyes of the girl above the grating.

'Don't run!' she cried. 'Fight. You must fight.'

He was almost dying of shame. This wasn't supposed to happen. He wasn't meant to lose and there weren't meant to be witnesses to his defeat.

'Fight,' she repeated. 'It's the way of things.'

The way of things. That's right, he was meant to stand and fight. It was in his nature as a hero. But he couldn't. Not against *that.*

'Please,' he begged, turning his face away from the girl in shame, 'somebody help me.'

The beast was careering through the tunnels, crashing, bellowing thundering through the maze. Its charge was hot, furious, unstoppable. It was almost on him.

Get me out of here!

'That's it,' he cried, throwing down his sword, 'I've had enough. Game over!'

2

Ripping off the mask and gloves, Phoenix bent double gulping down air like it had been rationed. The dank half-light of the tunnels was replaced by the welcome glow from an Anglepoise lamp in his father's study. He glanced at the score bracelet on his wrist. It registered total defeat: **000000**. For a few moments everything was spinning, the claws of the game digging into the flesh of the here and now. Then his surroundings became reassuringly familiar.

He was out.

*It **was** a game!*

'Well?' his dad asked, 'What do you think?'

'Mind-blowing,' Phoenix panted. 'It was all so real. It was like another world. I mean, I *was* Theseus. I went into the palace of the tyrant-king Minos. I could actually touch the stone columns, feel the heat of the braziers, smell the incense.'

He knew he was gushing, babbling like a little kid, but he didn't care. 'The king's daughter Ariadne helped me and she wasn't just an image on a screen. She was a real girl. Then I actually came face to face with the Minotaur. It was really happening. I believed it.' He shivered. 'Still do.'

'Oh, I could tell how convincing it was,' said Dad, enjoying the mixture of excitement and fear in his son's voice. 'You were screaming your silly head off by the end. I bet your mother thought I was killing you in here.'

Phoenix blushed then, beginning to control his breathing at last, he picked up the mask and gloves and traced the attached wires back to the computer where images of the labyrinth were still flashing away on the screen.

'It really was just a game?'

Dad pushed his seat back and gave a superior smile.

'That's all. Just a very sophisticated piece of software, hooked up to an even more sophisticated piece of hardware.'

Scared as he had been, Phoenix didn't want it to be a game. He wanted it to be real. Real and vibrant as the old legends had always seemed to him. He fingered the soft texture of the amazing gloves and mask that had created the illusion. 'And you get to play with all this great stuff for a living?'

'I certainly do. And there's a lot more to come. To quote my boss, Mr Glen Reede: *This is only stage one in the development of the ultimate game.*'

Phoenix stared at the screen and the figure of the Minotaur. Is that what he'd been afraid of? That ridiculous cartoon-strip monster blinking on the screen.

'Maybe now you'll quit complaining about moving to Brownleigh.'

That was asking a bit much. When Dad gave up his job at Compu-soft and accepted the lucrative offer from Magna-com, he'd fulfilled a lifelong dream. Only it was *his* lifelong dream. Phoenix and his mother had hated moving out of London, away from family and friends, especially when it meant re-settling in a one-eyed backwater halfway between Dullsville and Nowhere. Life's the game, thought Phoenix, a boring game of patience.

'We could have stayed in London,' Phoenix argued. 'After all, you're working from home. What was wrong with the house we had?'

'Where do you want to start?' Dad asked. 'The noise, the pollution, the rat race, the crime.'

Phoenix shook his head. The city had got Dad down, but he could keep his peace and quiet.

Brownleigh was a dump. No cinema, no sports centre, no railway station. There was nothing at all to do, and when it came to escaping the boredom, the buses to the nearest big town stopped at 10 o'clock. Phoenix was still trying to work out what people did round here. Maybe they took a chair out onto the pavement so they could watch the traffic lights change!

He'd gone from a city that never sleeps to a town that never wakes up. That was why he couldn't forgive his dad. London was what Phoenix craved – something big and important – and Dad had taken him away from it. Dad hadn't just pulled out of the rat race, he'd just about pulled out of life.

'Anyway,' said Dad, unplugging the mask and gloves from the phone socket in the PC, 'We're here now so you'd better make the best of it.'

Phoenix watched Dad carefully wrapping the experimental game equipment.

'There is something I don't understand,' he said.

'And that is?'

'You've produced this game so quickly. I thought it took months to get something like this off the ground, years even.'

'It does,' Dad agreed, 'with the usual technology. But this is several steps beyond the norm. Half the work's been done for me already. *More* than half. The company has developed a basic computer environment. It's so flexible that you can program in each new story line for a game in weeks. I take the story line lines your mum comes up with and, with a bit of help from me, the software just seems to grow into it.'

Phoenix frowned at the mention of Mum's story lines. Mum and Phoenix were two of a kind. They both had dreams, they both had a sense of destiny. Her dream was to be a writer – any kind of writer. She'd been trying forever to get published. First a romantic novel, then some poems, finally a short story competition, but she never got anywhere. She actually kept the rejection slips, as if they were some sort of stepping stone to success! Writing was just another disappointment, along with Brownleigh – and Dad.

Dad had no idea what was going on in Phoenix's head, and carried on regardless. 'I don't even need to come up with half the graphics. The images have already been stored in the computer's memory. I'm little more than a scene-shifter. I bring ready-made images and story lines into focus. Money for old rope, really. Glen Reede's the one who created this, he's the genius. I tell you, when this comes out at the end of next month, Reede's going to change the face of computer games.'

'Did you say the end of next month?'

'That's right,' said Dad. 'The advertising and marketing is already done. That's why I'm working all the hours God sends. It's one heck of a deadline, but Reede will make sure it's met. You can bet your bottom dollar on it. He's a giant. I just can't understand why I haven't come across his name before. No articles in *Computers and Computing,* no reputation to speak of. I'm guessing he's American, but there's no biog. on the Internet. He's come out of nowhere. Still, who cares so long as he's ready to have me on board.'

Phoenix smiled as Dad locked the game gear away. There was something very odd about Dad of all people creating games about heroes. Anybody less like a hero would be hard to imagine. He looked like the original computer geek, complete with untidy red hair, patchy, unkempt beard, corduroy trousers and a lumberjack shirt that strained to contain his thickening waist. There had been a time, in his early twenties, when he'd been a promising tennis player, but that seemed an awfully long time ago. Phoenix wasn't sure whether the old man tried to look like a nerd, or whether it just came naturally. Whatever his intentions, he managed to drive Mum mad with his eccentric, slobbish behaviour. He could have featured in a sitcom – Dads Behaving Madly. But he must have something going for him. He'd been head-hunted by this Glen Reede character, the multi-millionaire boss of Magna-com who had offered him a small fortune to join the company as a creator of mass-market computer games.

They'd done up the cottage with the 'golden hello' Dad had got from Magna-com.

That's it. He was a computer hero!

'So tell me,' Dad continued, 'as a fourteen-year old, you're a member of our target audience. Will it sell?'

'Sell! It'll go like hot cakes. A game you can actually get into—'

'Hey, that'd make a good advertising line: *The computer game you can* ***really*** *get into.'* Dad scribbled it down on a spiral-bound notepad. 'What about the mask and the gloves? Not too sweaty?'

'Not at all,' Phoenix replied. 'They're dead comfortable. The material is really soft. It's almost like a second skin.'

'That's the idea,' Dad explained. 'It's got to be comfortable and easy to get on and off, or the kids will think it's just too much trouble and stick with their old games.'

'Not much chance of that,' said Phoenix, still unable to take his eyes off the monitor screen. 'I mean, it felt like I was really moving around. The graphics were amazing.'

'As good as reality?'

'Better.' Phoenix blushed as he realized what he had said. 'You know, it's true. Stories can be better than real life.' He paused then, unable to resist the temptation to have a dig. 'Especially when real life means Brownleigh.'

Dad ignored the last remark. 'I'm not sure all kids are like you, mind. How many teenagers have their noses in a book of Greek myths half the evening? But a computer game on the other hand – this time they won't have their *noses* in a book, they'll have their whole selves in the story. That's what's been wrong with all these computer games so far. No matter how good the graphics are, you always know that you're in a game. But if you can convince your player that he is actually inside it, *living it,* then you're onto a winner.'

'I guess so,' said Phoenix, wilting slightly under Dad's tidal wave of enthusiasm. 'But it's got to be as good as the one I've just played. It's got to be a match for the real world.'

'Exactly,' Dad interrupted. 'Not so much virtual reality as *parallel reality*. That's what I'm doing now, getting rid of any fuzziness, any sense that this is an electronic entertainment. You can't get most kids off their Playstations now. But when this comes out, forget life. Everybody will have one in their living room. The game will be everything. In six weeks it will be a household name. It'll make us a fortune.'

'You're right there,' said Phoenix. 'It's an amazing

experience. I didn't just *see* the labyrinth, I was there. I could feel it, I could smell it. That's what made it so scary. How did you do that?'

Dad scratched his chin.

'To tell you the truth, I don't really know. You've got to remember, I'm only one part of a team. I play with the jigsaw. Other people provide most of the pieces.'

'Funny sort of team if you never get together,' said Phoenix. 'You've really never met anybody else from the company?'

'No, I haven't,' said Dad. 'Reede contracts everything out to people like me working from home. Maybe he doesn't want anybody getting a complete picture of the game. Whatever his reasons, I've only been given the top two levels, nine and ten, to do. I don't even know the names of the people doing the lower levels. It doesn't really matter. I just take the story lines, match them with the animated action I get and send them in. Magna-com does the rest, and does it at astonishing speed. These Greek myths seemed as good a place to start as any.'

They certainly were for Mum and Phoenix, who prided themselves on their Greek roots. Most of their relatives had settled in London, but they still exchanged Christmas cards with the odd uncle or aunt on some Aegean island. That was something else Dad had taken them away from when they left the capital – their past.

'Great plots, great monsters, great heroes,' Dad ran on, 'and in you and your mum I've got a couple of experts around if I need to pick anybody's brains. As for this feel-around technology, I don't know how Reede does it myself.'

Mum popped her head round the door. 'Are you two ready for something to eat? You've been stuck in here for two hours already.'

Phoenix glanced outside. It was true. Dusk was gathering over the ancient yew trees at the end of the lane. It was something he'd noticed about a good computer game. It seemed to be able to pull time out of shape, mould it and remake it the way a potter does a vase on the wheel. It could turn hours into minutes and minutes into hours. Phoenix had been known to spend a whole day at the screen, even begrudging the time spent on meals. Like most kids, he'd perfected the *just-five-more-minutes* routine. As he got up from his chair, he found himself thinking how grateful he was that he'd taken after Mum when it came to looks. In sharp contrast to his red-haired, pear-shaped dad, she was tall, slim and dark.

Mediterranean-gorgeous, as one of his mates back in London used to say.

'Aren't you shutting down?' Mum asked.

'No need,' said Dad. 'I'll eat and come straight back on. Deadlines, Christina.'

'Oh, you're not going to be on it all night, are you?' asked Mum.

Dad shrugged.

'One of these days,' she said, leading the way into the kitchen. 'We'll have a life. Work, work, work, that's all you care about. Go on, shut down. Just for an hour.'

Dad gave way. As he shut down the screen was filled with a sequence of numbers.

'What's all that?' asked Phoenix. It intrigued him, like the first part of a puzzle. 'There's nothing wrong, is there?'

'Beats me,' Dad admitted. 'Some sort of encrypted message, though you'd have to be an expert to crack it. One of Glen Reede's little secrets.'

But wasn't Dad an expert? Phoenix frowned. Here was something he didn't understand and he was willing to just gloss over it.

'So, what about the characters?' Dad asked over the kitchen table a few minutes later. 'Do they work?'

'Yes, I think so,' said Phoenix. It was hard to take him seriously with strands of cheese sauce dangling from his beard. 'But I've only played one episode of the legend, remember. Theseus is right. And Princess Ariadne, she makes Lara Croft look like a bag lady!'

'Oh, by the way, Reede has just released the title—'

'*The Legendeer,*' Mum said absent-mindedly, her eyes on the road outside and her mind a world away.

'Now how did you know that?' gasped Dad.

Mum started, as if wrenched out of a magical dreamtime.

'I've no idea,' she said, troubled by her own intuition. 'You must have mentioned it sometime.'

'No, that's impossible. It was embargoed. I—'

'Oh, does it matter?' snapped Mum.

They exchanged hostile glares. For some reason it mattered a lot.

'Anyway,' Phoenix interrupted in an effort to prevent a row. '*The Legendeer* is great. You were lucky getting the Theseus and Perseus levels to do.'

'Why's that?'

'Well, they're both boy heroes, about my age. I reckon they'll appeal to that target audience you're always going on about, teenagers.'

Dad frowned. 'Boy heroes, eh? You don't think they look a bit too old, do you?'

Mum smiled. 'It's a bit late to think of it now. Honestly, they put you in charge of developing the story line for the game, and you don't even read the source books properly. You're such a philistine, John.'

'Oh, come off it,' Dad retorted, 'It's a computer game, not a novel. I skip all the boring stuff.'

Mum raised her eyes. 'Boring stuff indeed! This is my Greek heritage you're talking about; truths that speak to me down a hundred generations. These are some of the greatest stories ever told. They're about reaching manhood, about young men growing up and proving themselves, surviving in a hostile world. They're about great friendship and crushing betrayal—'

Noticing the look of amusement on Dad's face, she faltered. He never seemed to take her seriously. Not her writing, not her ancestry. Maybe that's what she resented so much. She believed in the magic and mystery of things, the spaces between what could be explained, whereas Dad reduced everything to a series of provable facts.

'Besides,' she said abruptly. 'They've got two of the best

monsters in the business, Medusa and the Minotaur. That's what got you hooked in the first place.'

'I'll make a few adjustments then,' said Dad. 'I take it you won't mind being my guinea pig, Phoenix. You'll be prepared to play both levels as we make the finishing touches?'

'Are you kidding?' cried Phoenix. 'I'd love it.'

That's when he remembered the yellow eyes of the Minotaur and its ferocious roar. He'd love it all right, just so long as it didn't get *too* real.

3

But it was going to get real, and sooner than either Phoenix or Dad dreamed. There was a message hidden among those bewildering sequences of numbers, a coded signal that might have made John Graves think twice about carrying on working for Glen Reede at all. A dizzying parade of threes, sixes and nines was flashing across the screen as the computer shut down.

Did you enjoy your time in the labyrinth, my brave young Theseus? Did you feel the thrill of the dark, the enticing smell of your own death? How lucky you are to be able to come in on the most advanced levels. They're reserved for the players most deserving of a glorious demise. But you, you insignificant microbe, you get to face the greatest perils. What an oddity that your father is the most able programmer I've got, so you start at the top. Don't get over confident, though. I'm giving you a taster of the game, that's all. It is pathetic, really pathetic to watch **you**, *a mere boy, trying to stand up to my magnificent beast. I might let you tread the slimy stones of his realm a little longer, teasing you. There are no free rides in this game.*

I promise you – this is just the beginning.

4

Legends are not just one of my interests, they're my life.

Where did that come from?

Phoenix shook his head. Where *on Earth* did that come from, and why did he have to go and blurt it out in front of the whole class? Was he trying to make himself look a complete idiot? If he knew Steve Adams – and unfortunately it was one of his burdens in life that he did know him – he'd pay for that little outburst. What was he thinking of? It was one thing to swallow what Mum said about legends speaking to them down a hundred generations, and spend hours poring over dusty old volumes full of spoilt, cruel gods, courageous heroes and fabulous, blood-drenched monsters. It was quite another to show himself up in class like that. This was the world he had to live in, not some never-never land of temples and demons. That's what he'd done though, he'd made a complete idiot of himself halfway through double English. Look at me, the new kid, I'm after the Nerd of the Year award.

And this is what he said to earn it: *Don't you understand, Miss? These myths. They're not just stories. They're real. They show us as heroes. They're our true nature.*

That's what came of getting so wrapped up in Dad's *Legendeer* project. Phoenix had played the game three times in the last week and he'd started quite fancying himself as one of those heroes. Unfortunately, the very thought of Phoenix as a hero had Adams and his idiot hangers-on cackling fit to burst. Most of the boys in Phoenix's class wouldn't admit to reading at all. It didn't do much for your street cred. It was seen as a girl thing. And they definitely didn't believe that what they read was real. So what did Phoenix do? He actually announced to the whole world that books were *better* than life, that he saw himself as a Theseus or a Herakles.

With his flesh still creeping from the embarrassment of that awful afternoon, Phoenix dashed out of the school gates like a bat out of Hell. It was in danger of bringing on one of his sick headaches. They were the bane of his life. They would come from nowhere and last a few hours, completely draining him. He had had all sorts of hospital tests but the doctors had never been able to explain them. Or treat them. With the passing years, the family had learned to live with the problem. Headaches and embarrassment – what a life! Phoenix remembered the score bracelet he'd worn in the game. For the second time in as many days it would have registered the fatal numbers: **000000.**

A loser with knobs on.

Even being a loser wouldn't have been so bad, but Phoenix suffered from something else. An exaggerated sense of his own importance. All his life he had had this idea nagging away at the back of his mind.

I've got a purpose in life. Something big.

It just made the boring reality even worse. *Something big—*

He snorted. 'Sure, something like keeping out of Adams' way.'

The 221 bus was waiting at the bus stop. If I catch this one, Phoenix thought, maybe I'll be gone before he gets out of school. He sat watching the jostling groups of kids getting on. It soon became obvious the driver wasn't going to move off until the bus was full.

'Oh, come on,' said Phoenix. 'Go!'

But the kids kept piling on board. Eventually, he pulled a book out and started reading. It was the Greek myths, of course. Phoenix shivered as he remembered his performance in class. Geek myths would be more like it. After a couple of minutes he heard a tap on the window. It was Laura.

'Save me a place.'

She flashed her pass and shoved her way down the bus.

'You were miles away,' she said.

Miles? Centuries was more like it. In his mind he was already treading the labyrinth again. He hoped Dad would let him have another go that evening. He didn't care how scary the labyrinth was, he'd get that stupid Minotaur yet. He'd been talking to Mum, working out his moves, and he was sure he had a plan. Brain, not brawn, would conquer the beast. At least at home, in the privacy of the study, he could be a hero.

'Go on,' she said, digging him playfully in the ribs. 'What were you thinking about?'

Laura Osibona's friendship was about the only thing that made living in Brownleigh half-bearable. Her brown, almost black eyes sparkled as she fingered the book lying half-open on the seat.

'What's this, Phoenix?' she asked. 'Let's have a look. Oh dear.'

She pouted with mock disapproval.

'Not those ghastly beasties again.'

She was teasing, but Phoenix found it a lot easier to take from her than from Steve Adams and his mates. They used humour like a knife, twisting it until they drew blood. Laura, on the other hand, didn't have a cruel bone in her body.

Phoenix glanced at the book's drab olive-green cover, and remembered the clash of the Minotaur's hooves on the floor of the labyrinth. If only she knew what lurked inside those pages. Phoenix had never really read for pleasure. He read to immerse himself in worlds that seemed as real as the one he had to grow up in. Now the game was opening the door to them. Did he dare tell Laura? But Dad had sworn him to secrecy on the whole project.

Commercial confidentiality.

'Yes Laura, those ghastly beasties.'

It was a relief to talk to her, to make fun of his fears, cut his demons down to size. Much as he'd enjoyed it, the encounter with the Minotaur had spooked him good style. The only reason he felt ready to play again was because Dad's finger would be on the off button.

'The Concise Dictionary of Myths and Legends,' Laura read. 'Light reading, eh?'

She flicked through the pages.

'He looks like you,' she said, showing him the illustration of one of the legendary heroes.

'That's Theseus,' said Phoenix. 'Do you really think he looks like me?'

'Spitting image,' Laura confirmed.

Then she was nudging him along the seat.

'Well, are you going to let me sit down, or what?'

Between him and his school holdall, Phoenix was hogging the whole seat.

'Budge up, Phoenix.'

Phoenix! It wasn't just his monsters the other kids laughed at. He was even a victim of his own name. Didn't Mum and Dad know how important it was to fit in? Adams was having a field day with it. Bundling his holdall to the floor, Phoenix moved over to the window.

'Oh, great!'

'What's up?'

'Look who's getting on.'

Adams had just appeared with his usual bunch of cronies. The gang leader was lean and tall. A wolf in wolf's clothing.

'Take no notice,' said Laura.

Phoenix sighed. 'Easier said than done. They're staring.'

Laura took the news calmly.

'Let them. They're only jealous.'

'So they've got something to be jealous of, have they?'

Laura dug him in the ribs. 'Now that would be telling.'

Phoenix found himself smiling. They'd hit it off right from the start. Just when he was cursing his luck at ending up in such a tedious little town, full of no-hopers like Adams, Laura had arrived to make his day. Her best friend Kathy had been off so there had been a spare seat next to her. Kathy never got her place back. Phoenix and Laura had been inseparable since then. It set tongues wagging of course, but it didn't really bother him. They were meant to be friends and that was that.

But if they were friends, shouldn't he—? No, Dad would kill him. Oh, what the heck, this was too big to keep to himself. He gave Laura his in-confidence look.

'If I tell you something,' he began, 'do you promise to keep it to yourself?'

'Of course.'

Phoenix knew Dad would kill him, but he was dying to tell somebody about *The Legendeer*.

'I mean it,' he said. 'You can't tell a soul, not even Kathy.'

'I promise, you creep.'

Phoenix glanced at the kids around them. They were too busy with the latest gossip to take much notice.

'You know my dad makes computer games?'

'Yes, you told me.'

'Well, you should see the latest thing he's doing.'

'Why, is it good?'

'Good? It's amazing.'

Phoenix leaned forward conspiratorially.

'You know there are these games where you can wear a glove instead of using a control pad?'

'Sure. And you can get those Virtual Reality helmet things.'

'Well,' Phoenix told her excitedly. 'Dad's company has just come up with something even better. It's state of the art. It feels like you're right inside the game.'

Laura looked intrigued.

'What game?'

'It's called *The Legendeer*.'

Just mentioning the game caused a curious tugging at the coat-tails of his memory. Like Mum, he was beginning to think he'd heard the name before.

'Legends, eh? That should be right down your street.'

'It is. I've been helping Dad with the story line. I get to play Theseus going to the palace of King Minos to fight the Minotaur.' He knew he was gushing, but he didn't care. *The Legendeer* was something you just couldn't oversell. 'The game's incredible. King Minos' daughter Princess Ariadne helps me kill the beast. She looks as real as you or me. I'm talking flesh and blood, totally 3-D. You'd swear there were real people in the game.'

'Could I play it?'

Phoenix frowned.

'I'm afraid not. It's at the experimental stage. It's sort of secret.'

It was Laura's turn to frown.

'So, if you won't let me have a go, why are you telling me about it?'

Phoenix was beginning to wonder himself.

'I had to tell somebody. It's really cool. You don't just see the monster's lair. You can smell it, you can feel it.'

'That's impossible.'

'Not any more.'

Laura put her head on one side.

'You're having me on.'

'I'm not,' said Phoenix. 'Honestly I'm not. It's about the most exciting thing I've ever done.'

'Prove it then.'

'How do you mean?'

'I mean,' Laura said pointedly, 'if you want me to swallow this big secret of yours, you've got to let me play it.'

Phoenix was wondering how to get out of the hole he'd dug for himself, when Adams and his gang appeared in front of him.

'Hey, Free Knickers,' Adams smirked. 'That was a corker you came out with this afternoon. Nobody would believe me when I told them what a freak of nature you are. Now they've found out for themselves. Seen any ghosties and ghoulies lately? Had any books come to life? Go on Free Knickers, give us all a laugh.'

'The name,' Phoenix growled, 'is Phoenix.'

He could feel that twinge of headache developing into the familiar band of pain that had plagued him all his life. The slightest little thing could set it off, strong sunlight, nerves, loud noise. Then it was heat rashes and headaches. He'd often spent hours lying on the couch in a darkened room with a damp cloth on his forehead, listening to Mum turning away his friends with talk of, *one of his heads.*

'Phoenix, Free Knickers, whatever. What sort of name is that, anyway? Your folks hippies or something?'

Phoenix stiffened. That's exactly what Dad was, a throwback to the days when people wore their hair long and slopped around in tie-dyed shirts.

There was actually a pair of blue-tinted John Lennon glasses in a drawer somewhere. Laura was squeezing Phoenix's arm, making a silent plea for restraint.

'Don't rise to it.'

But Phoenix was stung. He was touchy about his nerdy little dad, the redhaired geek who used to turn up at his primary school wearing this giant, floppy ski hat. What an embarrassment that was! That's right, Dad *had* been a bit of a hippy, only twenty years too late.

'You shut your mouth, Adams!'

'Or what?'

Or nothing. Phoenix was angry. He wasn't suicidal.

'Leave it, Phoenix,' said Laura. 'Here's our stop.'

But Adams didn't know how to let go. He was like a dog with a bone. He was going to chew and chew until he got to the marrow.

'Just look at his face,' said Adams laughing. 'Lighten up, Free Knickers. No need to get uptight on me.'

Phoenix watched the mocking glint in Adams' eye and he hated it. He hated the reminder that he wasn't special after all, that he didn't fight demons. Not real ones. He hated Adams for being a common or garden small-town bully. He hated him, full stop.

'Take your hands off me.'

'Don't be so touchy, Free Knickers my old mate. Just sit there like a good boy while I have a word with the lovely Laura.'

Suddenly, Phoenix was seeing everything through a red mist. Good boy! Good *boy*. Adams' face, so cruel and taunting. His friends, urging him on with their jibes and laughter. Then

Adams was pushing against Laura, trying to make room for himself on the seat.

It's not that he really fancied her. Adams was quite a racist, and used to pick on Laura as one of the few black kids in school, but if he could use her to get at Phoenix he would. Phoenix glanced outside at the pavement. The bus was slowing down as it approached his and Laura's stop.

'You don't mind, do you?'

Adams taunted Phoenix, his thin lips curled. A smile should be a mark of friendship. With him, it was a weapon, as sharp and effective as a scalpel.

'No, of course you don't.'

Phoenix listened to the arrogance in Adams' voice. He was cock of the school, a boy used to getting his own way, even with the teachers who he was expert at winding up. So, Phoenix told himself, thinks he's fireproof, does he? His neck was burning with shame and fury, and the headache was building.

I can't let him get away with this.

'I was thinking, Laura, why don't you ditch old Free Knickers and come to town with me? Me and the lads will show you a good time.'

The bus was stopping. He couldn't let Adams get away with it, but what could he do? In the event, he didn't do anything. Laura had it in hand.

'Forget it, Steve,' she said, tossing her dreadlocked hair. 'Mum doesn't want me dating anybody at my age. Besides, you're the last boy I'd go out with.' A pause, then she was trying to get up. 'Excuse me, please. This is our stop.'

Phoenix imagined himself crashing his fist into Adams' leering face, but that wasn't his style. He *read* about fights or engaged in them in his on-screen battles with the demons. That was the best sort of fighting, the kind you could stop at the touch of the off-button.

As the gang stepped back, he followed Laura meekly off the bus, ignoring the sly kick in the calf, and burning with humiliation at the insults being shouted behind him.

'Just look at him,' sneered Adams. 'Hiding behind Laura's skirt.'

Hiding! Phoenix didn't want to hide. He didn't want to hide or run ever again. He'd sampled danger in the game. It made him think maybe he did have a destiny after all.

'I should have thumped him,' Phoenix grumbled as they reached the pelican crossing.

'And what good would that do?' asked Laura. 'You can't take on the whole gang. I can handle Steve. I've been doing it for years. I'm not some damsel in distress and you're no knight in shining armour.'

But I could be, thought Phoenix. If I mastered this game, I really could be.

5

'Is that you, Phoenix?'

'Yuh.'

Mum met him in the hallway. She put the ring-bind folder she was carrying down on one of the piles of marking stacked along the wall.

'Uh oh, what's wrong?'

Phoenix could hear Dad tapping away at the keyboard. It was getting to be the usual routine; Mum at her school work or her writing on the kitchen table, Dad in the study trying to get the game right. The one thing they never seemed to do was talk to each other. Phoenix wished they could give up work and get a life.

'Nothing's wrong.'

'Don't give me that. What's happened?'

'I told you, nothing.'

'It was Steve Adams again, wasn't it?'

Phoenix nodded.

'He didn't hurt you, did he?'

'Not exactly.'

'Then what exactly?'

Phoenix hated having to tell her. It meant reliving the humiliation.

'He kind of shoved us around. Me and Laura.'

'I knew it. He's a bad one, that Adams.'

Phoenix looked away. Tell me something I don't know.

'So, how many of them were there this time?'

'Four.'

'I'm going to have a word with that school. We don't have that sort of behaviour at mine.'

Phoenix thought it was hardly surprising. She taught ten-year-olds. He didn't want her causing trouble though.

'No, Mum,' he pleaded. 'Don't.'

Didn't she know that would only make things worse?

'Well, we've got to do something.'

Why? When they lived in London they had a neighbour who used to play his music at all hours. And at full volume too. Dad went round once and the neighbour started getting heavy.

'Want to make something of it?' he'd asked. Dad didn't.

And now, Phoenix thought, I'm following in the old man's footsteps. Big ideas, but no action.

'You just tell me if it happens again,' Mum said.

Phoenix gave a half-nod. It didn't mean a thing, but it seemed to satisfy Mum.

'What's up?' asked Dad, wandering in from the study. 'Were you two arguing?'

'Nothing you need to worry about,' said Mum. 'A bit of bullying. I'll handle it. You get on with your work and leave the real world to me.'

Dad glanced at Phoenix. His face said *Ouch*.

'Pop in and see me when you've finished here, son.'

After another five minutes of ear-bending from Mum, Phoenix escaped to the study.

'You OK?' Dad asked.

'Yes, I'm fine.'

He would have liked Dad to listen to his problems now they were out in the open, tell him how he'd handled this sort of stuff when he was in his teens. But Dad was no great shakes in the Man-to-Man Talk Department.

He carried on as if nothing had happened.

'Good. I've got something to show you.'

Dad was almost trembling with excitement. Part of Phoenix shared the thrill of a new toy, but another part of him hung back, still annoyed that Dad didn't want to listen to his problems.

'There!'

Dad was holding up what looked like a very flimsy diving suit.

'What is it?'

'Can't you guess?'

Phoenix shook his head.

'Here,' said Dad, jabbing a finger at the balaclava-like mask at the top of the suit. 'Recognize this?'

'It's the helmet I wore to play the game.'

'And these?'

Dad flapped the gloves at him. Phoenix was catching on.

'You mean it's a Virtual Reality suit?'

Dad winked.

'Better than that. We've created a *Parallel Reality* suit.'

Phoenix felt the material. It was just like the mask and gloves. A second skin. Except this time, it was an all-over skin. It was bound to make the illusion even more convincing.

'*You* made this?'

'Well, I e-mailed the idea to Magna-com and this came back.'

'When did it come?'

'Second post this afternoon. I could hardly believe it. The game is developing by the day.'

Phoenix stared at the suit.

'But they couldn't come up with something like this so quickly. They must have been working on it already.'

'Oh, I'm sure they were,' said Dad. 'But they're ready to try it out. With luck, this kit will be ready for launch day. It's much more advanced than the first equipment we tried. Want to play guinea pig?'

'What, now?'

Dad chuckled.

'No time like the present.'

Phoenix examined the suit.

'How do I get it on? I can't see any fastenings.'

Dad grinned.

'It took me a while to figure it out. Here.'

He guided Phoenix's hands to a barely-visible line down the front of the suit.

'Now, just pull it like you're opening a bag of crisps.'

Phoenix tugged and the suit opened with a barely audible hiss.

'What is it, Velcro?'

'I couldn't work it out myself. It doesn't feel sticky or anything. It's more advanced than Velcro, that's for sure.'

Phoenix put his feet into the suit and pulled it up to his armpits. He slipped his arms in then finally pulled the mask down, snapping it over his jawline.

'How does it feel?'

Phoenix looked around. His mouth and eyes were covered by a very fine gauze.

'I hardly even feel like I'm wearing it. Am I plugged into the PC?'

'Hang on. I'll hook you up now.'

Phoenix heard the purr of the PC as it stirred into life. He strapped on his score bracelet. He couldn't wait to re-enter the world of *The Legendeer*. No way was he going to register the Big Zero this time.

'Right,' said Dad. 'You're all set. Here, you carry on.'

Phoenix loaded the disc. Previously, he had gone straight into the labyrinth. This time it was different. Credits started flashing up on the screen.

Manufactured by: Magna-com International. Dir: Glen Reede.

Marketing: Arcadia Computers.

Copyright: Tartarus Applications.

Clues rolled onto the screen. Teasing signposts to the rules of the game. Phoenix smiled.

All Greek to me?

I don't think so.

The title sequence began. He stared at the screen with a mixture of anxiety and excitement as a horned face appeared. A thrill ran through him. Phoenix watched the strange figure emerge grinning from a boiling cloud. His hair was dark and wiry, streaked with grey. What's more, it came down his forehead to the bridge of his nose in a V-shape. His long, hooked nose was hairy too, and his skin was sunburnt and weather-beaten, scored with wrinkles and crow's feet. Most noticeable of all was his smile, wide, thick-lipped. He was the god of shepherds, prophecy and mischief – Pan. His hoarse, chafing voice scraped in the speakers. 'Welcome, friend, to the world of *The Legendeer.'*

Pan smiled. It was perfect. Phoenix had only played a snippet of the game until now. This was the real thing, complete with introduction and player's guide.

'Hello Pan.'

'Let me introduce you to my domain.'

Our domain, thought Phoenix as a sheer wall of rock rose before him, the summit swathed in mist.

'Behold,' ran the introduction. 'Cloud-dark Olympus. They say it takes an anvil nine days and nine nights to fall from Heaven to Earth.'

'Yeah yeah, I know all this. Get to the game.'

The game! No headaches any more. Phoenix was almost trembling with excitement.

'Far below, my dear disciple,' Pan continued, 'is dismal Tartarus, the land of dead souls. That sad country lies as far below Earth as Heaven stands above it. Do you remember how far, my friend?'

'Of course I remember,' Phoenix replied. 'Nine days and nights as the anvil falls.'

For a split-second he remembered Dad's presence in the room, but so what, he was enjoying himself.

'Your task is simple, player, you must go through the many labours of the hero, march forward through the very jaws of death itself and claim your place on High Olympus in the company of the gods. Are you ready to proceed?'

Phoenix smiled.

'OK Mister Pan, I'm hooked.'

As the screen faded out then back in again, the game's illusion started to suck Phoenix in. He was introduced to a vast mountainside shimmering under a blazing sun, and he wasn't looking at the screen any more. He was there, standing on the sheep-grazed slopes. Pan was present in person, man from the waist up, goat from the waist down. He was dancing on the mountain top, playing the seven-reed Arcadian pipes. And the strangest thought came to Phoenix: *I'm home.*

'Ready, young friend? Select your hero.'

Phoenix looked up. There they were, emblazoned on the sky, the heroes of antiquity: Herakles, Orpheus, Achilles, Jason, Perseus, Theseus. The list went on. They were arranged in groups. All but Perseus and Theseus were slightly faded. They couldn't be accessed.

'Fair enough. I'll take the boy heroes.'

Images of the heroes hovered in front of him. He remembered what Laura had said about the picture in his book. He inspected the heroes closely. Theseus bore him more than a passing resemblance. By touching the floating image, Phoenix selected Theseus.

'Starting at the top,' said Pan. 'Still, there's nothing like ambition. You are now Theseus of Troezen. Your father left you here when you were a baby. He is King Aegeus of Athens. You haven't seen him for fourteen years.'

Just my age, thought Phoenix. The game fits me like a glove.

'Now it is time to claim your birthright,' Pan resumed. 'You are the true and destined heir to the throne of Athens. Follow me, *Prince* Theseus.'

Phoenix – or was it Theseus? – felt that he was being teased. But he was hooked. He started to follow Pan along a dirt path between the cypress trees. The heat haze shimmered. He could actually feel it on his skin. And hear the scrape of the crickets. And smell the sheep on the hillside close by. The illusion was even better than the first time.

Besides the smells and sounds, he could actually taste the dust. Better than real life? No doubt about that.

'And here,' said Pan, springing on to a ledge of rock, 'I must leave you. Welcome to your first challenge.'

He pointed to a huge boulder.

'Roll back this rock and you will discover the tokens by which you will prove your identity to the King of Athens. Your epic journey begins here.'

Phoenix stared at the rock. It was impossible. At least, it should have been, but this was a game, and games are places where miracles can happen. He stepped forward and braced his shoulder against the rock. Straining every muscle, he shoved at the boulder. Nothing. Again, he was struck by the sheer reality of the game. This rock, it was physically there. He took a deep breath and planted his feet down hard on the sun-baked earth. As he heaved again, he felt his shoes sliding and scraping on the ground. This time it was moving. It was gradual at first, then the boulder was rolling steadily towards a steep slope. With a last push, Phoenix sent it bouncing down the hillside. He felt the score bracelet chattering away against his wrist. *I'm scoring.*

He knelt down to examine what was underneath – a pair of sandals and a sword. The ivory hilt of the sword bore the seal of King Aegeus, three entwined serpents. The score bracelet was recording still more points. He was on a roll. He weighed the weapon in his hand, remembering the grim trial ahead, his entry into the labyrinth to face the Minotaur.

His mind was concentrating on the beast that haunted the dark tunnels when a hand fell on his shoulder. His chest cramped in the agony of fear.

It's the game. It won't let go.

Suddenly, he knew what a heart attack must feel like. His head was pounding and his blood was on fire. He was looking at Dad's study through a boiling fog. And the pain! It was as if he was being torn in two, as if the game had penetrated him and was ripping his flesh as he came out of it.

'What's wrong, Phoenix? You look terrible.'

Phoenix finally focused on Dad's anxious face. He was about to tell him about the pain, but something stopped him. The game had got under his skin, and no matter how much it had hurt he had to play again. He'd been home, he'd felt the promise of his destiny.

'It's OK,' he panted, trying desperately to recover from the shock of the hand on his shoulder. 'You gave me a fright.'

'Seems more than a fright to me. You look awful.'

'Honestly, you took me by surprise, that's all.'

'Well, sorry if I gave you a start, Phoenix. There's a phone call for you.'

Reluctantly, Phoenix unfastened the score bracelet, peeled off the mask and started to wriggle out of the suit. There was sweat this time, the sour sweat of fear. And all for a phone call.

Phone call indeed! He'd almost forgotten the stone cottage in Brownleigh existed.

6

If numbers can groan, that's what they were doing as Phoenix went to get the phone. Dad decided to shut down. He knew all about teenagers' phone calls! As first one, then another of the multiples of three glowed on the screen, he wondered what they meant.

How dare you? the hidden voice was saying. *How dare you break off? You cannot walk away from the game so easily. There's a whole world waiting to play. You will have to learn respect, young warrior. You will have to learn to stand in awe of the game. It is part of you now, just as it is part of me. I felt it too when you broke free. There's a connection, something I haven't felt for so long. You were meant to play. Enjoy it while you can, boy-fighter. Soon, it will penetrate the soft underbelly of your undeserving world. There will be no peace for the innocent. You must play this game to the end. To the bitter end.*

7

Phoenix awoke the next morning to the sound of the breeze snapping the curtains. He felt desperately tired and his head was pounding. It was as though something was probing his mind, draining him of life. He was experiencing a deep, numbing exhaustion. What had the game done to him? It was a quarter of an hour before he was able to swing his legs painfully out of bed and make his way to the bathroom. Washing and brushing his teeth made him feel a little better and he could finally think.

'Of course, it's Saturday.'

The thought started to loosen the hold of his headache.

'Yes, I can play all day if I want to.'

He remembered how angry he'd been with Laura for dragging him off it with an uneventful phone call the previous evening. This time he was going to declare himself out of bounds for the whole day. Nobody, but nobody was getting him off the computer until he was good and ready.

'Morning,' he called to Mum as he made his way downstairs. 'Is Dad in the study?'

'Whoa, whoa,' said Mum, emerging from the kitchen in her towelling dressing gown, a cup and tea towel in hand. 'What's the big rush?'

'The game,' Phoenix replied, following her into the kitchen. 'I'm going to get some breakfast and play.'

'I think you might be in for a bit of a disappointment,' said Mum, taking a sip of coffee. 'Your dad went out about half an hour ago, taking that suit thing with him.'

'He's what?'

'He packed all that game stuff away and chucked it in the car. He must have been working until well after midnight, because I went up to bed at half past eleven. Don't ask me what he's up to. He went back to the game after you turned in, and he didn't say a word to me this morning.'

Suddenly, there was a huge aching space where all of Phoenix's expectations for the day had been.

'But Pan had only just introduced me to the game.'

Mum reacted as if she had suffered an electric shock. She seemed to mouth the word *Pan*. The mug she had been drying fell and smashed on the floor.

'Look at that!' she cried, running her finger under the tap. 'Now I've cut myself.'

Phoenix stared in disbelief. What a reaction.

'I'm sick of hearing about that game,' snapped Mum. 'I wish John had never started it.'

Phoenix gave her time to calm down.

'Did he say where he was going?' he ventured after a few minutes.

'You've got to be joking,' said Mum. 'He didn't even have breakfast with me. That father of yours, he's getting worse.'

'And he's taken the lot?'

Phoenix couldn't believe it. The one day he would have had the time to really get into the game. Him, the guinea pig. And Dad had gone off with all the gear!

'What am I supposed to do all day?'

Mum smiled.

'What you did before you had the game, I suppose. Read, go swimming, call on your friends—'

'This isn't London,' Phoenix objected. 'I've only got one friend here.'

'Call on *her* then.'

'I'd rather play *The Legendeer.*'

That look came into Mum's face, the one she'd worn when she dropped the mug. It was a moment or two before she managed a reply.

'Oh, stop moaning,' she said. 'It's only a stupid game.'

Phoenix turned away. Stupid? Nobody who'd played it would say that.

The rain had stopped by the time he reached the High Street. He'd waited all of three hours before giving up on Dad. There was no sign of him and he hadn't phoned. It was after Phoenix's third minor tiff with Mum that he decided to call on Laura. The sun came out, garish and dazzling on the damp streets. The heat only added to his bad mood. He had a heat rash spreading across his chest. He felt itchy and uncomfortable and a headache was lurking. He reflected on a lousy morning. Not only was he locked out of the study and unable to play the game, he'd also made an unwelcome discovery in the shed. The back tyre of his bike was flat and there was no puncture kit.

'Looks like I'm walking to Laura's.'

Or maybe he was running. He caught sight of Steve Adams and his mates making their way past the Post Office. Perhaps they hadn't seen him.

'Hey, surprise, surprise, if it isn't Free Knickers.'

So much for wishful thinking.

'Get him!'

There were five of them, and they were coming at a run. They fancied the odds and Phoenix didn't. Not this time. He remembered Laura's warning. Steve carried a knife.

'You've had it this time, Free Knickers.'

Phoenix looked hopefully at the pelican crossing. The news wasn't good.

Wait, it told him.

Adams was patting his jacket.

'You haven't got it yet, have you? You're not wanted here.'

A bluff, Phoenix hoped, but he wasn't about to call it. For once, it wasn't fear that drove him, it was something he'd felt in the labyrinth – the shame of being beaten.

'You stay right there,' Adams ordered.

Phoenix fixed his enemy with a stare. Ten yards and closing. He glanced at the crossing. Still on *Wait*. The Saturday morning traffic was more dangerous than Adams, but he threw himself into the road nevertheless. He couldn't give Adams the satisfaction of beating him.

Behind him he heard warning shouts and a cry of horror: 'The boy's crazy.' '. . . He's going to get himself killed.'

He was dodging and weaving, holding up his hand to the startled and angry drivers. He heard the squeal of brakes. A near miss. But nothing was going to stop him now. Struggling to the middle of the road, he took a gulp of fume-filled air and weaved his way to the far pavement. He'd made it, but only thanks to an emergency stop by a private hire taxi.

'You young idiot!'

'Need their heads looking at, these kids.'

But Phoenix wasn't hanging around to listen. He had to put some distance between himself and Adams' gang.

Without so much as a backwards glance he ran off, cut through the alleyway between the bank and the church and scrambled down the embankment on the disused railway line. A quick sprint across the biscuit factory car park and he was at the corner of Laura's street. The gang wasn't following. But he was out of luck at Laura's too. Nobody was in.

'Wonderful,' he groaned, 'Absolutely rotten wonderful!'

He was just turning back into the High Street, glancing nervously from right to left for some sign of Adams, when he heard a car horn. It was Dad.

'You're back then,' Phoenix said, sliding into the passenger seat. Much as he resented Dad's disappearing act, he kept quiet about it. He didn't want to jeopardize his chance of playing the game again.

Dad checked the mirror and glanced over his shoulder before pulling out into the traffic.

'Mmm.'

His voice sounded flat.

'Something up?'

'You could say that.'

Phoenix felt a twinge of unease.

'Has this got something to do with the game?'

Dad nodded and pulled up at the traffic lights which had just turned to red.

'I had to send the suit back this morning.'

'You did what! Why?'

Dad rolled up his shirt sleeve to reveal a long scratch on his upper arm. It looked raised and angry.

'How did you get that?'

The lights changed to green.

'That's what I'd like to know. One minute I was playing the game, the next there was this burning sensation right down my arm.'

Phoenix started, remembering the charge of pain that had run through his own body. He still hadn't mentioned it.

When the lights changed, Dad drove over the bridge and turned left towards home.

'But I didn't notice anything sharp.'

'Me neither. But something caused this. One thing's for sure, you're not going to use that game until I've got some assurances about its safety.'

Phoenix stood on the pavement while Dad locked and alarmed the car. His frustration boiled over. 'Typical,' he snorted. 'You get a bit of a scratch and you send the whole thing back. Haven't you got any bottle?'

'Look,' Dad replied, struggling to contain his temper. 'All the accessories are made of the same material. I'm not taking any chances.'

'No, you never do.'

'Now that's enough!'

Phoenix looked at the cut. He hardly cared about the danger. There was something in the game, something hidden and exciting. Playing was all that mattered.

'You spoil everything! First you drag us all the way out here to live, then you ruin the only good thing that's happened to me.'

Phoenix didn't like the sound of his own voice, there was a cruelty he didn't intend, but he was furious with Dad. The game was gone, a game that had started to become part of him.

Still fighting to keep a lid on his temper, Dad turned his key in the front door. There was a note from Mum on the hall table.

Gone shopping. Back in an hour.

Dad ran his eyes over the yellow Post-It, then turned to face Phoenix. 'There's something I haven't told you.'

'I can't wait.'

'Just listen to me, will you?'

Phoenix grimaced. He knew he was being horrible, but he couldn't help it.

'OK, I'm listening.'

'I'd got as far as Theseus' journey through the badlands on the way to Athens. You know where I mean?'

'Yes, where he has to fight the bandits.'

'That's it. Anyway, I had no problem with most of the bad guys. I got past Periphetes, the cudgel man, and Sinis who tried to tie me to a couple of trees to rip me in half. I was having quite a good time, wasting them. I was really clocking up the points – a superhero. Then it started to get . . . weird.'

Phoenix was intrigued, so intrigued he forgot he was meant to be angry.

'How do you mean, weird?'

'Well, at first it was just fun. You know, baddy jumps up, hero kills baddy. The mother of all battles is fun when you know nobody gets hurt. Then I came to this castle. An old man invited me in. He was called—'

'Procrustes. Yes, I know the story.'

'Then you'll know he has this cute habit of tying people to a magic bed.'

'That's right. If you're too short for it, he stretches your limbs. If you're too tall, he—'

'Yes, he cuts off your feet. Well, I wish I'd known about old Procrustes—'

'But you must have known,' Phoenix interrupted. 'You do the story lines.'

'That's what I thought,' said Dad. 'But it appears there's more than one of us working on the plot, even on my levels.

I'm not like you and your mother. I skim the [illegible] the exciting bits, the stuff that will make g[illegible] episodes. I'd never even heard of Procrustes an[illegible] bed. Anyway, you know the way you can touch a[illegible] things in the game, well it turns out you can eat and dr[illegible] well.'

'You're kidding!'

'Oh, believe me, you can,' Dad insisted. 'Every physical sensation seems to have been incorporated into it. I had quite a supper at Procrustes' castle, but the wine must have been drugged because I woke up being tied to the bed. And before you say it, yes, he was going to stretch me. Luckily, my hands were still free and I got loose. Then Procrustes came at me with a razor-sharp cleaver. That's when I felt the pain in my arm. But it's crazy, the game couldn't cut you.'

Phoenix wasn't so sure. He couldn't get the Minotaur out of his head. The yellow eyes, the bellow that shook walls, the blood-smeared skin. It's not that he'd wanted to run. He'd *had* to. Phoenix was starting to think the game had a life of its own. But he wasn't going to tell Dad that. He still wanted to play it again. Something else he had to do. It was time to placate the old man.

'Of course not,' he said reassuringly. 'It'll be a sharp thread in the suit, that's all.'

'Mmm,' Dad replied dubiously.

'I mean,' Phoenix said hurriedly. 'What else could it be?'

'That's just it,' Dad answered. 'I can't imagine. The only thing I know is that something was wrong with the suit and I'm not taking any risks. I've written to Reede, telling him what I think of his game.'

'You haven't!'

'Oh, I have. I told him I was quite worried about safety.'

Phoenix relaxed. *Quite* worried, was that all Dad could say? With a protest as weak as that, Reede would soon have him singing a different tune.

'I'm sure it'll soon be sorted out,' he said, anxious to play again.

[illegible]pe,' Dad murmured, gazing thoughtfully into the garden.

Phoenix smiled to himself. If he knew Dad, he was bound to do whatever Reede wanted. After all, Dad was no hero.

8

The family were in the living room the following morning when Dad sprang out of his chair and flew to the door.

'What's he doing now?' groaned Mum.

'Beats me,' Phoenix replied.

'Unbelievable,' came Dad's voice. 'Un-flipping-believable.'

Mum and Phoenix reached the hallway together.

'What is?'

He was kneeling on the floor, surrounded by polystyrene packing, rummaging in a cardboard box.

'This.'

He held up a new Parallel Reality suit. It was identical to the last one, only in red.

'That's funny,' said Mum. 'There's no parcel post on a Sunday. Did you catch who delivered it?'

'Not really,' Dad answered. 'All I saw was a van pulling up in front of the house. It was halfway down the road before I got to the door. And look at this, there are two suits this time.'

'Isn't there a letter or anything?'

'Not a dicky-bird. Just the parcel. Honestly, what sort of cock-eyed operation is this Glen Reede running?'

'A pretty efficient one, by the look of it,' said Mum. 'You've got to admit, it's impressive, getting the suit replaced in 24 hours.'

Dad didn't reply. Instead, he folded the suit and put it back in the box.

'I don't have to give him anything. Tomorrow morning, this package goes right back where it came from. I'm not so much as touching that program until I get cast-iron assurances about the game's safety.'

'Well, good for you,' said Mum. 'You stick by your guns.'

'That,' Dad told her as he opened the study door and stowed the package inside, 'is exactly what I intend to do.'

But the resolution only lasted a few hours. Dad got the e-mail from Reede about Magna-com's new safety measures at three o'clock. He was back-tracking by four.

'Damaged in transit,' he explained to Phoenix. 'A fine wire thread had worked loose. Reede's had the suit fully-lined to prevent a repeat. See.'

He held out the suit, displaying the new lining, a layer of fabric as fine and soft as the original.

'And I've got a cast-iron guarantee that the fault will be eliminated before the game's launch date.'

'I can't believe we've got the new suits already,' said Phoenix. 'They don't hang about, do they?'

'Not a bit.'

Dad's worries about the suit were quickly forgotten in the excitement of having the replacements but he was particularly enthusiastic about a new development announced in the e-mail. Whatever it was, it seemed to have tipped the balance. Dad was back on board.

'So do I get to have another go?' Phoenix asked eagerly. 'I *am* your guinea pig.'

'We both have another go,' said Dad, 'now there are two suits. I'm leaving nothing to chance this time. Wherever you go, whatever you do, I'll be right behind, shadowing you. The moment anything goes even slightly iffy, we're getting out.'

Phoenix thought it was an odd thing to say – *wherever you go*. After all, they would be right here in the study. Dad had made the point often enough himself; the sense of movement was an illusion.

'Could we just skip straight to the labyrinth? I want another crack at the Minotaur.'

'You're sure you want to?'

Phoenix nodded. Grateful for Glen Reede's e-mail, he slipped into the suit. And slipped was exactly the right word. There was hardly any friction at all.

Like a second skin.

'But before we start,' said Dad. 'Take a look at this. It's the next stage in developing the ultimate game, and it'll blow you away.'

He handed Phoenix a questionnaire.

'Go on, read it.'

'What, now?'

He was itching to get at the Minotaur.

'Yes, now. You won't be disappointed.'

'But what's it about?'

Dad smiled. 'Another innovation from the fertile mind of Glen Reede. You won't believe what he's come up with this time. He's not satisfied with the game as it stands. Now he's planning one that can be tailor-made to each individual player.'

'Never!'

Dad nodded.

'Imagine it. You send off a list of what – and who – you would have in your perfect game, and Magna-com will design it for you. I've never seen anything like this outfit. The ideas just flood out, and the technology is changing by the day. Astonishing.'

Intrigued, Phoenix started to fill it in straightaway.

'Look at this,' he said. 'A game for several players. You have to name your heroine and your villain.'

'Any candidates?' asked Dad.

Phoenix grinned. 'Oh yes.'

For heroine, he wrote *Laura Osibona*.

For villain, without any hesitation, he wrote *Steve Adams*.

For incidental characters, he jokingly added *John Graves*.

Completing the last question, about the cheats you wanted programmed into your game, Phoenix handed the form to Dad.

'Go on,' he said excitedly. 'Load the disc.'

Dad frowned.

'What did your last servant die of?'

'Boredom,' Phoenix quipped. 'Some idiot sent him to live in Brownleigh. Now can we get on with the game?'

Dad loaded the disc.

'Don't forget to skip forward.'

Dad nodded.

'The labyrinth awaits.'

9

It was dark in the palace of King Minos and it took Phoenix a few moments to get accustomed to the gloom.

'You there, Dad?' he whispered.

'Right behind you.'

They were edging cautiously down a flight of stone stairs.

'I thought we were starting at the labyrinth,' Phoenix hissed.

'We are. These are the steps leading down to the entrance. I should know. I helped design them.'

'And that light?'

Phoenix was pointing at a faint glimmer below them.

'Princess Ariadne,' said Dad. 'She's waiting with the ball of thread and the sword.'

'That's OK,' Phoenix told him impatiently. 'You don't need to tell me everything. I only wanted to know *where* I was. I know the legend better than you, remember.'

It was brighter at the bottom of the stairs. Torches stood in iron brackets, flaring with every whisper of breeze. In their flickering light he saw the dark-eyed girl who had watched him break and run. It was hard to believe she was no more than a graphic projection.

'Prince Theseus,' said Ariadne, approaching him. 'I was only able to slip away for a few minutes. My father is suspicious. Here.' She handed him the thread and sword. He felt the usual vibration against his wrist as his score built up. 'Take these. The thread will lead you back to the entrance. The sword—'

'Yes,' said Phoenix. 'I think I know what to do with the sword.'

When she saw Dad emerging from the blackness of the stairwell, Ariadne shrank back.

'Who's this?'

'This? Oh, he's my servant.'

Ariadne continued to dart suspicious glances at Dad. Reluctantly accepting his presence, she rested a hand on Phoenix's arm.

'May the gods go with you. Strike hard and strike well. Make the beast's death agony short. You must remember who he is.'

As Ariadne unlocked the door, Phoenix noticed Dad frowning.

'What?'

Dad shook his head.

Phoenix knew what he meant. *Not in front of the girl.* He waited until the door slammed shut before asking his question.

'Go on, Dad. What was that about? Something's bothering you.'

'It's what Ariadne said. She wanted you to kill the Minotaur quickly.'

'That's right. Don't tell me you've forgotten the legend, it's her half-brother.'

'Exactly,' said Dad. 'But I took that bit of the legend out. I thought it was too complicated for a computer game. I've been trying to keep it simple. I just wanted to cut straight to the action. Boy fights Monster, that'll do most kids.'

The Minotaur for one also wanted to cut to the action. No sooner were the words out of Dad's mouth than the beast was roaring menacingly in the dark depths of the maze.

'What's the big deal?' asked Phoenix. 'So somebody has added a few extra bits.'

'But this isn't *my* game. Phoenix, I'm calling this. Something's wrong.'

For a few moments, Phoenix wavered. Then, driving his own doubts to the back of his mind, he pleaded with Dad.

'Oh, come on. Just a few more minutes, and if you're still not happy, we'll call *Game Over*. That was the agreement.'

Dad looked doubtful, but finally nodded. Phoenix felt like

changing his mind a few seconds later. The beast was close, snorting and panting in the tunnels. Then it bellowed, a sound so loud and harsh that it buried itself deep into his brain.

'Give me the sword,' said Dad.

He was definitely rattled.

'No way,' said Phoenix, displaying his score. 'It gave me fifty points. Here, you can have the thread.'

He was already fighting an uphill battle with his own fear. He didn't need Dad making things worse. Did he have to be so jumpy? Phoenix breathed deeply, trying to compose himself. He knew every line of the beast's face. At the thought of those yellow eyes, he felt a rush of terror.

Only a game, he repeated again and again in his mind, it's only a game.

But every little thing that had happened so far had drilled the fear deeper and deeper into his brain. When the door had slammed shut, it was like a coffin lid being screwed down. And Dad's concern about the re-writing of the game, for all Phoenix's brave words, was worrying.

'That smell!' gasped Dad. 'I can hardly breathe.'

Phoenix knew what it was. It was the rank odour of rotting flesh. Maybe Magna-com were laying the special effects on a bit thick. It was stifling.

'Are you all right?'

He looked pasty.

'Not really.'

'Come on. Just a bit longer.

They were creeping forward, Phoenix crouching sword in hand, Dad playing out the thread. On they went into endless passageways, turning first to the left, then to the right, and never quite knowing the shifting whereabouts of the beast.

'I can hear it moving,' Dad whispered. 'It's behind us.'

Phoenix could hear the beast. It bellowed again, like a great ox, shaking the mortar between the stone blocks of the dungeon walls. Dust fell like fine, dry rain. Just like the first time.

'Listen!'

It was the unmistakable scrape of giant hooves on the stone floor. A moment later a dark muzzle appeared. Yellow eyes blazed through the darkness, vivid under the heavy brows.

'It's here. Phoenix, get ready, it's here.'

Phoenix could feel the hilt of the sword sliding in his clammy grasp. He was feeling the same urge to flee as he had the other times, but he had to overcome it.

Had to.

Come on, just do it. Make your move.

But the beast held its ground, targeting its victims with a long, cold, unwavering stare. The predator's stare.

'We can stop the game,' Dad murmured.

Are you sure about that, thought Phoenix, remembering the blinding pain last time.

'Give me a little bit longer,' said Phoenix. 'I can win. I'll do it this time.'

Then something flashed.

'It's armed.'

Phoenix watched in horror as the huge, sinewy arms swung a heavy, metal-studded club.

'That's not right,' Dad exclaimed. 'I didn't give it any weapons. It's got enough advantages already. I'm calling it, Phoenix. Somebody's been tinkering with the game. It's fixed.'

'Don't say that,' gulped Phoenix.

The beast stepped forward raising the club to shoulder-height, its upper arms bunching massively. Phoenix glanced at the score on his bracelet. Eighty points. He was going to defend them with his life.

'Come on then,' he said, gritting his teeth. 'This time I'm not running.'

With an ear-splitting roar, the beast swung its club shattering the sword into a dozen fragments. Phoenix stared in disbelief at his grazed palm and the shards of metal bouncing on the floor of the labyrinth. Then he turned his attention to the hideous face looming above him. His score was in free fall. The attack was wiping out his precious points.

'That's it,' yelled Dad. 'This time I'm definitely calling it. *Game over!*'

Seconds later, Phoenix and Dad were ripping at their masks, panicking a little when they took so long to give.

'I can't get it off,' cried Dad.

'I know.'

'You mean this has happened to you before?' Dad demanded, finally tugging it free.

Phoenix kept quiet about the pain he had felt, but he admitted the difficulty removing the mask. 'Yes, it has. When Laura phoned.'

'For goodness' sake. You've *got* to tell me when anything like this happens.'

'What, so you can stop me playing?'

'If that's what it takes to make the game safe, yes.'

Phoenix rolled his eyes.

'Typical.'

Dad chose to ignore the comment. 'That's another fault to report,' he grumbled, wincing slightly as he pulled his hand from the suit. 'Why on Earth didn't you tell me?'

Because I've got to play.

When they were finally free of the suits, they stood panting. Before they could exchange a word, Mum was at the door, anxiety etched on her face.

'What's happened?'

'It's nothing,' panted Phoenix. 'Just the game.'

'A game that's been interfered with,' said Dad. 'Something is very odd and I'm going to find out what.'

Phoenix said nothing. Infuriating as Dad could be, he was right about one thing. This was no ordinary game.

10

'I'm your what!' Laura clearly didn't know how to take the news. 'I'm your heroine?'

'That's right,' said Phoenix. 'I can't wait to see how this pegs out. I don't understand how you and Adams—'

'Hang on. What's Steve Adams got to do with anything?'

'Well, when I wrote down your name as the heroine, I gave Adams as the villain. But like I say, I don't see how it can work. I mean, if they're going to program people into these personalized games, they'll need a photo or something at least. Unless they start grabbing the real people themselves.'

Despite the slight headache he had been nursing ever since he got up, Phoenix smiled. That's the sort of thing Dad might be expecting. The mood he was in, he wouldn't even put kidnapping past Magna-com. It was incredible how seriously he was taking this game. He wasn't really to blame, though. *The Legendeer* was addictive all right. It made him feel more alive than he'd ever been. If pain couldn't keep him away, what could?

'Are you sure this is for real?' asked Laura. 'You're not making it up?'

'Of course I'm not making it up! What do you take me for?'

'Well,' said Laura, 'you did tell the whole class stories were better than life.'

'Yes, but that's—'

He looked around the people on the packed bus and realized that not one of them would be worrying about myths and monsters. It wasn't the sort of thing people thought about on a

Monday morning on their way to school or work.

'All I can say is, Dad is working on a game and it's as fantastic as I've told you. More so.'

Laura gave him a sceptical look. 'I never know how to take you.'

'Laura,' said Phoenix. 'There's one thing you should know about me. I *never* lie.'

He said it in all seriousness, so Laura's reaction was all the more shocking. She laughed. No, that's not quite the word for it. She gave a shrill whinny of a laugh that had half the bus staring at her.

'Sorry, Phoenix, but everybody lies.'

He stuck to his guns.

'I don't.'

'Then you must be some sort of saint.'

Not a saint, just somebody with a destiny.

'I'm telling you,' he insisted. 'Magna-com does exist, and Dad is involved in developing a personalized game.'

'So, you're telling me you can put me in your game?'

'Yes. And sometime soon they'll be able to customize you a game of your own.'

'OK, *The Wizard of Oz,* it's my favourite film. You could make something of that. I'll be Dorothy. You can be the lion looking for his courage.'

Phoenix frowned. He had enough with his headache without Laura winding him up.

'Now you're just being silly.'

'Oh, am I? Well, you just look at it from where I'm sitting. You tell me about this amazing game, but you won't let me play it.'

'I explained that,' Phoenix said. 'Dad would kill me if he knew I'd even told you about it.'

'Let's change the subject, eh?' said Laura. 'I don't want to quarrel with you. You're my best friend.'

Phoenix seized eagerly on her words.

'Am I?'

'You know you are.'

Phoenix wanted to hear more, but he'd reckoned without Steve Adams.

'Well, well,' he said. 'If it isn't the lovely Laura. And, oh dear, what bad taste you've got. What can you be doing with this deadbeat?'

'Oh, leave off, Steve,' said Laura. 'Don't you think this has gone far enough?'

'Oh no,' said Adams, the smile instantly leaving his face. 'I haven't even started. I'll have you, Free Knickers.'

Aware of Laura watching him, Phoenix decided to play it cool. 'Adams,' he said matter-of-factly. 'I'll choose my own friends, thank you very much.'

'You'll do as you're told,' said Adams. 'You think you're so clever, don't you, swanning in here like you own the place. Well, I'm going to show you exactly who runs Brownleigh. I'll be waiting for you tonight. And just to make sure you don't try to do a runner, I'm going to spread the word all round school. You and me on the wasteground opposite the gates. Don't even think about bottling out, or you'll never be able to hold your head up round here again. See you, Free Knickers.'

As Phoenix watched Adams making his way back down the bus, Laura caught his attention.

'Take no notice,' she said. 'He's all talk.'

'You sure about that?'

'Oh Phoenix! You're not going to do it? You're not going to fight him?'

Phoenix was struggling with the discomfort behind his eyes.

'It doesn't look like he's giving me much choice.'

Laura sighed.

'Well, I am. You walk away. Nobody will blame you. Steve Adams is a thug. Just give him a wide berth.'

'Oh, I will,' said Phoenix. 'If he lets me.'

Adams had no intention of letting Phoenix off the hook. All day long Adams' cronies were sidling up to him, reminding him that he was expected on the wasteground at 3.15. For once, Adams took a back seat in the continual goading.

'Don't let it get to you,' Laura told him during the lunch hour. 'You don't look quite right, you know.'

Phoenix was tempted to tell her it wasn't because of Adams. The headache he'd woken up with had turned into a general feverishness. His skin prickled and his eyes felt as if they were being pushed back into their sockets. Something told him this might have something to do with the game too. Even when he was little, the attacks had never been this frequent.

'It'll be OK.'

But the headache didn't let up, nor did the campaign. It continued throughout the afternoon with notes passed across the classroom.

'Ignore it,' Laura advised between lessons.

But by home time, Phoenix knew it would take a miracle to prevent the fight.

'Just walk away,' Laura pleaded as they headed for the school gates.

Phoenix smiled thinly. Because of the headache, he didn't feel like speaking, or even nodding his head. But ahead of him was a reception party of Adams' mates. A buzz of excitement was running through the crowds of schoolkids jostling past them. Everybody knew about the fight.

'Keep walking,' said Laura. 'I've told you before. He carries a weapon.'

But by the time he reached Adams' cronies, he knew there was no avoiding the fight.

'He's waiting for you,' they taunted.

Phoenix didn't even give them a glance.

'You're coming with us,' they announced, surrounding him.

The headache was a searing band of pain behind his eyes. He no longer had the strength or the will to resist. As he accompanied them across the road, he realized that Laura had disappeared.

'Surprise, surprise,' crowed Adams. 'Look who's here.'

'There's no need to do this,' said Phoenix feebly, struggling with the drumbeat in his head.

He tried to break out of the circle of onlookers, but they shoved him back in.

'Oh yes,' said Adams, rushing him, 'there is.'

Phoenix took the full force of the charge on his right side and was spun round. The world turned, sickening him to the core. He lost his footing and fell. As he hit the ground, for a split second he saw something. Not stars, but numbers. The numbers from the monitor screen.

What's happening to me?

It was as if the game was reaching out, calling him back.

For a moment, he was between two worlds.

Adams took immediate advantage, getting behind his opponent and pinning his arms. Phoenix struggled, but Adams had a powerful grip. Wriggling one arm loose, Phoenix prised Adams' hands off. The respite didn't last long. As Phoenix turned to face his opponent, Adams sprang at him, the force of the attack pinning him to the ground.

'You're going to regret ever coming to Brownleigh,' Adams snarled.

That was almost funny. Phoenix had been regretting it for months. Sitting astride Phoenix, Adams steadied himself, but Phoenix forced a hand under the other boy's jaw shoving back his head. He could feel Adams shifting backwards. The move soon had him half unseated, grunting with discomfort.

But Adams wasn't done yet. He crouched over Phoenix, punching hard.

'Get him, Steve!'

'Batter him!'

Phoenix's head was pounding. The oppressive heat was overpowering. Even worse was the smell – the choking animal musk of the labyrinth.

I'm going mad.

'Don't let him off, Steve!'

'Get into him!'

Phoenix was shocked by the savage beating he was taking, but he wasn't about to give up. He had more pride than that.

'Get off me!' He spat, blood dripping from his nose.

But Adams was in command. He twisted his fingers round Phoenix's tie and punched down into his face. That's when Phoenix started to retch.

'Look out Steve, he's gagging.'

Adams drew away. A moment later, Phoenix was suddenly, violently sick.

'Ugh, the disgusting pig!'

Phoenix was leaning to one side, coughing and spluttering. Once Adams had released him, he wiped his face and rolled over, feeling drained. He was looking up at the sky. Adams had gone. All Phoenix could hear were the retreating footfalls of the gang. As he rose unsteadily to his feet, he noticed Laura hurrying through the school gates in the company of two of the teachers. But he didn't wait for them. He didn't want to share his humiliation with anyone else. From somewhere he found the strength to run. He was in no mood to talk. He wanted to lick his wounds.

Alone.

11

Dad was the only one in when he got home.

'What happened to you?' he asked. 'No, don't tell me. It's that lad isn't it? What's his name?'

'Adams. You're not going to tell Mum, are you?'

'I think she ought to know, don't you?'

'She'll be straight down to school if she knows. She'll make things worse.'

'I don't see how. Look at the state of you.'

Phoenix continued to plead his case. 'She'll make a show of me.'

'That's daft talk.'

'What do you know?'

'I was your age once, you know.'

Phoenix sneered. 'Yeah sure, I bet you never had to put up with anything like this. Look, Dad, I just want to fight my own battles.'

'Not doing too well though, are you?'

'I'll be fine. Just don't blow me up. I'll never forgive you if you do.'

'You know what?' Dad said, his eyes flashing with hurt. 'Sometimes you and your mother treat me worse than the dirt on your shoes. What do I do that's so wrong?'

It was a good question, and one for which Phoenix didn't have an answer. He regretted his outburst.

'Sorry. I just want to sort it my own way. Give me a chance. Please.'

Dad examined Phoenix's face.

'Should be able to patch you up,' he said. 'Yes, you'll get

away with it. There'll be one or two bruises to explain away, so you'd better get your thinking cap on. A good excuse, mind. Something convincing.'

'So, you're not going to tell her? Thanks Dad.'

'No,' said Dad, 'I won't tell her. Despite what you think of me, I do understand. I've been there myself.'

Phoenix looked at him. He couldn't see it somehow.

'There is one condition though.'

'What's that?'

'You've got until the end of the week to sort things out with this Adams lad, or it will be me knocking on the Headteacher's door. Got that?'

'Yes Dad, got it.'

By the time Mum got in from her meeting, Dad and Phoenix were in the study. They'd sunk their differences enough to tackle *The Legendeer* together. Mum had to be satisfied with a grunted hello from behind the closed door. Once she had accepted that they were in for the duration, they put on their suits and descended into the labyrinth again.

'I'm going to win this time,' said Phoenix as they walked down the stone steps of King Minos' palace to meet Ariadne.

'Sure,' said Dad, 'you're going to win.'

But there was an unease in his voice. He couldn't forget what had happened last time.

Phoenix led the way to the bottom. It was the same as the day before. The torches flared, the dark-eyed girl approached them. He felt a rush of excitement – the game was underway. But the moment she started speaking, Phoenix too was reminded of the last time they had played.

Ariadne had departed completely from her usual text.

'You have to flee,' she said urgently, her normally sing-song voice little more than a strangled croak. 'Both of you. Get out of here. It's not what you think.'

'What do you mean?' asked Dad.

Ariadne glanced around furtively. 'I can't talk,' she said. 'King Minos' spies are everywhere.'

Phoenix found this disquieting. A note of imbalance had entered the game. Something wasn't right. Ariadne had said King Minos, and not *my father*. Very strange.

'But one thing I can tell you,' Ariadne concluded. 'This place is evil.'

Unease pinched the hairs on the back of Phoenix's neck.

'What are you up to?' he demanded. 'Is this a trick?'

Judging by the look on Dad's face, he was already having second thoughts. Phoenix had to act. The game was everything he had always wanted, something big, something extreme. Something to tell him he wasn't the sort of kid to get pushed around by the likes of Adams. Then he saw his chance. Just as Ariadne was about to speak again, the words seemed to strangle in her throat. She was holding the side of her neck as if she was in pain. That's when Phoenix remembered. The key to the labyrinth was where it always was, hanging from Ariadne's necklace.

'Come on, Dad. We're going in.'

Snatching the key from the gasping Ariadne, he turned the lock and plunged into the labyrinth. The score on his bracelet had already reached ninety. The best yet. Once inside the tunnel, he started creeping forward. It wasn't long before the beast's roar filled the maze.

'Roar yourself hoarse if you want,' said Phoenix. 'This time, I'm going to finish the job.'

As if encouraging him, the points display clicked on for no apparent reason, reaching the magic hundred. He'd scored three figures for the first time.

He reached the meeting of the ways and paused. He was still wondering which way to go when he felt hot breath on his neck. He cried out in spite of himself.

'No!'

But it was Dad.

'Don't creep up on me like that. That's the second time you've scared the life out of me.'

Dad was in no mood to apologize. His eyes were bulging and a vein was throbbing in his temple. He was beside himself.

'You young idiot!' he bawled. 'Pull a trick like that again and I'll ground you for a month. I thought I told you we weren't going into the labyrinth. Don't you think it's a bit funny when even the game's characters start warning you off? That poor girl needed our help. I think she'd had some sort of seizure. Do you realize that I had to leave her to suffer just so I could come after you?'

'She's all right,' Phoenix retorted, suppressing his own doubts. 'That's all part of it. You're not going to let the game win, are you? Don't you recognize a con when you see one? Look, I've scored 100 already. I'm not giving up now.'

'Phoenix,' said Dad. 'I'm not arguing with you. We're getting out of here.'

'Bottle out if you want,' Phoenix replied angrily, determined to find the courage he'd lacked in the fight with Adams. 'I'm staying.'

Dad had obviously decided he wasn't going to waste another word on Phoenix, because he started manhandling him towards the door.

'You're coming with me.'

'No,' cried Phoenix, straining against his father's grip. 'No I'm not, and you can't make me.'

Dad dragged him closer to the door.

'Oh, can't I?'

That's when he loosened his hold.

'What the—'

The door had shut behind them.

'It's locked.'

He pounded on it.

'Ariadne, can you hear me? Let us out.'

There was female laughter, but it wasn't Ariadne's gentle tones they heard. There was a razor edge of cruelty in *this* woman's voice.

'Who is that?' Dad demanded. 'Who's there? Stop playing games. Let us out. Now!'

But the laughter continued, reverberating in the darkness.

'That does it,' said Dad. 'Game over.'

Only the game didn't end. Instead, the beast bellowed its blood lust from the heart of the maze.

'Game over!' Dad repeated.

But the labyrinth was in no mood to let go. Terror was closing round them like a claw.

'Game over! Game over!'

The beast's cry echoed through the labyrinth, an insane series of thunderclap animal howls.

'Phoenix,' Dad ordered. 'Take off your mask.'

His hands were already tugging at the skin around his chin.

'What is this?' he said, his voice betraying real fear. 'I can't feel the join. I can't feel the mask at all.'

Phoenix tried. He too was lurching over into skin-prickling panic.

'Me neither.'

They could hear the beast stamping through the tunnels, dragging its club behind it.

'This is wrong,' said Dad. 'Very wrong.'

Now even Phoenix was having second thoughts. Horror was pounding in his heart.

'You out there,' Dad cried, beating the door with his fists. 'Whoever you are. This is no joke. Let us out this minute.'

For a moment Phoenix glimpsed eyes looking back at them through the hatch in the door, but they weren't the soft, brown eyes of Ariadne. These eyes blazed, just like the beast's. Somehow, they were made of the same primeval brutishness.

'We've got to run,' said Dad. 'If we stay here, it's got us cornered.'

Somewhere in the back of his mind, Phoenix knew this didn't make sense.

It can't hurt us. It's not real.

The terrible braying resumed, worse than ever.

It's a game, just a game.

But that single, common-sense thought was swallowed up by a tidal wave of terror. Fear coiled in the blackness then broke over them with unstoppable power.

'Phoenix! Move, this way.'

And they were running, running for their lives. He noticed the score on the bracelet. Eighty!

But how? Then he remembered.

'Dad! I've dropped the thread.'

He fell to his knees feeling for the string in the darkness. He hardly dared stretch out his fingers, for fear of brushing against the beast's gore-clogged hooves.

'Forget it,' said Dad. 'It can't help us now. Just run.'

They could hear the beast stamping somewhere close behind them.

'It's gaining on us. Run!'

They emerged into a large open space. It was hexagon-shaped. In the centre lay a filthy straw mattress. The heart of the labyrinth.

'Got to think,' said Dad. 'Come on, Phoenix, you like these games. What do you do when you're stuck?'

'Play a cheat, of course.'

'That's it,' said Dad. 'The cheats have been programmed in. But how do we use them?'

'You've got me,' said Phoenix. 'I mean, there's no keyboard. We're *in* the game.'

'That's it then,' said Dad. 'That means the cheats must be in it too. *Physically* in it.'

'Sounds good to me,' said Phoenix, his bravery crumbling as he clutched at straws. 'We've just got to find them.'

'Oh my!'

Dad's body was sagging against his, a heavy sack of despair. The beast had just appeared in the room.

'Dad,' Phoenix panted. 'You start looking. I'll try to keep him off you.'

For all the fear drumming inside him, Phoenix was still half convinced this was all some elaborate computer adventure. He could conquer the beast. And even if he lost, there was always another day.

Dad didn't share even a shred of Phoenix's hope. To face the beast was to die.

'Don't be so stupid—'

'I'm not,' Phoenix shouted. 'If you don't like my idea, try coming up with a better one.'

Dad hesitated, then reluctantly entered the nearest tunnel. Phoenix held the hilt of the sword tightly, and kept moving from side to side, skipping like an acrobat. He'd learned something from the last confrontation – don't take the beast on directly. He remembered the fragments of sword clattering on the floor.

If he could only avoid the murderous swing of the club, if he could just thrust under the Minotaur's defences. But the beast didn't give him time to think. It rushed him suddenly, flailing madly with the club. Masonry and dust flew in the gloom, pattering against the walls. Phoenix was overwhelmed. It was impossible to hold his ground under the frenzied onslaught.

'No, no-o!'

The score was down to seventy.

'Phoenix,' Dad called from the tunnel. 'What is it, what's wrong?'

The club whistled past his head. His score dropped to sixty.

'Dad. Help me.'

He could hear his father's footsteps in the tunnel behind him.

'Phoenix!'

The beast lunged again, smashing the sword from Phoenix's hands. He'd broken it like a toothpick.

The score was crashing. Fifty. Forty-five.

What am I doing? I'm a kid. I can't fight monsters.

Phoenix was hauling himself backwards, his feet lashing feebly at the oncoming beast.

Lowering its head, the Minotaur moved in for the kill.

'Dad!'

Then a surprisingly strong pair of hands was dragging him back. The deadly horns drilled into solid stone. With a shriek of rage, the beast twisted and tore at the floor. Mud, stone and foul water exploded around it.

'Run Phoenix,' cried Dad, relaxing his grip. 'Just run.'

Now they were flying, colliding with hidden walls and pillars in the blackness, but scrambling on, oblivious to the pain of a jarred shoulder or a bruised knee. And all the while the beast was coming, growling, snarling, roaring its hatred and its hunger.

'Dad,' Phoenix yelled suddenly. 'What's that?'

There was something in the wall. It was the size of a phone box, but in the shape of a kind of pyramid, a tetrahedron. It was silvery and distinct from the rest of the masonry and bore a bull's head symbol on the top. It was giving off an electronic buzz, the first reminder that this was, in fact, a game.

'That's it,' said Dad, hope rising for the first time in his reedy voice. 'It has to be. It's a terminal of some sort. It operates the cheat – the escape.'

The beast was at the end of the tunnel, dark and massive in the half-light. It seemed to hammer the air with its presence, shocking the breath out of its prospective victims.

'You first, son.'

Phoenix entered and felt a burst of energy around him.

'This is it,' he screamed, a cry that was half joy, half horror as the beast advanced.

'Then get through,' shouted Dad. 'And take my hand. When you get through, keep pulling. Whatever you do, don't let go.'

Phoenix hurled himself into the shimmering, yielding energy-burst, the gate between game and home.

'Don't let go!'

But the beast roared again, the rancid heat of its breath blasting into Phoenix's face. He screamed and threw himself through the gate – back into Dad's study.

To his horror, the room was empty. This time he and Dad hadn't been there at all, twitching in their PR suits. They had vanished bodily into the game.

Phoenix reached into the gate, but his fingers clawed at emptiness. He'd done it. He'd done the most terrible thing. He'd let go!

'Dad,' he shrieked, drowning in guilt. 'Dad!'

The gate was still shimmering, an oval of light in the study. It was still open. Phoenix thrust his hand into the light, reaching into the monstrous parallel world. Nothing. He stared at the computer screen. Dad was fleeing towards the gate. The beast was almost upon him. It was impossible to separate the two blurred figures.

'Dad!'

Then there was a dark shape in the gate. Dad? Or the beast? Phoenix fell back. Please, not that. In his panic, he almost pulled the plug from the wall. But Dad was still in there somewhere. He couldn't just abandon him. Then the shape took on recognizable form.

'Dad, thank goodness.'

'Phoenix,' Dad snapped. 'The suit, get it off. Now!'

As Phoenix peeled off the suit, Dad reached for the computer and switched off. The oval of light vanished. This time it really was game over.

He was running through the passageways again.

I have abandoned him, left him to his fate.

Behind him Phoenix could hear Dad's cries. The beast's bellows mixed with his screams.

It's tearing him apart and I have abandoned him.

Phoenix rested his forehead against the slimy stonework.

How could I?

I have to go back.

He retraced his steps through the gloomy tunnels, listening for a clue to the beast's whereabouts. But the maze was silent. He stumbled over something in the dark. Or somebody.

'Dad?'

He knelt down and examined the body, forcing himself to touch the bloodstained face.

It wasn't Dad.

Maybe I didn't betray you.

'Dad?'

He moved on, discovering four more of the beast's victims. He was seized by panic.

'Where are you?'

Then a shaft of light fell on his face. Dad was with Laura.

'You're alive.'

But they weren't looking at him. Their eyes were trained on a spot just behind him. He turned slowly. Two yellow eyes were staring at him. Hot, sickly breath was steaming from its nostrils. The beast! Phoenix watched in horror as its huge muscular arms curled round Dad and Laura, snapping ribs and grinding flesh.

'Phoenix,' they were screaming. 'Help us!'

He hung on to their arms but the beast was too strong.

'Don't let go. Please don't let go.'

But his courage failed. The beast vanished into the darkness with its fading victims.

'No!'

Phoenix sat bolt upright in bed. He was clammy with sweat and his head was pounding.

'What's happening to me?'

Moments later Dad came running into the room in his pyjamas.

'What is it? What's wrong?'

Phoenix felt stupid.

'It was a dream, Dad. I had a nightmare. Sorry if I woke you.'

The tension in Dad's face relaxed.

'Bad dreams, eh? I've been having a nightmare myself. I'm working through the game, then a terrible thought occurs to me. I'm not playing the game. *It's* playing *me*. I must be going crazy.'

'That goes for both of us.'

'Anyway, try to get some shuteye. It's been a wild day.'

Phoenix smiled.

'You can say that again.'

Dad walked to the door.

'Goodnight, son.'

But Phoenix didn't want to let him go without another attempt at an apology. Part of him was still playing the game. He could feel Dad's hand slipping from his grasp, his whole being filled with the agony of loss.

'Sorry I let you down. In the labyrinth, I mean.'

'Forget it.'

But it didn't sound like Dad had forgotten it. There was a curious hollowness about his voice, as if something had gone from him. Trust perhaps. Dad was about to close the door, when he paused.

'Forget the game too. You are not to go in the study. Do you understand that? Never.'

This time, there were no arguments. Just then, Phoenix didn't think either of them should chance playing again.

'Yes Dad, I understand.'

'I've had enough of this, Phoenix. That wasn't virtual reality. We were somewhere else.'

Phoenix nodded.

'Tomorrow morning I'm going to get to the bottom of all this. I'm going to find out exactly what Mr Glen Reede is playing at.'

'And if he won't tell you?'

'Then I'll find out for myself. I'll find out what's going on. Either that, or I'll destroy it.'

Even then, Phoenix couldn't shake the feeling that the game was part of him. He was the only one who could play and win.

'Dad, don't even try!'

'Why not? I've had it with Magna-com. I don't owe them anything. Anyway, I'm going to have one more go at understanding this game, then I'm telling Mr Glen Reede I'm finished with him.'

'You're resigning?'

'I'm thinking about it.'

Phoenix felt the weight of disappointment in his father's voice. The room filled with the distance between them. His voice shook as he answered, 'Goodnight, Dad.'

12

From the time of their return from the labyrinth, only Dad entered the study. He became a man obsessed. This thing was dangerous. He had to know just how dangerous. So John Graves set himself a task. He was going to crack the secret of the game, then he was going to destroy it. What's more, he knew that the numbers were a stepping stone. Crack their mysterious code and he would be on his way to thwarting Reede. So he alone stared at the encrypted message, he alone struggled with the numbers.

You'd like to read my thoughts, wouldn't you, John Graves? You'd like to pick my brains and then destroy me. I even had to remind poor Ariadne where her loyalties lie. That's right, suddenly it seems that my creatures would like to have a mind of their own. But the boy Phoenix has a feel for my world. No, more than a feel. That's right, our little Theseus has an instinct. Who knows, in time he could prove himself a worthy opponent. He is what I've been looking for, a believer, one I can use to test the game. The Legendeer *is his destiny. He knows it, I know it. Why not? I can't unleash the game for a month. I've been waiting this long, I can afford to be patient. A little sport, then it will be time to get down to the real business. Coming soon, the bargain of the century. My world for yours.*

John Graves continued to stare at the screen. Who knows, if he had understood even a little of the meaning of the procession of numbers, he might have worked with even greater urgency.

Phoenix tapped lightly on the door. 'Dad?'

'Can't talk now, son.' His voice was distant, as if he was speaking from another world entirely.

I didn't mean to betray you.

Why didn't I just hang on? Why did I have to let go?

'Are you working on the game? I—'

'Leave this to me, Phoenix.'

I can't leave it to you. I'm the one who plays the game.

'But Dad—'

Why wouldn't he listen? Suddenly, Phoenix didn't want to keep anything secret. Not the pain, not the sense of belonging. He had to stop Dad playing.

'But nothing, Phoenix. Leave me to sort it.'

So Phoenix walked on down the hall and dropped heavily on to the couch. Just like he had the night before and the night before that and the night before that. Except for a few snatched hours of sleep, Dad had hardly surfaced from his study since their last brush with the Minotaur. He'd said something strange once.

'I'm preparing a bomb for Glen Reede.'

After that, scarcely another word. He'd even started taking his meals in the study. Anything so that he could stay at the PC. Phoenix knew his father was getting himself deeper and deeper into something he didn't understand, and it scared him.

'I'd leave him to it,' Mum advised.

Phoenix groaned 'But how can I? I'm meant to be with him. It's my game as much as his. More. Dad doesn't know what he's dealing with.'

'Would you care to explain that?'

Frankly, thought Phoenix, I wouldn't. Somehow, the game gave him a sense of himself, of what he might be. It scared him all right, but he still felt he could beat it. He could be a hero. Not Dad though. He was an outsider.

'I'm still listening,' Mum said.

In some ways, she was the strongest of the three of them. She was quiet and modest, but her dark eyes saw right through her husband and son, and once she had made up her mind, she rarely changed it. Quietly, and without making a fuss, she held the family together even when the strains were as obvious as at present. Now that she sensed something was wrong, she wanted Phoenix to explain himself. He knew he had no choice.

'It's the feeling I get when I'm playing,' Phoenix told her. 'I belong there. I'm . . . I'm *home*. But how can I feel at home in hell? I must sound really stupid.'

'No, not really,' said Mum. 'It's our game. We all had a part in creating it, remember.'

'Not as much as we thought,' said Phoenix.

'I know what you mean,' Mum said. 'But you've got the same feeling I had when I was writing the script for your father. It wasn't so much that I was telling the stories. They were telling themselves *through* me.'

Phoenix met her look.

'That's it Mum, that's exactly it. We're part of this.'

He twitched open the curtains and stared outside where the trees were threshing in the strong night wind. Mum was a good listener and talking to her seemed to make everything clear. He told her about his forays into the game and the growing feeling that it was bigger than he was. She didn't say a word, but from time to time her eyes widened, especially when he mentioned the god of mischief, Pan.

'Hang on,' he said, as if thinking straight for the first time. 'What was it you said before?'

'About what exactly?'

'I know. You said it was *our* game, but it isn't. We've been fooling ourselves. Maybe we feel we're part of it, but I don't think we created the game at all. I don't think we created *any* of it. We retold a few of the legends, Dad played with the elements of the game, but we didn't do anything new. It was all there for us, ready-made.'

Mum gave him a questioning look.

'It seems so obvious now,' Phoenix continued. 'Sure, when we picked the Greek myths we thought it was our choice. But they were there at the top of the options, along with the vampires and all the other legends. We were bound to choose them. Do you remember what Dad said?'

Mum shook her head slowly.

'He said he was only a scene-shifter. Somebody else made the jigsaw. All he did was move the pieces around.'

By then, Phoenix might have expected Mum to be questioning his sanity but, instead, she was listening intently.

'Go on.'

Encouraged, Phoenix let the ideas spill out. All the things he'd half felt or half thought. *The Legendeer* was more than a matter of graphics and a story line. It always had been. It was a living thing, a thing with power and a life independent of the PC. The machine was a vehicle for the game, the sheath for its chrysalis stage, and that's all. *The Legendeer* was somehow both primitive and all knowing. It was able to reach out. It could twist time and space. It played the player.

'That's right,' Phoenix exclaimed. 'It's been playing us.'

Dad had mentioned it more than once, the way the game was constantly changing, evolving, the way bits were being added without his knowing it. It was obvious.

'The game's alive!'

The thought filled Phoenix with horror. He had been at war with himself for days. Part of him, the instinctive part, wanted to play, to fulfil his destiny. But the greater part of him was taking control. All he wanted was to take a hammer and smash the computer so nobody could ever play it again, so that nobody could ever put themselves in danger.

'Dad!' cried Phoenix. 'We've got to get him off that computer.'

Mum wasn't arguing. They hurried down the hall.

'John, talk to me,' said Mum. 'I'm worried about you.'

'Worried?' Dad repeated. 'No need to worry about me. I'm a big boy now.'

He turned the lock and opened the door slowly, until he was peering out at them.

'Look Dad,' said Phoenix, going for broke, 'I think the game's alive. It thinks. It does things. It could even be dangerous.'

Dad smiled grimly.

'Only just worked that out, have you?'

'So you know!' cried Mum.

'Oh, I know all right. I knew before either of you did.' He unlocked the door and looked at them. His eyes were hard, staring. 'Shall I tell you what I know? There is no Magna-com. There's no office, no factory, no nothing. Just a website and a bank account that pays me each month by computerized credit transfer.'

Mum reacted first.

'But I don't understand.'

'Well,' Dad confessed, 'that makes three of us. It's true enough. There isn't even a Glen Reede. Want to know what Glen Reede is? It's an anagram, a stupid kid's anagram.'

He handed Phoenix a sheet of paper.

The letters GLEN REEDE were rearranged to read LEGEN-DEER.

'That's why I'd never heard of him. He doesn't exist.'

'Slow down a minute, Dad. How do you—'

'What do you think I've been doing in here? I've been trying to build a weapon, an antidote to the poison in the game.'

Phoenix couldn't believe what Dad was saying. Perhaps the last time in the labyrinth had unhinged him.

'John,' said Mum. 'What are you talking about?'

'Well, the joke's on me,' Dad went on, ignoring her question. 'I'm working for a phantom. As for the game—'

'Yes?' Phoenix asked. 'What about the game?'

'Forget it,' said Dad. 'Look you two, I know this is strange, but I can handle it. I've got to get on with my work.'

'But what work?' Mum demanded. 'If there is no Magna-com, then who are you working for?'

Dad pinched the bridge of his nose. He looked tired.

'I only wish I knew. But there is a way to beat the game. I'll find it, you see if I don't. I'm not working for Glen Reede and Magna-com any more. I'm working *against* them.'

'And you can work against them tomorrow,' Mum interrupted. 'John, this is scary. You've got me worried – both of you. I don't understand this game, and I don't want to, but you can't work night and day on it. Just take a little time to think about it.'

Dad stared at her. He was wavering.

'Please. For me and Phoenix. You've got to break off. Just for one night.'

Dad was a few moments coming to a decision, but eventually he nodded. For the first time in months the three of them felt like a family.

He was in the labyrinth again. He was running this time, sprinting through the tunnels slapping his hands on the walls.

They must be here. They've got to be.

The cheats – they were the only means of escape.

But the beast was in there too, and it was close behind. Phoenix could hear it shifting through the darkness, stalking him.

'This way,' cried a voice, a muffled male voice. 'Make your way towards me.'

A helping hand, thought Phoenix. But where? He eventually tracked the voice to a grating in the ceiling.

'Dad?'

But it wasn't him. It was a boy's voice.

'Surprise, surprise!'

'Adams! What are you doing here?'

'Don't you remember, Free Knickers? You invited me in.'

Then somebody else was speaking. The voice this time was female. Laura? Ariadne? It belonged to a woman all right, but there was no warmth in it. It crackled with hostility.

'Here comes the beast, boy. Say your prayers, because it's just round the corner.'

Phoenix stood beneath the grating, panting with fright. Where was it? Go forward or go back?

What do I do?

Then the question was answered. It was there in the gloom, the huge heavy head visible first of all, then its shoulders, then the powerful arms and the enormous club.

'Don't leave me here!'

He turned and ran.

'Dad, Laura, anybody. Help me!'

Then he saw Dad. He was on the other side of one of those gratings. Somehow, he'd wrenched off the metal grille and was reaching down towards Phoenix.

'Get me out of here!'

'Take my hands,' said Dad.

'Don't let me go,' begged Phoenix as the beast closed. 'Please don't let go.'

Dad was hauling him up through the hole in the ceiling. His legs were dangling, dangerously close to the beast. He could feel his breath, the spray of its saliva.

Hold on to me, for pity's sake hold on!

But suddenly Phoenix was falling, crashing to the stone floor in front of the beast, his breath dashed out of his lungs.

Dad! You let me go!

Phoenix was detonated from his dream.

'A nightmare,' he breathed, relief overwhelming him. 'Another nightmare.'

He looked around the room, half-expecting the beast to attack again, a dream within a dream. But it was over. He was safe.

For now.

He swung his legs over the side of the bed and sat there for a few moments, before checking on the time. It was half past two. On a whim, he walked to the top of the stairs. Was anybody still up? The light was on downstairs.

'Mum?'

He said it quietly, just in case she'd turned in.

'Mum?'

He walked downstairs and stopped outside the study. The ceiling light was off, but the computer screen was flashing. Had Dad left it on? Phoenix was about to return upstairs when Mum came out of the kitchen.

'Phoenix,' she said. 'What are you doing up?'

'I had a nightmare,' he told her.

She nodded.

'We've brought a nightmare into this house.'

Phoenix followed her into the kitchen. There was a fresh cup of coffee on the table, sitting next to the contents of an old box. There were a couple of notebooks, dog-eared and faded. A fan-shaped pile of curling black-and-white photographs looked intriguing, but he still wanted to know about Dad.

'Is he in bed?'

Mum gave a long sigh.

'He tossed and turned for a couple of hours, then he got up again.'

'You mean he's back in the study?'

Mum nodded.

'I did my best—'

She broke off, almost in tears.

'Don't cry, Mum. He'll be OK.'

Why did I say that? How do I know?

'It's not just John,' she said.

She held up a photograph, dated 1969. It showed a man in his garden. Obviously Greece. Phoenix noticed the family resemblance.

'Who's this? A relative?'

'Your Uncle Andreas. My father's brother.'

'Andreas? You kept him quiet.'

'They were twins. So close. They thought each other's thoughts, felt each other's feelings.'

'So where is he now, this Andreas?'

'He's dead.'

Mum fingered the notebooks.

'The family always thought he was mad. Now, I'm not sure.'

'But why did they think he was mad?'

'He saw things – apparitions, ghosts. He had always been bookish and painfully sensitive. He was also obsessed with ancient mythology. Then he started to believe those gods and demons were talking to him.'

Phoenix felt a shadow fall across his heart.

'It's all in his journal.' She looked into Phoenix's eyes.

'There is more . . . Something you should know. All his life Andreas suffered debilitating headaches—'

Phoenix started.

'Listen, Phoenix, I don't know if this has got anything to do with the game, but your grandfather gave me Andreas' journal when we moved from London. He didn't explain why. He just told me to keep it in a safe place, and read it *if anything happened*. I think I always had an idea what it was about. I've got a kind of instinct, a sixth sense.'

Phoenix smiled thinly.

'I tried to shut it out, deny the strange thoughts that came into my head. But when you started talking about Pan, I got the journal out and read it. It wasn't long before I understood the truth.

'Andreas wasn't mad. All I knew about him to begin with was that the family didn't like to talk about him. He was a kind of black sheep.'

She stroked the back of Phoenix's hand, as if to reassure him.

'There was only one exception, your grandfather. They were twins, remember. Even when Andreas started slipping away from the normal world, seeing those things, my father knew in his heart of hearts that he wasn't mad.'

'But what did Andreas see?'

Mum pushed the photograph across the table.

'Look closer. Dad pointed this out to me when he gave me the journal. It's quite a mystery.'

Phoenix frowned. 'I don't—'

'Look behind him, in the shadows of the wall.'

Phoenix's heart missed a beat. The image was hazy and ghost-like, almost lost in the shadows cast by an orange grove, but there was no mistaking those features. It was the guide to the game – Pan.

'It can't be.'

'The photograph has been in the family for years,' said Mum. 'I had shut Andreas out of my mind until you told me what was in the game.'

'But what happened to Andreas?'

'His obsession with his ghosts, his demons, got worse. In the end, the family placed him in . . . an institution.'

'A madhouse!'

'A hospital,' said Mum, correcting him. 'No, why should I cover up for what they did? That's exactly what those places were then. The family put him away. He saw things and they put him away in a madhouse. All the years he was there, he kept on telling anyone who would listen that there was a nightmare world, and its creatures visited him. Poor Andreas. He died in that awful place.'

Phoenix gasped. 'The demons got him.'

Mum smiled.

'No, there was a fire.'

'That's terrible. But why didn't you ever tell me about it?'

'Maybe it's because I was shutting it out. Nobody wants to believe in demons, do they?'

She paused.

'There is something else though.'

'Yes?'

'Don't you see? The legends, the headaches. I didn't want—'

'You didn't want me to go the same way?'

She paused before moving closer so that they were sitting side by side at the table.

'There is one last thing I have to show you.'

She picked up a photograph which had been lying face down in front of her and turned it over.

Phoenix felt his senses swim. It was a portrait of Andreas, aged fourteen. Phoenix didn't just look like him. They were identical.

It was like looking in a mirror.

13

'Like to tell me about it?'

At the sound of Laura's voice, Phoenix looked up. The 8.30 a.m. school run was an ordeal at the best of times. Adams made sure of that. This particular breezy morning it was about as much as Phoenix could bear. Dad still hadn't emerged from his study. The entire night had slipped away without him so much as putting in an appearance. Judging by the look on Mum's face and her edgy, brittle way of speaking, she was as unsettled by Dad's latest escapade as Phoenix was. He'd gone way beyond eccentricity this time.

'I don't think he's even had anything to eat,' she'd said at breakfast, returning from a fruitless attempt at getting him out. 'And he's locked himself in. I don't care how important his work is, he can't stay in there forever.' But even a second visit hadn't roused him. In the end, she'd had to go to work.

Phoenix stared at Laura. Her mouth was moving, but he hadn't heard a single word.

'What did you say?' he asked.

'I was wondering,' said Laura, sitting next to him, 'whether you wanted to talk. Something's obviously bothering you.'

'I'm worried about Dad,' he told her.

'How come? I thought everything was coming up roses. You know, with this wonder game and all.'

Phoenix frowned. 'It's the game that's the problem.'

Laura listened while he stumbled through a garbled explanation of the week's goings-on. But when she interrupted him for the third time to ask him whether he wasn't exaggerating just a little bit, he lost his temper.

'What is it with you, Laura? Don't you understand? Something really strange is happening here. Can't you even imagine anything out of the ordinary?'

'Don't have a go at me, Phoenix,' Laura retorted. 'None of this is my fault, you know.'

Their raised voices were a gift to Adams. He detached himself from his mates at the back of the bus and made his way up the aisle.

'What's this?' he asked. 'Trouble in paradise? Don't tell me you're falling out.'

'Clear off Adams,' warned Phoenix. 'This is none of your business.'

'My, aren't we touchy this morning,' sneered Adams.

Phoenix glared back at him. He reminded him of the ancient spirit that hounded a man to death and beyond, Nemesis. Adams was *his* Nemesis.

'Maybe you need another lesson, Free Knickers. You've forgotten how to talk to your betters.'

Phoenix lowered his eyes. He was still smarting from the humiliation of the fight.

'I don't want any trouble,' he murmured.

He'd got enough with the game.

'You should have thought about that before you started hanging round with Laura.'

'Oh, grow up Steve,' said Laura.

Adams chuckled and returned to his mates.

'Can't you ignore him?' asked Laura. 'Just say nothing.'

Phoenix nodded.

'Anyway, forget Adams. I want to hear the rest of your story.'

Phoenix turned his head and scowled in the direction of Adams.

'There isn't much more to tell. Only that Dad hasn't come out of the study for ages.'

'Are you sure? I mean, he has to eat, sleep, use the toilet.'

'You don't understand. He's obsessed.'

That's rich coming from me, thought Phoenix. Even now I would be tempted to play again.

'You know what you need,' said Laura.

'No, tell me.'

'You need a change of scenery. Get out of the house. Forget your problems for a while.'

'Yeah? So how do I do that?'

'You could come to my house for tea tonight. I told Mum and Dad I'd ask you, and they said it was OK.'

'I'll have to phone Mum,' said Phoenix.

'No problem,' said Laura. 'Just let me know later if it's all right.'

The bus was pulling up outside Brownleigh High. As he stood up, Phoenix felt Adams' elbow brush against him.

'Be seeing you, Free Knickers. Soon.'

Laura was right. He did need a change.

'That you, Laura?' shouted Mrs Osibona.

'Yes. Phoenix is with me.'

The Osibonas emerged from the kitchen wearing aprons. Phoenix smiled. Laura had told him about them, the way they did everything together. Like a pair of love birds, he thought.

'Glad you could come,' said Mr Osibona, wiping a hand on his apron and offering it to Phoenix.

'Thanks for inviting me,' he said as they shook hands.

'This came for you second post,' said Mrs Osibona.

Laura took the large bubble-pack envelope and turned it over. She examined the sticker on the back as her parents returned to the kitchen.

'If undelivered,' she read, 'return to Magna-com Products Limited, PO Box—'

'Magna-com!' exclaimed Phoenix. 'What are they doing writing to you?'

'Only one way to find out,' said Laura.

But as she started opening the envelope, Phoenix grabbed her arm.

'Laura, don't.'

'Don't tell me,' said Laura, 'you're expecting a monster to jump out at me.'

'Of course not,' Phoenix replied.

But she wasn't far off.

'Let's see what it is,' said Laura. 'I like presents.'

There were two items. She pulled out the small plastic case first.

'It's a CD.'

'Actually,' Phoenix told her, examining the black case, 'it's a computer game. *The* game.'

Laura pulled out a larger cellophane wrapper.

'It is the game,' murmured Phoenix, giving the Parallel Reality suit a wary look.

'So this is the famous game,' Laura exclaimed. 'At last.'

But before they could continue the discussion, her parents called them for tea.

'No no,' said Mr Osibona at the end of the meal. 'Don't get up. We'll do the washing up.'

'When did you order this game anyway?' asked Mrs Osibona. 'I didn't even know you were that interested in them, Laura.'

Laura gave Phoenix a sideways glance.

'I'm interested in this one,' she said, making her way to the family's PC.

'I don't think this is very wise,' Phoenix ventured, following her on unsteady legs.

'Why?' asked Laura. 'What can go wrong?'

Phoenix inspected the inoffensive looking disc and the rather more threatening Parallel Reality suit. Even now there was a little voice inside encouraging him to play.

'You'd be surprised,' he told her, resisting the temptation.

Laura was holding the disc thoughtfully between her fingers. After a few moments she put it down on the computer table and started to rip open the wrapper that contained the suit.

'I'm going to have a go,' she said excitedly.

Phoenix felt his throat tighten. His mind was suddenly loaded with rushing images from his last expedition into the game. It was alive all right, and it was expanding its territory.

He was beside himself. Seeing the plug he reached down and yanked it from the socket.

'Phoenix,' gasped Laura, 'What did you do that for? Imagine if my parents had seen you.'

'Sorry,' he answered, knowing his reply was bound to sound completely over the top. 'But I had to. It was a matter of life and death.'

'Oh, p-lease,' scoffed Laura. 'Don't be so melodramatic. You just don't want me to play your precious game.'

Before their disagreement could escalate, there was a knock at the door and Mr Osibona popped his head in.

'Phoenix,' he said, 'your mum is on the phone.'

In a day of uneasy moments, this was the most disturbing. Even before Phoenix picked up the phone, he knew something was wrong. Instinct.

'Mum, what does she want?'

The voice on the phone was breaking.

'Phoenix, can you come home? I'm worried.'

'Why, what's happened?'

'It's your dad. He's vanished.'

'He must have left a note.'

'I'm telling you, the study's empty and he's gone without saying so much as a word.'

Phoenix remembered the game and Dad searching feverishly for an antidote to its poison.

Retaliation? It couldn't be. It just couldn't.

'I'm coming home right now,' he said. 'Oh, and Mum—'

'Yes?'

'Stay out of the study.'

14

Fifteen minutes later Phoenix was standing outside the study.

'I'm going inside.'

Mum looked at him doubtfully.

'It isn't long since you were telling *me* to stay out.'

'We've got to do something.'

Mum sighed.

'But I told you. He wasn't in here.'

'No, I mean before he . . .' His voice trailed off. There was no point reminding her about the *bomb* Dad had been preparing for Glen Reede. She was worried enough as it was. 'Before he left.'

Mum fixed him with the same cautious look.

'What if . . . ?'

Phoenix nodded. They were both harbouring the same crazy suspicion. Phoenix wasn't sure what to expect, but in the event the room was a disappointment. Everything looked just as it had several days earlier. There were a few scribbled notes in his pad, but they were completely undecipherable. With the exception of the coffee cup with its dark brown dregs, it would have been hard to notice any differences at all. The computer was on, but there was nothing to see, just the screen-save program flickering away with its now familiar lines of numbers.

'We should have smashed down the door,' she said. 'Anything to get him out of here.'

'Don't blame yourself,' said Phoenix. 'It was his decision.'

Phoenix turned to go. That's when he noticed the box that contained the Parallel Reality suits.

'Hang on.'

'What is it?'

'I'm not sure yet. I've just got to check something out.'

He lifted a suit, then rummaged in the polystyrene packaging.

'What's wrong?' asked Mum. 'What are you doing?'

'That's funny,' said Phoenix.

It wasn't funny. It was unsettling. The way charged air before thunder is unsettling.

'What is?'

'Well, there should be two suits in the box, and there's only one here. And one of the points bracelets is gone. You didn't move anything, did you?'

'No, nothing. It's all just as it was. Except—'

'Yes?'

Mum glanced at the computer.

'There was one thing I wondered about. That was on, just like it is now.'

'The computer?' Phoenix sat down on the swivel chair in front of the screen, unease turning to panic. 'You mean you didn't switch it on? It was still on from when Dad was using it?'

'I'm not sure—'

'Think Mum, this could be important.'

The crazy suspicion was haunting them both.

'You don't think . . . No, John wouldn't be so stupid.'

Phoenix held his hand up.

'Bear with me, OK? Now, cast your mind back. Was there anything on the screen when you came in?'

'Just give me a moment. Yes, got it!'

He already had an idea what she was going to say.

'It was the palace,' Mum began. 'A bull's head symbol on the walls. The palace of King Minos.'

Her eyes widened, as if her worst nightmare had been confirmed.

'I knew it,' murmured Phoenix.

The labyrinth. Where the Minotaur awaits, hideous, bloody, brooding.

'It can't be,' said Mum. 'No, it's impossible.'

Phoenix lowered his eyes.

'With the game, nothing's impossible.'

That's when the phone rang. Mum flew to answer it.

'Oh, it's you, Mrs Osibona. Laura? No, she's not here. Phoenix, do you know where Laura is?'

'No, I left her at the house.'

In his mind's eyes he could see her, standing by the PC, itching to play the game.

'Yes, that's very strange,' said Mum. 'But Phoenix tells me she was still at home when he left.'

Phoenix was about to volunteer more information when he heard Laura's voice.

So you are here. You followed me.

He went to the front door and opened it, but there was no sign of her. Phoenix frowned. He wasn't imagining it. He *had* heard her voice.

'So where—?'

That's when his heart kicked. He knew where her voice had come from. The study – from the computer's twin speakers. She was calling to him from *inside* the game.

Moments later he was sitting in front of the screen with the Parallel Reality suit spread out on his lap. He was staring in disbelief at the pictures on the screen. What he'd thought about Dad, it wasn't a wild theory at all. It was true. Chillingly true.

'Oh, Laura, didn't I tell you not to play the game?'

There on the screen, Laura was racing up and down a deserted beach, crying out at the top of her voice.

'Phoenix. Anybody. Can you hear me?'

He ran his fingers over the suit. It was a nightmare come true. The game was alive. It could reach out. But it didn't just reach into the fabric of time and place, *his* time, *his* place; it fed on them. It looked for its players, played its little game of cat and mouse, then devoured them.

'Phoenix. Someone. Help me. Help me!'

Laura's voice burst achingly from the speakers.

'Please.'

Phoenix knew what he had to do. His fingers shaking slightly, he snapped the suit open and stepped into it. All the time he was pulling it on, he stared straight ahead, dull-eyed. Like a sleepwalker.

'Phoenix!'

He sat in front of the screen and made a decision. The game had Dad and Laura. Now it wanted him too. But he wasn't going into it as a victim. Somehow, he knew he could conquer it. He was going in to fight. He looked at the figure of the teenage girl running in circles on an unknown beach and he made his grim promise.

'I'm coming, Laura.'

He drew the balaclava-style mask over his head and plugged the suit into the PC. Mum had just hung up on an anxious Mrs Osibona when she happened to see him through the open study door.

'Phoenix, no!'

But she was too late. A split second later the room was empty.

BOOK TWO

The Book of the Legendeer

THE LEVELS

Level Nine
The Gorgon's Stare

1

This time there was no choice. Before Phoenix, flashing against the azure sky, was a menu. Only one option was highlighted.

Level Nine: *The Gorgon's Stare.*

No sooner had he selected it than he was lying face down, clutching at damp, heavy ground.

I'm back. Back in the game.

He scrambled to his feet and took in his surroundings. He was standing on a beach with the sea wind booming in his ears. He started looking around for Laura. He didn't have to search for long.

'Oh, Phoenix!'

She took a few steps towards him then stopped abruptly.

'Tell me I'm not going mad. We *are* by the sea, aren't we?'

'That's right.'

'But how? I don't understand.'

'It's the game, Laura. It's all part of the game.'

Then he remembered his warning.

'I thought I told you not to play.'

She didn't reply. She was reaching down, plunging her hands into the waves of the incoming tide.

'But this is no game. It's real water, real sand.'

'Or parallel water, parallel sand.'

Laura fixed him with a withering glare.

'I don't know what you're talking about, Phoenix,' she said. 'All I know is that we're on a beach somewhere.'

And I know where, thought Phoenix.

'Phoenix,' said Laura. 'I'm scared. This isn't fun any more. Just get me home.'

'That's the whole point,' said Phoenix. 'I don't know how.'

'Can't you just press a button, or something?'

'I only wish I could.'

Laura was losing her temper.

'You got me into this, Phoenix. Now get me out.'

'Just calm down, Laura.'

'Calm down! I'm lost in some crazy computer game, and you tell me to calm down!

A trill on the seven-reed Arcadian pipes brought the argument to an end. Phoenix heard a familiar voice. It was the guide, Pan. He must have been watching them from his vantage point, perched on a rock overlooking the beach.

'You!'

'Now, is that any way to talk to your guide through this troubled land?'

Laura was staring at his cloven hooves and the wiry hair that covered his legs.

'What's the matter with you, girl?' he demanded. 'Never seen a satyr before?'

She shook her head slowly, her eyes widening.

'Are you for real?'

'Is anything, my dear? Is anything?'

Phoenix decided to try a more useful question.

'Is this Seriphos?'

'Of course it is. It is the destination you chose.'

Seriphos, home of Perseus.

'I see your faculties haven't deserted you entirely. What did you expect after all the times you fled from the Minotaur with your tail between your legs? You've been demoted.'

He inspected Phoenix.

'Oh, I do apologize. You don't have a tail, do you?'

'All right, all right,' Phoenix snapped. He was feeling sensitive about his failures in the labyrinth. 'Cut the jokes. So I'm playing the part of Perseus? That's lower than Theseus?'

Pan nodded casually.

'That's what demoted means.' From somewhere, he produced a pocket dictionary. 'Yes, demoted. Put down. Now just look at this. Put down also means killed. Quite apt, really.'

'So what happens now?'

'You fight your way back up. I'm afraid you scored less than impressively on level ten of *The Shadow of the Minotaur*. You had more than enough chances, but you barely tested the beast. It is the top level, of course, and you did keep coming back for more, but you failed so level nine it is.'

'What's level nine?' asked Laura.

Pan frisked gaily.

'Let me show you a trick. Go on, I'm dying to do it.'

Laura shook her head. 'No, I want to know what's in level nine.'

'That's just it,' said Pan. 'That's the trick.'

'Oh, let him do the stupid trick,' said Phoenix.

'Thank you,' chuckled Pan. 'I know you won't be disappointed.'

With that, he began to sniff and snort.

'What's he doing?' asked Laura.

She got her answer instantly, and in the most dramatic fashion, as Pan drew a twisting serpent from each nostril.

'Oh, that's disgusting!'

Pan clapped his hands at Laura's expression of disgust. 'But the best is yet to come,' he announced.

Immediately his hair started sprouting dozens of snakes.

'Going to tell her, Legendeer?'

Phoenix nodded grimly.

'Not got it yet, Laura? It's Medusa.'

The serpents retreated into Pan's scalp as quickly as they'd appeared.

'Exactly, *The Gorgon's Stare*. If you want to try your hand once more in the lair of the beast, you must first conquer the Gorgon, Medusa.'

'So, to get back to the palace of King Minos, I have to complete this level?'

'That's about the size of it.'

'What about Dad?' Phoenix demanded. 'You mentioned my dad.'

'Reach the heart of the labyrinth and your questions will be answered.'

'So he is in here?'

'Complete the game, Phoenix Graves. There is no other way forward.'

Laura turned to Phoenix.

'Is he trying to tell us we can't stop it?'

Phoenix gave her a sad smile before turning to Pan.

'Let's get this straight,' said Phoenix. 'I'm here because I failed as Theseus?'

'Oh yes, you got that right,' chuckled Pan. 'The labyrinth's far too hard for a beginner. Whoever let you try was either wicked or stupid.'

The thought flashed through Phoenix's mind. Glen Reede or Dad. But whatever he thought of Reede, it wasn't fair on Dad. He wasn't stupid. It's simply that he was out of his depth, like any normal person would be.

'No,' Pan continued. 'It's the Gorgon's head for you, my lad, and even that's a tall order. You need a bit of practice before you're ready to slay demons.'

As Pan pumped invisible iron, Phoenix remembered his miserable defeat at the hands of Adams.

'Call it a workout,' said Pan, completing his exaggerated bicep curls. 'Sure you're up to it?'

'I'm not sure of anything.'

Pan threw back his shaggy head and roared with laughter.

'And you're the hero? Can so much really be resting on such frail shoulders?'

Phoenix frowned. 'Look,' he said, setting his curiosity aside.

'You may be a god, but there's no need to rub my face in it. Just give me a clue. Where do we start?'

'First,' said Pan, 'those clothes. So other-world, so Earthly.'

With a snap of his fingers Phoenix and Laura's jeans and tops were replaced by white tunics.

'Togas?' asked Laura.

'That's Roman,' Phoenix told her. 'Chitons.'

'You should fit in better now,' said Pan, inspecting his handiwork.

'I doubt it,' Phoenix replied.

'Meaning?'

'You may not have noticed, but there's the little matter of Laura being black. Won't she stand out a bit in Ancient Greece?'

'She could be Persian,' said Pan offhandedly. 'The Hellenes don't care about skin colour.'

'She still won't pass for Persian,' Phoenix countered.

'It's a vast empire,' said Pan. 'Say she's from foreign parts. That usually works.' He turned it over in his mind. 'Yes, it ought to get you by.'

'Get us by!' cried Laura. 'I don't want to get by. I don't even want to be here. I want to go home.'

'Home!' said Pan from his perch. 'That could be difficult. It may take some time.' He picked himself up and turned to go.

'What do you think you're doing?' Laura demanded, beside herself. 'You can't just clear off.'

Pan winked.

'Oh, can't I?'

Then he was gone.

'What are we supposed to make of all that?' asked Laura. 'I mean, is he real?'

'Beats me.'

'Just a minute,' said Laura. 'Somebody's coming.'

Phoenix squinted against the strong sunlight.

'There are two of them,' he said.

'How will we explain who we are?' she asked.

Phoenix wanted to say he was the hero, but he wasn't sure whether he believed it himself.

Phoenix shielded his eyes against the strong sunlight and watched the approach of the two men through the heat haze. Two spearpoints, two sword blades. At the sight of their weapons and the face-pieces that gave an inhuman look to their helmeted heads, he felt his insides begin to dissolve.

'We'd better hide,' he said. Then from somewhere he found the courage to stand his ground.

'No, maybe not.'

That's right. I don't need to come up with a story. I'm Perseus. I ***am*** *the story.*

'Perseus,' they shouted. 'You're wanted at court.'

'Court?' whispered Laura.

'This island of Seriphos is an unhappy land,' Phoenix explained. 'It is ruled with great cruelty by a tyrant king. His name is Polydectes.'

'Tyrant,' Laura repeated, raising her eyes skyward. 'I might have guessed.'

'Just try to keep mum,' he advised as the heavily armed men approached. 'Let me do the talking.'

The game was there to be won, but they couldn't afford any mistakes.

'Oh, don't worry,' said Laura, 'I don't want anything to do with this madness. It's all yours, thank you very much.'

The soldiers arrived, sweating under their armour and helmets.

I have to find the words.

'King Polydectes isn't happy about you disappearing like this. He demands your presence – now.'

Laura gave Phoenix a sideways glance. She was obviously impressed that he'd got the king's name right. He was tempted to tell her that he knew the story into which they had been plunged, but precious little else. Somehow he didn't have the heart.

'Who's this?' asked one of the spearmen.

'She's—' Phoenix remembered Pan's advice. 'A servant,' he explained, struggling to overcome the shake in his voice. 'Brought from foreign parts.'

He quite enjoyed the look of suppressed fury on Laura's face as he delivered the line. Servant! The main thing was, it satisfied the two soldiers.

'Well, let's be having you, young Perseus.'

They fell in line behind the two soldiers. Phoenix was wondering about a strange tattoo on both men's necks, when one asked him a question.

'Been up to any mischief today?' he asked.

There are questions which disarm you, and neither Phoenix's books nor his newly found intuition gave him a defence against this one.

'Mischief? What sort of mischief?'

The second soldier laughed out loud. His helmet tilted back, revealing the tattoo. An owl.

'What sort of mischief, he says! Drinking, brawling, carousing, your usual style, my laddo. What sort of mischief indeed! The sort that could see you locked up in the palace cells for ever and a day. I tell you, you've done it this time, you young scamp.'

Laura gave Phoenix an enquiring look, but he was stumped. He dug deep to discover what he was supposed to have done – what Perseus had done – but he came up empty-handed.

It was the first soldier's turn to make conversation. 'I don't think that mother of yours is doing herself any favours, either. I can't think of another woman on this island who would turn down King Polydectes' hand in marriage. She's brave—'

'Or very foolish,' his companion interrupted.

'Your mother,' Laura hissed. 'What are they talking about?'

'Not *my* mother,' Phoenix whispered back. 'The mother in the game – Perseus' mother. I'm just playing a part, remember. Never lose sight of one fact – this is all part of the game.'

Laura frowned. Phoenix squeezed her upper arm in a gesture of reassurance.

'Just trust me.'

The court of King Polydectes was less a palace than a fortress. Its forbidding battlements were guarded by sentinels carrying tall spears and massive, elaborately wrought shields. Scarlet banners fluttered from the ramparts. Ominously, black standards flew alongside them. The mark of death and mourning. As he followed in the footsteps of the soldiers, Phoenix could feel his legs turning to mush. It was one thing finding the words, one thing *playing* the hero, but heroes have to fight. The horse hair crests that nodded on the shining helmets of the soldiers only added to the air of menace. Phoenix took in the scene and remembered Perseus' mission.

How can I deliver the head of the Medusa? I'm just a kid.

The first guard broke in on his thoughts. 'There you go boy, take yourself inside. I wouldn't like to be in your shoes.'

That makes two of us, thought Phoenix as the guards brought them to the entrance of the palace.

'What are you waiting for Perseus? You know your way from here.'

Phoenix stared. I do? He took in the massive, hostile fortress. The monstrous battlements swam before his eyes. But it wouldn't have been wise to voice his doubts.

'Yes, I do.'

He led the way inside, out of the glare of the late afternoon sun. The gloom of the marbled interior rushed to embrace them.

'Now where?' asked Laura.

Phoenix looked around. There were corridors to left and right and a broader one still that led straight ahead. For all the dread that was mounting inside him, he had to sound in control. For Laura's sake.

'There.'

They were walking under an ornate archway. The crest at the centre caught his attention. The head of the Gorgon. He felt the reassuring chatter of the points bracelet as his score mounted.

'Yes, this is it.'

'But how do you know?'

He pointed up to the Gorgon's head, then to the huge doors.

'It's no broom cupboard, that's for certain.'

Laura smiled for the first time since they had entered the game.

'That guard,' she said, 'he said you'd done it this time. Done what?'

Phoenix shrugged.

'I just wish I knew myself.'

Time shuddered to a halt as they hesitated outside the doors.

'Phoenix?'

Her expectant look made him ache.

What if I let you down.

Then the inevitable guilt.

Like I did Dad.

He braced himself for his entrance and pushed. It was as if he had walked on a grave. The court of King Polydectes occupied a vast hall. Its dark, cavernous depths were lit by braziers that towered over the sentinels who were standing to attention around the walls. Carved reliefs displayed the three Gorgons, the sisters of evil who dwelt at the end of the world. The die was cast. Polydectes sat on a raised platform flanked by his bodyguards. He lounged on his throne, only his eyes shifting. He had a wolf's face, lean and clean-shaven, and it was no comfort that his black hair was greying slightly. Polydectes had the look of a ruthless hunter. Age only testified to experience, and cunning. But it wasn't the king who struck fear into Phoenix's heart. In the centre of the hall there was a long couch where a body lay, as if in state. It was the corpse of a youth his own age, anointed with oil, dressed and adorned with flowers, wreaths and bronze jewellery. The lifeless face, partly masked by its burial trappings, looked strangely familiar. For a moment Phoenix was convinced that he recognized its features. Then he dismissed the idea as quickly as it entered his head.

Don't tell me this is what Perseus has been up to?

A black shroud covered the corpse to the chest. Phoenix caught the eyes of Polydectes. The old wolf's gaze was flitting from the corpse to Phoenix and back again. The youth had died at the hands of Perseus all right. The game had already dealt him a losing hand.

I'm a—

'Murderer!' yelled an old man who had been standing by the body.

A woman, probably the boy's mother, rushed forward and raised her hand to strike Phoenix.

Only the intervention of a burly guard stopped the attack. Phoenix was aware of Laura watching him, but he stared straight ahead.

'Pray silence for the king!' bellowed a guard.

Phoenix watched anxiously as Polydectes rose from his throne.

'Well, young Perseus, serious charges have been laid against you.'

'Murderer!' the old man roared again. 'Lord Polydectes, I demand justice.'

The cry was taken up by every member of the dead boy's family. Phoenix shrank back, wanting to protest his innocence, but unable to utter a word.

'Justice! Justice!'

It was as if the whole thing was choreographed. Parts in a play, thought Phoenix, you're all playing parts.

Polydectes raised his hand.

'I weep for you and your loss.'

Weep, Polydectes? Since when did tyrants weep? Phoenix only knew about this king from the legends, but he already detested the wolf's face. And Polydectes had the false smile of a hypocrite and a cheat. Hatred flared in Phoenix's heart. For the first time, he felt ready to plead his case. Hatred was strength.

'There you have it, Perseus. Do you see the result of that temper of yours? What began as a tavern brawl has led to the death of a young man of good family. I have been patient with you for your poor mother's sake, but you must see that my hands are tied. A bereaved father craves justice.'

At last Phoenix found his voice.

Hatred is strength.

'Lord Polydectes,' he began haltingly, feeling his way. 'I am sorry for a family's loss, but I plead my innocence.'

'Innocence!' cried the dead boy's father. 'Half a dozen men saw you draw your sword. Half a dozen saw you strike and the point darken with blood. Assassin! Murderer!'

Clinging to what he remembered of the legend, Phoenix doggedly continued his defence.

'Let the son of Cronus, wide-browed Zeus decide my fate. I throw myself on the mercy of the gods. I call on the gods of high Olympus to weigh my life on their scales.'

Phoenix could scarcely believe his own words. It had taken a struggle to dredge them from the depths, but once found, they tripped easily from his tongue.

Polydectes joined the grieving family by the body. He snaked one arm round the shoulder of the sorrowing mother. It was a comforter's embrace, but the eyes of the tyrant showed through the flimsy pretence.

As if you care!

'There is only one penalty for murder in my kingdom—'

'Death! Death!' cried the mourners, right on cue.

'Aye,' said Polydectes. 'Death it is, but my verdict must wait. We are about to bury this victim. This is a solemn and a sacred act and I forbid any unseemly quarrelling during the rites. I will give judgement after the funeral.'

To the beat of a drum the funeral procession began to file out of the hall. Laura looked at Phoenix hesitantly. He simply held out his hand.

'What is all this?' she asked.

'The next episode in the game,' he told her. 'This whole level is devoted to Perseus. That's what Pan told us. The tyrant Polydectes wants to force the mother of Perseus into marriage. Only the hero stands in his way. Something tells me this is a put-up job. Polydectes is getting me out of his hair so he can go ahead with his wedding plans.'

'By sending you on an impossible mission?'

Phoenix nodded.

'Medusa.'

Laura shook her head. 'I keep pinching myself. I just need to wake up and I'll be home. Like Dorothy in *The Wizard of Oz.*'

'Forget it,' Phoenix told her. 'There's no Yellow Brick Road here. We're working in the dark, but this much I do know. Once the game has begun, we've got to play it to the finish.'

Laura stared at him.

'The game is insane, Phoenix. What can we do against all this?'

Something was stirring inside him. A strength and a knowledge given him by his love of the myths. But would it be enough?

'We think, that's what we do. No matter how terrifying it gets, it is still a game. There must be ways to build up our power. There will be cheats too. That's the point of the game. The player has to have a chance. What would be the point of playing otherwise?'

'Are you sure about this?'

No, not by a long shot, but he didn't tell Laura that. As the cortege made its way to the cliffs that overlooked the sea, the sun was beginning to set. Bats were flitting restlessly among the wind-twisted trees. Soon, they were proceeding by the light of blazing torches in the hands of the guards. Wispy showers of sparks were illuminating their way. Ahead of them, where the pall-bearers were climbing steadily to the highest point on the cliffs, an enormous pyre had been built. Phoenix couldn't help but marvel at the intensity of his sensations. A priest was leading the lamentations, addressing the crowd.

'Stand and mourn at the pyre of our poor, murdered son. With sacred honey, oil and wine I anoint him.'

He raised a knife above the shoulders of an ox standing tethered in front of him.

'With the blood of this animal I honour him.'

The knife fell. A few moments later the bloodstained hands of the priest were holding up the animal's heart. Phoenix smelt the woodsmoke and felt the breeze on his cheeks. The illusion of reality was stronger than ever. Terrifyingly strong. There was something else, too. The priest had the same owl tattoo on his neck as Polydectes' guards. Phoenix had spotted it when the old man raised the sacrifice above his head.

'High Olympus, accept our offering.'

Soon the pieces of meat were being roasted on the fire. The fat spat and hissed like a nest of vipers. Phoenix blinked as the flames caught and the acrid smoke began to sting his eyes. As the fire mounted higher and the sun sank in the sky, the funeral came to an end.

'What now?' asked Laura.

'I don't know.'

He had been too busy trying to solve a puzzle. What sort of cremation is it when they don't burn the body?

'Laura,' he asked, 'did you actually see what happened to the dead boy?'

She looked at him for a moment, then her eyes widened.

'You're right, they didn't put him on the funeral pyre. There's something very fishy about all this.'

'Yes, like a corpse who isn't dead, maybe.'

And an owl-tattoo that was being worn like the brand of a secret society. Some of the mourners also bore the mark. Before Phoenix could explore either mystery any further, a guard approached.

'Follow me, Perseus. King Polydectes wants to see you in his private apartments.'

They were following the guard when Laura tugged at his sleeve.

'Phoenix, look.'

The King's Chancellor was dropping handfuls of coins into the mourners' eager hands. The corpse – that partly disguised, but strangely familiar corpse – was the first to hold out his hand.

'He's paying them off,' Phoenix exclaimed. 'I knew it. The whole thing *was* a put-up job.'

'But how do we prove it?'

'Laura,' he said, 'this is the tyrant's court. He has absolute power. What he says, goes. We don't prove anything.'

The guard prodded them away with his spear. Minutes later they were being ushered into the king's presence.

'Who's this?' Polydectes demanded as Laura followed Phoenix inside.

'My . . . companion,' he stammered.

Laura managed a sarcastic comment. 'I'm a slave.'

The king looked unhappy about her interruption. The girl didn't know her place. No equal opportunities in this world!

'Mmm.'

Phoenix was the next to speak. 'You wanted to see me, Lord Polydectes.'

There was no shake in his voice this time. The fear was still there, but there was something else. Something that might prove even stronger. A sense of belonging.

That's it. I'm home!

'I like you Perseus,' he said, the oily delivery making a nonsense of his words. 'I would welcome you as a son. That is, of course, if your dear mother were to agree to my proposal of marriage.'

There was a noise to his left. From behind a heavy curtain a woman appeared. For a second Phoenix's heart skipped. Could it be? Had she read the note and followed him into the game? But it wasn't *his* mother.

Though she bore Mum a passing resemblance, this was Danaë, mother of Perseus. Phoenix remembered his own advice. Never lose sight of one fact – this is a game. He took the woman's hands and smiled. He felt he owed her something. Danaë looked back, drawn and unsmiling. Her pale eyes were troubled pools. Something passed between Phoenix and Danaë. He could feel her feelings. Fear of the tyrant. Horror at the thought of being his.

Polydectes cleared his throat and started to speak.

'The penalty for murder, as you know, is death. I am however moved by your plea for mercy. I also wish to spare your poor mother any anguish.'

Phoenix looked into Danaë's haunted eyes. He could feel her

disgust for the tyrant-king, her captivity. What he'd give to wipe the smile off the tyrant's face.

'You have thrown yourself on the mercy of the gods,' Polydectes continued. 'All that remains is to strike a bargain. Name the trial you will undergo to atone for your crime and I will accept your plea for mercy. And remember, only the greatest trial of courage can cleanse your sin.'

Phoenix didn't have to search his memory this time. Thanks to Pan, the legend was clear, and with it the next step in the game.

'At the end of the world,' Phoenix declared, 'there is a cave. In this cave dwell three monstrous sisters, the Gorgons.'

Danaë gasped. Her hands were gripping Phoenix's so tightly that the pressure was causing him discomfort.

'The Gorgons,' said Polydectes, licking his lips. 'You're aiming high, young Perseus.'

Phoenix saw the hunger in Polydectes' eyes. It filled him with terror, but there was something else. He was *alive*. Every inch of him blazed with life. I have to aim high, he thought. There is a game to be won.

'With serpents for hair,' he cried, his voice ringing boldly round the chamber of Polydectes.

'Teeth that can tear their prey in half and eyes so terrible that they can turn a man to stone, the Gorgons are a match for any hero. Do you agree, Lord Polydectes?'

The king's beady eyes were sparkling with delight. He could almost taste the boy's blood.

'Oh, I agree. I agree.'

Enjoy yourself now, Polydectes, thought Phoenix, casting a reassuring glance at Danaë. I won't forget this trumped-up charge, and that living corpse. You will live to regret your deception.

'Let's strike the bargain then,' he declared. 'Two of the evil sisters are immortal and can't be killed. I will bring you the head of the third, the horror-eyed Medusa.'

'Done!' roared Polydectes.

'On two conditions,' Phoenix said, interrupting.

Polydectes was almost beside himself. In one fell swoop he would have the hand of Danaë and be rid of Perseus.

'Name them.'

'There will be no marriage until I return.'

Phoenix read the tyrant's eyes. He knew the fate of all who had challenged the Gorgon. There would be no boy to return.

'Agreed. What is the second condition?'

'By delivering the head of the Medusa, I will have proved my innocence.'

Yes, and won through to the next level of the game.

'You strike a hard bargain,' said Polydectes. 'But I agree. Done! When does your mission begin?'

Phoenix broke away from Danaë and looked Laura straight in the eye.

'Immediately.'

'You depart this very night?'

'Tonight.'

2

On the other side of the monitor screen, there were tears in the eyes of Christina Graves. Her first thought was to destroy the computer, to smash it to pieces and end the nightmare. But she knew in the same split second that taking a hammer to it would solve nothing. The very idea of a game that swallowed its players alive was insane, but it had happened. Her son and husband were in there, lost among the mists of a bygone age. It was no accident either. She ran her fingers over the photographs and journals that told the story of Andreas' life. Destiny was at work here, and it was painting on a canvas much greater than her imagination.

What a performance! the numbers declared, unread and unheard, *Oh, you would have been so proud, my sorrowing Christina. That was your boy speaking. I actually felt like applauding. That's right. I wanted him to get the better of that old scoundrel Polydectes. It's been such a long time since I found a worthy opponent, and now it has come in the form of an unshaven boy! What were the chances? Do you know what I will do, Christina? I will let you see him. Now, weeping mother, look through the numbers and see your son.*

With that the screen cleared and there was a familiar figure on a desolate clifftop.

'Phoenix,' cried Mum, her face flooding with joy. 'My Phoenix!'

But Phoenix didn't hear. He had been sitting on the clifftop for an hour, maybe more, staring out to sea when Laura asked the obvious question.

'What now?'

The dark waves rolled in and Phoenix listened sadly to the boom of the wind and the crash of the tide. Salt mixed with woodsmoke and stung his eyes.

'Phoenix, what do we do?'

'I don't know.'

'You don't know!'

It had sounded good, all that stuff about returning with Medusa's head. In the king's apartment, carried away by events and swept along by his sense of destiny, Phoenix had actually believed it. The instinct had been strong in him. But here under a starry sky that sense of being home had drained away leaving only fear and uncertainty. He didn't feel one bit the hero. Sitting at a computer keyboard, he could be a giant. But this was different. He was a fourteen year old boy in a foreign land, maybe even a foreign world, no more than a speck of dust under those blue-black skies. What did he know about killing monsters? Demon slayer indeed.

'But you said—'

If there was one thing worse than Phoenix's realization of his own weakness, it was Laura's trust in him and the thought that he was failing her.

'I know what I said.'

He pulled at a loose thread in his tunic. It reminded him of a loose thread in another suit.

'I've always been the same. When I was little there was this ditch at the bottom of the garden. I knew I could jump it. I was special, you see. I've always had that feeling inside me. So I jumped. Guess what?'

Laura was way ahead of him.

'You fell in.'

'That's right, Laura. I fell in. That's me – head in the clouds, feet in the mud.'

'But you sounded so convincing in there,' Laura complained bitterly. 'We're supposed to go to the end of the world, aren't we?'

'Yes.'

'And?'

Phoenix stretched out both arms, as if displaying the vastness of the land and their own puny size. 'What do you see, Laura?'

'The sea.'

'And?'

'The sky, cliffs, a city. What are you getting at?'

He allowed his head to sag between his arms.

'Unless you're clairvoyant, or you've got an A-Z of ancient Greece handy, we've got a bit of a problem.'

'And that is?'

'The end of the world, I don't even know where it is.'

Phoenix had barely finished when the trill of seven-reed pipes and a loud cough behind him brought him to his feet. A familiar figure stumbled clumsily out of the velvet night.

'Pan, you scared me out of my wits.'

The usual mischievous grin, then a question.

'Am I to understand that you are lost?'

Laura took over.

'We certainly are.'

'Then look no further. I am here to serve you.'

Phoenix was ready to go along with the game, but Laura had other ideas.

'Serve?' she cried. 'And how exactly does that work? Let me get this straight. You're a god, right?'

Pan mulled this over.

'For the purposes of the game, yes.'

'And you made all this happen?'

'Now that,' said Pan, 'isn't strictly true. I am your guide. That is all.'

'All?' cried Laura. 'But you're a god. I thought you were superhuman.'

'Superhuman?' Pan chuckled. 'Now that's a thought.'

'What do you find so funny?' Laura demanded. 'We've been spirited away by this stupid game, and all you can do is laugh. Where are your powers? Can't you just magic us to the end of the world and get this over with?'

Pan scratched his scraggy beard.

'You must understand what you are dealing with. I have knowledge, some power too. But I am a very minor god. I am, like you, part of the game and subject to its rules. This is a world where gods exist, but it isn't *about* them. It is about the men and women who play the game and the ways in which they work out their destiny. I can't decide the outcome. Only you can do that.'

Laura stood up, waving her arms.

'But this is crazy! The game's about men and women, you say. We're kids. What are we supposed to do?'

Pan gave her a sideways glance.

'Simply this. You must play the game to its conclusion.'

'But can't you just call it off?' Laura asked. 'What if we say sorry?'

She shouted up to the sky.

'Can you hear me anyone? We didn't mean it. We just want to go home. This is all a mistake.'

Pan shook his head.

'It's no mistake. Phoenix is a player. He had his fair share of warnings on his little forays into the labyrinth, but he didn't take them. He was given every chance to walk away, but he couldn't leave it alone. He chose his path. This is his destiny.'

Phoenix listened. Pan was right. The die was cast.

'So what's the next move?' he asked.

Pan gave one of his unsettling smiles.

'Mine is the power of prophecy,' he said. 'I know your destiny within the rules of the game. You must slay the Gorgon, Medusa, and return with her head to the court of Polydectes. I can point the way. As for the rest, that is in your own hands. You must find the courage to make the kill.'

'But what's the point of all this?' cried Laura. 'Why can't we call it off? Why can't we just go home?'

Pan scowled.

'You forget, child. This is a *game*. Your minds must be as clear as a mountain stream. There have to be tactics, strategy, a gameplan. Most of all, there has to be thought. Though this world may play the sweetest tune, you must never fall for its terrors or its delights, never confuse the game with reality.'

Phoenix had listened patiently until then. But that phrase, *never confuse the game with reality,* it wasn't right. He suddenly remembered the photograph of Uncle Andreas, and the strange figure in the background.

You, Pan. It was you.

'Use the myth as your pole star,' Pan ran on, unaware of the questions that were assailing Phoenix. 'It is an aid to navigate your way in treacherous waters. It is not, in and of itself, the whole truth.'

Phoenix was about to interrogate him about the ghostly apparition in a garden in Greece, when Pan cowered, as if spooked. He lowered his voice, eyes darting to left and right. There was a definite catch in his voice. Fear ruffled his hair like a spirit wind.

'My work is done for now. Prepare yourselves, the Olympian is coming.'

Phoenix looked out at the black sea breaking on the rocks below, the sea-spray mounting the cliffs, and shivered. He watched Pan scurrying away and turned his gaze out to sea.

I know who is coming.

'Laura, look.'

The clouds were parting and a startling figure was sweeping down from the sky. Though the form was human, its presence was immense. Its coming charged the air with a dark intensity. Laura must have felt it too because she shrank back.

Phoenix gave the presence a name. 'The goddess Athene.'

The goddess was armoured, her high-domed silver helmet reflecting the moon's glow. She was bearing a sword and spear. Hovering before them, she started speaking. 'You are Perseus?'

Phoenix remembered the way Pan had spoken. *For the purposes of the game, yes.*

He just said. 'Yes.'

'And you are pledged to bring back the head of the Gorgon, Medusa?'

'Yes.'

'Though it could threaten your very existence?'

A note of uncertainty crept into his voice.

'Ye-es.'

'The gods salute your courage, Perseus.'

My courage!

Phoenix remembered lying on his back, looking up into Adams' leering face. He remembered failing Dad.

What courage?

'If you are ready to accept your mission, I will furnish you with the tools.'

But for all the shaming images that haunted him, Phoenix knew that there was something else inside him. A steel, a conviction that he had a destiny.

'Then give them to me,' said Phoenix. 'I'll do my best to find the courage.'

As Athene led him to the mouth of a cave, Laura continued to hang back.

'There,' Athene announced, drawing back a cloth. 'Your weapons.'

She listed them. There was no need. Phoenix knew it the way a blind man knows his home. By a kind of second nature.

From Athene herself, a burnished shield in which to see a reflection of Medusa without having to look into her terrible eyes. Eyes that could turn a person to stone. From the Stygian nymphs, a pair of winged sandals, a helmet of invisibility and a magic wallet – a heavy leather bag – to carry the Gorgon's head. Finally, from Hermes, messenger to the gods, an adamantine sickle to kill Medusa.

As Phoenix ran his eyes over the weapons he heard the welcome chatter of the points bracelet. His score was climbing.

'There is no further help I can give you,' said Athene, turning to go. 'The winged sandals will take you to the town of Deicterion in Samos. There you will see representations of the Gorgons. Remember their images well, Perseus. Of the three foul sisters, only Medusa is mortal. Do not attempt to kill her sisters Stheno and Euryvale. Such a mistake would surely cost you your life.'

Phoenix nodded.

'From Samos you will journey to Mount Atlas. There you will find the Graeae, the sisters of the Gorgons. You will discover from them the whereabouts of Medusa.'

With that, the goddess was gone, returning to the storm clouds that were racing over the crashing sea. Phoenix was examining the weapons when he heard footsteps.

'You're armed,' said Pan. 'That's good. That's why you were chosen to play. The knowledge is strong in you. But by itself, even knowledge is not enough. It is courage above all that you must discover. When you fled the labyrinth, you exhausted almost every ounce of your life force doing it. If your courage fails again you lose. I hope you understand me well, I am talking about life and death. If you run this time you lose *all*.'

He closed his eyes and breathed the night air deeply, giving Phoenix time to take in this information. And time to prepare his question about Uncle Andreas.

'The only way to conclude the game,' Pan resumed, 'is to complete this level and return to Knossos to face the Minotaur. You have the time it takes for the moon to cross the sky thrice over. By then you must have Medusa's head or you may not proceed.'

Phoenix smiled.

'I understand.'

Pan turned to go.

'There is something.'

'Go on?'

'I would like to know how you came to be in a garden in my world fifty years ago.'

Pan stepped back as if suddenly unsteady on his cloven hooves. His eyes narrowed. It was some time before he managed a reply. 'It's a good question, but one I am sadly not at liberty to answer.'

'Not at liberty! What sort of answer is that?'

'It is the answer of a servant. Win the game, and you will have all the answers you want.'

'But—'

Before Phoenix could complete his sentence, Pan had vanished.

Laura followed him into the darkness, then asked, 'What was all that about?'

'All I know,' Phoenix replied, 'is that there's only one way out of here. We win the game, we find Dad and we go home.'

Laura pointed to the five things Athene had brought.

'How do you know they even work?'

'Pan seemed pretty impressed.'

'You're not telling me you trust that . . . that . . . that old goat?'

'I don't see we've got much choice.'

'But Phoenix, he got us into this. What if it's all his crazy idea? What if *he's* the enemy?'

Phoenix tried to explain. It was the way he'd felt ever since he first played the game.

I was made to play. I am the slayer of demons, the Legendeer.

He watched the expression on Laura's face. She still thought it was all an illusion.

Well Laura, you want proof? I'll give you proof.

'Phoenix, what are you doing?'

He started strapping the winged sandals to his feet.

'Oh no, you've got to be joking.'

'Stand back, Laura.'

He strode to the edge of the cliff.

There's only one way to make you believe me.

'Please Phoenix, don't do this.'

He stared down at the black, crashing waves and the jagged rocks. The boy that had been beaten by Adams wouldn't dare. The boy who had let go of Dad's hand would just sit on that lonely cliff forever. But he wasn't that boy. Not any more. He was becoming so much more. Laura was pleading with him.

'Please.'

I am better than that boy. I am reborn.

Stretching his arms up to the sky he threw himself over the edge of the cliff.

'Phoenix!'

He plunged into the darkness. The night wind was crashing against his face, stinging his eyes. The rocks were rushing up at him. So rapid was his fall, he could feel his flesh being tugged from his bones.

'Phoenix!'

Laura's voice was lost in the wind. It was almost over. He could feel the lash of the sea spray on his cheeks, the smack of salt on his lips. Then, as quickly as it had started, the downward plunge ended and he was sweeping upwards, light as a feather.

He was airborne!

'Can you see me, Laura, I'm flying!'

He swept high into the air, dizzy with the sensation of weightless flight.

'Didn't I tell you? I knew Pan could be trusted. I can fly.'

Then he was diving down, tracing circles round the astonished Laura.

'Still think Pan's a fraud? Well, do you?'

'I don't know,' said Laura doubtfully.

Phoenix dropped to the ground and walked forward. The score on his bracelet had rocketed to **550**.

'There's just one thing, Phoenix,' Laura said. 'What about me?'

'What about you?'

'You could call it a transport problem. We're short of one pair of magic sandals.'

Suddenly, Phoenix had the answer to everything.

'I conquered the night sky, didn't I? I defied gravity, didn't I? You simply take my hand and we'll cross the skies together. To the end of the world.'

Phoenix could see his destiny. It wasn't something beyond him, out of his reach, something decided by the game. It was his to grab hold of.

'I don't know, Phoenix. It looks dangerous.'

'Of course it's dangerous,' he cried. 'I've smelt the stench of death in the labyrinth. We have both heard the treachery in Polydectes' voice and seen the lengths he will go to to get what he wants. This whole world is dangerous.'

Laura was staring, wondering if Phoenix had gone completely mad. But he wasn't mad, he was reborn. Brownleigh, that stupid, boring little town, was dead and gone. That's right, thought Phoenix, this world of enchantment and monsters isn't the myth, *Brownleigh is.*

He raced across the wiry scrub grass to the cave where Athene had laid out her gifts. Bundling the helmet and sickle into the leather wallet and strapping the shield to his back, Phoenix strode towards Laura holding out his hand.

'Are you ready?' he asked. 'Ready for an adventure to the end of the world?'

3

The first thing Phoenix saw by the dawn light the following morning was the interior of the shepherd's hut where they had sheltered for the night. Laura was still asleep, her nose pressed deep into the yellowish-white fleece that she had wrapped tightly round herself. The second thing he saw made him jump for joy. Food. Fit for a king. Better, for a hero! Cheese, coarse brown bread, olives, grapes, oranges, even a jug of watered wine. Very watered. Their provider obviously didn't want them drunk! There was only the faintest scent of goatskin to give a clue to his identity.

'Laura. Hey, Laura. Breakfast is served. Courtesy of the very minor god, Pan.'

He watched Laura's eyes open at a squint. They were puffy with sleep, but opened wide the moment they registered the breakfast table.

'This is a dream. It has to be!'

'It's no dream—'

The moment the words were out of Phoenix's mouth, he realized something else.

No dream.

For the first time in days he had slept easy the night before, cradled by his new identity. The headaches had gone. The hero had woken refreshed. He sprang on to the table and started to dance around the platters.

Through a mouth stuffed with bread and cheese, Laura managed to speak. 'What's with you?'

Phoenix jumped off the table, grinning broadly.

'Those nightmares, Laura, about letting Dad down. I didn't have one last night.'

Laura was unimpressed. The next words she uttered were bristling with indignation. 'No wonder.' She pointed at the blazing light that was streaming through the open door. 'The nightmare is out there. Or have you forgotten where we are?' She swallowed the mouthful of food. 'And what we have to face?'

Phoenix poured two tumblers of wine, listening to the liquid cluck against the side of the earthenware cups. If what Laura saw through the open door was a nightmare, what he saw was a thrilling new world. *His* world.

He did his best to disguise his delight in his surroundings as he replied flatly, 'I forget nothing.'

Laura contradicted him. 'Oh, yes you do.'

'Like what?'

'Like what my parents are thinking. They'll be worried sick.'

Unsure how to reply, Phoenix made his way to the door with a bowl of bread, cheese and fruit.

'We should be in Deicterion by nightfall.'

'How do you know?'

He strapped on the winged sandals. Athene's gifts reminded him of his identity. He was the Legendeer now, in the form of Perseus.

'The moment I put these on I knew all sorts of things.'

'Such as?'

'Deicterion is a lawless town. A wild west frontier post, if you want. There will be bandits and cut-throats. Try not to look anyone in the eye. It wouldn't be a good idea.'

Laura shook her head.

'Can't I just wait here until you get back?'

'No. We have to stay together. You're here for a purpose just like me.'

'Oh, here we go again. What purpose?'

Phoenix mumbled his next few words like a guilty schoolboy.

'You're here because of me. Remember the questionnaire I told you about?'

Laura gave a slow nod as if realizing what he was about to say.

'I named you as my heroine. You're not here by accident. It's fate. That's got to be it.'

Laura stood digesting the information for a few moments, then downed her wine without another word and walked to the spring to splash water on her face.

'I don't suppose Pan ran to a toothbrush?'

Phoenix laughed. The world of Brownleigh had been left behind, and with it the routines of school, home – and toothpaste.

'You'll have to scrub them with your finger.'

He gave her a few moments to finish, then reached out his hand.

'Are you ready to go?'

Laura gave his sandals an uncertain glance.

'Are you sure this is safe?'

'We flew together last night.'

It was as though he was born to fly. He skipped on wave tops and climbed halfway to the stars, taunting the wind and the wide-open sky. And all the while Laura was clinging to his hand with a vice-like grip.

'Yes, and my heart was in my mouth.'

Scared? Phoenix smiled to himself. You don't know scared, Laura. At the other end of the world three sisters are waiting. They know the hero is coming. They were born to await my coming. Their golden wings beat steadily in the putrid air. Their bronze hands stroke the petrified forms of adventurers who came before and were foolhardy enough to look into the Gorgons' eyes. The sisters wait and sniff the west wind like three hounds of hell. Their tongues hang out and loll against their leathery jaws. They know I am coming and they are ready, waiting. At the thought of the Gorgons, his nerves jangled. Terror and expectation were fighting inside him like wildcats in a sack. The old Phoenix told him to stay, to hide in a corner.

But I am better than that.

'Ah well,' he said at last, 'if you want to stay, then that's your choice.'

Laura's eyes sparkled.

'One thing though.'

'Ye-es.'

'You know the old saying?'

'No, but I'm sure you're going to tell me.'

Phoenix cleared his throat and glanced meaningfully at the flocks grazing on the hillside. 'Where there are sheep, there are Cyclops.'

'Do they really say that?'

He crossed his fingers behind his back.

'Absolutely.'

'And there are Cyclops round here?'

Time to lay it on thick.

'A single giant eye, two rows of bone-crunching teeth, a twenty foot tall frame of muscle and brawn. Yes, the brotherhood of the Cyclops roam these hills.'

Laura gave him a very long frown and took his hand.

'Let's go.'

It was the strangest thing. Phoenix didn't have to imagine Deicterion. He *remembered* it. The shadows of this new world must have been gathering around him ever since he was born. There was no rhyme or reason to it, but the hazy images were definitely memories. He was recalling things from beyond recorded time.

Deicterion was a walled town, its rough streets almost deserted as the braziers began to flare in the gathering dusk. An owl shrieked and swooped into a cypress grove, its hunter's song piercing the night. Phoenix thought of the strange tattoos.

'It looks quiet enough to me,' said Laura as they passed beneath its brooding battlements.

'Except for the owl.'

Don't let appearances deceive you, Laura. Remember Pan's

advice. It is a game, all a game. We won't leave this place without staring danger in the face. Perhaps even death.

'What was that?'

Laura was agitated, her head snapping round.

'We're being followed,' he told her, 'but you already knew that.'

Laura didn't want him to know that she was spooked by the quiet streets and the muffled footsteps behind them. She edged closer nonetheless. He liked the brush of her arm against his.

'I can't see anybody, Phoenix.'

He eased a rush light from its holder on a house wall. 'Take this,' he said quietly. 'When I tell you, throw it.'

He expected roughnecks spilling from taverns, brawling youths tussling in the streets, not this unsettling silence. The quiet gnawed at him.

'There!' said Laura. 'Something moved.'

Phoenix had seen it too. He slid the adamantine sickle from where it hung at his belt.

'It's a boy,' he whispered. 'Somebody our own age.'

Gravel scraped under the stranger's feet.

'Now!'

Laura tossed the rush light into the dark alcove. As it struck the ground, the glow revealed a familiar face.

'Adams!'

'What are you doing here?'

'You should know the answer to that. After all you invited me in.'

Phoenix stared. 'The questionnaire!'

Adams nodded. 'Clever boy.' A sly grin flitted across his lips. 'Not very alert though, are you? We've met before.'

Phoenix stared at him. Then the penny dropped. 'It *was* you. You were the walking corpse in Polydectes' palace.'

Adams crossed his arms over his chest and closed his eyes. 'It was a lovely service, if I say so myself. There's nothing like a good funeral, especially when it's your own.'

His eyes popped open and his expression changed. 'A

funeral, eh? Now isn't that a good idea. I let you off easily the last time we fought. Now it's for keeps.'

He drew a short, stabbing sword and struck out at Phoenix. 'Surprise surprise!'

Phoenix parried the blow with the sickle. Adams was taken aback by the speed of Phoenix's reflexes. Surprise yourself, thought Phoenix. We're not outside the school gates now. Adams lunged again, his blade once more clashing against the sickle. Phoenix saw the flash of dismay in his opponent's eyes and disarmed him with a slashing blow. Adams stared in disbelief as his sword clattered on the ground and shattered into fragments. It was a very different Phoenix he was fighting. Then with a guttural command, he scrambled away.

'Get them!'

With the start of the attack, Phoenix's senses had been sharpened. He was hearing intensely and feeling every twitch of his muscles. His brain filled with the sound of running feet. Armed men were spilling from the darkened doorways. Five, ten, fifteen. He'd got his roughnecks. In his lust for the kill, one man was outpacing the others. His unbuttoned jacket revealed a familiar blue mark on his throat, the owl tattoo. Phoenix's curiosity was aroused, but there was no time to worry about it. He had to bring the attacker down in the space of a single heartbeat. The adamantine sickle hissed as he wielded it, dealing the assailant a glancing blow. The youth crumpled to his knees with a groan, then fell at Phoenix's feet. He was elated by his success, especially when it added fifty points to his score.

'His sword, Laura, get his sword!'

'What am I supposed to do with it?'

There was no time for a martial arts lesson.

'Anything, just so long as it looks like you can do some damage.'

'But I don't—'

'Focus Laura. Remember, play it for what it is – it's a game.'

The next two assailants were upon them. Phoenix dropped the first with a swing of his glinting blade. The second hesitated and took the flat of Laura's sword in his face. The points bracelet was frenetically rattling up the score. Phoenix was starting to enjoy himself.

'Don't drop your guard,' he yelled. 'Just hit the target.'

In the melee, bodies were falling like cut flowers. The skirmish ended with raucous shouts and running feet.

'That was so easy!' Laura exclaimed. 'We're not fighting real people. We can't be. It's like cowboys and indians. Bang bang, you're dead, then everybody gets back up again.'

Phoenix wasn't so sure. He restricted himself to a neutral comment. 'We're clocking up points in the game. We can't just face Medusa cold. We have to build up our power.'

'But how do we know if it's enough?'

'Good question,' said Phoenix. 'I wish I had the answer.'

With that, he walked away.

'Where are you going?' Laura asked nervously.

'I have to take a look at something.'

He examined the first attacker. He wanted to see the tattoo. He turned the fallen youth's head to one side and inspected the mark. As he bent forward his victim groaned.

'He's coming to.'

The moment the youth regained consciousness, he gave a startled cry. Phoenix had the sickle at his throat.

'Tell me about this.'

The youth put his hands together, as if pleading for his life.

'This tattoo, what's it for? What does it mean?'

His captive began to stammer out a plea for mercy. 'Don't ask. Please don't. It will cost me my life.'

Phoenix dismissed the look of horror. He was play-acting, like the mourners at Polydectes' court.

'Don't be stupid,' said Phoenix. 'I just want to know about the tattoo. I've seen it before. What's it for?'

But before he could force a reply out of the youth, there was a loud thud from inside his throat. Hands reached for Phoenix and tore at his tunic.

'Please. Help me. I don't . . . want to . . . die.'

His eyes rolled back, showing the whites, and his head lolled.

The words gargled grotesquely in his throat. Just a game, Phoenix kept telling himself despite all the evidence of his eyes. It's just a game. But a hideous black bruise was spreading on the youth's neck and a trickle of blood was spilling from his mouth. This was all too real.

'I don't believe it,' said Phoenix, lowering the dead boy's head to the floor and drawing back. 'Something killed him.'

'What do you mean, killed him?' Laura demanded. 'It's cowboys and indians. Everybody gets back up.'

'Maybe that's what we thought,' said Phoenix. 'But this isn't faked.'

He stared at the body in horror.

'It's like a bullet went off *inside* him.'

Laura cut him short with a sharp cry. He felt her hands pulling at his tunic.

'Phoenix!'

Just as he was wondering what had got into her, an arrow head carved a path through the night air, smashing into a lintel and splintering the timber. Laura had reacted quickly, pulling him back with unexpected force.

The points bracelet clocked up an extra fifty points. His reward for cheating death.

'How many points would we have lost if the arrow had got you?' she asked.

'The lot,' Phoenix panted, a new understanding flooding through him. 'I'd be dead.'

All that time he thought he'd got the game sussed, he'd just been kidding himself. Forget cowboys and indians. His first feelings had been closer to the mark. It was real. The arrow head had been a lethal weapon. The game was for keeps.

'But—'

'Listen,' he interrupted. 'I don't get it either. OK, so a game's a game, but dead is dead.'

He tugged at the arrow's shaft.

'There's nothing virtual about this reality. Feel.'

While Laura examined the arrow, he pressed his back against the door.

'We're too exposed here,' he whispered urgently. 'Where's the door handle?'

Laura was the one who found it and they tumbled into the building. There was no time to take in their surroundings. The sound of running feet alerted them to another attack. Then a smirking face – Adams' face – appeared at a window.

'You did well,' he said. 'Better than I would have expected.'

Their fight was in both their minds.

'But it isn't over yet,' he chuckled.

Firebrands were being flung into the building, sizzling as they hit the floor.

'Surprise, surprise!'

By their flaring light, Phoenix and Laura began to make out the features of the room. Tall jars were stacked against the far wall. Phoenix plunged his hand into the nearest of them.

'A granary,' he told Laura. 'We're in a food store.'

'Phoenix, there. A back door. We can still escape.'

Too easy. Their besiegers would have had it guarded from the start of their attack.

'Listen Laura. They'll be expecting us to try the back way. When I give the signal, ease it open just the slightest amount then get right away from the door.'

'What are you going to do?'

He smiled. It was an unsteady smile. He was out of his depth but learning fast, drawing on the memory that couldn't be a memory, picturing sword-play in a quiet grove.

'I should have thought of this earlier.' He took the helmet of invisibility from the leather wallet and put it on, praying it would work. Hauling a grain jar over to the nearest window, he prepared himself for battle.

'Now!'

As fingers squeezed round the door Phoenix used the jar as a stepping stone up to the window sill and jumped down into the alleyway. The sickle did its work again, leaving the enemy, who hadn't even seen him, face down in the dust. The helmet worked.

'Phoenix!'

He reached the half-open door to see three men closing in on Laura. She was swinging the sword and backing off. They were enjoying the sport. Time to make an entrance.

'If it's me you're after,' he announced, 'then I'm here.'

The trio span round. Phoenix took pleasure in their confusion. They made for his voice but they were stabbing thin air. Under the cover of invisibility, he struck once, twice, three times with the sickle. With each cut of the ferocious blade, the points display registered another score.

'Let's go, Laura.'

They fled down the main thoroughfare of Deicterion, expecting more attacks at any moment. But none came. A hush descended.

'Why did they give up?' Laura asked. 'We didn't get them all.'

Phoenix was none the wiser. But give up they had. It's as if they had wanted to bring them to this place. Anxiety mounted inside him.

He slid off the helmet.

'I don't like this, Laura.'

She was just as jittery. Unable to believe the fight was over she made her way to a corner – and screamed.

Phoenix gazed upon the hideous faces looming towards them and breathed a sigh of relief.

'It's all right, Laura, they're not real. This is what we came for.'

In the stone walls of the town, three huge reliefs had been carved, matching the ones at Polydectes' court.

'The Gorgons.'

He had seen his share of illustrations of the legends, of course, and made his own sketches. But none were ever anything like this, not even those at Polydectes' palace. There was so much more detail. Each of the sisters had the body of a woman, but resting on a serpent's tail instead of legs. They were winged and their hands were armoured claws. Their hair was set in ringlets made of living, writhing snakes. But it was the face of the Gorgon that was the site of its terror. She had tusks like a wild boar and there was something that reminded him of the Minotaur. She also had the killing teeth of a big cat, a lion or tiger. A swollen rope-like tongue spilled from her mouth. But there was one detail that couldn't be shown in the giant carvings – her eyes. The sculptor hadn't even made an attempt to portray the eyes that could turn a man to stone. He had left his creatures eyeless.

Beneath each of the sisters, a name was carved. Stheno, Euryvale and Medusa.

4

Some hours into Christina Graves' lonely vigil at the computer she made a discovery. While watching Phoenix sitting on the clifftop, she happened to consult her watch. Seven-thirty. She observed the arrival of the goddess, the night spent in a shepherd's hut, the fight at Deicterion. Then she looked at her watch again. Still seven-thirty. She shivered right down to the marrow of her bones. It had to be a mistake. The watch had stopped. But she knew that was too simple an explanation. The clock on the wall registered exactly the same time.

'Stupid woman!' she declared after a few moments. 'Of course, it's seven-thirty in the morning. I've been up all night.'

But no sooner had the thought crossed her mind than she was forced to think again. Darkness hadn't fallen at all. She hadn't had to switch on the light.

'But this is—'

While one part of her was trying to come up with a rational explanation for the vice-like stillness around her, another – the deeper part – had raced ahead to a more incredible one. She walked around the house, trying to disprove her own suspicions. But her first intuition had been right. Not only had her watch stopped at seven-thirty. So had the hall and kitchen clocks, the bedside alarm and the digital displays on the micro-wave, oven and video. She even switched on the TV, only to see Homer Simpson, hands locked around Bart's throat forever.

'I'm going mad.'

She glanced out of the window. A scream froze in her throat. Everything was caught in a freeze-frame. Cars, people, clouds, leaves, everything trembling on the cusp of suspended time. She tried the door. The handle and lock were jammed, sealed in that single, timeless moment.

Seven-thirty.

She had no choice but to return to the computer where the screen saver had clicked on, launching the endless rows of perplexing numbers across the screen.

Doing nothing to hold back her tears, she pressed her right hand against the monitor and sobbed out her pain. She was lost – just like John and Phoenix.

Maybe you are beginning to understand. There is only one time. The time of myth. It is your time, the time so carefully calculated down to a fraction of a second by sophisticated atomic devices, the time displayed on millions of clocks, that is imaginary now. The game is real, your world a dream. Time will move forward only when I will it.

It was noon next day before Laura and Phoenix reached the foothills of Mount Atlas. Another night had passed without dreams, without the labyrinth. Most of all, without fear. Curious, thought Phoenix, I've started to realize just how deadly the game is, and I'm not scared. I was born to complete this journey. The greater the fear, the greater the reward in facing it down. The same world that is making Laura so angry and afraid is allowing me to breathe again. For the first time since he had arrived at Brownleigh, furious at having to leave London, he felt truly alive.

'Looks like Pan got here before us,' he remarked, indicating the feast of meat and fruits laid out on a bronze table.

Laura was looking at the inviting fare, but she didn't rush forward like she had the first time.

'Something wrong?'

Laura ran a hand over her face.

'I need some answers,' she replied, unhappiness clouding her voice.

You and me both, thought Phoenix. I am the adventurer, the hero, the Legendeer, but I have entered a vast and very black cavern armed with the smallest of torches. For all my sense of belonging and excitement, I am part blindfolded. There is so much more darkness than light.

'What is all this, Phoenix? First it's a game, then it's real. The fight we were in, did we hurt those people? Was it cowboys and indians, or what?'

She waved her arms at the vastness of the sky. 'Somewhere out there my parents are worrying themselves sick about me. And I'm worried about them too.'

Phoenix lowered his eyes. His too.

'Sorry Laura, but I just don't have any answers.' He remembered the lifeless eyes of the youth he'd been interrogating, the gathering pool of blood pillowing his head. 'One thing we've both learned, you can't trust the game. This is a cruel world. Terrible things happen here.'

Laura sat heavily on a grassy knoll, resting her arms on her knees.

'Do you have to tell me something I already know? I just want to understand what's happening here. Did those people really die?'

What did Pan say? For the purposes of the game, yes.

'They died.'

Laura had been asking more in hope than belief.

'But it was too easy. Are you sure that sickle thing really works? I mean, back home they have war games. They use paint guns and stuff. Even grown men do it.'

Phoenix gave a scornful laugh.

'Paint guns, eh?'

He produced the sickle and brandished it to show the glint of its razor's edge.

'Set me a test.'

Laura looked round.

'That tree.'

One stroke of the blade and there was nothing but a stump where the sapling grew. Phoenix found himself laughing out loud.

'What tree?'

He walked over to the bronze table. Suddenly, there was a

storm inside him. Laura wasn't the only one who was worried. Phoenix wanted to smash things, tear them down.

'Want another demonstration?'

He brought the sickle down hard on the bronze table, making Laura jump. As it split, the plates of food slid to the centre.

'Satisfied?'

He glared at Laura, then seeing the look on her face, he immediately regretted his show of temper. He'd started acting like Adams.

'I'm sorry.'

She accepted the apology with a brief nod. Then there was another question.

'What about Steve Adams?' she asked. 'What's he up to? If all this is real, then he could have got us killed.'

'I do have an explanation,' Phoenix told her. 'Adams said it was the questionnaire that brought him here. He must have been sent a pack of software, just like you. Now the game is following my instructions to the letter. Me as the hero, you as my heroine, Adams as the villain. And Dad—' He felt a tug of regret. 'I put his name down too. He'll be here somewhere.'

'This is really hard for me, Phoenix. You fit in here. I don't.'

Fit in. Yes, he did. He *was* the Legendeer.

'You're doing just fine, Laura,' Phoenix told her. 'The way you handled that sword. The way you saved me from that arrow. The way you've kept your nerve all along.'

He didn't know how to tell her, but ever since they'd met their hearts had been beating to a single rhythm.

'I'd be lost without you.'

She smiled.

'Let's eat.'

A few moments later Phoenix was pointing out their next destination with a crust of bread. He pictured the inhabitants of the mist-shrouded slopes. The Graeae, sisters of the Gorgons, but bearing no resemblance to the snake-haired predators who lurked in poisonous mists in a cave at the end of the world.

Three Gorgons – powerful, savage, unconquered. Three Graeae – withered, ancient, wretched.

The Graeae were the wasted remnants of their former selves, little more than bags of bones. They lived their lives bickering constantly, forced to share one eye and one tooth. Maybe they dreamed of their sisters and envied them the terror they stirred in the hearts of men.

'But why do we need them?' Laura asked.

'Nobody has ever returned from the Gorgons' lair to tell of its whereabouts,' Phoenix explained. 'Only the Graeae can set us on our way.'

'But why would they betray their own sisters?'

'Because,' he answered, 'without the eye they are doomed to eternal darkness. Without the tooth they will hunger forever. We have to steal the only things that are precious to them.'

Laura gave him a nervous look.

'This is going to be grotesque, isn't it?'

'Very.'

He could almost hear the air shuddering in Laura's throat.

'Then we'd better get it over with.'

The image Phoenix had of the Gorgons blazed up again in his mind. He circled the summit of the mountain slowly, peering down through wispy clouds. There was a warning here. Laura clutched his hand even tighter. 'Something wrong?'

'I don't know. It's this picture I keep getting in my head. No . . . I've got it. Of course, they're onto our scent!'

The Gorgons were sniffing the wind, that's how they knew Laura and Phoenix were coming.

And the Graeae too, if he wasn't mistaken.

'We've got to land downwind of the creatures.'

Laura gave him a wary look. 'If you say so.'

They edged down the slope towards the three marble thrones of the Graeae.

'There!'

It was them, all right. Three bags of bones, husks of living things. Toothless, sightless, reduced to arguing over a single eye and a single tooth, they scrabbled and clawed at each other, demanding their turn to see or to eat. One of the twisted beings reared suddenly. 'Sisters, what was that?'

'Nothing. I know you, you crone. You didn't hear a thing. It was just a ruse to steal away the eye.'

'Calling me a liar, are you, you pathetic worm? It *is* my turn with the eye.'

Their fight resumed.

'Cheat!'

'Liar!'

But then their squabbling broke off again.

'No, there it is again. He's coming, sisters. The one who was prophesied – the boy of Seriphos.'

Phoenix glanced at the startled Laura and winked. He was so alive.

'Skirt round to their left,' he whispered. 'When I give the signal, I want you to create one almighty commotion.'

Laura bit her lip, as if he'd asked her to balance the whole world on her thumb, and crept away through the undergrowth. She'd had enough stomach for the street fight. This was a different matter.

Phoenix, on the other hand, was in his element. The part he was playing *was himself. I'm coming, ladies. It's I, the boy of Seriphos.*

The three of them were raised on their haunches, sniffing at the breeze. And all the time they were snatching the eye, taking turns at scanning the mountainside for any sign of Phoenix.

'You'll never find the cave of the Gorgons,' cackled one.

'No torture will break we three,' said another. 'There is a blood bond here.'

Laura had got behind them, averting her face. She couldn't bear to look at the malformed sisters. Phoenix drew the sickle and slipped the shield from his back, turning it upwards like a dish. Then he raised his arm and dropped it immediately. Laura started dancing, shouting, yelling for all she was worth.

The Graeae were falling over themselves to get a look at the strange girl.

'Who is it?'

'What's she doing?'

'Where's the eye? Let me see.'

The eye was being passed from hand to bony hand. Phoenix watched as one twisted claw reached out, then he leapt forward.

'Mine, I think.'

With a flick of the wrist, he used the sickle like a spatula, tossing the eye and the tooth into the air.

'Thank you kindly.'

He watched the eye roll round the shield and come to a rest in the middle. The tooth rattled beside it.

'Now ladies, time to bargain.'

The Graeae were thrown into a frenzy.

'Give them back!'

'You'll pay for this, boy.'

'Wait till my sisters get hold of you. They will rip you open like a fig.'

As Laura shrank back in disgust Phoenix waited for the sisters' anger to ride itself out.

'Now,' he said finally, when they had exhausted themselves with their raging and cursing. 'The location of the Gorgons' cave, if you please.'

'It'll do you no good.'

'I don't know why you're in such a hurry, boy.'

One rubbed her scrawny stomach.

'The sisters will give you a fine welcome.'

'Munch you.'

'Crunch you.'

'Gobble you up.'

Phoenix rolled the eye and the tooth round the shield.

'Hear that? I could deposit them half a world away. Mmm, I quite like the idea. You've got good hearing, haven't you? Imagine, you could listen to them as they fall into the sea. Plop! Such a lovely sound.'

Another frenzy, then the Graeae resigned themselves to defeat.

'Very well, we'll tell you boy, but little good will it do you.'

'Are you in such a hurry to die?'

He'd had enough of their abuse.

'The location, please. Now! Or you'll never see the eye or the tooth again.'

'I'll tell you,' said one. 'On one condition. I have the eye first.'

'No,' shrieked her sister. 'Me, Me!'

More squabbling, then bit by bit they spat out the directions to the Gorgons' lair in the Land of the Hyperboreans. Satisfied with his day's work Phoenix tossed them their prizes. 'Here.'

The last Laura and Phoenix saw of the Graeae was a tattered mass of rags, scrambling in the mud and the dust, and all for an eye and a tooth.

Night fell once more and Phoenix was at peace with himself. He wasn't afraid. His nightmares had gone. The headaches too. His lifelong torment was over. A meteor flashed over the mountain tops. There was a silence, completely unbroken by any sound except the scrape of the crickets. Until Pan put in one of his appearances, that is. Phoenix made himself a promise.

This time you don't get away without telling us the truth.

You're going to answer my questions.

'It's about time you turned up,' said Laura.

'A profitable day?' asked Pan.

'If you mean, have we found the cave, the answer's *yes*.'

'That's good,' said Pan. 'That's very good. It keeps the game going. Let's see your score.'

He examined the bracelet.

'Very impressive. Here, a present for you.'

He handed something to Laura.

'A flare? In ancient Greece?'

'You forget,' said Pan. 'This isn't Greece. At least, it is one possible Greece. This is the world of the game. And, as Phoenix has already discovered, you're allowed the odd cheat. That's what makes it all so entertaining. It's the wobbles that make the high-wire artist interesting.'

Pan sidled up to Laura and laid his head against her shoulder.

'Do you like adventure, my pretty?'

Laura flinched at his touch. He grinned and sprang back, producing a knife and holding it to his own throat.

'Back off,' he barked in a Chicago-gangster voice, 'or the goat gets it.'

Phoenix stared. What is this? Maybe Laura's right. He isn't what he seems. Laura simply shook her head at Pan's antics. Then the pair of them gasped. The blade that Pan had pressed against his own throat had produced blood, a single scarlet trickle stringing into the briar-work of hair on his chest.

'Stop it,' said Laura. 'You're making me sick.'

'Just high spirits,' said Pan, staggering.

'You're drunk!' exclaimed Laura.

'A little tipsy,' said Pan, 'but that's my nature. We can't escape our nature, can we Phoenix?'

Phoenix could only stare, wondering what he meant.

Remembering the flare, Laura gave it the once-over and shook her head. 'But what am I supposed to do with it?'

'I'm sure you'll find a use for it. I hear it will illuminate the blackest night.'

Phoenix let him prattle on for a while then launched himself into his questions.

'What does the owl mean?'

Pan blinked, clearly taken by surprise.

'You're an intelligent boy,' he said, recovering himself. 'The owl is the symbol of Athene.'

'I know that,' Phoenix retorted. 'I mean here, in the game.'

'Now what do you think it is?'

'Oh no,' Phoenix warned him. 'You're not fobbing me off. You owe us an explanation. What's going on?'

Pan inspected his filthy, jagged fingernails casually.

'The world is turning. Stars flash and mortals wonder.'

'Cut it out,' snapped Phoenix. He drew the symbol in the dust, the perched owl. 'I saw it on some soldiers.'

'And that priest,' Laura added.

'And the boy fighter in Deicterion.'

Pan was acting stubborn. 'Then ask him.'

'I can't. He's dead.'

Pan yawned. 'Very well. It can't do any harm. The owl belongs to the game, and if you bear the mark of the owl then you too belong to the game. Surely you've worked it out by now. There is a world here which dances to one man's tune. There is but one Gamesmaster. His pawns do as they are told. By terror or by bribery, they do the bidding of their master.'

'And if they refuse?'

'Then they must wear the mark of the owl. If they dare defy the Gamesmaster's will again—'

'They die.'

Pan nodded. 'It is the way of all flesh.'

Pan made as if to go.

'One more thing,' said Phoenix. 'Tell me, Pan. Tell me about Uncle Andreas.'

'Andreas,' said Pan thoughtfully. 'Now I haven't heard that name in such a long time.'

'You visited him,' said Phoenix, pressing him. 'I want to know why.'

Pan's dark eyes blazed, stabbing deep into Phoenix's soul, branding it with the stamp of fear. 'If you know Andreas,' he spat, 'then you will find the answer inside yourself. You only have to look.'

With that, Pan stole into the night.

5

Next day, Phoenix and Laura rose at dawn and set off to complete their journey, heading westwards into the Land of the Hyperboreans.

Phoenix could feel Laura's eyes on him. 'Nervous?'

He nodded. It was an unnecessary admission. There was no disguising hands that were moist with perspiration. *Somewhere among the dismal mists of these endless grey hills the sisters are scanning the sky and sniffing the air. They are making themselves ready, waiting for me.*

As he descended with Laura through dense, reeking clouds he felt something, a tick-tick-ticking against his wrist.

Laura sensed his concern.

'What's wrong?'

Phoenix was staring in horror at his points bracelet. 'This is impossible!'

The display was chattering away as their score went into freefall.

'We're losing our power. Our points total is being wiped out.'

'But why? I don't understand.'

Phoenix found himself looking around, as if expecting somebody to pop up and give him an explanation. It didn't make any sense. They weren't under attack. Neither of them had been hurt. So how could they be losing points? Eventually the fall in the points score slowed, then stopped tumbling altogether.

'What have we got left?' Laura asked.

'It's bad news,' Phoenix told her. 'We're down to a few hundred.'

'So we're—'

'In the red zone. Mortal danger.'

But why? He shivered, as if aware that something terrible had happened.

'Are you all right, Phoenix? You look awful.'

'I feel awful. I mean, to have lost a score as big as that. From hero to zero. And without any sort of fight. It took the whole skirmish at Deicterion to build it up. What's done it? I mean, what can be worth the lives of a dozen street fighters?'

What indeed? Phoenix imagined the street fighters thrown into the pan of a giant scales. But what could be balanced against them?

'Oh no, it can't be.'

'What?'

'Dad,' said Phoenix. 'Reede's killed him.'

'Reede?'

'Glen Reede, I told you. It's him, or whoever's in control of this crazy game. It has to be. He's killed Dad for working against it. For preparing his bomb.'

'Phoenix,' said Laura. 'Calm down. Number one, you don't *know* he's dead, and number two . . .' Her voice trailed off.

'Go on,' said Phoenix. 'What's number two?'

'Let's face it,' Laura told him. 'We're not even sure any of this is real. What if—?'

'What?' Phoenix demanded. 'It's all a dream.'

He knew better. He could still feel the clash of steel in the fight at Deicterion. The legend was real. In fact, it was the only thing that was real any more. They were living in a world of legend.

'Think you're going to wake up like Dorothy in *The Wizard of Oz*? Think you're going to click your ruby slippers and fly away home? Grow up Laura, you saw that fighter in Deicterion. That wasn't cowboys and indians. He was dead Laura, and he was going to stay dead. We're playing for keeps.'

Then the world that had once been everything, was nothing. A dead ball of clay. Pointless.

'Dad,' he groaned. 'This is all my fault. I gave him the idea for the game. And I let him go.'

Laura shook her head and walked to the edge of a crag. She made a brave attempt at changing the subject.

'Do you think it will affect the mission, losing all those points?'

'It must do. All the points we'd built up, they were bound to help us. They were a cushion against disasters. With that score under our belt, I was on fire. I really was the Legendeer. Now—' He passed his hand over his face. 'I just don't know.'

'So do we go on?'

Phoenix deposited the shield and leather wallet on the ground.

'Looks like there's no choice. We have to fulfill our mission. Dad's life depends on it. If—'

If he's still alive.

'Ours too, I expect. Maybe a lot of others besides.' Then everything was coming together. His sense of destiny, his growing power, his rage to fight back. 'So let's prepare ourselves for battle.'

But when Phoenix loosened the drawstring on the wallet, he cried out.

'What now?' murmured Laura.

'The helmet of invisibility, it's gone.'

'It can't have.'

He passed her the wallet.

'See for yourself if you don't believe me.'

Phoenix closed his eyes and saw his destiny. Somewhere close by the sisters were waiting, licking their lips and sensing the hero's setback. Their golden wings glowed with satisfaction. It would soon be over.

We're waiting, boy. Come and do your worst.

It was Laura's turn to despair.

'But it doesn't make sense. You slept with it under your head like a pillow. Nobody could have taken it.'

Phoenix turned his face towards her.

'The game took it.'

'What, you mean Pan? I never trusted him.'

'No, not Pan. The game was always much more than any one player. It's playing with us. I don't understand it yet, but I know that the points don't lie. We've suffered a defeat. The helmet is the price we have to pay. It's too much, Laura. It's all too much.'

Laura gave the wallet one last inspection.

'What's this? Oh, I might have guessed!'

'What is it?'

She handed Phoenix a note. *Surprise surprise.*

'It wasn't the game, at all,' she cried, seizing on the scrap of paper. 'Don't give up, Phoenix. Don't you dare give up. It wasn't destiny. It was Adams. He did this.'

Phoenix watched Laura. She was trembling with anger.

'Maybe I don't know much about fighting monsters,' she said. 'And I don't know what makes this stupid world tick. But I do know this. Adams is human, and we can fight him.'

'I don't think there's any choice about the matter,' said Phoenix, subdued.

He felt another click on the bracelet. Five more points gone.

'This is worse than I thought,' he murmured.

Laura didn't speak. Instead, she waited for him to explain. For all her stubborn rage, the avalanche of setbacks was getting to her.

'It's something Pan said,' Phoenix told her. 'We don't have forever to get the head of Medusa.'

'So how long *have* we got?'

Phoenix repeated Pan's words. 'By the time the moon has crossed the sky thrice over. That's tonight.'

Five more points clicked away.

'Do me a favour,' he said. 'Count to ten.'

Laura had just reached ten when the score fell another five points.

'I was right, the game's being timed.'

Dazed by the turn of events, Laura covered her ears with her hands.

'Don't tell me any more,' she sighed. 'Just decide on a plan of action and we'll do it.'

Phoenix couldn't help but smile. There was a heart as true as steel inside Laura, and thank the stars for it.

'We've no time to spare,' he said. 'We can't wait any longer. We've got to do it now.'

All the while they were creeping forward towards the Gorgons' cave, the words of Pan were running through Phoenix's head.

The myth is a pole star to navigate your way.

And his second, more ominous piece of advice.

By the time the moon has crossed the sky thrice over.

Phoenix went through every detail he had ever read about the Perseus story and listed them mentally.

Medusa is my target. Pick the wrong Gorgon and I will be killed.

I mustn't look directly into her eyes. I can only look at her reflection in the shield.

When I sever the head I have to keep clear of Medusa's blood. It burns like the most powerful acid.

Then he came to one detail that chilled his blood. The helmet of invisibility would hide him from the Gorgons' stare. Except it wouldn't. It had gone. And all thanks to Adams.

He's no minor irritation, thought Phoenix. The game has him now. He is no longer just a small town bully, he really is my Nemesis.

Laura peered over a ridge.

'Is that it?'

'That's it.'

'But who are all those people?'

In the choking mist there were silhouettes of ten, maybe twenty still figures.

'All the adventurers who came looking for the Medusa.'

'But what are they doing?'

'Doing, Laura? They aren't doing anything. They're dead, victims of the Gorgon's stare.'

Laura's eyes narrowed.

'So they're—'

'Statues. People have come here many times to slay the demon, but every one of them has looked into her eyes and suffered the same fate. She turned them all to stone.'

Laura peered through the stinking fog. 'And we're going in *there*?'

'Like I told you; we've got no choice.'

Another click on his score bracelet. Five more points gone.

'See?'

'And if we don't complete our mission in time?'

'Then we lose,' Phoenix answered, 'or worse.'

He checked the sickle and slid his arm through the strap of the shield.

'Now stay close to me.'

His heart was pounding, but it was even worse for Laura. At the thought of what lay ahead, her legs were giving way under her. Her earlier determination was crumbling.

'Phoenix, I'm not sure I can go in there.'

'You must.'

'But why? This is your quest, not mine.'

He took a deep breath.

'I've told you, Laura, like it or not, you are part of this.'

'Phoenix, I just can't.'

He looked her straight in the eye and spoke to her as simply and directly as he could, 'Laura, you're not the only one who's afraid. I need you.'

She bit her lip and gave the briefest of nods. They started to move forward through the poisoned air.

'Here,' Phoenix whispered. 'Hold this over your face.' He passed her a piece of cloth.

'Where did this come from?'

'Let's just say my chiton is a bit shorter today.'

By now they had reached the forest of petrified souls.

Armed men caught in the moment of terror when they

looked into Medusa's eyes, sorceresses who had begun – but never finished – their spell to cast out the demon, even fantastic animals frozen to the spot where they came across the Gorgons. Over the years rain had worn away an arm here, part of a face there. But one thing remained in every one of the faces, the expression of utter horror at the sight of the foul sisters.

'Do you really think we have a chance?' Laura gasped, her voice coming out in snatches.

'Of course. I wouldn't be here otherwise.'

There, the words came easily. But would courage follow?

'Now, not another sound until we leave the cave with the Medusa's head. It could cost us our lives.'

Laura took him at his word. But her next attempt at communication almost dislocated Phoenix's shoulder. The thump to get his attention sent a stabbing pain through his arm and neck. Turning questioning – and wounded – eyes towards her, he was directed to movement around the mouth of the cave. The Gorgons.

'Sistersss, he is here.'

Instinctively, he flattened himself against the sodden, slimy earth. Laura followed suit.

'Hiding, boy? That won't help you. Sooner or later you must show yourself.'

He rolled on to his back and drew the sickle. Motioning with his head, he willed Laura to follow him through the mist.

'There!' came the voice of Medusa. 'I hear him. He is coming.'

Her sisters were sniffing the air. Like dogs. And excited as dogs. They were rearing, straining to catch sight of the hero.

'Yes, yes, it's true. He is coming. I can almost taste his flesh.'

Phoenix kept his gaze turned from Laura. The last thing he needed was to betray his growing terror. Keeping their step as light as they could on the spongy ground, they scurried between the Gorgons' petrified victims and cowered behind a boulder at the cave's mouth. They were to the left of the sisters and slightly behind them. While Phoenix struggled to control his breathing he became aware of Laura staring round, alerted to something behind them. He gave a questioning frown. She shrugged in return.

'Show yourself, boy.'

'What'sss the matter? Too frightened? Yes, that's it, isn't it? The skin is creeping off your bones, isn't it? You wish you were a babe again, in the safety of your mother's armsss.'

The other Gorgons took up the refrain. 'Mummy, mummy.'

'Did you know?' Medusa rasped. 'That's what the warrior does at his death. Yes, you heard me correctly, boy. As the big, bearded hero crawls through his own blood, he starts calling for his mother. Mummy! Mummy!'

Phoenix tried to shut out their sly, wheedling voices, but he couldn't help himself. He saw Mum's face. Danäe's too.

The sisters joined the chorus. 'Mummy! Mummy!'

Then a cackle of triumph.

'Let's get this over boy. What's one more childless mother in this world of pain?'

I don't need to listen to you, you twisted demons, thought Phoenix. I know your game. You want to plant the terror inside my head, to freeze my muscles and kill my courage. I can't let you. I mustn't.

But the noise was getting to Laura. She was still darting glances behind her.

For crying out loud, Laura, the danger's over there. Right in front of you.

He tapped her on the arm, almost scaring her out of her skin. Waiting a moment to let her steady her nerves, Phoenix pointed to a recess deeper inside the cave. She nodded. But as they scrambled over the slippery rocks he lost his footing and fell heavily.

'There,' Medusa declared triumphantly. 'I have him, sistersss.'

Phoenix shuddered at her snake-slithering approach and tightened his grip on the sickle.

She'll be upon me any second.

'Welcome boy, welcome to my home, your mausoleum.'

He twisted his head and looked into the shield. Her form towered over him, the movement of the snakes writhing its way inside his brain. He drew back his arm to strike but the blow never fell. Instead it felt as if somebody had hit him hard on his wrist. The sickle span across the cave's uneven, water-logged floor.

'Phoenix,' Laura cried, throwing caution to the winds. 'That's what I was trying to tell you. Somebody has been behind us all along, stalking us.'

Half paralysed with fear at Medusa's approach Phoenix found it hard to take in what Laura meant.

'Listen to me,' Laura continued. 'The helmet didn't just disappear. It was stolen. Somebody's using it against us. Here in the cave, we have an invisible enemy. And I think you know who.'

Phoenix felt the rush of air as Medusa lashed out with a bronze claw, and he threw himself out of her reach. Scrambling to his feet, he retreated to a shelf of rock.

'Of course,' he panted, 'Adams.'

'That's right,' came a voice, a boy's voice like his own, just beginning to break. 'Surprise surprise.'

'You again.'

But there was no time to dwell on his unwelcome arrival. The Gorgons were on the move, encircling Phoenix. In the corner of his eye he could see Laura crawling forward, reaching for the sickle. Just as she was closing her fingers around the handle, it skipped away as if it had a life of its own. Adams again. Phoenix could hear his footsteps, but how to find him? Backing away from the Gorgons, he found himself standing knee-deep in water.

That's it, that's how to see him!

Using the wallet, Phoenix scooped up a bucketful of the stagnant liquid and waited.

'This is a poor fight,' Medusa taunted. 'Can this really be the hero we were promised? The others put up a much better fight.'

Ignoring the words, Phoenix focused on Adams' footsteps. There! Without a moment's hesitation he flung the water and watched it splash off his invisible form. Hurling himself at Adams, Phoenix pinned him to the floor and wrenched off the helmet.

'I could kill you for this,' he yelled. 'I could kill you, Adams!'

But Adams wriggled free and made a dash for the cave. Attracted to the movement, all three Gorgons set off in pursuit.

'You all right, Laura?'

'I'm fine, but what about Steve?'

Phoenix pulled on the helmet.

'What about him?'

'I know what he's done, but you can't let them kill him.'

Why not? He'll only come back to haunt us.

'Phoenix,' Laura cried, as if reading his mind. 'He's sly and he's nasty. But look what's happening. They'll rip him to shreds. He doesn't deserve that. He isn't evil.'

Phoenix picked up the sickle.

'All right, I'll save him.'

Climbing to the highest point in the cave he shouted a challenge to the sisters.

'What's the matter? Picking on small fry?'

His heart was thudding in his chest. Either this was very brave, or very foolish.

The Gorgons span round and Phoenix took refuge in the shield's reflection. He could make out the approach of their monstrous forms. Satisfied that Adams had made his getaway, Phoenix prepared for battle. He recalled what he'd seen in Deicterion and etched every detail of the Gorgon, Medusa in his mind.

He had to choose the right sister. But as he readied himself for the fight, his heart turned to ice.

Outside the cave the light was fading, replaced by dense, moonless night.

'Phoenix,' cried Laura, realizing their predicament. 'It's nightfall.'

How would they ever recognize Medusa in the dark?

6

The nightmare had returned. Phoenix thought he'd been scared before, but this! Every moment filled him with hopeless, gut-melting horror. It was like being back in the labyrinth, dragging his fear through the darkness. Every sound seemed closer. He could make out the slide of the Gorgons on the waterlogged bottom of the cave, the hiss of their serpent-wreathed hair, their taunting shrieks.

'No escape now, boy. Don't think the helmet of invisibility will save you. We can smell you, boy. We can smell your fear.'

'No way out,' the second Gorgon told him. 'Do you know your fate, boy? Your dying will not be quick. First we will destroy your mind, then we will devour the rest of you. Do you know what we've got in store? It's not the forest of statues for you. No, we've a special treat. First, you will hear us feed on the heart of the girl, then we will come for you.'

I know what you're after, thought Phoenix. You want me to call out to Laura, to give away my position. But I'm not falling for it. Hear me, you monsters? I won't do it.

'Show yourself, hero, you know that time is running out.'

Phoenix glanced at the points display. Only fifty points left. Time was indeed running out. He peered into the gloom. One of the Gorgons had installed herself at the mouth of the cave to prevent their escape. He could make her out quite clearly. But what about the others? They were moving unseen through the deeper dark of the interior. They could be anywhere. He heard movement to his right. The Gorgons? And what if it was Adams? What if he'd come back to finish the job? Phoenix felt the bracelet click again. Forty-five points left. Time had almost run out. The task was enormous. He felt the hero in him detaching itself. His power to think and act was being stripped from him. He couldn't go on.

And if we lose, what do we lose?

Maybe it would be better to throw down his weapon and show himself.

He was desolate. All he wanted to do was surrender to the Gorgon's stare.

Do we just lose the game, or our lives as well?

No, he thought, his mind rejecting his cowardice. I can't just sit here. Got to fight. He edged towards the noise, raising the sickle ready to strike. As he reached out, he heard a yelp of panic. Thank goodness, it's Laura.

Got to reassure her. 'Shh. It's me.'

'Phoenix! What do we do now?'

But his mind was blank. Laura was unarmed. What *could* she do? Then his thoughts were interrupted by the voice of Medusa.

'Come sister, he is here. I smell him. Yes, I smell his fear, the sickness, the sourness of it.'

Phoenix could just about distinguish two hideous shapes. But which was Medusa? He found himself backing deeper into the cave. Laura was moving too, retreating at his pace. His thoughts were racing.

How do I tell one sister from another? How?

Forty points left.

'Can this be the hero?' came Medusa's voice. 'This wretched boy cowering in the dark? Surely not.'

Unnatural laughter filled the cave, echoing into the depths of Phoenix's soul.

'Listen to him, sister. The coward can hardly breathe.' Then the thin, insinuating voice was replaced by a deafening roar. 'SHOW YOURSELF!'

'SHOW YOURSELF!'

'SHOW!'

The echo boomed around the walls of the cave, the

vibrations quivering inside his skin. There was no escape. The display clicked to thirty-five.

'Time's almost out.'

'Phoenix, we have to do something.'

But fear had him by the throat. He could only think of one thing. Escape. An end to the terror.

'Where are you, little hero?' called the sisters. 'Scary in the dark isn't it? You never know what's next to you?'

'They're right,' Phoenix panted. 'We need some light.'

'Light,' said Laura excitedly. 'But we've got light. The flare Pan gave me.'

'What's that? What's she saying sistersss?'

'Light, what does the girl mean?'

The Gorgons were worried. For the first time doubt crept into their voices.

'Laura,' Phoenix whispered, 'you must be onto something. They're scared.'

Terror was beginning to relax its grip.

'When I give the order,' he told her. 'Set off the flare and cover your eyes.'

Their score was down to thirty.

He braced himself, measuring the distance to the two looming shapes in the darkness. Turning his back, Phoenix looked down at the polished surface of the shield.

'Now!'

The intense light of the flare exploded into the cave, sending stabbing pains through his eyes. For a moment he was utterly blinded, then he turned to look at the shield. He could see them, the Gorgons.

Is that her?

Shorter than her sisters, her tongue protruding more grotesquely, the writhing pattern of snakes denser and more revolting.

Is that her?

The score hit twenty-five.

'Phoenix, what are you waiting for?'

Yes, that's her. It's got to be. Strike. Do it now.

The bracelet began to flash. Twenty. Fifteen.

Scurrying sideways like a crab, Phoenix kept his neck twisted and his head turned away from those terrible eyes. He looked into the burnished shield. Pausing only to squash one last doubt he swung the sickle.

The score glowed ominously. Ten points.

With a cry, Phoenix struck an upward blow, putting every ounce of fear and anger into the thrust – fear and anger *and courage.*

A shriek of pain crashed round the cave, as pitiful as it was hideous, the death throes of Medusa.

Five points.

Again, strike again.

Measuring his blow, Phoenix sliced through flesh, muscle, bone. He beheaded the Gorgon. But in doing so he unleashed a scalding torent of tarry, venomous blood. The points bracelet was racing, the vibration fairly drilling into his wrist.

'Laura. Get back.'

They hurled themselves out of the way of the blood-venom and watched fascinated as it burned through the stone floor of the cave.

'Is it safe?'

'I think so. Only one way to find out.'

Reaching for the severed head he felt the twist of the snakes over his wrist. Forcing down the temptation to be sick, he bundled the head into the wallet.

His score was still mounting.

'Laura, let's go.'

But the battle wasn't over. Laura was screaming.

'Behind you!'

Phoenix felt the beat of wings, the grief-stricken snarl. One of Medusa's sisters was mounting her own attack.

'Laura, my hand. Grab it. Now!'

The sandals took them into the air just as the Gorgon's claw shattered the boulder in front of them. The force of the blow sent them spinning, and knocked the helmet clean off Phoenix's head. For the second time he had no disguise.

'Don't let go. Whatever you do, Laura, hold tight.'

'Phoenix, the third Gorgon. Where is she?'

He could see the second sister sliding after them, too far away to pose a danger. But the third? She'd left her place at the mouth of the cave. Why?

'Look!'

The stagnant water beneath them was beginning to boil. Suddenly, the Gorgon's head erupted through the floor sending rocks hurtling across the cave. Her face loomed violently in front of them.

'Shut your eyes, Laura. Whatever you do, don't look.'

Locking his eyes on the shield's reflection, Phoenix searched for the cavemouth and escape.

The way out. I don't see it. I DON'T SEE IT.

He was tempted to turn his head. The Gorgon was reading his mind.

'That's it, boy, turn. You want the way out? Well, let me help you. This way. You just have to look this way.'

But the Gorgons didn't wait for him to turn. They gathered over their dead sister, then mounted their attack, rising on their serpent tails and snapping with their jaws. The sound was deafening, like iron doors slamming over and over again. Soon Laura's cries and Phoenix's own added to the din in the cave.

We'll never get out!

The closest of the sisters coiled herself then hurled her grotesque frame upward in a determined assault. A sharpened tusk sliced through the skin on Phoenix's shoulder.

'Hunh!'

By hurling himself backwards Phoenix managed to prevent serious damage, but the pain was burning all down one side. He remembered Dad's wound in the castle of Procrustes. If he still harboured any doubts, the attack ended them. The game was real all right.

We're finished.

Phoenix was struggling to avoid the second of the Gorgons when he glimpsed a silvery glow.

Of course. The moon. Ready to cross the sky for the third time.

'Laura,' he cried. 'The moon. Look at it. The moon is up.'

There was no more time for delay. Seizing the moment, they swooped out into the chill of the night. Their score was back in the thousands and mounting rapidly. They skipped over the moonlit clouds.

Victorious!

They were back over Deicterion when Phoenix began his descent.

'Phoenix, what are you doing?'

'There's something I have to see.'

'But what about those streetfighters? Why put ourselves in danger again?'

She gestured at the bloodstained cloth on his arm.

'Especially with that wound.'

Phoenix pointed to the carving of the Gorgons.

'Because of that.'

He led her to the giant representation.

'It's Medusa,' she said. 'But we don't need the carving any more. Why—'

'Look,' Phoenix told her. 'At the base. It didn't mean anything last time.'

There was a number. A *score*. Five thousand.

'Check the display,' Laura said excitedly.

'5005,' Phoenix read. 'But what's the winning score?'

He found himself wandering along the alley that skirted the city wall. Laura moved ahead of him.

'Phoenix,' she said suddenly. 'Come here.'

Another carving, as massive as that of the Gorgons. This time it pictured the Minotaur.

'But there's no score.'

'There is here,' said Laura.

In the corner of the carving there was a small detail. The door to the labyrinth, and below it the number 7000.

'Seven thousand!' Phoenix cried. '*Seven* thousand to enter

the labyrinth. But what else have we got to do? How do we score that? We're 2000 short of our target.'

'Here's your answer,' Laura announced, walking further along the wall.

Phoenix reached her side and ran his fingers over the numbers. Two thousand. Then he traced the lines of a familiar face. The tyrant-king of Seriphos.

'Of course,' Phoenix sighed, remembering the myth. 'Another has to die. Polydectes.'

7

Back in John Graves' study, Phoenix's mother was laughing hysterically, great blobs of tears spilling over her cheeks and dropping from her chin. She wanted to run to somebody, hug them, tell them that her boy was all right. But there was nobody to tell. They were all mummified, entombed in a single, unchanging instant of time. For once the voice in the computer had no words to commemorate Medusa's death. Instead, as if to mourn her passing, the screen images blurred and the sequences of numbers raced more madly than ever, throbbing and pulsating until Mum had to shield her eyes.

'Don't go wrong now,' she cried as she lost sight of Phoenix.

There was a flash and every clock in the house started ticking simultaneously. Time had started again. Mum hadn't noticed. She was trying to make the computer work.

But the flash wasn't a technical fault.

It was a cry of despair.

Inside the computer, something was screaming.

There were no black flags over the tyrant's palace this time. As Phoenix and Laura approached Polydectes' citadel, there was gaiety in the air. Red banners vied with yellow, snapping in the strong sea breeze. They dropped to earth in the cover of an olive grove.

'Are you sure you're ready for this?' asked Laura.

'My arm, you mean? It's fine. A bit stiff, and that's easing.'

He weighed the Gorgon's head in the leather wallet.

'You know what we have to do?'

He saw Laura's downcast eyes and felt some sympathy. Killing a man in cold blood is hard.

'We're so close to completing our mission. We have to do it.'

'But it's so calculated. To turn a man to stone. And without giving him a chance.'

'It's no more than we did to Medusa.'

Laura showed signs of frustration. 'She was a monster.'

'And so is Polydectes.'

'Maybe,' said Laura. 'But even if he is, he's a human one.' She rested a hand on his arm. 'What's he done that's so terrible? He wants to marry Danaë. Hardly a capital offence. And OK, he set you up, but it's all part of the game. Adams has done worse, but we didn't try to kill him. Let's face it, Phoenix. How do we know he's a tyrant? Because the legend says so. How do we know we have to destroy him? Because the game says so. Everything is because the game says so.'

Phoenix continued to cling stubbornly to his plan of action.

'That's enough for me.'

'Well, not for me. You've said it yourself. The game is cruel. You can't trust it.'

'Don't you think I know that?'

They faced each other, angry and tense.

'Ask yourself one simple question, Laura. Do you want to stay here forever? Do you?'

'Of course not. It doesn't mean we have to do this. It's wrong.'

Giving a snort of exasperation, Phoenix stormed off to the cliff's edge. He felt the wind on his face and he knew he was right.

Polydectes must die!

He span round. 'Why can't you understand? You're not home in Brownleigh now. Mum and Dad aren't there to sort it out. You can't phone 999. Normal rules don't apply here. You learn the ways of the game or you perish.'

'What makes you so right all the time?' Laura retorted. 'You're not infallible. I was the one who knew there was somebody in the cave, not you. I thought of the flare, not you.

And there was the arrow. I pulled you back then, too. I've saved your life more than once, remember. What makes you think you know everything?'

'All right,' Phoenix yelled back. 'I'm human. I make mistakes. But I'm the only one who can get us home. I'm the Legendeer. Don't try to stop me, Laura. Polydectes must die.'

Laura turned away. There was no bridging the gulf between them.

'Do what you have to.'

'Here,' Phoenix snarled, tossing the shield and the sickle to the ground. 'I'm leaving these with you.' He slipped off the sandals and threw them to Laura. Finally he hoisted the head of Medusa on to his shoulders. 'You could still come with me.'

'No,' said Laura, her back still turned to him. 'Not this time.'

Without another word, Phoenix set off for the palace with his gruesome wedding gift. By the time he had reached the outer battlements the marriage feast was beginning. He heard the blare of trumpets and the beat of drums. Flower petals were being showered on the arriving guests. He looked up at the maids emptying baskets of petals over the crowds and scowled.

I am coming, Polydectes.

He was at the doors to the great hall before he was challenged.

'Young Perseus, eh?' said the guard. 'I didn't expect to see you again.'

'I return to give Lord Polydectes his wedding present.'

He raised the leather wallet.

'Then you'd better go inside, though Olympus knows what King Polydectes will make of it. He thinks you're on a quest for Medusa's head. I ask you, a boy sent to slay the demon.'

Phoenix smiled.

'You know me and my idle boasts.'

The guard smiled back.

'I do that. In you go, lad.'

The hall was full of Polydectes' guards and hangers-on. Of all the people in the hall, only Danaë was innocent. Phoenix made his way to her side.

'Lady Danaë,' he whispered. 'When I begin to speak, avert your eyes.'

She stared at the wallet.

'You mean—'

'Yes, I succeeded in my quest.'

She slipped away from the table without a word and retired to a recess where silken curtains hung. Satisfied that she was safely out of the way, Phoenix strode towards King Polydectes' throne.

'Polydectes,' he declared, 'I return with the Gorgon's head.'

Polydectes turned, and all his guests with him.

'You dare walk back into my court?' he cried, baring his wolf's teeth. 'And with some tall tale about bringing the Gorgon's head. You'd better be a good runner, boy, because my guards will chase you all the way back to the end of the world, or wherever you've been hiding yourself.'

Laughter rippled through the crowded hall.

'But it's true,' Phoenix insisted. 'I have the head.'

More mocking laughter.

'Lords and ladies of Seriphos,' Phoenix shouted. 'Invited guests. You have a choice before you. I swear that I have here the head of the Gorgon, Medusa. King Polydectes seems to doubt me. Let's have a game. All those who believe the king, stand with him. All who trust me, stand at my side.'

There was raucous laughter from the guests as they moved over towards Polydectes.

Phoenix's side of the hall emptied steadily until he stood alone.

'There you are, boy,' boasted Polydectes. 'That's how many believe in the boy-hero. Do your worst *hero*.'

Phoenix did as he was told. He reached into the wallet and produced the head of Medusa. He watched with satisfaction as horror registered in the eyes of every one of Polydectes' court. In the time it took to blink an eye, a fantastic transformation had taken place. Skin that was tanned and soft turned as wrinkled as an elephant's hide. As hard as granite. Where there had been a hundred laughing guests, a hundred stone statues now stood.

Phoenix was returning the head to the wallet, smiling grimly at his growing points score, when Danaë emerged from the recess.

'Lady,' he told her. 'You are free.'

She took his hand, but not to thank him.

'Listen,' she said urgently. 'I may only have minutes.'

She lifted her hair to display an owl tattoo.

'That's right. I could die on the spot for talking to you. But too many lives hang in the balance. I wish I could have found the courage earlier. I have to say my piece, whatever the cost. Enough of this play-acting. Nobody can be free until the Gamesmaster is destroyed. Even if you kill the Minotaur, you won't have won. Know this, Legendeer. The labyrinth is not the end.'

'How can you be sure? How do you know about the Minotaur? How do you know? You're—'

'There's no time for that. Listen to me, and listen well.'

She leaned forward and whispered in Phoenix's ear. 'Only one man knows how to win the game. Find him and you will free us all.'

'But who?'

There was a sudden, sickening thump in Danaë's throat. Her lovely pale eyes rolled back and her breath rattled in her throat. The soft, reassuring voice was drowning in blood.

'No!' cried Phoenix.

He cradled the dying woman.

'Please. Don't die.'

She smiled, blood staining her gasping lips.

'Too late. But the man who can beat the game. It's your father.'

Then came a desperate struggle for breath, before the moment of dark crisis came, and she died.

Don't die. Don't leave me.

Phoenix slumped to his knees. He was alone and crushed by

Danaë's death. Phoenix was still taking in what Danaë had told him, wondering about the identity of the Gamesmaster, when he heard the palace guard arriving at the run.

'Treason!' they cried. 'Treachery against the king.'

In fury at the death of Danaë, Phoenix showed them the head and they cried no more. Ten more statues had joined the hundred in the hall.

'Laura,' he called, reaching the path that led down to the beach. 'I'm back. It's over.'

There was no reply.

'Laura,' he shouted again.

His heart began to race.

Why doesn't she reply?

He started to run.

'Laura!'

As he reached the sands his worst fears were confirmed. Written on the beach in letters three feet high was a chilling message:

SURPRISE SURPRISE.

THE LEVELS

Level Ten
Into the Labyrinth

1

'Laura!'

Phoenix had scoured the barren beaches of Seriphos for hours, but there was no sign of her. He even staggered into the waves, beating the water with his fists. All to no avail. He was no hero now, just a boy alone. It was even worse than that. Now that he'd known real friendship, the loss of it weighed even more heavily. It was as if part of him had been ripped out and his whole body was outraged by the gaping, throbbing wound. He sank to his knees by the message written in the sand

SURPRISE SURPRISE.

I could kill you, Adams.

This time Phoenix really meant it. Wherever there was danger, wherever there was evil, Adams was there to give it a helping hand. Beyond the screen, in a backwater like Brownleigh, he had been a small town bully. Here, under the influence of the game, he was deadly. He was Reede's disciple. Dad might hold the key to the game, but, like Laura, he was a minor player.

It's a two-player game, Adams, and it is between us.

You ***are*** *my Nemesis.*

A terrible thought struck him.

'And it's all my fault. I invited you in!'

When Adams entered the game he started drinking from evil's cup. There was no doubt any more, he had become intoxicated with the taste. That was it. The two boys were enemies to the last beat of their hearts, the last breath in their bodies.

More than just a game? Adams, you don't know how much more!

Phoenix patted the wallet containing Medusa's head. Kill him. Maybe he should.

He dug his fingers into the silvery sand and felt utterly broken and defeated. He was as sorry for himself as he'd ever felt in his life. He wanted to curse the gods, or Reede, or whoever was making this crazy world turn, but he wasn't going to give them the satisfaction of hearing his misery echoing over the booming tide. They thought they were so clever with their game, didn't they? They had their hero, somebody to put through every trial. Now they had their villain too, to track him all the way. Adams and I, Phoenix thought, we're two sides of the coin, adversaries in a lethal game.

He thought of Danaë dying and Laura kidnapped. Every ounce of his growing confidence had evaporated.

I can't stand it any more. It has to end. It's all too much. I want out.

But how *could* he escape? And how could he leave without Dad and Laura? It was only then, as he abandoned hope of ever finding her on the island, that he gave the beach a proper investigation. What he had missed before now became obvious. It was the footprints. His own, of course. Then Laura's. A set for Adams. Then there was the imprint of a pair of cloven hooves.

Pan.

Laura had been right about him all along. At best he was an unreliable guide, at worst— He didn't like to think about it. Phoenix sat watching the tide roll in, wondering what to do next. He was beginning to realize how great a setback he had suffered. It wasn't just Laura he had lost. The flying sandals were gone, the helmet, shield and sickle. Every single thing that told him he'd made progress in the game. But it couldn't end here.

I won, didn't I?

So why hadn't he moved on to the next level? Why was he still stranded on Seriphos? He checked the points display. There! All seven thousand points. His sense of injustice boiled over. He had to face the Minotaur one last time. He had to destroy the creature that haunted his dreams.

But how?

He was at his lowest ebb, staring at the writing in the sand and feeling his loss like pain, when he heard something, a high, piercing screech. High above, swooping from the cloudless sky came a great bird. Like an eagle, but even bigger, with a wing span at least twice as wide. The bird was tracing vast circles in the sky. Phoenix watched fascinated as it glided closer, a huge predator with the most brilliant plumage he'd ever seen – blue, purple, scarlet and gold.

'The phoenix! You're the phoenix aren't you, my namesake. The bird who rises from the ashes.'

He watched spellbound as the great bird swooped over the sands. Phoenix raced after it, on and on, round the rocky headland towards a stretch of beach he hadn't seen, never mind explored. As he staggered exhausted around a screen of rocks, he cried out. On the beach, the phoenix had built a funeral pyre. Phoenix watched as his namesake bound together the ingredients of the pyre: aromatic plants, incense and balsam, threaded into a nest of twigs and branches. He breathed in the scent, mysterious yet familiar, the mingled odour of life and death. He was becoming drowsy, exhausted by the events of the last few days.

He re-ran them all in his mind: the fight at Deicterion, the beheading of Medusa, his revenge against Polydectes, and now Laura's kidnap. He was slipping into a hazy dreamstate, half waking, half sleeping.

Playing the game . . .

. . . the stench of the underground prison . . .

. . . its endless passageways . . .

. . . THE ROAR OF THE BEAST!

Phoenix was shocked awake. The nightmare had returned. But he didn't feel horror – he felt hope. Propping himself up on one elbow, he began to focus on the scene before him. The fire of life and death was scorching the sands. Smoke was billowing into the sky, roaring flames dancing at the water's edge, burning with such fury that the tidewaters boiled. And there at its heart was the great bird, beating its wings in the red and orange of the fire. He could feel the flames licking around him, but he didn't burn. It was a gentle, healing fire. As he looked through the acrid smoke he saw a familiar figure, come to witness the event.

Pan was standing at the water's edge, silent and watching.

Now Phoenix understood. The bird's death was his rebirth. There was more than evil at work in this legend world. There was good too, and it was working through him. As the bird's dying screech filled the sky Phoenix saw his arms fading, becoming transparent.

Through the woodsmoke Pan gave a brief, cryptic nod, as if formally witnessing the Legendeer's progress, then strode away into the surf.

At last! Phoenix was moving to the next level.

2

Another quest, another forest of black flags snapping in the sea breeze. Phoenix shook his head. Death hung over the game like a cloud.

'Hey! HEY!' Phoenix shouted to a passing street urchin. 'Where am I?'

The boy scratched his head. 'Are you serious?'

'I just want to know where I am.'

'Look around you,' he said. 'What do you see? Only the greatest city in all Greece, beloved of Pallas Athene, sorrowing Athens itself.'

Though he was sure from the moment he stepped on to the street exactly how the boy would answer, Phoenix still needed to hear it from his lips.

'Why sorrowing?'

'Where have you been, stranger? Because King Minos demands his tribute, that's why. This year, as every year, seven youths and seven maidens will be transported to the palace of Knossos on a black-sailed death ship. Every well-born family in this city has lost a son or a daughter. There in the palace of merciless King Minos, the razer of cities, they will be thrown to the beast that dwells in the labyrinth.'

Phoenix breathed deeply. Now he knew why the nightmare had begun again. He had almost come full circle, to resume his mission where he had broken off and fled in terror.

Where I begged for my life.

He felt his cowardice keenly. He had abandoned Dad, left him to his fate. There was only one way to make amends. He had to be the hero he claimed to be, the Legendeer. He'd played Perseus to the end, and played his part bravely.

He'd conquered the Gorgon, Medusa and destroyed Polydectes. There was only one way to make amends, he had to win the game.

'Which way to the royal palace?' he asked.

But the boy was staring past him, eyes widening. Phoenix turned and saw what he was looking at.

'Pan.'

He strode to the shadowy recess where his guide was waiting.

'Another of my tricks, Legendeer?'

Phoenix didn't reply. Instead, he watched as his guide's nose swelled into a monstrous snout and his head sprouted horns.

The Minotaur.

Returning to his normal state, Pan spoke, but without the gaiety he had displayed in his earlier appearances.

Can it be?

You are actually beginning to fear me?

'Welcome to the next stage of your journey.'

Phoenix returned Pan's gaze coldly. He remembered the prints on the beach. He was in the presence of a treacherous god.

'Where's Laura?'

'She's for you to find,' Pan replied without a trace of emotion in his voice. 'It was your carelessness that left the girl prey to the fates.'

'Me!' cried Phoenix. 'You dare to blame me. Why—'

Pan waved away his furious protests.

'I am sure you have worked out where you are,' he said. 'And who.'

He eyed the wallet carrying Medusa's head and stroked it lightly.

'You won't be needing that here, Legendeer. It is time for the hero to take on a new form. Hail to thee, Theseus, heir to the throne of Athens.'

Phoenix was about to pepper Pan with questions when he

was cut off by the sound of a procession. Drums beat and trumpets blared.

'The king?' he asked.

There was no reply. Pan had gone. Phoenix found himself standing in the front row of a growing crowd, drawn by the approach of the royal party. But there was no cheering, no applause. The mood was sombre. Every building flew a black flag. After a few moments, he discovered the boy he had spoken to before Pan's appearance.

'What are you?' the boy asked, glancing back at the recess. 'A god?'

'No,' said Phoenix with a smile. 'Not a god.'

The boy didn't seem reassured by his answer.

'The death ship,' Phoenix asked, 'when does it sail?'

'Tomorrow, at dawn.'

There was no time to lose. Phoenix remembered the words of Pan. *Use the myth as a pole star to navigate your way*. He turned the legend over in his mind. King Aegeus of Athens fathers Theseus in a distant town called Troezen, but doesn't stay to see him born. He leaves the boy a sword and a pair of sandals hidden under a great rock to remember him by. When Theseus is approaching manhood, he rolls back the stone and discovers the secret of his birth.

Remembering the way Pan had stroked the leather wallet containing Medusa's head, Phoenix felt inside. In place of the gory trophy he discovered the hilt of a broken sword and an ancient pair of sandals.

Phoenix looked at them. The belongings of Aegeus that had lain concealed under the boulder in Troezen.

My destiny.

If I'm to win the game I must claim my destiny.

An advance party of soldiers was marching into the square, carrying black flags. 'Make way for King Aegeus and Queen Medea.'

Phoenix then stared at the king, aging and bowed. There was nothing for it. He had to make himself known. If he could slay the Gorgon, he could speak to the king. He stepped forward and immediately drew the attention of three of the king's bodyguards.

'Wait,' Phoenix cried as they converged on him, swords drawn. 'I wish to petition the king.'

The soldiers glanced round at Aegeus.

'Let the boy speak.'

'My name,' he announced, 'is Theseus.'

A murmur ran through the crowd. The king leaned forward, examining every inch of Phoenix's face.

'I come from Troezen to claim my birthright as your son and heir to the throne of Athens.'

He saw the eyes of the king's wife, Queen Medea burning into him. Those eyes, he'd seen them before . . . somewhere . . . Thrown by the piercing stare of the queen, Phoenix struggled on. But even as he spoke, he was unsettled by those scintillating, black diamond eyes.

'I have travelled many days and many nights to reach your court.'

'Your coming has been announced,' said Aegeus. 'The Oracle spoke of the boy-hero and his deeds. We have been waiting for your arrival.'

Phoenix knew exactly what to say. None of his reading had been wasted. Time to draw on it now. He recalled his and Dad's first attempts at this level.

'I came by the coast road, a bandit-ridden place. I defeated Periphetes the cudgel man, Procrustes with his magic bed and Sinis who ties his victims to trees. I destroyed a wild sow and the thief Scirion.'

In truth, Dad had done all that, but the tale came to his lips as easily as treachery to those of Adams. They were both becoming skilled in the ways of the game.

'Finally, I mastered Cercyon the Arcadian and Polyphemon, butcher of travellers.'

'Great adventures indeed,' said Aegeus. 'And travellers will long sing your name. May the reputation of great Theseus echo down the hallways of time. But what is your mission?'

Before Phoenix could answer, Medea began to speak.

'Welcome, bold Theseus. This mean street is no place to greet a hero. Come to the palace this evening. We will prepare a banquet in your honour.'

Her words were welcoming but her scheming eyes blazed with hatred. He could feel her power like an electrical charge in the air.

'We will speak further then of your adventures and your claim to the throne.'

Aegeus clapped his hands.

'Guards, conduct our visitor to his chambers and make him comfortable. We will see you tonight, bandit slayer.'

It was as he passed Medea that Phoenix caught the glare of her eyes again. Now he knew where he had seen them before. It was there, in the labyrinth, among the blood and the splintered bones. It was *her* eyes he'd seen staring down at him through the bars of the grating.

3

Two hours later Phoenix was standing at the window of his room, watching darkness fall over Athens. The death ship sailed the next day, and he had to be on board. Somewhere, the game had Dad and Laura. Phoenix remembered all the cruel things he had said to Dad, and the night filled with regret. But remorse wasn't going to solve anything. If any of them were ever to get out of this nightmare, he had to reach the labyrinth. He stared out across the paved square where huge braziers were burning, tossing showers of sparks into the twilit sky. Along the broad avenue that led to the palace, great black flags billowed in the strong sea breeze. A breeze that blew all the way to Crete and the lair of the beast. It could probably smell his fear already.

Suddenly, Phoenix froze. The hinges of the door to the chamber were creaking. Continuing to stand at the window, he felt on the table next to him for a weapon. His fingers came into contact with a large plate. The creaking had stopped, but muffled footsteps were approaching across the floor.

Just a little closer.

Half turning, Phoenix glimpsed a raised hand and a glinting dagger. Spinning round and kicking out his right leg, he tripped his assailant.

'Adams.'

In a reversal of their fortunes back home, Phoenix was sitting astride Adams, pinning his shoulders. No headaches now, he thought. Not one since I entered the game. For all the horror, I've never felt so alive. He tossed away the plate and recovered the dagger that had spun from Adams' hand.

'What are you doing here?'

Adams struggled in vain to get up.

'Playing my part,' he said, accepting defeat and lying back. 'I am Prince Medus, son of Medea and Aegeus. Your rival.'

My rival. What else?

'I should kill you right here,' snarled Phoenix.

Adams didn't show a grain of regret. No fear, either. In fact, he was as arrogant as if he were the one sitting astride Phoenix.

'What, and sign poor Laura's death warrant?'

A lump came to Phoenix's throat.

'Laura's here?'

'Let me up and I'll tell all.'

Reluctantly, Phoenix released his arch enemy. Adams didn't seem to mind being overcome so easily. That alone made Phoenix cautious.

'Tell me.'

Adams led him to the window and the black flags rippling against the stars.

'Those flags. They're for Laura.'

'You mean—'

'When the death ship sails tomorrow, she will be on board. But don't fret. You'll be seeing her tonight.'

'At the feast, you mean? How?'

Adams reclined on a couch, munching grapes. 'Tell me what you remember of the Theseus story.'

'I'm not going to—'

'Just tell the story, Legendeer. Remember, the myths are your guide.'

Back to that again. Telling stories of gods and demons. But that was his role. Adams was right; he was Phoenix, the Legendeer. He started the telling.

'King Minos is the ruler of Crete. Many years ago his son Androgeus visited Athens, but he was murdered in this very city. In revenge Minos waged war until a tribute was agreed. Every year seven youths and seven maidens are loaded onto a death ship and taken to the city of Knossos in his kingdom.

There they are fed to the Minotaur. The bones of his victims litter the floor of his maze. How am I doing?'

'You have the story to a tee,' said Adams. 'But I expected nothing less. That is exactly how King Aegeus told it to me. Here's the first bit of news. Laura has been chosen as one of those maidens. She'll be shown off with the others tonight.'

'This had better be the truth,' Phoenix warned.

'Oh, it is,' continued Adams. 'Now carry on with the story.'

'King Aegeus, Theseus' father, rules Athens, a city burdened by the terrible tribute. He marries twice, but there is no heir to the throne. Medea, his third wife, is a sorceress. She bears him the son he has craved, Medus—'

Adams stood up and took a bow.

'Yours truly. I'm the witch queen's son.'

Adams was barely recognizable as the small town bully he had once been. The game had transformed him. Such was the power of evil. But it had transformed Phoenix too.

Am I better, he wondered, or simply stronger? As he watched Adams, Phoenix saw a pattern. His enemy was part of a magical trinity of evil. Variations on a single monstrous name.

Medusa . . . Medea . . . Medus.

Of all the many heads of evil, these three loomed the largest in Phoenix's imagination. Medusa the Gorgon dies, Medea the sorceress rises in her place. Finally, waiting to ascend the throne, there is Medus. As the sorcerer-prince, Adams was now locked into the game. Evil would continue in an uninterrupted line.

'You can't win, you know,' Adams said smirking. 'Think about it. If old Aegeus declares you his heir, then the Queen's son remains second in line. And believe me, Medea isn't the kind of woman to accept second best.' He strode towards the door. 'Enjoy your meal.'

Phoenix watched Adams go and sat turning the warning over in his mind. He was taking it seriously. Anything that was in the legend was part of his destiny. At the banquet tonight, the Queen would try to poison Theseus. He thought of the witch-queen and her hate-filled eyes. Yes, she planned to kill him.

As Adams' footfalls faded down the corridor, Phoenix inspected the contents of the leather wallet. The hilt of the sword was beautiful, twin serpents delicately carved into the ivory. Along with the sandals, it was his safeguard. The moment King Aegeus recognized them, he would accept him as his son. Then on to the labyrinth and the Minotaur, the key to finding his real father. Phoenix shouldered the wallet and waited to be fetched. The banquet would be another test.

He was in the tunnels again, running through the gloom. The beast was on his heels. He saw a sword on the floor and reached for it. But as he picked it up, it came to life in his hand. A snake, many snakes! They were twisting, slithering up his arm. This was no sword. He was holding the head of Medusa.

'No!'

He shook loose the chains of sleep, and sat up. There was a sheen of cold sweat on his skin. Would the nightmare never let him go?

A knock on the door swept away the last dusty cobwebs of drowsiness.

'Theseus, Prince of Athens. You are summoned to the palace.'

He followed the guard through the palace gardens and into the great hall. He remembered Polydectes and smiled at the thought of his silent, petrified court.

'Welcome, young Theseus,' said Aegeus. 'Take a seat at our table.'

Phoenix ran his eyes over the guests and stopped at a teenage boy watching him with malice-filled eyes. Adams.

'Ah,' said Aegeus, registering Phoenix's interest. 'This is my son Medus.'

Phoenix exchanged nods with Adams then gave the woman beside him a wary glance. The witch-queen, Medea.

'Before we eat,' said Aegeus. 'I have a sad duty.'

He raised a hand and the palace guards ushered in the

fourteen Athenians who were to die at the hands of the Minotaur. Laura was the third in the group.

'Youth of Athens,' Aegeus proclaimed. 'It is with a heavy heart that I salute you. Once in a twelvemonth, I bid farewell to the flower of this city as they lay down their sweet lives in the slaughterhouse of cruel King Minos. Be brave, my children. You surrender your fine young lives so that the citizens of Athens may sleep easy in their beds, free of war and dreadful slaughter.'

The fourteen stood in a line, facing the guests. There was fear in their faces.

'Now, Theseus, you have a tale to tell.'

'I do, King and father. I—'

'Before you continue,' Aegeus interrupted. 'A toast to the courage that brought you to my court.'

Phoenix saw Medea lean over to the king. Phoenix felt a twitch of foreboding. A maidservant charged his goblet. Medea whispered in her husband's ear. Adams watched the exchange between king and queen and smiled. Phoenix knew what they had in store for him.

'Hail to you, great Theseus,' cried Aegeus. 'A toast. To the slayer of bandits. Theseus of Troezen.'

Phoenix's heart kicked. The wine. Was this the poison? He stared at Laura and mouthed the word.

Poison.

For a moment her face wore a puzzled frown, then she understood. Yes, poison for the hero.

'Hail to you, great Aegeus,' Phoenix cried, raising the goblet.

He hesitated.

'Drink, brave Theseus,' said Adams. 'This banquet is in your honour.'

'Yes,' Medea added. 'Down your cup.'

Another glance at Laura. What did he do now?

'King Aegeus,' she said suddenly. 'May I speak?'

Surprised, Aegeus gave his consent. 'Tomorrow, you will make the greatest sacrifice for your city. You have leave to speak.'

All eyes turned towards Laura. It was Phoenix's chance. Leaning forward he tipped the goblet over and watched as the wine ran off the table. Adams was watching too. Just as he was about to call for more wine, Phoenix reached for the jug from which he filled his own cup.

'This will do fine,' he said with a smile.

Laura was stumbling through a feeble speech of praise for Aegeus, but it had done the trick. The wine, with its lacing of poison, was running through a crack in the tiled floor.

'Before I drink this toast,' Phoenix said, smiling triumphantly at Adams. 'Let me show you the proof that I am heir to the throne of Athens.'

But when he reached into the leather wallet his face drained of blood. The trinity of evil: Medusa, Medea, Medus. Instead of the sword hilt and the sandals, he felt the serpent hair of Medusa! The score bracelet registered the danger facing him. He was losing points.

'What is it, Theseus?' asked Medea, a smug satisfaction showing on her face.

'Is something wrong?' asked Adams.

Their voices were gloating. At the very moment when Phoenix thought they'd done their worst, they had turned the tables again. He saw Adams tapping a leather wallet just like the one he was holding. Somehow they had made a switch.

'Well,' said Aegeus, suspicion written into every wrinkle of his tired old face. 'May I see this proof?'

Phoenix's mind was thrown into tumult. If he produced the head, anyone who saw it would die. A grotesque picture burst into his imagination, of the boy-hero turning to stone before the entire gathering. Even worse, of an entire court destroyed, and with it any hope of completing the mission.

But how was this done? Phoenix met the eyes, the burning eyes, of Medea, and he remembered Adams' boasts. This sorcery was her work. He exchanged glances with Laura. This time there was nothing she could do. She was all out of ideas. It was time to turn the tables.

'Great Aegeus, I understand that my arrival must be of concern to your wife, the queen. After all, it is her son who stands to lose a throne. The wallet is hers.'

Seeing the look of shock on Medea's face, he felt his power growing. In a bolder, more assured voice, he addressed her. 'Lady Medea, would you examine the proof?'

He handed the wallet to the startled queen. She stared panic-stricken at the heavy leather bag. It was the turn of her flesh to crawl at the macabre trophy inside.

'I—'

Her eyes met those of Phoenix. The hatred burned stronger than ever. She knew she had been outwitted. Closing her eyes, she rested a hand on each of the wallets. Phoenix felt the charge of a strange power in the air. Her magic was doing its work. She had switched the wallets again. Unfastening the drawstring, Medea emptied the sword-hilt and sandals on the table.

The score bracelet chattered reassuringly.

Raising his goblet in triumph, Phoenix toasted Aegeus. 'To you, King and father.'

'By the gods of great Olympus!' cried Aegeus. 'It's true. You *are* my son.'

He stared at the sandals and sword-hilt then at the goblet in Phoenix's hand.

'No!' he cried. 'Don't drink.'

He rushed to dash the cup from Phoenix's hand.

'The drink is poisoned. I thought you were an imposter. I swear to you, my boy, this was the queen's doing. She told me you were a lying knave, come to kill me.'

Phoenix let him dash the cup with its harmless liquid to the floor. It was part of the legend, after all, so why deny the old man his place in it? As the king embraced him, Phoenix looked across at Adams. He made a suitable son for Medea. He shared her thirst for malice. His eyes burned with the same hatred.

4

As the morning mists cleared from the port of Athens next day, Phoenix found himself standing among a great crowd. It had been a night of rejoicing. Aegeus had embraced him as his rightful heir, Prince Theseus of Athens. Phoenix had come through, he'd played his part to the full. He was the toast of the entire city. Fires had been lit on every altar in all the temples of the city. Images of the gods had been heaped with gifts. The air was still filled with acrid smoke where oxen had been slaughtered and roasted in sacrifice to Olympus. Now the citizens of Athens jostled for a place at the harbour. There remained one last ceremony to perform. The banishment of a traitor. Two ships were being prepared at the quayside. The death ship to Crete and the ship of exile – Medea's ship.

'Queen Medea,' said Aegeus. 'You have shared my life, but you are now a proven traitor. You have been found guilty of the vilest treason. You have tried to poison Theseus, my first-born son and rightful heir to the throne of Athens. You tried to poison my mind against him, telling me he was a spy. Or, worse still, an assassin. Do you have anything to say before you are cast out?'

Medea and Adams were standing together, under armed guard.

'You old fool,' Medea said, her voice crackling with fury. 'Who are you to banish me? My power is greater by far than yours. I should have ruled here, not you. As for you, Theseus, relish your victory now because your fate is betrayal and black despair.'

Along the quayside, Laura flinched. The sorceress stood

proudly, her long hair flying in the wind. There wasn't a trace of shame.

'Hear me, Theseus. You are cursed. You and all who follow you.'

Aegeus shook his head sadly.

'I loved you Medea, as wife and queen . . . and mother to my son Medus.'

He looked at Adams, who turned his face away. He'd played the part long enough. He belonged to nobody but the spirit of evil that powered the game.

'Now I must lose you both.'

'You never had us,' raged Medea. 'With my spells I made you love me. You poor old fool, you were my puppet. That's all.'

Aegeus seemed to reel under the impact of her acid tongue.

'Enjoy your triumph Theseus,' shrieked Medea. 'But don't forget, another ship lies in this harbour, and when she sails she will carry the broken heart of Athens with her. Cast me out if you will, Aegeus, but you will never live to enjoy your new-found son. The Minotaur will avenge me.'

All eyes turned towards the black-sailed ship lying at anchor further along the quay. The celebrations of the night before seemed to evaporate. The death ship was ready to sail, bearing away fourteen of their sons and daughters. Aegeus waved to the crew of the first vessel that was to carry Medea into exile.

'Set sail. Convey this faithless witch across the sea. Begone, outcast.'

'Banish me then,' yelled Medea, flinging wide her arms. 'But hear this, Aegeus, there is no jail on Earth that can hold me, no shackles that can bind me. Circe, my mother, taught me the arts of mysteries of the sorcerers. I fly with the raven, swim with the shark, slither with the viper. Come the turn of the year the throne of Athens will be empty and you will be at the bottom of the sea. That's right, Aegeus, your broken body will be picked clean by the crabs, and I will return to set my son upon the throne.'

The ship carrying Medea was setting sail. But most of the

crowd were already turning their eyes towards the death ship. Aegeus led the procession to the black-sailed vessel.

'My heart is heavy this day,' said Aegeus. 'I have lost a queen and an heir. Now I must bid farewell to the flower of our youth.'

Laura was shuffling on to the ship. Phoenix knew what he had to do. His destiny lay in those endless, twisting passageways across the sea. He raised his voice against the wind.

'Wait! This cruel tribute has to end. Athens must no longer give up its children to die in the labyrinth.'

'What can we do?' asked Aegeus. 'It is the will of Zeus who delights in thunder. We dare not deny the dark-browed Lord of Olympus. Have you any idea what happened the last time we refused tribute? Famine and earthquake laid waste to the land. Our streets were littered with the dead. Would you have me bring the wrath of the gods down upon Athens a second time?'

'I am not talking about refusing tribute,' Phoenix told him. 'Let *me* be the tribute.'

He stepped forward and grabbed one of the youths boarding the ship.

'What's your name?'

'I am Themon.'

'Return to your family, Themon. I'm taking your place.'

'No, my son,' Aegeus cried, 'I cannot permit this sacrifice. What if you should perish?'

'Didn't I clear the coast of bandits?' Phoenix demanded, playing his part with gusto. 'Didn't I expose Medea as a sorceress and traitor?'

His mind was back in Seriphos and the exploits of which he couldn't boast. Didn't he destroy Medusa and the court of cruel Polydectes too?

'It is my destiny to face the beast in his lair. I must do this, or Athens will groan under the burden of her loss for generations to come.'

More importantly, Phoenix, Dad and Laura would be trapped in this savage world forever.

Aegeus conferred with his courtiers.

'Very well, you have my blessing for your adventure. But promise this, you must return safely to Athens.' He waved to his servants. 'Take this with you.'

They tossed a heavy bundle on to the deck of the ship.

'What is it?'

'A white sail. When you kill the beast, hoist it in place of this black one and I will know you're safe. I shall be atop that cliff waiting for you.'

He turned and beckoned a grey-haired man from the crowd. He was the priest of Poseidon, god of the sea. The priest washed his hands in a silver bowl and scattered grains of barley on the flames of a brazier. He raised his arms and shouted an order. 'Bring the offering.'

A bull, its great head swaying, was led on to the quay.

'Lord Poseidon, son of Cronus and Rhea, you who command the waves, grant safe passage to our sons and daughters and their safe return.'

Having slain the animal the priest cast some of its hair on the flames. Phoenix watched the spectacle for a few moments then walked towards Laura. Before he could reach her, he was alerted by a cry of dismay from the crowd.

'The queen has returned. Look! It's Medea!'

In the billowing smoke above the sacrificial flame, the witch-queen's features were forming.

The crowd fell back in terror.

'Cowardly Athens. You retreated from the armies of Minos the Conqueror. Now fall back before my wrath. Gaze upon your sons and daughters for you will never see them again. Soon, they will be as dead as the crew of this ship of exile.'

Aegeus stepped forward but she cut him short.

'Yes, you too Aegeus, bid farewell to your son. You wish to know his fate? Then watch.'

Sparks showered from her eyes and fell upon the carcass of the bull where it lay. New life breathed into the dead body and it began to rise. But a terrible transformation was occurring.

Rising man-like on two legs, the bull's haunted eyes sought out Phoenix.

'Look upon this creature,' cried Medea. 'Tremble at the Minotaur's strength. Fear him for he will soon crush your bones and feast on your broken flesh.'

In an instant she was gone and the bull was once more lying dead on the ground.

'Don't go,' Aegeus begged.

'I have to,' Phoenix told him. 'It's my destiny.'

As they prepared to set sail, he confided in Laura.

'My destiny,' he repeated. 'And my nightmare.'

The nightmare came that night. Phoenix's courage failed again. This time there were other faces in the darkness. Not just Laura. Danaë was there, Aegeus too. All trusting him. All betrayed by him.

But I didn't fail! I didn't betray anybody!

Then in the dream-haze, Dad turned to face him, not the twinkling-eyed John Graves who had been so excited about *The Legendeer*. This was his ghost. His eyes were dead, drained of life. His freckled skin was bleached and cold.

'You betrayed me,' he groaned. 'And you will betray them too.'

And Phoenix was screaming, screaming until the sunlight filtered between his eyelids and he caught sight of the black sail billowing overhead.

'Phoenix.'

The scream went on and on.

'Phoenix, wake up.'

His eyes filled with Laura's face, staring down at him.

'The nightmare?' she asked.

Of course it was the nightmare. It was never going to let go. She sat beside him on the deck of the ship. A seagull wheeled overhead, eerily echoing Phoenix's scream.

'Are you ready for this, Phoenix? Are you sure you can kill the beast?'

'I don't know.'

'You're thinking about Medea's curse, aren't you?'

'That,' Phoenix replied. 'And Dad.'

He shuddered at the dead-eyed John Graves who had accused him in his dream.

'I still don't get it,' Laura sighed. 'What is going on here? It doesn't make any sense.'

'I know,' said Phoenix. 'Sometimes I think this is just a game. But no computer program could be this real. Or this evil. We're in another world. We must be.'

'And it's a world we're going to get out of,' Laura said defiantly.

Phoenix hung his head. 'Are you sure about that?'

Laura looked impatient with him for a moment. Then her face came to life.

'I almost forgot. It's the reason I came to wake you.'

'What is?'

'You'll have to see this for yourself.'

He followed her into the quarters below decks, where the rest of the ship's sad cargo were sleeping.

'Look.'

Phoenix examined all twelve sleeping passengers. No wonder Laura wanted to see.

'All of them!' he gasped.

Laura nodded.

'Every one.'

Phoenix continued to stare. It was true. They all bore the same mark. An owl tattoo.

'This *is* a real world,' he said. 'I've always known it. But there is an intelligence at work here. Reede, the Gamesmaster, the gods, call it what you wish, but this intelligence is playing with every one of us as if it were a game.'

Laura listened without a single interruption. He had spoken of an instinct, an inkling. Now it was growing into knowledge.

'Just think of it,' said Phoenix. 'Everybody's playing a part. I was Perseus, now I'm Theseus. Adams was Medus. What's more, the game never ends. Nothing has changed since the time of the legends, fifty, a hundred centuries ago. The people of this world are condemned to play over and over again, for all time. They're frozen in an age of terror. But what if somebody decides they don't want to play any more? What if they want out?'

Laura frowned. 'Go on.'

'There was that lad in Deicterion. He refused and the game did something to him. Danaë tried to tell me something and she died the same way. And it's all got something to do with this tattoo. That's why nobody breaks free.'

He was interrupted by the captain.

'I hope you slept well,' he called. 'We've reached our destination.'

Laura and Phoenix were the first to scramble up on deck. The other passengers followed them to the ship's rail a couple of minutes later. They assembled along the bulwark, gazing at the coast of Crete.

'Look!' shouted one of the sailors. 'To starboard. One of Minos' warships.'

Phoenix watched the warship's oars slicing through the waves. It was coming to bring them into harbour.

My destiny is reaching out to me.

But the warship wasn't the only thing out at sea that day. The waters began to boil before them, turning blood red. The other passengers fell back in horror. Within moments the cause of the scarlet stain became obvious.

'Surprise surprise!'

Phoenix watched the scene as if he were witnessing a third funeral pyre.

'I'd been expecting him.'

His Nemesis was approaching. Riding a chariot, drawn by dolphins, Adams and Medea were closing in on the ship.

'So,' Medea said, 'here you are Theseus, hastening to your death.'

Now Phoenix could see why the sea had turned red. In the bloodied waters he began to make out human features. Faces appeared first, with eyes staring and lifeless just as Dad's had been in Phoenix's dream.

'It's me,' cried Laura. 'Me and—'

'I know,' Phoenix murmured. 'Every one of the fourteen human sacrifices.' He glanced at the others. 'All of you.'

But Medea hadn't finished yet. Dipping her hand into the gory soup, she pulled out a familiar head. Laura screamed. The other passengers fell to their knees.

'The prince!' they cried.

Phoenix could only look at the bold, young face as if he was looking in a distorted fairground mirror. He was staring at his own death mask.

Medea turned her chariot and headed for the shore.

'I'll take my leave of you now,' she shouted gaily. 'I want to make sure of a ringside seat. I want to watch your face as you die.'

Nobody spoke.

Not one of them.

Each was facing their destiny in their own way.

5

Within the hour they were standing on Cretan soil, seven youths and seven maidens, chained to one another. They were guarded by fourteen soldiers, each carrying a brightly-patterned ox-hide shield, a murderous-looking javelin and a sword. On the cliffs above there were as many archers testing their bowstrings. Minos was taking no risks with his tribute.

'All hail Lord Minos,' one of the soldiers cried suddenly. 'Great King, law-giver, conqueror of Megara, master of Athens.'

Phoenix felt the prick of a spearpoint in his back.

'Kneel craven Athenians, bow your heads before your lord.'

Laura bristled. 'Lord indeed. He isn't *my* lord.'

The protest earned her a brutal kick in the back which sent her sprawling to the ground. The incident was seen by a tall, bearded figure in maroon robes. Judging by the way the crowd divided to let him pass, it could only be one man – Minos himself.

'Is she giving you problems?' he asked the soldier.

'No Sire.'

Phoenix could see Laura's eyes flashing.

'Then why are you mistreating the prisoner so?'

'She was defiant. She refused to swear allegiance, Sire.'

Phoenix's heart turned over. She had slighted Minos, King of Crete, conqueror of Athens. She could be put to the sword on the spot.

'Hail, King Minos,' he declared, pushing forward as far as his chains allowed. 'The fault is not my friend's. I have encouraged her in her pride.'

'And you are?'

He was about to play his trump card, claiming special status as Theseus, Prince of Athens when a familiar voice broke in.

'He is Theseus of Troezen, the bandit slayer.'

'Why thank you, Medea,' said Minos. 'I take it you two know each other.'

Medea glared at Phoenix with her blazing eyes.

'Oh, we know each other, King Minos. The boy is responsible for my banishment.'

'Well, well,' said Minos, stroking his beard. 'Two royal visitors at my court. The gods have blessed me. They have indeed.' He turned to Laura. 'Get up girl. Save your proud gestures for the Minotaur.'

Phoenix stretched out a helping hand, but Laura was determined to get up by herself.

'Come here, Theseus,' Minos ordered. 'Let me look at you.'

Phoenix stood before the King.

'So you are the bandit slayer, the hero of Athens. Medea has recounted your exploits. I am impressed, young prince. And to have offered yourself as part of the tribute! I wonder, is it courage or madness?'

Phoenix had asked himself the same question a hundred times!

'This should be good sport, Theseus. Never has such noble blood quenched the thirst of the beast.'

Phoenix managed his own gesture of defiance. 'I did not come to satisfy the appetite of the beast, King Minos, but to slay it.'

A murmur ran through the crowd until it was cut short by a noise from beneath the earth. Below their feet the ground trembled with a terrible roar, half-animal, half-human. It sang of savagery, but of sadness too. In the darkness the beast awaited them.

'Tut tut, Theseus,' chuckled Minos. 'I fear you have upset our monstrous son.'

The roar had penetrated Phoenix's soul. He could feel his courage draining away.

'Now, Theseus, I am sure you are tired after your voyage. Let me conduct you to your chambers.'

Phoenix was about to follow when he remembered his companions.

'What of them?'

'Why, they will be held in the dungeons until—' His eyes twinkled. 'Until feeding time.'

Phoenix stopped short.

'Then I will share their quarters.'

'So an Athenian with spirit. Very well, you shall all enjoy chambers in my palace. I can afford to be generous.' He gave a knowing wink. 'Besides, it will only be for one night.'

Another roar from the demon prison below.

One night, then we meet face to face.

Laughter rippled through the crowd. Two voices laughed loudest and longest – those of Adams and Medea.

Minos was as good as his word. When he said they would enjoy chambers at the palace, he really did mean enjoy. Tables were set with cooked meats, wine, fruit, vegetables, bread and cheese.

'I feel like a turkey,' grumbled Laura. 'Being fattened up for Christmas.'

'Christmas?' Phoenix exclaimed. 'I wish we had that long.'

'The king said we had one more night. When *exactly* do we go to the labyrinth?'

Did she really want to know?

'Tomorrow, at dawn.'

Laura took the news calmly, but she was unable to finish her meal. Phoenix was trying to think of a way to comfort her when there was a loud knock at the door.

'Prisoners, be upstanding for His Highness Lord Minos, Great King, law-giver.'

Laura shook her head. 'Do they have to go through this rigmarole every time?'

Phoenix smiled.

'Yes, Laura, every time. The rules of the game.'

Minos walked in followed by the members of his court.

'Prince Theseus,' he said. 'Pardon me for interrupting your meal, your *final* meal, but I wanted you to meet my family and my court.'

Phoenix stood and approached the king.

'Let me introduce my wife, Queen Pasiphaë, my sons Catreus, Deucalion and Glaucus.' Minos paused. 'And the flower of my court, my daughter Ariadne.'

Phoenix felt a shudder of recognition. He felt Ariadne's eyes on his face, the same eyes he had seen the first time he played the game.

Minos stroked his daughter's hair. 'Sweet Ariadne. So fair, so *loyal.*'

The princess shuddered at his touch. But Minos took little notice. He was keen to say his piece.

'The Fates are cruel indeed, brave Theseus. The bandit-slaying Prince of Athens and the Princess of Crete. In another time this would have been a match made on Olympus, a marriage to unite our warring lands.'

The introductions ran on and on. Phoenix avoided Medea and Adams. As he approached the end of the line he was hard-pressed to stifle a yawn. Then Minos pulled a master stroke.

'Last but not least, great Daedalus.'

Phoenix turned, then snapped to attention.

'Da—'

It was Dad, but the familiar green eyes cut Phoenix short with a warning glare. No emotion, no embrace. They had to continue to play their parts.

Minos was in a hearty mood. 'I see you recognize the name of our wise friend.'

Flustered by Dad's presence, Phoenix stammered out a reply.

'Yes, Lord Minos, I know of Daedalus. Who doesn't? He is the talk of all Greece. Hail to you, great inventor and architect of the labyrinth.'

Hail to you, ***father****.*

'You seem excited, young Theseus,' said Minos, the corners

of his mouth twitching with a sly grin. 'You don't look like a man enjoying his last night on this Earth.'

At the King's words Phoenix's doubts returned. He found himself glaring at Adams and Medea and saw the cold smiles on their faces. What were they up to?

Laura joined him and glanced at Minos and his courtiers. 'What is this?' she whispered. 'Do they have to watch us eat?'

Phoenix was about to reply when Ariadne detached herself from the rest of her party. She wandered around the room, finally drawing close to Phoenix. As she passed, a tiny piece of paper dropped from her sleeve and landed beside him. A sudden joy flowed through him. How could he have forgotten the legend? Ariadne would be there with sword and twine, helping him. She would be their salvation.

The myth is a pole star to navigate my way.

'Let them have their fun,' Phoenix told her, reassured by the meeting with Ariadne and Dad – or should it be Daedalus? 'We're going to have the last laugh.'

It was late and the court of Minos had left. While the lights were being extinguished in the corridor and the guard changed, Laura made her way to Phoenix's side.

'What was all that about earlier? How are we going to have the last laugh?'

'Remember what Pan always said, Laura? *Use the myth as the pole star to navigate your way.*'

Laura gave him an indulgent smile.

'I'm not likely to forget, am I?'

'Remember Princess Ariadne?'

'Mmm, what's she? The love interest?'

Laura seemed a bit nettled. So, she'd noticed the princess. Not jealousy, surely?

'I suppose she is actually,' Phoenix replied, enjoying teasing her. '*For the purposes of the game.*'

'Mmm.'

Laura *was* bothered.

Phoenix produced the note that Ariadne had slipped to him. Laura was determined not to be impressed. She barely raised an eyebrow.

'What is it?'

'I'm sure you've guessed already. The part of the story I'd almost forgotten.'

Maybe he'd been too paralyzed with fear by the prospect of returning to the labyrinth to remember.

'Ariadne falls in love with Theseus.'

Laura rolled her eyes.

'Of course she does.'

'Oh, stop it. This is good news, Laura. It's the most famous part of the legend. The labyrinth has been constructed as an impossible maze. Daedalus made it that way. But between them Ariadne and Daedalus come up with a plan to save Theseus and his companions. That's what the note says. They're coming. Soon.'

'Daedalus? You mean your dad?'

Phoenix nodded.

'So answer me this. If he can rescue us now, why didn't he do something earlier?'

'I don't know,' Phoenix admitted, as images of their previous flight in the labyrinth started to trouble him. 'The important thing is, they're planning a rescue.'

'Let me guess, a helicopter.'

'Now you're just being silly. No, it has to follow the rules of the game. In the legend Ariadne gives Theseus a ball of twine and a sword. Theseus ties the twine to the door of the labyrinth and plays it out behind him. He uses the sword to kill the beast and follows the thread back to the entrance.'

He was buzzing with excitement, but Laura wasn't so sure.

'I don't know. Remember how hard it was to defeat Medusa. You've said yourself that the Minotaur was too strong for you. I mean, how many times have you run from it?'

'I'm not running any more,' said Phoenix. 'This time I intend to win.'

'What's changed?'

'This, for one,' said Phoenix, waving the points bracelet under her nose. 'We've built up a huge score. I'll win this time. I know it.'

'But what if it's a trick?' Laura asked. 'We can't expect anybody to bail us out. Not the architect, and not a lovesick princess. No, it's just too sudden, too convenient.'

Phoenix was furious with her. He'd been so happy. He'd convinced himself that they were almost home. How could she doubt him? Didn't she realize? He *was* the Legendeer. He stormed to the window in a fit of pique and stared out across the sea. Was it too much to expect your best friend to believe in you?

'I've been patient with you, Laura, but I've got to say it. You don't know what you're talking about.'

He was about to tell her a few more home truths when he heard footsteps echoing below him. By the torches on the battlements he was able to make out a band of soldiers marching two chained prisoners away. A new horror clawed at his insides.

'No, this is impossible.'

But there they were, caught in the torchlight from Minos' palace, the princess and the architect. It was them, Dad and Ariadne, accompanied by four guards.

'What is it, Phoenix?'

'Dad and Ariadne. They're being taken away under guard. I don't understand. They can't be. They're the ones who are supposed to help us.'

He wracked his brains, trying to make sense of it. His hands flew up to his face, tugging at his skin, as a fever of panic ran through him. Now he was stammering, as if begging Laura to make everything right.

'The legend's clear. Ariadne falls in love with Theseus. She enlists the help of Daedalus. The string . . . the sword . . . I'm not dreaming. Laura, that's the way it is, the way it has to be. It's the only way we can hope to complete the game.'

Loud laughter filled the room. Phoenix and Laura turned to see the far wall bulging, becoming molten and fluid. Two faces emerged, familiar faces, Adams and Medea. The laughter was louder now, it circled them like a pack of hyenas.

'The way it *should* be,' cackled Medea. 'The way it would have been if I hadn't had a word in the ear of King Minos. Forget all those things you heard in Athens, my prince. He is a sweetie, really, old Minos. He would do anything for a sorceress in need.'

'You mean—'

'My dear Theseus, you don't think I would allow an interfering girl to upset my plans, do you? Poor little Ariadne, she's no match for me. Or that dried-up fool Daedalus. Haven't you grown out of happy endings yet? It's been fun watching your silly face light up with joy, thinking you were saved, then seeing the dawn of realization, that you're going to die all the same.'

'You witch!'

Medea purred like a cat.

'Thank you for the kind compliment, Theseus. Goodnight, sweet prince. Sleep tight. I am trusting you to provide us with some fine sport tomorrow. Put up a good fight, just so long as you lose.'

As the faces faded from the wall, Adams yelled his parting shot.

'The game is up Theseus. Or should I say *Phoenix*? Ariadne and Daedalus locked away where they can't interfere. All hope gone. The will of the gods is done. Surprise, surprise.'

6

Beyond the screen, in that old world once more frozen in time, the voice in the machine was speaking its impenetrable code.

The will of the gods is done. Poor, poor Phoenix expecting me to play fair. To think, you really expected Ariadne to come along with her string and sword. Not this time, Legendeer. This myth-world is faithful in every detail to the tales you love. As you put it yourself, a universe frozen in time, playing out the old truths again and again. But it is still **my** *myth-world, and these creatures are my subjects, my pawns to be moved as I wish. Now tremble before my power, Legendeer, for I am the angel of death come to pass over your house and your world. I know now that it is no accident you came into my world. We are bound together, you and I, champions of our savage gods. Two sides of destiny's coin. Then let us flip and see which of us finishes this game face up.*

Christina Graves meanwhile watched her son trying to sleep. She longed to reach out and touch his cheek. If the pain of loss she felt for her husband was sharp, this agony was worse still. To see her son going through such ordeals and be unable to help him, it was the most terrible torture she could suffer. Unable to tear herself away from the screen, she had barely eaten in days. She felt light-headed, her mind switching from one thing to another as she tried to make sense of what was happening to her family. From time to time, she flicked through Uncle Andreas' journal, continually rereading his story. She ached to hear the dead man's voice, echoing down the years. She traced his descent into hell as he saw the demons beating at the door of his world and was labelled as a madman for trying to raise the alarm. But the section she pored over longest was the one about his headaches. The part where he believed he suffered *because he had been born in the wrong world*.

That was it. All these years, the family had closed their eyes to the truth.

Andreas had been right all along. There was another world, maybe many worlds. But life there danced to a different, more macabre tune. Time didn't run foward generation after generation, it seemed to turn in an endless loop. Man and monster alike, they were condemned to wage an endless struggle, waiting for time to start again.

Then Christina understood. There was a way for time to continue its forward march.

'Oh, sweet heavens,' she murmured.

Because that way was to break out of the myth-world altogether and continue the struggle in this one.

Sleep was hard to come by, at least for Laura and Phoenix. They talked in hushed tones until the early hours, but in the end even Laura was lying curled up – restless and tossing it's true – but sleeping nonetheless. As for their twelve companions, they had fallen asleep immediately. They had even slept through the appearance of Adams and Medea. Phoenix found himself padding across the room, examining the owl tattoo that they all bore. Could that explain the depth of their sleep? It was a blessing, of course. At least they didn't have to dream and live out the terror in the tunnels below.

He grimaced despite himself. 'It's no dream now. It's real.'

All hope gone. Somewhere in the bowels of the palace, two people lay chained, the only two people in the world who could have helped him, the princess and the architect. Phoenix raised his eyes to greet the first glimmerings of dawn. Smoke was rising from the kitchens as the servants prepared breakfast for the court. He watched it plume heavenward and he remembered the funeral pyre on the beach at Seriphos.

When the bird had come, when he'd been given renewed hope.

'Gone,' he said with a sigh.

Discouraged and weary, Phoenix leaned his back against the wall and slid down to the floor. There he rested with his head on his knees.

'So what's left?'

In answer to his question, an unwelcome guest entered the room. Phoenix turned his face to the wall.

'What's this, Legendeer?' asked Pan. 'Aren't you happy to see your old friend?'

'Friend? You're no friend. You serve *him*, the Gamesmaster.'

'I serve the greatest power. I serve that force which can break out of this timeless prison.'

Phoenix turned his eyes towards Pan.

'You serve evil.'

'I serve life,' Pan retorted. 'When you and your kind are just memories, this thing you call evil will still be there. Andreas' blood runs in your veins all right. You're a sentimental fool just like him.'

'So you did visit him?'

'I tried. *We* tried. But the wall between the worlds was too strong. There was no way to pass through. My kind could only appear to him as shadows of ourselves, ghosts if that's what you want to call us. Then we found the magic that could thin the walls to breaking point.'

'The game!' cried Phoenix. 'You mean the game, don't you?'

Pan nodded gravely.

'A strange irony, isn't it, that this computer, this buzzing box, this highest point of your technology and science, the discovery that made you *civilized*, it's the very thing that will set free our power. Your computers, the most complex machines you have invented, they will open the gates to us. Then your world, your smug, flabby world will be ours.'

Phoenix stared in horror at his tormentor.

'You won't be hearing from me again,' said Pan. 'Destiny awaits you. Listen.'

In response to his words, a key scraped in the lock. Soldiers marched into the room, stirring the beast's victims.

Phoenix knew what was left.

Death.

Medea and Adams followed the soldiers into the room. They watched the reddish glow of the dawn spreading across the mosaic floor around the fourteen Athenians.

'What's the matter?' Adams asked sarcastically. 'Something bothering you, *Theseus*?'

The captain had no time for pointless banter. 'Look lively. The Minotaur's getting restless. He wants his breakfast.'

'Yes,' said Adams triumphantly. 'And guess who's the first course.'

Within minutes they were moving downwards, always downwards, negotiating a stone staircase into the stinking darkness. Phoenix felt the cloying, musty heat of the labyrinth. His nightmare was rushing up to meet him.

'Are you all right, Phoenix?'

He gave Laura a nod, but his heart was thudding and his knees seemed to buckle at every step. In the Gorgon's cave it had been Laura who had gone faint with terror. Now it was Phoenix's turn. He was walking on legs that were so rubbery and so weak they could hardly support him.

How can I face my destiny? I don't have the courage.

'All hail King Minos!' barked the captain of the guard as they reached the bottom of the last and steepest flight of stairs. 'Bow your heads, Athenians.'

While Phoenix and Laura's twelve companions sank obediently to their knees before the King, they stood upright, looking straight ahead. A few well-aimed kicks at the back of their knees and the two friends were also forced to kneel.

'Still defiant, Prince?' asked Minos. 'We'll see how your Athenian pride serves you in there.' He stabbed a finger in the direction of the labyrinth.

'I've seen this show of bravery before, remember. That's

right, the others were like you, breathing fire as they stood at this door. But once they got in there—'

He rapped loudly at the metal-studded wooden door, stirring the Minotaur deep in his lair. 'Oh, they sing a different tune then.'

Minos bent, bringing his face close to Phoenix's, then repeating the operation for Laura's benefit.

'I've heard them begging, screaming, whimpering. Yes, even the strongest of them.'

Laura scrambled to her feet.

'You're no king,' she cried. 'You're a monster.'

'No, my dear, the monster is in here.'

It was almost time. The entourage of King Minos was filling the area outside the labyrinth. Medea and Adams were there, hungry for sport. But Minos still had one surprise in store.

'Before you leave us, brave prince, perhaps you wish to bid farewell to your only friends at this court.'

He gestured to his guards and Dad and Ariadne were brought forward, struggling and resisting.

'Such good timing, don't you think? Here they are, freshly returned from their short stay in my dungeons. Such loyal friends to their sovereign.'

Phoenix managed a smile for the architect and the princess.

'How touching!' Medea chimed in gleefully.

'Yes,' Adams agreed. 'It's enough to bring a tear to my eye.'

'Let me go too,' Dad cried. 'My place is with them.'

Minos gave a smile of satisfaction. 'So, you want to die together. Why not?'

But before Dad could join Phoenix, Minos had a parting gift. He raised his sceptre and pressed it to the prisoner's throat. It sizzled like a brand. When Minos removed it, the tell-tale owl tattoo was left imprinted on the throat of John Graves.

'That's just in case you should escape the Minotaur,' said Minos.

'Escape the Minotaur,' Medea repeated, to raucous laughter. 'What an imagination you have, Sire.'

Still wincing from the pain, Dad joined Phoenix and Laura, and they walked slowly towards the door. The captain of the guard was jangling his bunch of keys, searching for the one that would unlock the nightmare. He turned the key.

'Ready, Sire.'

The guards were prodding the Minotaur's victims forward at swordpoint when Adams rushed forward and whispered a parting taunt in Phoenix's ear.

'How do you stop a bull charging, Phoenix?' His eyes twinkled. 'Why, cut up his credit card, of course.'

Phoenix tried to throw a punch but missed, falling against the guard holding Ariadne. She reacted quickly, snatching the soldier's sword and handing it to Phoenix. He looked into her dark eyes and smiled.

The legend may yet run its true course.

The disarmed guard tried to snatch back his weapon, but Minos called him back.

'Let him have the tooth-pick,' he chuckled. 'For all the good it will do against the beast.'

Phoenix closed the fingers of his right hand around the sword's hilt and felt the reassurance of cold steel. The great door slammed behind him and he stumbled into the gloom, feeling the walls slimy against his left palm. As he searched for the others, he heard the sound he'd dreaded for so long. The key was turning again, locking them inside the labyrinth.

'Phoenix?'

It was Laura's voice.

'Over here.'

It was quiet in the maze, the silence as complete as the blackness of the tunnels.

'I'm shaking.'

He felt for Laura's hand. She was as cold as ice.

'Me too,' Phoenix whispered.

'Just try not to let it show,' said Dad, joining them. 'They want us to put on a show. They want to hear us beg for our lives. Don't give them the satisfaction.'

The beast shattered the silence with an earth-shaking roar. He was beginning to move, his bull's hooves thudding monotonously through the tunnels.

'This way,' said Dad. 'Everybody, this way.'

'Are you sure he knows what he's doing?' Laura whispered to Phoenix.

'I'm not sure of anything.'

They reached a meeting of the ways. There were four openings.

'Now where?'

The beast's roar echoed down the gallery they'd just left.

'As far from that as we can get.'

Phoenix and Dad were leading the group into a shaft which sank quite steeply downward.

'They're leading us to the beast,' cried one of the youths suddenly. 'How do we know we can trust them?'

'Please,' begged Laura. 'We have to do as they say.'

Phoenix leaned forward and whispered in Dad's ear.

'Where have you been?'

'I've been in Minos' dungeons,' Dad replied. 'That's where Glen Reede treated me to a full account of his plans.'

'You've met him! But he doesn't exist.'

'I know. Put it this way, I met the spirit that goes by his name, the Gamesmaster. He treated me to a computer link-up, a kind of e-mail written on the air.'

It was Laura's turn to quiz him. 'So what does he want?'

Phoenix already knew, but he let Dad tell his tale.

'The usual stuff you get from madmen. Conquest. World domination. Do you know what I and all the others on the team have been designing? A two-way door. Think about it, if we can go into the game, then why can't the game come out to us?'

As Phoenix remembered Pan's words, Laura stared in disbelief.

'That's right. How did he put it? Yes. *In a few months every teenager on the planet will be playing **The Legendeer**. Each individual will face his or her own personal Armageddon. One* *minute some wretched teenager will be slaying demons, the next the real thing will be there in his bedroom.'*

Suddenly, Phoenix could see it all in his mind's eye. The two worlds, the thinning wall, the numbers that were more than a series of coded messages – they were an entry code.

'There's going to be a games console in every room,' said Dad, trying to come to terms with what he had heard. 'The game is so convincing everybody will want to play. Think what this means. This will be unlimited terror, a war of annihilation waged from inside your own home. Reede's created a fifth column of demons to destroy us from within.'

Laura's voice was shaking. 'And this is possible?'

Dad looked around at the labyrinth.

'Are you going to tell me it isn't?'

'Dad,' said Phoenix. 'I hope you've got a plan.'

'Oh, I've got a plan all right,' Dad answered. 'If the Minotaur gives us enough time to carry it through.'

'What have you got in mind?' Phoenix asked, but the frightened youth interrupted Dad's reply.

'No,' he shouted, his voice hysterical with fright. 'I won't do it. It's this way. Who's with me?'

One girl detached herself from the group.

'I don't trust the Prince, either.'

Without another word, the frightened pair disappeared down a third tunnel, the only one of the four which was glimmering with light.

'Come back,' cried Dad.

'He's right,' said Phoenix. 'It's a trap. The light's only there to make you think there's a way out.'

'It's no use, Phoenix,' Laura told him gently. 'They're beside themselves with terror. You can't stop them.'

The group were edging forward, starting occasionally at the ear-splitting bellowing that seemed to burst out of the darkness like a cannon going off.

'They were right,' bleated another of their companions. 'We're walking into danger. I wish I'd gone with the others.'

'Don't be a fool,' Phoenix snapped. 'We've got to stick together.'

He had barely finished speaking when the darkness erupted with the shrieks and screams of the pair who had broken ranks. Amid their desperate shouts and cries came the sound of gurgling, of throats filling with blood. The beast had them now.

'There,' Phoenix told the group. 'That's what happens if we strike out on our own. We have to trust . . . Daedalus.'

'That's it,' said Dad, admiring his son's quick thinking. 'Play the game to the end.'

'But where are we going?' asked Phoenix. 'Is this it – the bomb for Glen Reede?'

Dad nodded. 'Remember the cheats?'

'Yes?'

'Well, I think that terminal is the key. It led us home once. We've just got to find it. Then it's my turn to play. As you said, a bomb for Glen Reede.'

'You do what you have to,' said Phoenix, certain of his destiny at last. 'I'll handle the Minotaur.'

They had edged forward another twenty or thirty paces when a shaft of light blazed unexpectedly into the maze.

'Enjoying yourself, my prince?' asked Medea, her mink-dark eyes fixing him. 'And what's this, there are fewer of you now. Dear me, how careless.'

There was sobbing in the gloom behind him. The youth who had been complaining earlier rushed forward and threw himself to his knees under the grating.

'Please,' he begged in a quavering voice. 'Don't leave us here to die.'

He pointed an accusing finger at Laura, Phoenix and Dad.

'They're the ones to blame, not us. Let the Minotaur have them instead.'

And Phoenix was angry. Angry because he remembered the dream when he'd been paralyzed by fear. Angry because he remembered begging to get out. Angry because he could see so much of himself in this whining youth. But I've been changing, he told himself. Now the transformation must be complete.

From zero to hero.

'Get up,' Phoenix ordered. 'It won't do you any good.'

'That's right,' said Medea. 'It won't. But it's so much fun to watch.'

A rush of footfalls in the darkness, heavy, cloven hooves clopping close behind them, and it wasn't Pan.

'Come on,' Dad urged. 'This way. Quickly.'

They were running too, their breath spilling out in tortured gasps. The roaring of the beast seemed more distant now.

'Get your breath back,' Phoenix told them in hushed tones. 'And don't say a word. We have to listen, try to work out where he is.'

'What's the point?' came a desperate reply. 'He'll get us anyway. There's no way out, not for any of us.'

Phoenix wanted to knock the words back down the lad's throat. He confined himself to a sharp retort. 'That's enough!'

Phoenix was listening, trying to discover the whereabouts of the Minotaur, when Laura drew him aside.

'What are we doing, Phoenix? If we carry on like this, it's just a matter of time before it finds us.'

'Don't you think I know that? Dad, there isn't much time.'

'This way. It's round the next corner.'

They reached the silver tetrahedron with its bull's head symbol. Just as Phoenix was daring to hope, Dad spoke, chilling him to the core.

'Now,' he said, producing a razor-sharp knife. 'You must cut my throat.'

7

'You want me to do what?' cried Phoenix, horrified.

'I've had it with them,' gasped the panic-stricken youth who'd been thinking of running. He was appalled by what he'd just heard. 'I'll find my own way out.'

The sound of running feet echoed through the maze. Two, maybe three of the group were following him, fleeing through the passageways. Dad looked sadly after them, then gripped Phoenix by both arms.

'You saw what Minos did to me.'

He drew back the collar of his tunic to expose the owl tattoo.

'Now stop arguing, Phoenix. You know what this is. If any of Reede's pawns resists he destroys them with this. You have to cut it out quickly or I'm dead.'

'Cut it out? But are you sure that'll work?'

'Who knows? But I have to try. If I don't do anything, I'm a dead man.'

Before Phoenix could argue any more, a second chorus of shrieks was crashing round the walls of the labyrinth, followed by more grunting and bellowing. More death.

Laura was speaking again, breathless and concerned:

'Phoenix, we're depending on you. Do it.'

'Do it,' ordered Dad, forcing the knife on Phoenix. 'Now. Before anybody sees what we're doing.'

Another roar, louder than ever. The beast was going for the kill. A hidden door flew open behind them, timber splintering, dust showering them, and shards of metal flying through the air, pricking and slicing at skin. It was there, right among them.

Phoenix was going to face his destiny.

'Laura,' he shouted. 'You've got to help Dad. I'll try to keep the Minotaur off.'

Phoenix sensed Dad and Laura in the stifling darkness, their love. It was a bond of steel. There was still hope. It gave him the strength to face his nightmare.

'Let me see you,' he shouted.

The beast's hands were clawed and covered in tough, wiry hair. Phoenix felt the brush of its thick, impossibly powerful fingers and his flesh shrank in panic from its touch. It blundered blindly past him, pacing, searching for signs of life. Finding none, it resumed its hunt, its hooves thudding dully in the dark.

'Laura,' Phoenix hissed. 'How are you doing?'

'Nearly got it,' she said. 'It's an implant, just under the skin. Fortunately, it's shallow.'

The survivors of the beast's attacks were cowering behind them and nobody was protesting any more. The fate of the others had put an end to all resistance. It was an obedience dictated by terror.

Hurry up, Laura.

The roaring of the Minotaur began again, right behind them.

'Laura?'

'Done!'

Phoenix saw her fingers on the knife. Dad appeared, holding a blood-stained cloth to his neck.

'Now,' he said. 'Time to put an end to this.'

But the words were no sooner out of his mouth than the hot, stinking breath of the beast blasted into Phoenix's face.

'Get back,' screamed Laura.

'Not this time,' said Phoenix. 'I'm done with running. It's time to make a stand.'

He grasped the hilt of the sword.

'How do you stop a bull charging? Answer. You cut up his credit card. And everything else!'

The Minotaur was so close he could see its yellow eyes, the

black muzzle, the razor teeth in the mighty, grinding jaws. Gathering the survivors behind him, Phoenix lashed out with the blade, tearing through skin and hair. Phoenix felt the welcome pulse of the score bracelet.

'Keep it off,' cried Dad.

He had pulled something from the lining of his tunic, the size of a coin. It was a miniature CD.

'The bomb?' asked Phoenix.

Dad nodded.

'A computer virus. If I'm right, we will have about a minute to escape through the terminal before it begins to work and closes the gate for ever.'

Phoenix nodded. All he had to do was to give Dad time to use it.

'Let's finish this,' he said.

The Minotaur grasped its weapon, the giant, studded club. As Phoenix crouched, facing the beast, Dad ran to the wall. His fingers were trying to prise open a panel on the terminal.

'Come on,' he cried to the others. 'This will fit in here somewhere.'

The Minotaur made its move, rushing them, swinging the club in huge arcs, dislodging bricks from the walls and uprooting stones from the floor.

'It's no good,' yelled Laura, tugging at the panel. 'It won't budge.'

The club was swinging again, forcing Phoenix to flatten himself against the wall, then again, making him throw himself flat on the floor.

As the beast lumbered forward, he rolled across the slimy paving. He could see spots of the Minotaur's blood in the puddles. But it didn't terrify him. Enranged by the sword-cut, it was flailing about without purpose.

'Try again, Laura!' cried Dad. 'This is definitely a terminal. It's the connection between the ancient powers and modern technology. This disc will fit somewhere. It's got to.'

The club swung, the downdraft brushing Phoenix's face.

Now for the death blow, he told himself preparing to strike.

'We've tried everywhere,' groaned Laura.

'Keep going,' Dad panted, refusing to give in.

Phoenix slashed with the sword, cutting the beast on the arm. Driven mad with pain, it staggered into a corner. But just as Phoenix raised his sword in a two-handed grip, ready to deliver the final blow an arrow struck the hilt of the sword, slicing through the skin between Phoenix's thumb and finger.

As Phoenix crashed against the wall, the sword spun from his hand.

'Mr Graves!' screamed Laura. 'I think I've got it.'

Meanwhile, Phoenix was crawling across the floor, slithering away from the club, grasping for the sword. The club struck him a glancing blow, impacting muscle and bone. He was on his knees, pain coursing down his left side.

'Yes, that's it,' yelled Dad, momentarily oblivious to the peril facing his son. 'That's it!'

The beast had Phoenix. Twisting its fingers through his tunic, it lifted him off the floor and snorted its hatred into his face.

That's when Phoenix heard a weapon hissing through the air. He saw it flash in the half-light. His sword. In Laura's hands. Phoenix was twisting and turning in the Minotaur's grasp, trying to win enough time for her to strike. The beast was staring at him, as if seeing something of itself in Phoenix, his human part. There was no bellowing now, just a hoarse snorting as the beast examined Phoenix's face.

'Now, Laura!'

But still she didn't strike. Phoenix was dangling in the beast's clutches.

This is it; my nightmare, but I didn't run. I stayed. I fought.

Maybe I have to die, Phoenix thought. But at least I wasn't a coward. I've stopped running.

Half expecting the Minotaur to finish him, he closed his eyes and yelled out a desperate plea. 'Laura!'

She stabbed with the sword, hard into the Minotaur's thigh but she couldn't force the blade through the dense slabs of muscle. The beast roared nonetheless. As it twisted to face its attacker, Laura hacked at its ankles. Stung by the unexpected blows, the beast reeled round, releasing Phoenix. One great fist sent the entire group of Athenians tumbling like skittles. Staggering over to Laura, Phoenix closed his hand round the hilt.

How do you stop a bull charging?

'Face me, beast!'

Weary from its wounds, the Minotaur staggered.

'The gate's open,' shouted Dad. 'We can get through.'

Phoenix felt his destiny intense within him and lunged at the Minotaur. Driving the blade upwards and inwards, he felt it grate against the beast's ribs. Then the huge body sagged and its eyes misted over.

Curling backwards, it fell heavily where so many of its victims had fallen before.

'Dead?' asked Laura.

Phoenix stood over the massive frame of the Minotaur.

'Dying.'

He saw bewilderment and pain in its yellow eyes, then the long sigh as they closed.

'It's over.'

Dad was waving them towards the terminal, now transformed into a shimmering gateway back home.

'Come on, you two. We've won.'

'That's right,' came a girl's voice. 'You've won. Now go from this terrible place while you can.'

Ariadne was looking down at him through a grating.

'Come with us,' said Phoenix.

'I can't. You have to leave me behind. It's the legend – my destiny. I belong here.'

'Are you sure?'

'I'm sure.'

Phoenix returned her smile.

We've won.

But he'd counted without Adams. Phoenix glimpsed him out of the corner of his eye, drawing his bow.

'Surprise, surprise.'

The arrow sang in the stale air before hitting the brickwork, just a hair's breadth from Phoenix's head.

'How did you get in here?'

'Have you forgotten the strength of Medea's magic?'

Having loosed his last arrow, Adams drew his sword. He appeared possessed, stabbing and slashing in a blood rage, his features contorted in hatred. Two sounds filled the passageways, the clash of swords as Phoenix met him blade to blade, and the rush of air through the gateway.

Dad and Laura were already inside the gate, holding out their hands.

'Come on, Phoenix.'

But Adams wouldn't accept defeat. What was left of his human side seemed to be shrivelling as he stormed forward, sword flashing. He belonged to the myth-world now. He was rapidly becoming a demon creature himself.

Phoenix was struggling to parry the onslaught, but there was the gateway between the worlds beckoning him. It was now or never. He could almost hear the virus doing its work. Phoenix mustered all his strength as he dashed the blade from Adams' hand and pushed him into them. As they staggered back, Phoenix cuffed his Nemesis across the face and tried to haul him into the gate by the scruff of the neck.

'You've had your fun,' he said. 'I thought death would be your punishment, but there's something worse. You're going to go back to being a small-town loser. You're going home.'

Phoenix glimpsed Ariadne in the background. In a moment of horror, he remembered the black sail. But it was too late. King Aegeus' part in the legend would remain unchanged. Grief-stricken, he would fall to his death.

Taking advantage of Phoenix's hesitation, Adams wrenched himself free and fell back into the myth-world. Like Phoenix, he had chosen his destiny. Then everything was fading, fading away. All Phoenix could see was the golden haze, and shimmering within it the numbers. The game dissolved around them and they were back in the study.

Level complete.

Game over.

Epilogue

Six weeks later, Phoenix was leading his way up a dusty path past an overgrown and neglected orange grove. He paused to take in his surroundings. For a brief moment his mind turned to Adams. For weeks, the police had been searching the woods and dragging the canals in the vain hope of finding some trace of him. But Phoenix soon dismissed thoughts of Adams and his distraught parents. There was nothing he could do for them, any of them. Behind him, through the heat haze, Phoenix could see the waters of the blue Aegean. He thought of a grief-stricken King and his resting place beneath the waves.

'How far now?' he asked.

'Just over that hill,' Mum replied.

'Thank goodness for that,' panted Dad, mopping his brow. 'I'm done in.'

But Phoenix was anything but. He broke into a run. In a few minutes, he would be there, in the garden of Uncle Andreas, where Pan had once stood.

'Don't expect too much,' Mum told him. 'it's been abandoned for years.'

'There has to be something,' shouted Phoenix. 'I've got to know what this is all about.' He could see the journal entry. The few devastating lines about the headaches.

The more I think about it, the sickliness, the band of pain, the strange waking fever that has been with me all my life, the more I realize that it has something to do with the ghosts. When they gather, when they step out of the shimmering light and speak to me, then I understand. I belong to their world.

I always have. For all time, I will be a stranger inside my own skin. I have a mission. For every ghost that believes in life and justice and warns me of the dangers of the gate, there are others who are filled with death and destruction. They are knocking at the door.

But they will not pass me. I am the Legendeer. My task is to keep the gate closed, to keep out the demon legions. Though it breaks my heart every day of my life, I will never give up my vigil. To leave my post would be to abandon this world to horror.

Phoenix looked back. 'I have to discover who I am.'

'Everybody said Uncle Andreas was a madman,' Mum had said, setting down the journals. 'He died without a soul believing him.'

But we believe you now, Andreas, thought Phoenix as he forced himself into a final sprint over the brow of the hill. Then there it was, the garden with its stone wall, and the house. It wasn't much to look at. The roof tiles had gone and the timbers were rotten. The front door had long since been smashed in. It was a picture of dereliction.

'There has to be something,' Phoenix said out loud.

With that, he stepped through the doorway. A few moments later, his parents arrived.

'Phoenix,' called Mum. 'Where are you?'

'Here. In the back room.'

Dad had finally caught up. 'Have you found anything?' he asked.

'Come and see.'

Then all three of them were standing in the room, stunned to silence. Painted on the walls were images of Pan, Medusa, and the Minotaur. But that wasn't all. All around them, scrawled in a frenzy were thousands of numbers, all multiples of three. The language of the computer game.

Hundreds of miles away, at that very moment, the Osibonas were completing their early evening routine at the Graves house, drawing the curtains and putting on the lights. A precaution against burglary while they were away. Laura paused for a moment in the study. If only her parents knew what she'd been through.

All that horror, all those demons, and as far as her parents were concerned, none of it had happened. Days of terror had flown by in a mere second of recorded time this side of the screen. So that was how things stood with Laura. Every day she stumbled through the usual routines, still hearing the snarl of madness from that other world, and all the while she had to keep her nightmares to herself. Laura shied away from touching anything. Though John Graves had destroyed the PR suits and the rest of the equipment, she was still wary of approaching the computer.

'Is it over?' she murmured out loud.

'What did you say, Laura?' asked Mrs Osibona.

'Nothing, Mum.'

'Hurry up, we're going now.'

'Coming.'

But as the Osibonas closed the front door behind them, the computer purred into life. By the time they were getting in the car, the very same sequences of numbers that Phoenix was reading on a whitewashed wall in Greece were flashing in this empty room back home. And as Mrs Osibona turned right on to the High Street, the numbers were racing across the screen, pulsating with menace.

So you think you've won, Legendeer? I may have abandoned my attempt to enter your world by the front door, but there are other ways in. Dozens of them. You think you're secure? You think your world is safe? Well, think again.

For every world like yours, for every planet spinning self-satisfied on its axis, there are five, ten, twenty myth-worlds. And they are not stories, Legendeer. They are real, as real as you are. Even now I am knocking at the door of another world like yours. And when I'm done there, when my demons have visited every home and plucked out their owners' hearts, then I will come for you.

Then, in the maelstrom of swirling numbers, the voice added its final warning:

You don't need to be asleep to have nightmares.

VAMPYR LEGION

PROLOGUE

The Attack

They attacked an hour before dawn.

Daybreak or dusk, at the trembling crossroads between day and night, that's when they always came, the times when their enemies' defences were most likely to be down.

It was the way of the Legion.

Bird's Eye saw them first. It stands to reason. That was his way – to see. He was the boy with the sight. He didn't actually *see* them, of course. Not in the way most people think of seeing, the physical interaction of light, pupil, retina and optic nerve. His sight was so much more fine-tuned than that, a spirit thing. Mysterious too – a living, growing part of him, after all these years still surprising and new. That grey winter's morning the sight exploded into his brain like a dumdum bullet, the advance shadows of the Legion bursting into his half-awake mind and yanking him to his feet with all the force of an electric shock.

'Mother, Tom, Captain Lawrence, it's started. They're back!'

Images of the invaders were overloading his mind. The black flutter of the Legion's airborne troopers, the grey ghosting of the Wolvers. Sounds that filled his every waking moment, and many of his sleeping ones too. They used to come in small groups: twos, threes; fives or sixes at most. Now it was tens, dozens. He trembled to think what might lie in store.

A second shout to alert the others.

'They're here!'

Then the adults were scurrying round the room, shouting, crashing over the makeshift furniture, snatching up their weapons, taking over from the boy in that way adults do, but eternally grateful for his gift of sight. Bird's Eye was a boy who could see for miles. He saw every road and building and living thing, and much more besides.

'Tom, Ann, brace yourselves,' said Captain Lawrence as he loaded his revolver. 'This could be bloody. But win or lose, I aim to send a few of them off to Vampyr heaven.' At the bitter laughter of his comrades, he chose his words more carefully: 'Very well then, Vampyr hell.'

In his former life the tall, moustachioed adventurer had been a military man, a commissioned officer. Since the coming of the Legion, he'd become a Vampyr hunter, living outside the law and outside society, stalking the city's demons. His life hadn't always been like this. He had once had a dream of career and family. But the dream soon vanished, the way his own young family had vanished. That was the reason for his crusade. The Vampyr tornado had broken over his wife and three children. Nobody was safe. Worse still, the attacks were becoming ever more frequent.

'It's going to be all right, darling,' Ann told her son, at the same time loading a bolt into her crossbow. 'We've defended this position before.'

It was true. They had. Twice that night, in fact. But it was going to be different this time. The sight told Bird's Eye as much. There was nobody left to man the forward defences. Front line, rearguard: suddenly they were more or less the same thing. Just small knots of fighters pulled back into the corridors of the labyrinthine building, ready to fight the final desperate action. Their beleaguered band had suffered terrible losses. Losses! Bird's Eye told himself he would never forget what that word really meant, the people who'd gone down fighting.

Heroes.

'Here they come,' said Tom Beresford, his cheeks puffing with fright. He'd once been stationmaster on the Great Western Railway, a pencil-thin beanpole of a man, armed with a home-made crossbow and a length of lead piping. Despite all Ann's pleading, he'd insisted she keep her pistol. Bird's Eye didn't exactly know why he did that, why Tom was prepared to put her life ahead of his own, but there was no time for questions. Seeing Tom gripping the lead pipe in his bony fist made Bird's Eye shudder. He knew that if it came to hand-to-hand fighting they were already dead. Their enemy was as strong as steel. As unfeeling too.

'Our chaps have opened up,' said Captain Lawrence. 'Hear them?'

Bird's Eye listened to the snap and zing of their bullets. But the snipers crouching by the sash windows of the old mansion house couldn't prevent the familiar thump, thump, thump of clawed feet landing on the roof. There had to be a dozen of them. It was round one to the Legion. This time there were too many Vampyrs to hold off with sniper fire alone. After that they heard the frenzied scratching at the outer doors. The Wolvers had arrived, claws penetrating the oak panels like diamond-tipped drills. Both units of the enemy commando were engaged. When it was time to storm the defensive positions, it would be the Wolvers first. They were the advance guard, the moon-born, the rippers. They were used to storm the enemy lines. Then it would be the turn of the elite fighters, the Vampyrs themselves.

If I have to fall here, Bird's Eye thought, I want the Wolvers to take me. It will be savage, and it will be bloody, but at least it will be over in seconds. It was different with the Vampyrs. They bit, they drank. If you were lucky, you died there and then. Otherwise, you faded slowly with the fever. What some called *the contagion*. It could take days to die, possibly even weeks, but by the end you were begging for it to be over.

The contagion left you as mad as a sewer rat and desperate

for death. Bird's Eye had seen its victims, creatures so ravaged with pain they looked like translucent ghosts on their beds. Most unspeakably of all, some of the Legion's victims had themselves been transformed into warriors of the undead, servants of the Legion.

'Destroy them,' said Tom, talking to the defenders beyond the walls. 'Obliterate them all.' He gave an uneasy smile. 'When I was reading about Vampyrs and Wolvers as a boy, I never thought I'd have to face them in the flesh. I thought they were just stories then, you know, like the Bogey Man. Never for a moment did I expect to see them for real. Leastways, not in this world.'

'Nobody did,' said Captain Lawrence. 'If I'd been asked to place a bet on how the world would end, I wouldn't have put my money on the contents of a lurid Penny Dreadful.' He broke off abruptly, unable to speak over the gut-wrenching sound of men begging for their lives, then their pitiful screams as the Wolvers did their work. No more sniper fire. The Legion was mopping up on the upper floors.

'They're inside the building,' murmured Captain Lawrence, 'Let us pray that our defences hold.' Bird's Eye exchanged glances with his mother. She'd made a determined move for the door.

'I should be up there,' she said. 'I don't want anybody fighting my battles for me. I've got to face them. It's my destiny.'

'Forget it, Ann,' said Captain Lawrence, cutting her short, 'You and young Robert are all that's left of the Van Helsing line. Your survival is our number one priority.'

But why is my family so important, wondered Bird's Eye. What had he missed while he was away at boarding school?

Lawrence pre-empted Ann's protests with a raised palm. 'No Ann, that's my final word.' And so it was. They had no choice but to stay there, holed up in their dank cellar.

Bird's Eye took in the shabby walls and he could feel the pressure of the Legion's attack. He was shut away, hoping to live but expecting to die, and horror was sealed inside that awful place with him.

Captain Lawrence was still reminding Ann Van Helsing of her importance. 'Your survival is our number one priority. Please don't argue the point any further.'

Ann nodded, and Bird's Eye watched her as if she was made anew. She was more than just his mother. She was Ann Van Helsing, Vampyr hunter, prophet of doom, and she'd seen this catastrophe coming. Unbeknown to her son, she'd been part of the Committee of Nine all along. Only in the last few weeks had young Robert, Bird's Eye to the Vampyr-hunters, gradually begun to understand just who she was, and what his grandfather had been before her. Now, as far as anyone knew, Ann was one of the Committee's two surviving members. The other seven were lying slain in their graves, or missing, presumed dead.

'Oh my,' said Tom, flinching at the dull thunder from above, 'Will you listen to that?' The corridors of the middle floors were echoing with a furious volley of rifle shot.

'Hold them,' said Captain Lawrence, urging his comrades on. 'Just keep them off for another hour, hold on until daybreak. You can manage one brief hour, can't you?'

It was during those agonizing minutes, when the battle was still hanging in the balance, that Bird's Eye got the sight again. Somebody was watching him. He turned his head to the left then to the right, as if expecting to discover a hole in the wall, and, pressed to it, a peeping eye.

'What is it, Bird's Eye?' asked Tom. 'Another premonition?'

Bird's Eye nodded slowly. There was someone, a shadow, there was . . . *him.*

Somebody faded and blurred, like an unwanted intruder in a wedding photograph, brushed out to save the blushes of the guests. He was standing at the end of a lonely parapet, atop a mist-wreathed castle. About him there rose a symphony made of Wolvers' howls and the shriek of hundreds of glossy black ravens.

'The lair of the Beast,' murmured Bird's Eye. Noticing everyone staring, he blushed. But nobody made fun of him. There had been a time when people had scoffed at the sight, but it was proving too useful too often. He'd earned the trust of the entire band.

'What's wrong?'

'I don't know,' Bird's Eye admitted. 'But I've got the strangest feeling that we're being watched.'

It was true – they were. But not by the Legion, and not by hidden spectators either. The eyes that watched them were looking on from a realm of darkness more complete than the blackest night. They belonged to the architect of the demon invasion. It was a hopeless game Bird's Eye and his comrades were playing. They were predestined to lose, predestined by *him*.

'Try keeping it to yourself, my boy,' Captain Lawrence advised. 'You keep talking that way and you're going to have every man Jack of us spooked.'

Bird's Eye nodded, but the feeling didn't leave him. He was being watched all right. The curious thing was, he had a notion he'd get to meet the watcher one day. More than a notion, *a knowledge*.

'The firing's coming closer,' said Tom, combing back his thin blond hair with the fingers of one raw-boned hand. Bird's Eye found himself staring at Tom's other hand. It was shaking. 'I know lad, I'm scared. I don't mind admitting it.'

'We're all scared,' said Ann. 'Every single one of us. There's no shame in fear. Not when there's something to be afraid of.'

Overhead, the interval between shots was getting longer. They all knew what that meant. The Legion was closing in. Soon they were able to make out the spit and clatter of crossbow bolts. Now it was bow against fang and claw.

'Do you hear that?' said Ann.

'This is bad,' said Tom, approaching the door and inspecting the dents made by the Wolvers' claws. 'Really bad.'

'Get to your places everyone,' said Captain Lawrence, seeing the splintered wooden panelling. 'Something tells me we're going to have company sooner than expected.'

The corridors overhead echoed with screams, and the noise of running feet. The next sounds that could be heard came from the approaches to the cellar. *Their* level. The wolf was at the door. The terror was approaching. Soon it would crash over them like a hurricane. Captain Lawrence held the revolver in a two-handed grip. Tom hung on to his crossbow and tucked the lead pipe in his waistcoat.

Ann drew her gun. 'We're going to hold them off,' she said. 'You see if we don't.'

Tom tried a smile, but it just wouldn't take on his ashen face. His jaw was frozen into a tight grimace. Fear had him by the throat and the shakes were so bad he could hardly stand. His legs had turned to water.

'What did I tell you?' Captain Lawrence barked, feeling the sense of resignation all around him. 'To your posts, everyone. What is it with all of you? Do you really want to feel those suckers gnawing at your necks? Of course you don't; you want to live just as much as I do.'

It was the sort of speech he had given on the battlefields of two colonial campaigns, but never had the enemy been so cold, so ruthless, so elemental. Never had the words sounded so false. 'Well, just hold on to that,' Lawrence continued, going through the motions. 'You want to live, don't you dare surrender. Don't you ever give up.' He stormed up to Tom, as if warning him that when it came to being scary a Wolver had nothing on Captain James Lawrence. 'Do I make myself clear? Nobody here is going to simply lie down and die. Not while I've still got breath in my body.'

Bird's Eye and Ann climbed on to a wooden barrel. This was the escape route, if all else failed. It was pushed against the wall, giving access to a coal hatch. A woman or a child might just be able to squeeze through. There was no hope for a full-grown man. Ann and Bird's Eye were reluctant to use it. It would mean abandoning their comrades.

'This is it,' said Tom hoarsely as the corridors fell silent. 'The defences are down.' A tear spilled from his eyes. His son Harry had been out there. 'We're all that's left.'

There was a long silence.

'Come on, you infernal fiends,' growled Tom, shouldering the crossbow. 'You have taken my boy, my only son. I've nothing left to live for now. Only revenge. What are you waiting for? Do it.'

The seconds ticked away. Captain Lawrence shifted his feet, taking his weight first on the left then on the right. 'Is it over?' he murmured.

Ann glanced at Bird's Eye. He shook his head. 'I see blood.'

'Get ready,' Ann ordered.

The door crashed open with a thunderclap, then the Wolvers were spilling snarling into the cramped, candle-lit cellar. They were killing machines, their huge shoulders built to act as battering rams, their man-trap jaws capable of breaching walls. The Vampyrs followed, hissing and screeching. The room resounded with hellish battle-cries. In such an enclosed space, the noise was unbearable.

Captain Lawrence opened up, bringing down two Wolvers with fast, accurate shots. A third was moving behind him, but Ann shot it and moved to finish it off with mallet and stake. Tom slew one of the Vampyrs with his crossbow, the bolt's impact spinning it round on its heels, a hideous scream catapulting from its throat. But the Legion was attacking in force and they were overrunning the hunters' positions, penetrating the defensive lines with their ferocious speed. Captain Lawrence was the first to fall, knocked off his feet by the impact of a Wolver's pounce.

A pair of Vampyrs joined the Wolver.

Bird's Eye yelled inside himself. *Get off him. Get off!* But no sound came. All he could see were Captain Lawrence's legs kicking wildly as he tried to tear the suckers from his throat.

'Hang on, James,' cried Tom, advancing and firing the bow into the chest of the closest Vampyr. But before he could reload a Wolver detached itself from the group around Captain Lawrence and sprang. In a grey snowstorm of snapping and tearing it was over. The bow and the lead pipe clattered across the floor.

No! The silent scream jolted hard inside Bird's Eye. 'Mother, we've got to do something.'

She nodded and ran forward, grabbing the lead pipe and locking it over the throat of one attacking Vampyr. She wrestled with the sucker for a few moments than slapped a stick of dynamite into Captain Lawrence's palm.

He managed an anguished smile then waved her away. 'Don't hang around on my account. I'm bitten, Ann. Finished. Just get out of here.'

Another Vampyr drew its thin, almost colourless lips back and steadied itself, ready to make a strike at Ann and add her to the Legion's long list of victims. But she was alert to the danger, pumping a shot into it at close range, then dispatching the fallen ghoul with a stake.

'Let's go,' she cried, shoving Bird's Eye towards the hatch with all her strength as the Legion gathered for the final assault: the move that would give them their main prize – Ann.

'But what about Captain Lawrence?'

'There's no way back for him now,' said Ann. 'But he's going to leave this world the way a soldier should. He knows what to do.'

As Bird's Eye followed her into the darkness of the overgrown garden, the last thing he saw was Captain Lawrence lighting the fuse on the dynamite. Then they were racing through needle-sharp thorn bushes and stumbling over criss-crossed tree roots. Ann cursed her long skirts.

Bird's Eye could still feel the eyes of the watcher on him. He was still thinking about him when the dynamite went off, whip-cracking across the cellar and belching fire, smoke and murderous shards of glass into the garden. The bushes behind the backs of mother and son were shredded by a hail of glass and debris. Bird's Eye wanted to testify out loud, to say goodbye to Tom and Captain Lawrence and hear the words ringing out across the sleeping city. But the words never came.

That was the moment they burst through the foliage and onto the mist-dampened pavement. They were on a poorly lit street in west London.

'Don't look back, Robert,' said Ann, hitching up her skirts. 'Just keep running.'

Bird's Eye peered up into her earnest face and smiled thinly. That's when he felt the watcher's presence, stronger than ever.

He's the one. All this is his work.

They gained the corner. But, to their horror, the nightmare was not over. Immediately in front of them, a Wolver was crouching, ready to pounce. Bird's Eye had been so preoccupied, he hadn't registered its presence.

'Mother,' he murmured as the Wolver advanced. 'Just in case we don't make it, I love you.'

BOOK ONE

The Book of the Game

In a few months every teenager on the planet will be playing . . . Each individual will face his or her own Armageddon. One minute some wretched teenager will be slaying demons, the next the real thing will be in his bedroom. Shadow of the Minotaur

1

A universe away there was another teenage boy. Though Bird's Eye didn't know it yet, their destinies were bound together like the strands of a cable, fragile on their own but immensely strong when combined. It would be some time before their paths crossed, but when they did it would be in a fight to the death.

Maybe even beyond.

But that was in the future, and just then Phoenix Graves was more concerned with the present. He was a tall, athletic-looking boy, dark-haired and sallow-skinned. He looked much older than his fourteen years. There was something about his face, a premature seriousness and intensity. He had grown up before his time. In the late afternoon light that lanced across the kitchen, he was reading a computer game magazine as if his life depended on it. A single sentence leapt out at him.

'Death of a computer game designer.'

At first there had been nothing in the latest issue of *Gamestation* to alarm him. Quite the opposite. Phoenix had flicked through the usual features: Hot Stuff, Game Gear, Specials and Cheats before starting on the Reviews. He had turned the pages with some apprehension, before opening the centre spread on the kitchen table. One review in particular made pleasant reading:

The Minotaur bellows in the depths of the labyrinth. The Medusa hisses in the depths of a distant cavern. You are embarking on *The Legendeer: Shadow of the Minotaur*, our five-star hit of the autumn. This is super-charged mythology for *aficionados* and novices alike. You don't need a fistful of GCSEs to enjoy this game, just nerves of steel! The 3D graphics are sleek and convincing and you will be gripped by the astonishing realism of the game environment.

Phoenix smiled. He had played the game. How he had played it! In fact, he had been the first person to log on to *The Legendeer*. His dad had had a hand in designing it, and had used Phoenix as a human guinea pig. But it was the next line which turned his slight, wary smile into a triumphant laugh:

The only disappointment will be that the widely rumoured revolutionary game kit, the Parallel Reality suit giving a feel-around, fear-around sensation has failed to materialize, causing some embarrassment to its manufacturer Magna-com. The suit was meant to give the gamer the illusion of being right there *inside* the game. But don't be put off. PR suit or not, *The Legendeer* is as hot a spine-chiller as you will play this millennium!

Phoenix smiled. He knew why the Parallel Reality suit had failed to materialize.

Because I played and I won.

I went into the game and ripped out its heart.

The game is dead, long live the game.

He had waited for this news for weeks, tossing and turning in bed, remembering how he had played. And how the game had played him! He crossed the floor to get a Coke from the fridge, before continuing to browse through the magazine. A sense of self-satisfaction had started to flow through him. He turned to a new page. That's when he saw it, a single column of seriousness amongst the racy gabblespeak of the rest of the magazine.

OBITUARY

CHRIS DARKE (1961–2000)

The editorial team of *Gamestation* are saddened to hear of Chris's early death. Chris Darke designed some of the finest games ever released, from *Time Commando* to the legendary *Death Racer V*.

At the time of his death, Chris had just been head-hunted to take the already successful *Legendeer* series to new heights.

Seamless and innovative, Chris's all-action style has thrilled millions of gamers. Our sadness at the news of his death is all the greater given the circumstances. Tragically, Chris met a violent end in his home, by person or persons unknown.

Phoenix frowned as he reread, trying to unpick more information from this briefest of articles. 'It can't be. I won. It can't start all over again.' He almost ran down the hallway and into Dad's study. It took him a couple of minutes to find the cardboard box containing the Parallel Reality suits. Then there they were, the accessory that would transform computer games, actually taking you into the worlds the designers had created. The suit he held up was tissue-thin. It looked like an all-in-one diving outfit, but more flimsy. Phoenix pulled it open, listening to the familiar hiss of its velcro-like fastening. A sound like the serpent in the garden.

'Not again. It can't begin again.' He glanced at the points bracelet that flashed your score. The crystal display was blank. Finally he examined the balaclava-style face mask attached to the top of the suit. It still gave him the creeps. A clinging, inhuman face. It was as expressionless as death. The thought of ever putting the thing on again filled him with disgust.

But he didn't have to. It was over. Wasn't it?'

While he was repacking the suit, he heard the door. 'Mum? Dad?' There was no answer. Somebody was there, but they weren't answering. There was something about the silence that put him on edge.

He hurried back down the hallway. 'Mum?' He found her in the kitchen, going through her handbag. 'Mum, what's wrong?'

She threw the bag down in exasperation. 'I had a train timetable for London. Where can I have put it?'

'London,' said Phoenix. 'Why London?'

'It's your grandfather. He is very ill.' Phoenix stared at her, demanding more information. 'It's cancer, Phoenix. Grandpa's got cancer.'

'Has he got to have an operation or something?'

A catch came into Mum's voice. 'There's nothing they can do, except ease the pain. It's terminal. He's going to die.'

Phoenix continued to stare. He was thinking of the kindly old man who had come to London in the sixties to make a living, and built a Greek restaurant business out of nothing. 'I'm sorry, Mum.'

She put her hands on his shoulders, and looked into his dark brown eyes. 'Listen, I only heard an hour ago. Your grandmother got me on my mobile at work. It was a terrible shock. I'm going down to stay with them for a few days. They need all the support they can get right now. You'll be fine with your dad.'

Phoenix smiled. 'Of course I will.' The obituary piece in the magazine was still hovering somewhere at the back of his mind, but it no longer seemed so important. He certainly couldn't burden Mum with it now.

'I'm going to pack,' said Mum, snapping a purple band round her mane of raven-black hair. 'Would you do a quick tidy-up?' In a crisis, Mum always resorted to tidying up. It was one of her coping strategies. She indicated the magazines strewn on the table. 'You can put those in your room for a start.'

As Phoenix gathered up the mags, he was desperate to tell her that it might not be over. That the deadly game had come back to life.

Phoenix had cleared the surfaces and was washing the dishes when Dad burst through the door.

'Is Mum back?'

'Yes, she's upstairs packing.'

'She's told you then?' Phoenix nodded. 'This is all we need. After . . .' His voice trailed off. 'Still, at least that's over.'

Phoenix followed Dad with his eyes. *But what if it isn't? What if it's about to begin all over again?*

Six weeks ago – is that all it was? – he had worn that Parallel Reality suit the magazine had talked about, felt it clinging as though it was a second skin, creeping around him like the tendrils of some monstrous plant. He had played the game. Maybe the magazine was right. Maybe *The Legendeer* had been rendered safe, a mere entertainment.

But those few short weeks ago, it had been all too real. It had transported him physically into a world of demons, monsters and savage gods. He had learned that losing the game meant losing your life.

'Phoenix?' Dad was calling from the top of the stairs. 'I'm going to run your mum down to the station. Would you stay and wait by the phone? I'm expecting a call from that job interview.'

Phoenix watched his parents hurrying off. He waved sadly. Mention of the job interview brought it all back. When Dad had worked for the mysterious games company Magna-com, he had helped develop *The Legendeer*.

When he had played the game and found out that it was really playing him.

Just like Chris Darke.

Dusk was gathering by the time Dad pulled into the driveway.

'Dad,' said Phoenix meeting him at the front door, 'there's something I have to show you.'

'Not now, eh?' said John Graves. 'I'm tired and I'm hungry.

Did you take a call about the job?' Dad wasn't thinking demons. He was thinking mortgage. Phoenix winced. The job. He should have mentioned that first. Butter the old man up with the good news.

'Yes, you got it. They're sending you a contract in the next post.' Dad smiled weakly. Mum's news had obviously taken the shine off his success on the job front. 'I could whip up an omelette for you,' said Phoenix, keen to make amends. 'Ham and mushroom be OK?'

'Son, you're a life-saver. That would be great. I'll take a quick shower while you're rustling it up.'

Phoenix listened to the spit of fat in the pan and the sound of water running in the bathroom. He hated having to wait, but he knew it would be wise to hold back on the obituary, at least until Dad had eaten.

'Your mother's devastated,' said Dad, padding across the kitchen in his dressing gown still towelling his shock of ginger hair. 'She hero-worships her dad. They're such a close family.' He hung the towel over the radiator. 'Looks like we'll just have to muddle along without her for a while.'

'Coffee?' asked Phoenix.

'Love one.'

Phoenix approached the table, stirring a mug of instant. 'Dad, I need to show you something.'

John Graves immediately recognized the tone of voice. 'Not in trouble at school, are you?'

'No,' said Phoenix, 'School's fine. I'll get it.' He returned with the magazine and laid it on the table in front of Dad, open at the review page.

'What am I supposed to be looking at?'

Phoenix pointed to the obituary for Chris Darke. 'That.'

Dad shook his head. 'And . . . ?'

'Read it, Dad,' Phoenix, pleaded. 'Read it properly. There. *The Legendeer*. It's the same thing that happened to us.'

'It can't be,' said Dad. 'We stopped him . . . it . . . whatever it was that dragged us into that awful game.' But try as he might, he couldn't deny what was there in front of him in bold print. 'I don't believe it,' he said. 'Not again.'

But it was true. It had begun.

Again.

2

The supermarket was packed the following evening. It was the only one in Brownleigh and the entire population of the small market town seemed to be there.

'No wonder your mum comes back in such a state,' said Dad. 'It's like the chariot race from *Ben Hur*. I swear some of these trollies have scythes attached. Still, let's see if us boys can make a decent job of doing the shopping.' Phoenix saw through the forced gaiety. Dad was trying to keep both their minds off the game.

'I'll tell you what you've forgotten,' said Phoenix, consulting the shopping list they had drawn up. 'Milk. It's two aisles back.' He was one of those three bowls of cereal a day teenagers so milk was a big deal. Dad started to manoeuvre the trolley. 'No,' said Phoenix, 'I'll go. How many should I get?'

'Make it two,' said Dad. 'Only the four-pinters, mind. Those big six-pinters don't fit in our fridge.'

Phoenix nodded and backtracked. As he turned the aisle, his heart missed a beat. There, right in front of him was Steve Adams' mother. Seeing her unexpectedly like that brought to mind the key players in the deadly game he had entered. Phoenix, Dad, Laura . . . and Adams. Phoenix turned furtively and was about to make his way back to Dad when she spotted him.

'Just a moment. It is you isn't it? You're the Graves boy. Please wait.' Phoenix just wanted to escape. 'I know you and Steven didn't get on, but if you know anything, anything at all, you have to tell me.' Phoenix was aware of other shoppers turning and staring. 'Please, just the slightest detail you forgot to tell the police. It's been weeks. I can't bear not knowing what's happened to him.'

Phoenix wanted to tell her what he knew. But how? How do you explain to a mother that her son has been transported into a world which dances to Evil's fiddle – and that he loves every minute of it! Phoenix remembered the last time he had seen her son. The moment when Adams chose to stay in the game, rather than come home.

'I'm sorry, Mrs Adams, but I haven't seen him.' His reply, so obviously a lie, provoked a change in Mrs Adams. Her eyes narrowed. Phoenix saw her suspicion. 'You do know something, don't you?'

In his mind's eye, Phoenix saw Adams retreating into the darkness, returning to *him*. 'No, Mrs Adams. Honestly, I don't know what's happened to him.'

'Please,' she said. 'I can see it in your face.' She opened her purse. 'Money! I can pay you. How much do you want?'

'Mrs Adams. Please don't.' She was advancing on him, purse open. Then there was another voice.

'Margaret!'

Mrs Adams turned, and seeing her husband, she immediately burst into tears and buried her face into his shoulder. 'He knows something, Brian,' she sobbed. 'I'm sure he does. But he won't tell. How could he be so cruel?' Mr Adams patted his wife on the back and gestured to Phoenix to go. On shaky legs, Phoenix found his way back to Dad.

'So where's the milk?' Phoenix stared dumbly at his empty hands. 'Well?'

'I ran into Mrs Adams. She started giving me the third degree.'

'You didn't tell her anything, did you?'

'Of course not, what could I say?'

Dad sighed. 'The shopping can wait another day. I'll come back by myself tomorrow evening. When the coast is clear.'

Phoenix nodded gratefully and they made for the exit.

He couldn't put thoughts of the obituary and the game out of his mind. The following evening, after Dad had gone out to make the return journey to the supermarket, Phoenix slipped into the study and searched for Dad's copy of *The Legendeer*. It wasn't hidden, or locked away. The game really was harmless.

It wasn't without misgivings that Phoenix downloaded it, but there was nothing to arouse his suspicions. The labyrinth where he had fought a life-and-death battle with the Minotaur, the cavern where he had beheaded the Gorgon, Medusa, they were graphic images on the screen. Vivid and scary, but not real.

Now for the real test, he thought. Slowly, with the sort of care you devote to something very precious, or very dangerous, he donned the PR suit, plugging it into the computer. The suit was the passport to terror. Phoenix remembered the way he had been transported into the game, the brilliant portal of light, the flashing numbers. This time, nothing happened.

Nothing at all.

The gate is closed. There is nowhere to go.

With relief pulsating through him, he slipped off the suit, folded it, and put it back in its box. 'Round one to us,' said Phoenix out loud. 'But what about round two?'

Had he returned to the study just five minutes later he would have got his answer. The computer was on. It had switched on by itself. What's more, the screen was covered with a familiar blizzard of marching numbers. It was the encrypted code from another world, a spiralling sequence of threes, sixes and nines. It was the demon inside the machine, and this is what it had to say:

So you want to play?'

Then I, the Gamesmaster, will be happy to oblige.

It has been a while, Legendeer, at least as far as you are concerned. To a youth of fourteen summers, the weeks pass slowly. But to one such as I who was there before the pyramids and will remain long after the sun burns out, weeks or months amount to no more than a speck of dust in the eye of time.

Do you miss the clash of battle, the thrill of terror? Or is it fear that draws you back? Fear of me. Fear of what I can do.

You feel my presence still, don't you? Every time a flame gutters, every time the wind moans, every time you switch off the light, you sense me behind you. Every time the computer hums, you feel my presence.

The Gamesmaster.

You are right to be afraid. You quite ruined the first round of the game, but if you imagine you have conquered me then think again.

In my long march to rebirth and freedom, I have suffered many setbacks.

Even so, my latest plans are well-advanced.

Here I come, ready or not.

3

Phoenix felt something as he passed the doorway to the study the following evening. How to describe it – a chill, a tingling, a touch maybe? It was one of those moments when the walls of safe, everyday reality come down to reveal the shadows beyond. But he had no time to dwell on the unsettling sensation. The chirrup of the telephone was insistent. 'OK, OK, I'm coming.' He covered the mouthpiece and called down the hallway into the living room. 'Laura, would you get me something to drink?'

He heard her shifting out of her chair. He marvelled for a moment at the contrast in the house. First, there was the ordinariness and predictability of its routine. He could locate where anybody was simply by the way the floorboards creaked. Then there was the disturbance that gnawed at its heart, the possibility of a gate to terror suddenly opening.

'Hello? Mum! Good to hear your voice. How's Grandpa?'

'Not so good. He doesn't grumble much, but he isn't a bit well. He gets tired easily. He's lost weight, too. It's terrible seeing him like this. He was always such a strong man. Invincible, or so I always thought.'

'When are you coming home?'

'That's what I was calling about. Is Dad in?'

'No,' Phoenix replied. 'He's got a meeting at work.'

He heard Mum's breath catch. 'Of course, the new job. It slipped my mind completely. I haven't even congratulated him. There hasn't been room in my mind for anything except your grandfather. You must think I'm very selfish.'

'No, I don't,' Phoenix replied. 'Any message for Dad?'

'I'd like the two of you to come down this weekend. Grandma would appreciate it.'

'Sure,' said Phoenix, 'I'll tell him.'

'You wouldn't mind coming down?'

'No Mum, not a bit.'

'Papa's been asking after you. He mentions you in the same breath as Andreas.'

There was a moment's silence.

'Grandpa actually said his name?'

'Yes. That's twice in a few weeks. It must be the illness. They say looking death in the face makes you relive your past.'

Andreas. It was a name that meant so much in the family. Finally Mum spoke again. 'Any news at your end?'

Phoenix let the events of the last two days run through his mind: the obituary, the encounter with Mrs Adams. Neither of them were what Mum wanted to hear just then. 'No, we're managing fine. Dad's even done the ironing. Shirts and everything.'

'That I'd like to see.'

Mum sounded weary. The hollowness in her voice made Phoenix's heart ache. 'I'll go now, son. Ask Dad to phone me back about the weekend. Promise you won't forget?'

'Promise.'

Phoenix returned to the living room, hurrying just a little as he passed the study door. He could feel the darkness reaching out to him.

'Your mum?' asked Laura, holding out a can of Seven Up.

'Yes. She sounds really down.'

'I'm not surprised. Did you mention what's happened?'

Phoenix looked at Laura, taking in the dreadlocked hair, the deep black-brown of her skin, the slightly blueish tone that showed under the electric light. She was tall and striking, one of the headturners at Brownleigh High. 'How could I? She's got enough on her plate.'

Laura tossed a copy of *The Guardian* on to the coffee table.

'That's it. Two weeks' worth of newspapers and not a single mention of Chris Darke.'

'And your Dad doesn't keep them any further back?'

Laura shook her head. 'He's a stickler for routine. A leftover from his time in the Nigerian civil service. Keeps them exactly two weeks, then gives them to the paper collection. I suppose we should try the library next. It'll have to be the weekend, though. Our parents won't want us going into town straight from school.'

Phoenix nodded. 'We can't do much about it until Saturday.' He glanced down at the newspapers. 'Still, it was worth a try. I just thought we might strike lucky.' Then he cursed, low, under his breath.

'Now what?'

'I just thought, I won't be able to go to the library this weekend. I'll be in London. You know, my grandpa. There's no way I can get out of it.'

Laura smiled. 'I'll do the research. I'm very capable.'

It was Phoenix's turn to smile. Just how capable he had discovered when they played the game. She had endured all the terrors of the myth-world and come out smiling – just! That wasn't capable, that was heroic.

'I know you are. I'd like to have gone along with you.'

'I'll manage,' said Laura, before changing the subject. 'Phoenix, how far do you think Chris Darke got with the game?'

'No idea. There isn't much to go on. Yet . . .'

'Yes?'

Phoenix searched for the words. 'Sometimes feelings are stronger than facts. It's this instinct I have inside me. It tells me to be on my guard. Something's coming.'

'You're scaring me.'

Phoenix toyed with his drink. 'I'm scaring myself. You won't believe what I've done, but I've had my PR suit on again.'

'Whatever for?'

'I suppose I wanted to convince myself the game really is harmless. That it wasn't going to start all over again.'

Laura leaned forward. 'Did you? Convince yourself, I mean.'

Phoenix shook his head. 'All I did by touching those things was to bring it all back. The labyrinth, the poison cave, the fear. The Gamesmaster's still out there, Laura. I can feel him. It's anything but over.'

Laura shuddered involuntarily. 'Hey, look at the time. I'd better go.'

Phoenix stood at the door, watching her disappear into the evening mist. He was at a loss after that, flitting from one thing to another, unable to settle. Dad wouldn't be home for hours and the emptiness of the house made him anxious. He thought about doing his homework, but he just couldn't concentrate. He switched on the TV and spent ten minutes channel-surfing, before giving it up as a bad job. Three times he visited the kitchen, picking at peanuts and taking a couple of bites out of an apple before dropping it into the bin. In the end there was only one thing which would put his mind to rest. He climbed the stairs to his parents' room and crossed the floor to Mum's bedside table. He slid open the drawer and took out the journal.

Andreas' journal.

He carried it downstairs and started to read.

Andreas was Grandpa's twin brother. Their story was unremarkable enough at first, just two boys growing up in rural Greece. Then came adolescence. Grandpa did all the normal things: he got into mischief, had fights, became interested in girls. Andreas was different. As the years went on, he became withdrawn and suffered long bouts of ill-health. Some days he was paralysed by merciless, blinding headaches and would spend the daylight hours lying in a darkened room. Then, when he was fourteen, the haunting started, the visions that drove him to the brink of madness. Despite constant nightmares and long spells of illness, he managed to become a schoolteacher. Everyone hoped that, once Andreas had grown to manhood, he would leave his strange moods behind. He didn't. They just became longer and more intense. Phoenix opened the journal.

I want to sleep, read one entry, *to close my eyes and never open them again. I see them all the time now, the magic numbers, the demons. It is more than I can bear.*

'The numbers,' Phoenix said out loud, 'That's the link.'

Gradually, the days when Andreas seemed possessed multiplied, while the good days, the days when he could function as an ordinary man became fewer and fewer, eventually dwindling almost to nothing. Finally, it all became too much. Andreas suffered a breakdown and was committed to an asylum.

'But you weren't mad, were you?' Phoenix murmured. 'Or else I am, as well. The headaches you suffered, I have them too. The nightmares that haunted you, I've experienced them. The things you saw. I've seen them too. I saw them in the game.'

Phoenix read the tell-tale entry, the page he had read and reread so many times since first playing *The Legendeer.*

The more I think about it, the sickliness, the band of pain, the strange waking fever that has been with me all my life, the more I realize that it has something to do with the ghosts. When they gather, when they step out of the shimmering light and speak to me, then I understand. I belong to their world. I always have.

For all time, I will be a stranger inside my own skin. I have a mission. For every ghost that believes in life and justice and warns me of the dangers of the gate, there are others who are filled with death and destruction. They are knocking at the door. But they will not pass me. I am the Legendeer.

My task is to keep the gate closed, to keep out the demon legions. Though it breaks my heart every day of my life, I will never give up my vigil. To leave my post would be to abandon this world to horror.

'But a computer game that relives my family's past,' said Phoenix. 'How can that be?'

There were no answers in that silent house, only questions.

What was the link between a tormented schoolteacher in Greece in the 1960s and a macabre computer game almost forty years later?

What would Andreas have said if he had seen *The Legendeer*? Most importantly, how could his family have deserted him and locked him up like that? A man who was lucid and sane, imprisoned in a madhouse cell.

Phoenix sat back and closed his eyes. The family's trip to their home village came flooding back. He saw the cypress groves and the low stone walls surrounding Andreas' house. Then the house itself. The pictures of demons, numbers all over the walls.

No wonder they thought you were mad.

'But you were the only one who was sane,' said Phoenix. He closed the journal, but he couldn't close the cover on the family secret. It would always be there, the knowledge that in the terrifying spaces between everyday reality, there were other, parallel worlds. And in those worlds all the nightmare creatures that have stalked the minds of men go in search of prey.

And we are their prey.

Dad got home just before eleven. He was having to work late and even then his day wasn't done. The office was an hour's drive from Brownleigh, ninety minutes in the rush hour. He found Phoenix sleeping fitfully on the couch. Moving quietly across the floor so as not to disturb his sleeping son, John Graves switched off the TV and sat opposite. He had been there a couple of minutes before he noticed the grimy volume beside Phoenix on the arm of the couch.

'What's this you've been reading?' he murmured. Casting his eyes over the page, he paused, apprehension stealing through him. Unlike his wife and son, he couldn't read

Greek, but he could read the scrap of paper Phoenix was using as a bookmark. On it, Phoenix had translated an entry which read:

At least I know that, no matter how they haunt me, there is no way the demons can infect this beautiful world of ours.

John Graves slowly shook his head. 'If only we were so sure,' he said, 'if only it were true.'

4

It was just after seven o'clock the following evening when the front doorbell rang.

'Who's that?' said Phoenix, consulting the wall clock. 'Not double-glazing salesmen again.' He was in luck. The smiling face that greeted him on the doorstep belonged to Laura.

'Guess what I've got?' she said, waving a scrap of paper under his nose. 'Only Chris Darke's phone number.'

'You're kidding! I thought we'd agreed we wouldn't be able to get to the library on a weekday.'

'I didn't go to the library. But I happened to mention the story to Dad.' She held up her hand. 'Don't worry, I didn't give anything away. Dad remembered it. He's got one of those minds. Always does really well on quiz programmes. Anyway, it was there locked away at the back of his mind. He remembered the Darke murder and where it happened, so I called directory enquiries. Three Darkes listed, only one a C. Darke.'

Phoenix led her inside.

'OK,' she said, 'So do we call?'

Phoenix glanced at the number on the crumpled piece of paper. 'S'pose so.'

'You don't sound very enthusiastic.'

'What do we say?' asked Phoenix. 'Mrs Darke, could you confirm that your husband was killed by demons; you know, the ones that live in the computer game he was designing?'

'It's your call,' said Laura. 'You're the one who's convinced something's happening.' Phoenix took the number and laid it on the hall table. Instinctively, he glanced at Dad's computer, the doorway into the Gamesmaster's myth-world. Laura followed his gaze. 'Spooky, isn't it?' she said. 'Considering what happened last time.'

Phoenix bit his bottom lip and lifted the handset. The thought of hordes of demons massing on the other side of the screen prompted him to action. 'I still don't know what to say.'

'Can't help you,' said Laura. 'I wouldn't like to do it.'

Phoenix punched out the number. When the phone was picked up at the other end, his throat went completely dry. 'Mrs Darke?' he asked croakily.

'I'll get her.' It was a boy, nine or ten maybe. 'Mum,' he called. 'It's for you.' Phoenix and Laura exchanged glances, then Mrs Darke was on the line.

'Hello?'

'Mrs Darke, you don't know me, but I read about what happened to your husband . . . in *Gamestation* magazine.' He hesitated, wondering how to continue. 'I wonder, could you tell me about the game he was working on?'

The voice at the other end was suspicious. 'Who is this? Did you know my husband?'

'No, I didn't. But I think we've got something in common. I know about *The Legendeer*. Do you know if he finished it?'

Suspicion had turned to fear. Mrs Darke's voice was full of emotion. 'If this is some sort of sick joke, I don't think it's funny. Who are you?' Phoenix looked at Laura. This was going seriously wrong. 'If you call again, I'll be contacting the police. Do you understand?'

'Yes,' said Phoenix, 'I understand.' He replaced the phone.

'That was a bit of a disaster, wasn't it?' said Laura, stating the obvious.

'On a scale of one to ten,' said Phoenix, 'it was zero. She thought I was a crank caller.' They were still standing by the telephone when they heard a car pulling into the driveway. 'That'll be Dad,' said Phoenix, 'Don't mention any of this. He'd go ballistic.'

'Hello? Phoenix?'

'Hi, Dad. We're here.'

'Oh, hello Laura. I didn't know you were coming round again.'

'Spur of the moment,' said Laura. The small talk was interrupted a moment later by the shrill ring of the phone. Dad picked up.

'I beg your pardon? A call from this number? Are you sure?' He glanced at Phoenix.

'Oh great,' groaned Phoenix. 'She must have rung 1471. Call-back.'

'He asked what?' exclaimed Dad. 'I really must apologize, Mrs Darke. Yes, most upsetting. Don't worry, I assure you it won't happen again. Yes, yes, I'll speak to him. Do accept my sincerest apologies.'

Dad replaced the phone and glared at Phoenix. 'Have you taken leave of your senses? You rang Chris Darke's widow!'

'I had to know, Dad. I had to be sure . . .'

Dad opened his briefcase and flourished a manila folder. 'If you'd bothered to ask, I've looked into it already. There was no reason to go upsetting the poor woman.'

Phoenix stared back in disbelief. 'You checked up! But I thought . . .'

'That I wasn't interested?'

'Something like that.'

'Just because I haven't talked about it much, doesn't mean I'm not concerned.'

It was Phoenix's turn to be angry. 'You could have told me!'

'Yes,' said Dad, a hint of guilt in his voice, 'I suppose I could. I've had so much on my mind. The new job, your grandfather . . .'

'So what have you found out?'

'Come into the living room and I'll show you.'

They were able to piece together Chris Darke's story from the newspaper clippings and snippets from the various game magazines. Darke had been headhunted by Magna-com to produce their latest game, a sequel to *The Legendeer.*

'It was so strange finding out about Darke,' said Dad grimly, remembering the torment the game had dragged him into. 'It was like reliving what happened to me. Though Darke didn't know it, he was stepping into my shoes. Only he didn't know how dangerous it was.'

'Vampires,' said Laura, reading the excerpts.

'I beg your pardon?'

'The game. It isn't the Greek myths this time. It's vampires.'

'Oh, I see. Yes, seems the Gamesmaster is moving on to a different set of legends. Maybe by defeating him we made that last world useless for his plans.'

'But just look at the new one,' said Phoenix. 'A parallel world peopled by the undead. And trying to break into the land of the living.'

Laura shuddered. 'If anything, it sounds worse than last time.'

'Look here,' said Dad. 'Darke already had a working title for it – *Legendeer 2: Vampyr Legion.*'

Phoenix scanned the cuttings gloomily. 'I knew it wasn't over.'

'We're luckier than Darke,' said Dad. 'We got out alive. Poor man. What a terrible way to die.'

Laura and Phoenix exchanged glances. 'Is there something you haven't told us?'

Dad tugged nervously at his russet beard. 'The police found him lying on the floor of his studio. There's a mention in one of the reports of him being at his work-desk at the time of the attack. Reading between the lines, I'd say he was wearing his Parallel Reality suit, and it was still plugged in to the PC.'

'You mean he died while he was in the game?' asked Laura.

'No, not in the game. There were signs of a struggle in the studio. A broken lamp, some overturned furniture. He fought for his life, but not while he was in the world of the game. His killer had followed him back.'

'A demon? But how?'

'Not a demon,' said Dad. 'If they could break through, the Gamesmaster would already have won. No, not a demon but somebody who serves them.' He handed Phoenix a cutting from a local newspaper. There were two leads not mentioned anywhere else. One was an intriguing rumour of cult involvement, that had been kept out of the rest of the coverage. The other mentioned the sighting of a youth in his teens leaving the house.

'I know it seems stupid,' said Phoenix. 'But for a moment I actually thought it might be Adams.'

'Now that is paranoia,' said Laura. 'Even Steve couldn't do something like this.'

'Are you sure about that?'

It was a while before any of them spoke and when Phoenix finally broke the silence it was to utter a single word:

'Vampires.'

5

That Thursday night was the last Phoenix and John Graves would spend in the house before travelling to London. As the small hours of Friday morning dawned, an eery electronic glow filled the study. It touched the cardboard box containing the PR suits, the storage units, the bookshelves, the curtains. The computer switched itself on again, conducting its sinister monologue in the dull, dead silence. The only sound was the wheezing of the north wind outside.

Bravo Legendeer!

So you know about Darke. He got too inquisitive, and curiosity killed the cat. That's right, Darke wasn't satisfied developing the game. He had to stick his nose in where it wasn't wanted. Just like you once did.

But Darke didn't have your luck. He saw, he ran, he died. He completed the game on the night of his death. It has gone for pressing. I am just weeks away from victory, and there isn't a thing you can do to stop me.

Enjoy the bliss of ignorance. Sleep while you still can.

6

The drive home from London was a quiet affair. Even at the best of times, visiting a sick relative wasn't going to be easy. But these weren't the best of times. Grandma had cried most of the time, retreating upstairs to keep her lonely vigil over Grandpa. Great aunt Sophia had glared at everyone, as if daring them to mention her *other* brother. It was as if they had spent the entire weekend at Grandma's avoiding one name, Andreas. Mum had cooked, fussed and made endless cups of coffee, anything to keep busy. Dad found himself a chair in the corner of the living room and buried himself in a book. As for Phoenix, he'd scanned the family photographs, imagining Grandpa's twin brother, Andreas, the family member nobody ever mentioned. But he didn't say his name either. Instead he brooded, wondering how the family could have allowed him to be locked up like a madman, somebody they were supposed to have loved. Now, as the miles rolled by, neither Mum, Dad nor Phoenix felt much like talking. Each of them was, in their own way, preoccupied with matters of life and death. Instead of talking, they kept their minds busy, Dad with his driving, Mum with a poetry anthology and Phoenix with his vampires. He had just reached a chapter which seemed to have more to do with military hardware than with myth.

> The crossbow, or arbalest, (he read) one of the key killing tools of the vampire slayer. It is a means of delivering a stake through the demon's heart from a distance and with the force of 20 men. Used in war and sport in medieval

Europe, it consists of a wooden stock, with a bow made of wood, iron or steel crossing it at right angles. The bolts it fires are known as quarrels.

A little further on, an excerpt from a particularly lurid short story made him sit up. It was a reworking of the old vampire theme, but with a fascinating difference.

'Know this, Fernando,' said the old priest. 'The vampyr has neither fear of the holy cloth, nor of the crucifix. The cross it fears is yonder bow, set in the shape of the crucifix. Waste not your time throwing holy water. To destroy the creature you must drive a point directly through its heart, rend its corrupted body asunder or expose it to the blazing intensity of sunlight. Those are the three paths to victory over the Beast.'

Phoenix immediately relayed the information to his parents, expecting them to greet it with the same fascination he had.

'What *are* you reading?' Mum asked. 'Dear me, hasn't this family had enough of demons?' The moment the words left her lips the atmosphere in the car changed. Dad became more intent on his driving. Phoenix buried his face in his book, angry with himself for letting his tongue run away with him. 'What's happened?' Mum demanded, her voice filling with dread. 'What are you keeping from me?'

'Nothing,' said Dad. 'Honestly, it's nothing.'

'Don't treat me like a child,' said Mum. 'I knew there was something when I phoned home. You were so tight-lipped, Phoenix. Not like you at all.'

'Just drop it, eh, Mum,' said Phoenix.

'No,' she retorted. 'I will not drop it. I am as much part of this family as either of you. I have lived this nightmare as much as either of you.'

Phoenix caught Dad's eye in the rear-view mirror. They exchanged a brief nod. It was time to come clean. After all, it was Mum who had revealed the truth about Andreas, Mum who had witnessed Phoenix's previous adventures on the computer screen. They had all shared the first chapter of the terror. They would face this new episode together.

'We'd better talk,' said Dad. 'I'll pull in at the next services.'

In the end, Phoenix thought it better to let Dad do the explaining. Leaving his parents speaking in hushed voices over two hot chocolates, he wandered round the building. After drifting aimlessly for a few minutes, looking down at the speeding lanes of traffic then strolling round the telephone boxes and cash machines, he found himself at the entrance to the shop. He browsed along the bookshelves then moved on to the magazine racks. He honed in on the new edition of *Gamestation* straight away. Of course, the last Friday in the month. He had his copy on order. It would have been lying on the hall mat all weekend, waiting for him. But there was no way he would be able to hang on until he got home.

Imagine if there were something in there, a mention of Darke or the game. He had to know right away. As he laid the magazine on the counter, he couldn't help but think it was some sort of sick joke. Demons, man's most ancient fear, were at the door. And what was going to let them through? Only our most modern and sophisticated technological advance – the computer.

'That'll be three pounds fifty,' said the woman behind the till. 'Computer games, eh? My son's really into all that.'

That's the trouble, thought Phoenix. Everybody is. He re-ran the nightmare vision. In a matter of months, maybe even weeks hundreds of thousands of kids, maybe even millions, would be sitting in front of a computer game, battling its demons. Then the demon would take form. That was the endgame: millions of demons pouring through millions of computer screens.

A world invaded.

A nightmare triumphant.

No sooner was he out of the shop than he tore off the cellophane wrapper and discarded it. News. Nothing there. His heart started to beat a little more slowly.

Reviews. Still nothing. It took two readings to satisfy himself that he was right, but there was no doubt about it. *Vampyr Legion* wasn't on sale yet.

We've got time.

He had reached page 62 before he came across the section which would turn his blood to ice. It was a glossy pullout called 'In the Pipeline'. And there it was, the news he had been dreading.

Magna-com's latest is ahead of schedule. *Vampyr Legion,* the much-anticipated second part of the *Legendeer* series should be in the outlets soon, just in time for Christmas.

If anything, the tragic and mysterious death of its original designer, Chris Darke, has only added to the interest around its launch, giving the state of the art game a money-spinning air of notoriety. After *Shadow of the Minotaur,* we know what to expect from Magna-com, great 3D graphics and story lines to make you quake.

The only question now is: will they finally be able to introduce the revolutionary Parallel Reality suit? Our sources tell us that *Vampyr Legion* really will slay us!

For a moment Phoenix could barely breathe. It was coming. *He* was coming. The Gamesmaster's boast, that soon demons would pour from the screen of every computer, was about to come true.

'Christmas,' he said, not noticing an elderly couple watching him with some amusement. As he dashed off to tell his parents the news, the couple exchanged smiles.

'Kids,' said the old lady. 'They live in a dreamworld all their own.'

'I know,' her husband replied. 'You'd swear it was real.'

7

'I beg your pardon?' said Dad, as if unable to believe his own ears. He put down the bundle of mail he had just picked up off the hall mat. 'You did what?' The conversation they had begun on the motorway was still in full flow as they walked into the house.

'I wore one of the suits,' Phoenix replied, 'I was worried by the Darke obituary.' He saw Dad's expression change. He decided to avoid a row. 'At least that's the way it seemed. So I decided to check the game out for myself.' He said it as if hooking himself up to *The Legendeer* was the most natural thing in the world.

'Have you forgotten what happened the last time you wore one of those things?' Mum said. 'I had to watch helplessly while you . . . You could have been killed. Oh, Phoenix, how could you? And without telling us!'

Despite the third degree, Phoenix couldn't help noticing Dad staring intently at one of the letters in the pile he had dropped onto the hall table.

'But I knew it was safe,' Phoenix retorted. 'At least, I was 99 per cent sure. You said it yourself Dad; by beating the Gamesmaster last time round we destroyed the threat.' Dad had taken the letter and slipped it into his pocket. He looked startled when Phoenix said his name. 'We turned the first part of *The Legendeer* into an ordinary game,' Phoenix said, irritated by the way Dad was continuing to leaf through his letters. 'Even with the PR suit on, nothing happened.'

'No,' said Dad, 'But it could have done. You took a stupid risk.'

But you know I wasn't in danger. What's going on here? Why are you so upset? Phoenix saw something new in Dad's face, blind, unreasoning fear. All of a sudden, disappointment had turned to anger.

But why?

'Don't make excuses, Phoenix,' Dad snapped. 'You were forbidden to ever wear those infernal suits again.'

'You can't just blame him, John,' said Mum. 'I thought we'd agreed to destroy them. Then nobody could play.'

Dad looked away.

'John, why didn't you?'

There was a long silence.

'I know why,' said Phoenix. 'You weren't sure, were you Dad? You thought, maybe it wasn't all over. Maybe it was going to start all over again. That's it, isn't it? You thought we might have to return to the world of the game one day.'

Dad looked suddenly older, his face lined and grey. 'Yes, maybe I did.'

'And you were right. If we don't go into his world, how *do* we fight the Gamesmaster?'

'We find Darke's colleagues,' Dad replied. 'We find the game's manufacturer. We tell them what we know. I know you don't think much of my efforts, Phoenix, but that's what I've been trying to do.'

'But it isn't enough,' cried Phoenix. 'You can find as many designers and programmers as you like. The Gamesmaster will always come up with somebody else to carry on his work. We thought we'd won last time, but we hadn't. We've got to go back into his world and finish the job. The myth-world is real, Dad, as real as this one. You know that feeling when you get up in the night, and you think something's behind you? Well, it isn't our imagination. It's true. There's a nightmare world right behind us, *many* nightmare worlds, and every one as real as this one. That's where the battle is to be won or lost.' But Phoenix himself was fighting a losing battle. Mum delivered the fatal blow.

'No Phoenix, your dad's right. We have to try his way first. If we can't stop the game's production, then we can try your way.'

'Yes,' Phoenix said desperately, 'And by then we will have wasted so much time, nothing will be able to stop him. Could you live with that on your conscience?'

'Listen to me, Phoenix,' said Dad, his face set. 'Whatever happens, you are not to touch the PR suits. Do you understand me?'

'I understand, but what's the big deal? It's not like we've even got a copy of the new game.' There was a moment's silence, as if Phoenix had sworn in church.

'I've said all I've got to say, Phoenix. You let me follow up my leads and you keep out of the study. Do I make myself clear?'

Phoenix tried to argue back, but it was no use. With his parents putting up a united front, he was beaten.

'Sure Dad, it's crystal clear.'

When Phoenix went up to bed at half past ten, Dad was shut up in the study, hammering away at the computer. Phoenix imagined him opening files, sending e-mail, cross-referencing leads. In short, he would be working feverishly, trying to convince himself he was doing *something*. Phoenix sat in his room, resenting his parents for deceiving themselves, he knew trying to beat the Gamesmaster from outside wouldn't work. The Gamesmaster wasn't a virus, a rogue piece of software. He was no artificial intelligence. He was the demon-lord, and the computer was merely a way to open the gate between his world and ours.

'If I can't do it with you,' Phoenix said, 'Then I'll have to do it without you.' He sat a while with his elbows on his knees, face buried in his hands. Then, straightening up, he came to a decision. 'I have to return. I have to track him to his lair, destroy the architect of the game.'

But how? Without a copy of the game, he was shut out, doomed to sit and wait for the storm to break over his head. When Phoenix finally fell asleep, he was worn out, exhausted from wracking his brain for a solution. Whatever he thought, however he turned it this way and that in his mind, without a copy of *Vampyr Legion* there could be no battle. And without battle, there could be no victory.

8

Downstairs in his study, John Graves worked into the night. But not the way Phoenix thought. The moment Dad locked himself in the study, he pulled the letter from his pocket. It was a small, brown bubble envelope. He held it up to the light, inspecting the postmark. After a moment's reflection, he tore it open and read the letter.

Dear Mr Graves,
I'm sorry I was so off-hand with you when you rang me back. I am sure you can understand my distress. After my husband's murder, I didn't know who to turn to, who to trust. Is this what the killer was after?

Dad slid the small disc from the envelope and read the Gothic script: *Vampyr Legion.*

I think the killer got away with the original disc, the one Chris was working on, but he made a back-up copy and sent it to his parents for safe keeping. He had been worried for a long time. He had begun to take all sorts of precautions. I thought it was paranoia. How wrong I was! Chris's dad returned the disc to me at the funeral, so here it is. I have to admit that I don't understand what's going on and why this game led to my husband's death, but you have convinced me that you should have the disc. I am putting my faith in you, Mr Graves. I want you to bring Chris's murderer to justice. Maybe that way I can begin to sleep at night.

Yours sincerely,

Ruth Darke

Dad turned the disc between his fingers. He found his attention drawn first to the computer, then to the PR suits in their box. 'What now?' he murmured. 'What now?'

Out in the garden somebody was moving. Over six feet tall, of athletic, muscular build, the stranger was staring intently at the Graves' house. In particular, he was watching the light burning in the study. He took a step forward, compulsively clenching and relaxing his gloved hands. He watched all that night, standing under the flashing stars, the waxing moon, the rushing stormclouds. He saw the study light go off and moved slowly towards the house. Then, just as he reached the window, the light was switched back on. The stranger slipped back into the shadows, darkness against darkness.

Phoenix heard Dad making his way upstairs at about four o'clock. Everything that had happened in the last few months had made Phoenix a light sleeper. Sometimes he would wake up on the hour every hour. Was it the thoughts racing through his mind that jerked him awake, or the nightmares that came to call every time his head touched the pillow?

'Won't sleep now,' he grumbled, and switched on his bedside lamp. He reached for the vampire book, and opened it at the description of the crossbow. As he reread it he felt a draught, a breeze that seemed to sing across the room without even disturbing the curtains. 'Stop it,' he told himself, 'You're just imagining things.'

But as he read the brief chapter, it was as if he was seeing with new eyes. He started to interpret it differently, absorbing the facts as if they were a list of instructions. Each illustration fell into place, disassembling then reassembling the slayer's tool step by lethal step.

'I could make this,' he said excitedly. 'I could actually make this.' Then, a split-second later, the excitement faded from his face. 'But what would be the point? I will never be able to use it. Not without the game.' He put the book face down on the cover and pillowed his head on his palms.

'You're out there,' he said, speaking to the shadows and the cracks on the ceiling, the hints of darkness that crouched all around him. 'I beat you once, but that was only a skirmish, wasn't it? The real battles are still to come.' He could feel the presence. He was downstairs in the circuit boards and the memory of the computer. He was in the sighing wind and the grotesque faces the darkness made on his wallpaper.

You're even in my head.

Then all of a sudden there was something else in his head.

Dad slipped something into his pocket.

Phoenix jerked upright. 'That's right, he did.' Then the realization:

'It was a letter.'

Phoenix closed his eyes and tried to bring it to mind. A package, a small brown package. Then his eyes flashed open.

It couldn't be.

Could it?

Phoenix waited until the clock read 4.33 before he slipped out of bed and made his way downstairs. The worst moment was when he had to turn off the burglar alarm. Even though he closed the door to the cupboard that housed the alarm box, each time he pressed the key it seemed to yelp more loudly. But nobody came downstairs. He was in the clear. Padding down the hall in bare feet, Phoenix paused at the study door.

The lock. What do I do about the lock?

But almost before he had time to think, Phoenix saw the entire lock assembly as if it were part of a child's puzzle. He hurried to the kitchen, came back and rummaged until he found what he was after. Armed with a thin bladed knife, he set about picking the lock. After two or three agonizing minutes, it sprang open. Without ever wondering how he could suddenly spring a lock, he shoved the door open. Once inside, Phoenix searched the computer table, the desk, even the chaotic piles of paperwork.

Nothing. Then his eyes fell on Dad's briefcase. He rattled the catches. It wasn't locked.

The rest was simple: replacing the disc with a blank from Dad's store, copying the words *Vampyr Legion* on to the label in as good an attempt at Gothic script as he could manage, relocking the door and resetting the alarm. Phoenix was back in his room by five o'clock. With the disc safely hidden under a loose floorboard, he slept soundly.

No nightmares this time.

9

Phoenix wasn't going to be hurried. The game could be a trap.

But what if the trap can spring both ways?

He viewed *Vampyr Legion* without wearing the PR suit. He did everything consciously, systematically. Now that he had the disc, he was transformed. He had a say in his own destiny. He wasn't going to dash in headlong, as he had with *Shadow of the Minotaur*. He watched it all, the whole of Level One, from the moment the Vampyrs landed on the mansion house roof, through the frenzied battle in the cellar, to Captain Lawrence's brave sacrifice, and Ann and Bird's Eye's escape.

But that's all he did.

He watched.

He watched mother and son spilling onto the street, half-daring to think they were safe, then confronting the moon-born beast that shook its silver mane and howled eerily. Finally he watched them freeze, Ann and Robert Van Helsing, the Wolver, even time itself, waiting for him, Phoenix, to enter and set it in motion once more.

It hadn't been easy. Every fibre of his being itched to be there, standing between the two fugitives and their unearthly pursuer. But Phoenix had learned how the Gamesmaster thought, how he played with time and space. What the demon-lord was after was *engagement*, a connection with Phoenix's world, his coveted prize. And Ann and Bird's Eye were the bait. So Phoenix bided his time.

I don't need to hurry. I can wait for the connection.

And he had discovered it. It was the moonlight. What else

would it be in a tale of vampires and werewolves? The Van Helsings were hurrying through London's Edwardian streets, their shadows cast crisp and dark by a full, white, swollen moon.

'And our full moon is in two days,' said Phoenix. 'That's when the two worlds come into line. That's when we will write the remaining levels together, you and I, my old enemy.'

Phoenix continued his preparations patiently and in secret. He didn't drop a single hint to Mum or Dad, or even to Laura, his partner in the last adventure.

This time I'm going alone.

Nobody to worry about. Nobody to care about.

It's just you and me, Gamesmaster.

The precious interlude between getting in from school around 3.30 p.m. and Mum arriving from work around 4.30 p.m. became his time. That's when he combed the game for details, that's when he watched every movement of the Vampyr and the Wolver, how they sprang and how they attacked. That's when he moved around the study, shadowing their moves, inventing feints and strategies of his own.

It was also then, in the gathering twilight, that he fashioned the slayer's tool – the arbalest. He did it with a craftsman's eye, carving, mitring, honing. He prepared stock and bowstring, trigger and lever, groove and quarrel. Each part he made with meticulous care, laying it aside just before Mum walked through the door. There was no haste in his work. He was measured, steady. He felt his destiny as if it were as heavy and as solid as the stock of the crossbow. His last task was to give this killing cross a name. Finally, he had it.

He christened it 'Angel of Death.'

10

It was the night of the full moon.

Phoenix had never felt so focused on anything in his life. His concentration never flagged. Not when Mum mentioned Andreas quite unexpectedly over breakfast. Not when Laura questioned him anxiously about the game. He fielded their questions confidently, without once arousing their suspicions. Unbeknown to them, he had the disc, he had the PR suits, he had the will to fight. Nothing fazed him. His mind was on that evening's work: the suit that clung like a second skin, the disc that would open the gate between the worlds, the Angel of Death that would sing for him in battle.

I'm ready.

He did feel a pang of regret as he said goodbye to Laura at the top of her road. She had been with him on that first journey, and she had never been less than brave and resourceful. There was a time when she seemed to belong to the myth-world almost as much as he did. But this was his call. Destiny beckoned him, and him alone. He couldn't afford sentimentality. The stakes were too high. The Gamesmaster was pitiless. In the past he had used the people Phoenix cared about against him. Now it was time to tread the darkness alone. He glanced at his watch. 3.30 p.m. All the time in the world to lay everything out, to prepare himself, then to enter the game. But a shock awaited him when he let himself into the house.

'Dad!' Panic ripped through him. His plans were unravelling in front of him.

'Hello Phoenix.'

Phoenix was suddenly very aware of the Angel of Death hanging behind the chest of drawers, the disc under the floorboards, the darkening of the sky and the imminence of the full moon. 'But what are you doing back so early?'

'I've been waiting for you. I found something out today. About Chris Darke. It confirmed what we've both suspected.' Time was ticking by. Time that was precious. 'That stuff about a cult slaying. I finally managed to speak to the reporter who wrote the piece for the local rag. She took some persuading, but I eventually got her to spill the beans. Off the record, of course.'

Why didn't Dad just get to the point?

'There were puncture marks on his neck, Phoenix. Chris Drake had been bitten. Not by an animal. This was savagery beyond belief, deep, fatal gashes that gouged right into his shoulder. His body was completely drained of blood.'

Phoenix had barely listened until then. He'd been willing Dad out of the door so that he could make himself ready. But this!

'A vampire bite?'

'Looks like it. Of course the police have it down as the work of a madman. How could they imagine anything else?'

Phoenix was thrown into confusion. 'But how can that be? The demons can't break through. If they could, it would all be over by now.'

'I've been asking myself the same question, Phoenix. All I can tell you are the facts. Chris Darke was found dead in his own house, killed by a vampire bite.'

Phoenix could feel his pulse racing, the blood hammering in his head.

'You've got to be careful, Phoenix. The killer might come here.'

'Why would he?'

Dad looked flustered. He wasn't going to tell Phoenix he had the disc.

And I'm not telling you that you don't!

'I don't know, but if he were to come, just get out.'

'Don't worry Dad, I will.'

All the while they had been speaking, John Graves had been as jumpy as his son. 'Just be careful.' Dad glanced at his watch. 'I've got to get back to work. I've got a meeting at five. If I hit the motorway before the rush hour, I ought to just make it back in time.'

'But why did you go to all the trouble of coming home? Why didn't you just phone me?'

Dad shook his head. 'I had to tell you face to face. You were right. This isn't over, not by a long chalk. I'll see you tonight, then.'

'Sure, tonight.'

But you won't see me tonight. By then I will be gone.

To another world.

Phoenix watched Dad accelerating away down the road. He stood at the window a while, allowing his heartbeat to return to normal. It was time. There was no going back.

11

Laura was in a lousy mood. She'd forgotten her maths textbook and had had to run all the way back to school. She had had to almost beg Mr Owen, the caretaker, to let her in. Now, almost an hour late, she heard footsteps behind her, then a boy's voice calling her name. She turned.

'Phoenix? I thought you'd gone home ages ago.' Her smile vanished the moment she looked back. The road behind her was quite empty. 'Phoenix?' She wasn't imagining it. She had heard footsteps right behind her, familiar ones. Phoenix playing tricks. It had to be. He'd often waited around for her like this.

'Phoenix,' she repeated, 'This isn't funny. Come out.' Nervousness crept into her voice. Was it Phoenix? It wasn't like him to carry a joke on this long. He wasn't like other boys. Teasing wasn't in his nature. He was serious, loyal. It was while she was looking down the road, peering through the slight evening haze, that she heard the footsteps again. She knew now that, whoever it was, it wasn't Phoenix. He wouldn't do that. He wouldn't circle her the way a predator stalks its victim.

'Who's there?'

She wasn't a confident teenager any more. Here, on the lonely street, she became a little girl again, unsettled by the nameless menace around her. Fright was rippling over her skin. She was paralysed, scared to stand still, terrified of turning round.

'Why are you doing this? It isn't fair.'

Then it happened. Something brushed against her, barely making contact, but it was enough to make her gag on her own terror. A scream fought to escape from her throat, then clogged and died. She couldn't run, she couldn't scream.

'Who are you?' Those were her words, but the thought that was in her mind was:

What are you?

Pull yourself together, girl, she thought, you've been scared before. And by worse than this. But the presence was powerful. A raw, vengeful, pent-up power was there. Something familiar, but transformed. Something ordinary, yet alien.

You won't be weak, Laura, she told herself. You're going to run. That's the top of your street over there. You're going to turn and you're going to run. On the count of three.

Run! Before she could go even a few strides, her way was blocked. By a youth.

But more than a youth. A teenage boy whose lips drew back in a sneer, whose eyes flashed blood-red in the oncoming night, whose body seemed to blot out the milky whiteness of the rising moon.

Her heart went limp in her chest. Despair filled every fibre of her being.

'You!'

12

Phoenix didn't feel Laura's terror. He didn't hear her muffled scream or the scrape of her shoes as she was dragged away. He had work to do. He hurried to his room and took his rucksack from the top of the wardrobe. He felt around. Already inside were the things he'd bought for his mission: a mallet, steel tent pegs, strong line for sea fishing, several high-power torches. Fastening a utility belt purchased from the local DIY shop round his waist, he loaded the pouches. Before pulling his long top over the belt, he inserted the final item in his armoury, a small hatchet he had found in the garage. It was still as good as new. Phoenix quickly packed the result of his work over the previous few days. The sharpened stakes, the bolts, finally the Angel of Death itself. It was only as he turned to go that he became aware of the chill in the room.

'But I didn't leave a gale blowing through it like this.' The hairs twitched at the back of his neck. He stared at the wide open window. Phoenix flew to the loose floorboard where he had hidden the disc. Still there. Next he checked the room for evidence of a search. Nothing was disturbed. Everything was as it ought to be.

Everything except the window. 'Oh, snap out of it. Everything's here.' His sense of mission took over again. Slipping the rucksack over one shoulder, he ran to the study. Depositing the heavy backpack on the computer table, he pulled the PR suit from the box. Daylight was fading. The afterglow of the sun was a blood-red stain on the clouds. He slipped on the suit. That's when the first anxiety came. He couldn't help himself.

Experiencing that sliding closeness, the way the material seemed to grow into his skin, fuse with it, he felt fear flooding through him.

Keep your nerve, Phoenix. Now of all times.

He reached for the face mask that completed the suit. He was about to attach it to the suit when he made the discovery.

The second suit was gone!

He put his hand into the box. No doubt about it. This time he wasn't just afraid. He was filled with hopeless, gut-melting horror. This wasn't, this couldn't be Dad. Phoenix's nerves jangled. The window, the missing suit. What was happening?

Then came the moonglow. The dark seemed to fall back in awe of the full moon. 'No time to think about this now. I have to act. Before it's too late.' Pulling the mask tight over his face, he closed the last fastening and plugged the suit into the computer. While the disc was downloading, he pulled on the rucksack and waited. He watched the screen clearing and the first images of the game starting to flicker across it. But the evening wasn't done with its surprises yet. When it came to the game, everything came in threes.

First the window, then the suit, now . . . the message on the screen. Phoenix reeled as if under an axe blow.

A single word repeated. A stupid catchphrase that had become a byword for danger and betrayal.

Surprise surprise.

'Adams!'

My enemy. My nemesis.

Phoenix instinctively reached for the lead that linked the suit to the computer. Something was terribly wrong. There was still time to yank it out, time to call the whole thing off. His fingers closed round the lead, then just as quickly released it.

'No, I won't back out. So what if you're waiting for me?' As the golden light began to spiral out of the computer, shimmering with myriads of numbers – threes, sixes, nines – he clenched his fists. He squeezed until his nails were almost gouging his flesh through the thin material.

'I will fight you!' he cried. 'Fight you all!' For a moment the entire study was suffused with pulsating light then, without a sound, the brightness died.

Phoenix was gone.

BOOK TWO

The Book of Sight

1

Bird's Eye could feel his heart hammering, his skin tingling with fright. Then the crawling sensation was right inside him, setting off the panicky rat-a-tat-tatting of his heart. It was there in front of him and his mother. Tall as a man, but possessing infinitely more power, its steel-hard spine arched, its jaws bared, dripping blood and thick, viscous saliva.

The night-killer.

Wolver.

'Your crossbow?'

'Tom took it.'

Mum's face was set, her lips pinched into a thin, almost white line. 'I've got the revolver,' she hissed. 'But there are only two shots left.'

Bird's Eyed knew they wouldn't be enough. He had seen enough rippers to know they could take five, six or even more shots and continue their attack almost without interruption. The Wolver radiated menace. It was a giant; a grey, walking nightmare.

'Get behind me, darling. I'll try to hold him off to cover your escape.'

'No,' said Bird's Eye, 'I won't leave you.'

'You must! There is no sense in us both dying on this street.'

'I won't go!'

The Wolver paced from side to side, fire-red eyes piercing the night.

'Stinking hell-fiend,' snarled Bird's Eye. 'What's it waiting for?' Something rustled in the bushes. Bird's Eye felt his breath ball up inside his throat.

'Sucker,' whispered Mum, as the creature emerged from the mansion house garden. It had somehow survived Captain Lawrence's dynamite. Just. One taloned arm had been ripped away completely, leaving the shoulder socket exposed. White bone, grey flesh, dark blood. Its hideous face had been shredded by shrapnel and glass fragments. One eye was reduced to a mess of thick, tar-black Vampyr gore. But its murderous apparatus of attack was still intact. Razor talons, gleaming fangs.

'Sweet heavens!' gasped Ann, revolted by the spectacle.

Bird's Eye met her gaze. He knew what she was thinking. There was only one way to save them both from an appalling death. The revolver. It had two bullets in the chamber.

One for the mother. One for the son.

'Do it,' Bird's Eye told her in a voice that was firm, but stripped of hope. With the ripper and the sucker closing, Ann pressed the gun to his temple. He closed his eyes.

'No!' A strong yet youthful voice whipcracked through the evening air. 'Hit the ground!'

It was an unfamiliar command, but the Van Helsings got the drift, hurling themselves full-length on the pavement. Bird's Eye heard quick, agile footsteps as the newcomer raced across the road. A second sound followed immediately, that of the Wolver's powerful frame thudding onto the cobbled carriage-way. Bird's Eye saw a crossbow bolt sticking out of the beast's breast. The quarrel had pierced the ripper's heart.

The one-armed Vampyr stopped to examine the Wolver. There was no sympathy, only curiosity. Then the sucker locked onto the stranger, hissing and snarling its hatred. As the sucker prepared to attack, Ann raised her revolver and pumped both bullets into it. The Vampyr clutched its rib cage, watching the black blood oozing through its long, clawed fingers.

Then it leered.

It was a gesture of contempt. It tensed and hurled itself at

Ann. Instinctively, she flung an arm in front of her face, but the death-lunge never came. The sucker was down, a crossbow bolt sticking out of its side.

'Mother!' Bird's Eye yelled. 'I see another. The one who was missing from the cellar.' They'd wondered about the absence of the brood-master. 'A master Vampyr.'

'Run!' the stranger ordered. 'Get away from here.' The Van Helsings hesitated. 'I'm loaded and you're unarmed. Leave me to handle it. Go that way. Wait for me down by the river.'

Ann examined the adolescent boy who was giving orders with such remarkable authority. His manner, his speech, the cut of his hair, they all looked strange. But where was he from? She thought she had met all the Committee's European contacts. How could so adept a hunter be unknown to her? And how old was he? Fifteen, sixteen?

'We can't . . .'

'Please don't argue. Just go. I'll follow in a few minutes.'

2

Phoenix looked along the deserted street, first to the left then to the right. Bird's Eye had mentioned a Vampyr, a master. So where was it? Brandishing the Angel of Death, Phoenix poked the bolt into the bushes that overhung the garden wall. He glimpsed the scorched, shattered wall where the dynamite had gone off. Everything was still. There was no sign of movement anywhere. He was seeing things.

Taking advantage of the respite, Phoenix edged over to the Wolver. Gingerly, he knelt down and pulled the bolt from its side. Time to recover the tools of his trade. Wiping the blood off on its fur, he slipped the bolt back into the makeshift quiver in his belt. He glanced at his wrist, noting the score he had already built up on his points bracelet.

As if it were a game.

For a moment, Phoenix marvelled at his own composure. It was a feeling he had had in his first adventure. Not helplessness, not oppression, but a contradictory stew of terror and exhilaration. He had thrown off his own world as if it were an old coat, too tight, too worn, too familiar.

I'm born to this.

But the rules of the game had changed since that first foray into a myth-world. The Gamesmaster had dispensed with most of the trappings of the game. There were the points, but could he trust them? Might they not be just one of the Gamesmaster's deceptions? The demon-lord had stripped the game down but Phoenix was ready. He was continuing to retrieve his bolts for round two. Ruthless efficiency would be his strategy from then on. 'Now for the one I put into you, Mr Vampyr.' Phoenix's eyes scanned the street nervously as he knelt and tugged at the second bolt. This one was tougher to shift. 'Come out.'

That's what it happened. The Vampyr's unmutilated eye opened, making Phoenix's words die in his throat. With a hiss like water on a red hot hob, the sucker sprang, surging up like lightning, dashing the crossbow from Phoenix's hand.

The quarrel couldn't have pierced its heart. Why didn't I check?

Using his left hand to fend off the Vampyr, Phoenix felt for his hatchet with his right. But one hand was never going to be enough to stay the demon's frenzied assault. A spasm of pain jolted through Phoenix. The Vampyr's talons slashed at him, its blood-red eyes staring into his. It came at him, a scything of claws, a lunging of teeth. Phoenix thought he had got himself ready, but nothing could have prepared him for this. He saw the colourless lips draw back, revealing lethal fangs.

'No!'

He was squirming and flailing, fighting for his life. The points score was tumbling. Even with only one arm the creature was too strong for him. Phoenix could feel his strength draining away, but with one last effort he managed to yank the hatchet out of his belt and smash it into the Vampyr's chest. He felt its body rock, the honed edge of the axe-head crunching bone and cartilage, but its grip on him didn't ease even one tenth. Phoenix felt hope seeping out of him.

Csssss!

The Vampyr's mouldering face was so close, Phoenix was assaulted by the oily smell of death. Rotten-sweet, the stench of decay was almost overpowering.

'Get it over with then,' yelled Phoenix, feeling the hatchet bouncing harmlessly off his assailant's rotting, maggoty chest. But instead of completing the kill, the sucker loosened its grip on him and stepped back.

Why?

Two words provided the answer. 'Surprise surprise.'

Phoenix went cold. Adams. And then he saw her. 'Laura!' Adams was holding her by the hair, wrenching her head back brutally. 'So that's why you took the PR suit,' said Phoenix. 'To transport Laura into this hell, to use her against me.' Then a frown came over his face. 'But you didn't need to take it from the study,' he said grimly. 'You didn't need to come to the house at all. The Gamesmaster's factory is mass-producing them ready for the launch. Why take it from under my nose? Why leave that message?'

Then came the realization. 'You wanted to boast, didn't you? That's it, you wanted me crushed, you wanted to tell me you'd won.' He glanced at the points bracelet. His score was low, but it was still above survival level. 'Well, you haven't. I'll never give up.'

Adams affected a yawn. 'I'm not surprised you found your way through the gateway,' he said. 'My master expected as much. In fact, we welcome it.' He twisted his fingers through Laura's hair, making her cry out.

'Leave her alone,' warned Phoenix. 'If you want to fight somebody, fight me. I've beaten you before and I'll do it again.' He was trying to sound confident, but his heart had dropped through a trap door. There was something different about Adams. Phoenix couldn't believe how he had changed. The features were still those of the fourteen year old boy who had been his rival at school, but he looked taller, more powerfully built. His face was set into a mould of savagery. He was wearing a tunic that harked back to former times. He was dressed all in black, his jacket studded with iron.

'How long is it since we met last?' asked Adams.

'Six weeks.'

'Six short weeks,' sighed Adams. 'You won't imagine what I've seen, what I've done.'

Phoenix gave him a suspicious stare.

'You don't believe me, do you?' said Adams. 'So tell me,

how do you think I got like this?' He roared with laughter. That's when Phoenix saw the fangs.

'You're one of them!' he cried, his skin clammy with fright.

'A Vampyr? Why yes, so I am, for the purposes of this game. Not just any old Vampyr either, I am master of my brood.'

'Are you all right, Laura?' asked Phoenix, ignoring Adams' boasting.

'Well,' said Adams, relaxing his hold on her slightly. 'Aren't you going to answer him?'

Laura fixed him with a look made in equal parts of terror and contempt, then shouted, 'Run Phoenix. Save yourself!'

'Do you know,' Adams sneered into her face, 'I don't think your little playmate's going anywhere.'

The one-armed Vampyr had moved behind Phoenix, blocking his escape. It was unnecessary, Phoenix had no intention of fleeing. 'What do you want, Adams?'

'What do you think? On this, the first day of renewed hostilities, I will accept nothing less than unconditional surrender. A first step towards my master's rising.'

'You think I'm going to stand by while you get the game into every home. Think I'll give in and abandon the world to the demons? You don't know me very well, do you Adams? You can drop dead.'

Adams tapped his fangs and brandished his claws. 'Sorry,' he said, engaging in a show of gallows humour. 'But in a sense I already did that.' He chuckled at his own joke, then forced Laura to her knees. His talons pinched her flesh. The school bully had evolved into something that was barely human. 'What does it take to get some sense out of you, Phoenix? Maybe I should feed sweet Laura to our friend.'

The one-armed Vampyr looked interested, cocking its mutilated head and coming closer to Laura.

'Leave her alone,' snapped Phoenix.

Adams tutted. 'You're not in a position to give me orders.' Adams' voice had changed, filling with a low thunder. This too was new, true evil replacing the mischief of old. 'I don't think so, Phoenix. I've chosen my path, and my mentor. I left Brownleigh and our playground scuffles behind long ago. You will find that I have undergone a complete transformation, and I adore the new me. I think it's time you grovelled. That way, I may make the end merciful.'

He brandished his blade-like talons. 'One slash and I will open her throat from ear to ear. Now what have you got to say for yourself?'

'Don't touch her . . .'

'Oh, what next?' drawled Adams. 'You're so predictable. How does the speech go? *Lay a hand on her and I'll never rest until I make you pay.* You've watched too many movies, Phoenix. Well, forget it. This is the real world. The good guys don't have to win. Back in the old world I would have to face the consequences of my actions. Here . . .'

He spread his arms. 'Here I can do exactly as I wish, without fear of retribution. Hear that, I can do what I like. Don't believe me? Then watch.' His clawed hand stroked Laura's cheek, then ran slowly down her throat. A drop of blood oozed from the first slight nick he cut into her neck. The one-armed Vampyr moved in, intoxicated by the scent. It was thirsting after her. It wanted to feed. 'See how he looks at her, Phoenix, that wild, savage craving. Think I should give him a little taste? Just enough to make her one of us.'

'Get off her!'

It wasn't Phoenix's words which stopped Adams in his track, but a crossbow bolt that drilled itself right through his clawed hand. The bolt jolted Adams back, pinning his hand to the wall.

'Laura, run!'

She didn't need telling twice. Struggling free, she raced towards Phoenix, shouting a warning. 'Behind you,' she screamed.

Phoenix's eyes had been drawn to Adams squirming on the arrow. He had forgotten the one-armed Vampyr. Seeing Ann

Van Helsing wielding the Angel of Death, he appealed for help. 'Shoot!'

'No bolts,' cried Ann. 'I've just shot the one you left primed.'

Phoenix squeezed the handle of the hatchet. It slid in his grip.

Strength, don't fail me now.

He swung the axe with all his might into the Vampyr's face, taking its remaining eye and splitting open its skull. Bone crunched and jelly burst, black blood spilling into its evil mouth. Phoenix had recovered his will to win. Sheathing the hatchet he produced mallet and tent pin and hammered the pin into the sucker's heart. He felt skin and bone pop and heard the sickening gurgle in its throat. He drove it in hard and true, leaving no room for error. As he drew back, he wondered at his own ruthlessness. He was standing panting over the dead Vampyr when Laura shouted again.

'Phoenix, look . . .'

Adams had wrenched his hand from the wall and was slowly drawing the bolt, a shriek of pain bursting from his lungs. Phoenix raced across the road and snatched the Angel from Ann. Within seconds he had loaded and fired the quarrel, the bolt thudding into Adams' shoulder, doubling his agony.

'Now move,' Phoenix ordered, leading Laura and the Van Helsings from the scene.

3

'What made you come back?' panted Phoenix, quickly glancing behind for some sign of Adams.

'I saw the suckers,' Bird's Eye explained. 'The master and the legionary.'

'Saw them? How?'

Ann smiled indulgently. 'He doesn't mean see with his eyes. With his mind. Robert has a second sight. He has possessed it from infancy. He would be sitting in his playpen up in the nursery and I'd hear him say: *Grandfather*. Moments later there would be my father's familiar rap at the door. When he was six or seven, he once burst into tears. He claimed to have witnessed an old horse crumple and die on the road. I thought it was just his imagination. Days later I was to discover that the incident had occurred several miles away, something he couldn't have known about any other way.'

'I see the way a bird sees,' Bird's Eye explained. 'It's as if I'm up there, gliding on the air currents.'

'Hence the nickname Bird's Eye,' said Ann.

'Only I don't see things sharply,' Bird's Eye continued. 'They're not pictures. I see the shadows of things. I have to read them correctly. It's something I'm getting better at as I get older.' Phoenix felt something stirring inside him, a deep unease, and he knew better than to dismiss his instincts.

'OK,' he said dubiously. 'So if you're as good as you say, what's at the end of this alleyway?'

'It doesn't work like that,' said Bird's Eye. 'I don't choose the sight. It chooses me.'

Phoenix gave Robert Van Helsing another long, appraising look. 'We've got to get off the streets,' he said. 'I think I've only slowed Adams down.'

Ann nodded. 'Follow me. We will take the omnibus to Limehouse. I know of lodgings there, somewhere we will not be traced. The rooms are modest, but the landlady is a friend of the Committee. We will be safe there.'

Phoenix gave the street a final inspection. It seemed unlikely that they would be safe anywhere.

The omnibus ride was an uncomfortable affair. Uncomfortable because of the poorly upholstered seats. Uncomfortable because of the stares they were attracting. The game had transformed their clothes, but it couldn't do much with the colour of Laura's skin or her beaded locks. Phoenix looked out on to the streets of this unfamiliar London, a city at the crossroads between the nineteenth and twentieth centuries. The petrol-engined cars, taxis and buses vied with horse-drawn cabs and hansoms for every inch of bustling roadway.

'You went without me,' Laura whispered, more than a trace of accusation in her voice. 'Have I done something wrong?'

Phoenix glanced at the Van Helsings. 'It's not that I don't trust you,' he said. 'You know better than that. I didn't want you being used against me.'

'The way Adams used me, you mean?'

Phoenix gave a half-smile. 'He was a step ahead of me, wasn't he?'

'It isn't the old Adams. What's happened to him?'

Phoenix shook his head. 'I don't know. He was always a nasty piece of work, but nothing like this. I thought he was a bit of a buffoon really. I don't think I was ever actually scared of him. Now . . .' He remembered the curved fangs, the glinting talons. What was human in Adams seemed to have all but fallen away, leaving only the kernel of wickedness. '. . . I don't know.'

They were interrupted by a breezy shout from the conductor. 'Inkerman Street. All passengers for Inkerman Street.'

A pack of ragged boys tumbled down the stairs from the upper deck, laughing and hitting one another with their caps. Two old workmen grumbled and tutted and scraped their hobnailed boots on the floor. Ann leaned forward and tapped Phoenix on the shoulder.

'This is where we get off.'

Number nine, Inkerman Street, wasn't the flop house Phoenix had been expecting. It was a clean, well-kept, if sparsely furnished rooming house. The landlady, Mrs Cave, greeted Ann with an embrace and a kiss on the cheek. 'My dear,' she said warmly. 'I'm so glad to see you here.'

'Alive, you mean?' said Ann.

'And you, my dear Robert,' Mrs Cave continued. 'You're growing into such a fine, handsome young man.' She tousled his blond hair, and led them into a large kitchen. She stood with her back to the black-leaded range. Ann took a chair beside her.

'Are there any other lodgers this evening?'

'No, we are quite alone here.'

'Good.'

'I feared for you, Ann,' said Mrs Cave. 'After the dreadful news about poor Mr Bloch.'

Ann saw Phoenix's querying look. 'Bloch was the seventh member of the Committee to die,' Ann explained. 'You do know about the Committee?'

'I can make an educated guess,' said Phoenix.

'The Committee has been coordinating our efforts to resist this Vampyr plague,' Ann told him. 'At first we had our successes, but in the last few months we have suffered reverse after reverse. More and more nests of suckers, fewer and fewer fighters to destroy them. It has been dreadful, Mr . . .'

'My name is Phoenix Graves. This is Laura Osibona. First names will do.'

'Well, Phoenix,' she began, hesitating over the curious name, 'It began with my father, founder of the Committee.'

'Professor Van Helsing was the first man to warn of the Vampyr plague,' Mrs Cave interrupted. 'A great man.'

'He was ambushed and killed in central Europe. He died in Dracul's lair.'

'Dracul?'

'Lord of Vampyrs. Progenitor of the evil host. After Father's death, everything seemed to crumble. One after another, the leaders of our society fell, and all the while the Legion of demons grew in power. You find us at a low ebb, I'm afraid. But enough of us, how did you come to join the cause?'

Phoenix drew up a chair. 'You promise you will hear me out?' he asked. 'Even if what I have to say flies in the face of everything you believe to be true?'

At the end of the telling, Ann Van Helsing glanced at her son. 'Robert?'

Bird's Eye closed his eyes. For a few moments he appeared to be resting. When he reopened his eyes, he looked dazed. 'I think he is telling the truth,' he told her. 'Even now we are being watched. It is as though we are trapped, being controlled almost.' There was truth in Bird's Eye's vision. A world away, an anguished John and Christina Graves were watching their son's progress on the monitor in the study. All around them, the world was caught in freeze-frame. There was only one time now; the game's time.

'That's the computer,' said Phoenix. 'It's the gateway from my world into yours.'

Ann stood up and paced the tiled floor. 'Even that is not the most difficult thing to accept,' she said. 'From girlhood, I have accompanied my father into all kinds of crypts and castles. I have seen wraiths and ghouls and the shape-shifting creatures of the night. I have seen Hell in all its manifestations. It is but a short step to believe in other worlds. What I am unable to accept is that all of us here . . .' She indicated Mrs Cave and Bird's Eye. '. . . and all our comrades are unwitting pawns in some demon-lord's plan. Are you really trying to tell us that all this, our entire world, is a mere game and that we are a monster's playthings?'

'What would that make us?' Mrs Cave protested, 'Rows of clockwork toys waiting to be wound up? You insult us.'

'No,' said Phoenix, 'I'm not saying that.' He took a deep breath. 'Look, I'm sure that even here, in a myth-world, people can choose their own path. They *can* fight the Gamesmaster as you are doing. If that were not true, then everything truly would be lost.' He looked directly at the Van Helsings. 'What I am telling you is that he is always in the shadows, manipulating you. He aims to rule all worlds. Yours, mine and whatever other worlds lie out there, as yet undiscovered. And if you really want to know why you have lost so many of your comrades, it is because he has outwitted you all the way. Believe me, I have seen it before. Within your ranks, there may be people who, whether knowingly or not, act on behalf of the Gamesmaster. That is how he gains control. It is not only the horror, though that is real enough. He can control minds, twist thoughts, make people dance like puppets. Your world already dances to his tune. I won't let mine go the same way.'

Ann reeled at the revelation. 'Traitors! My father, all my friends were sacrificed by traitors?'

Mrs Cave started up from her chair. 'It's not true!' she cried indignantly. 'No, I won't have it. It beggars belief.' She turned on Phoenix. 'How do you know he can be trusted, Ann? What do you know about him? There were no traitors in our society. It is an insult to the men and woman who have given up everything in its service. Who could have known enough to destroy the organization? Only the Committee of Nine itself! With the exception of yourself, Ann, and one other, they are all dead.'

Mrs Cave built herself up for one last rebuttal. 'Are you pointing the finger at Ann, or at dead men?' she demanded. 'No Sir, there are no traitors. Unless, that is, you are the one the demon-lord has sent.'

4

The lights were still burning in Mrs Cave's lodging house at three in the morning. Though the gas lamps were turned down to afford some rest to tired eyes, nobody thought of climbing the stairs to bed. The cause of their restless vigil was Bird's Eye's sudden declaration:

'Evil is awake this night.'

Once dusk began to gather and shadows stole down the alleyways outside, Bird's Eye had been overwhelmed by a sense of foreboding. Evil was awake, and it had its eyes open. It was watching them, waiting to strike.

'What's that?' asked Laura, during one of the many lulls in conversation. All eyes turned in her direction.

'I didn't hear anything,' said Phoenix.

'And I didn't see anything,' said Bird's Eye.

Laura resumed her seat, knowing that her words didn't carry the same weight as Bird's Eye's. 'Sorry,' she said. 'Jumpy, I suppose. Maybe they just won't come.'

'They'll come,' said Ann. 'I trust my son's insights.'

Suddenly, Laura shot bolt upright, knocking her chair over. Everybody started. 'There it is again,' she said, eyes round. 'I'm not imagining it. I did hear something. Why can't any of you hear it?'

Phoenix cocked his ear. Outside in the darkness there was a scraping, crackling sound. 'Laura's right.'

Mrs Cave frowned. 'Well, I can't hear anything,' she said dismissively.

Phoenix disagreed. 'There is something. I'll . . .'

Nobody got to know what he meant to say next. At that very moment the back and front doors of number nine Inkerman Street were smashed in simultaneously, splinters of wood and metal fittings flying everywhere. The crash of the doors was accompanied by a nerve-shredding cacophony of shrieking and snarling.

'Arm yourselves!' Ann screamed.

Mrs Cave had provided a well-stocked arsenal. The deadly apparatus had been laid out ready. In the space of a few seconds, everyone was armed with a crossbow. Stakes, mallets and a pair of pistols also lay on the table, ready for use. They moved quickly to their places, following a rough sort of plan.

Ann and Bird's Eye were standing either side of the door which opened onto the hallway. Laura and Mrs Cave were kneeling behind the overturned table, using it as an impromptu barricade as they covered the back way. Phoenix chose not to join either position. Instead, he reserved the right to act according to his instincts. He stood in the middle of the floor, looking down the hallway. That's when he saw the first Vampyr. Its bleached, high-domed head was quite hairless. Its eyes were dark red points among the multiple folds of its wrinkled face. Its thin, colourless lips were drawn back to reveal stiletto-thin, razor-sharp fangs. As it advanced, he shot his first bolt directly into its chest. He knew before it hit the floor that it was dead. But one kill was never going to halt the Vampyr assault. The Legion cared nothing for its casualties, only for their master's victory.

'More this way!' yelled Laura.

They were pouring in through the scullery window, swarming towards their prey. Three of them. Laura got the leader, but as she tried to reload, she screamed. Danger had come from an unexpected source. Mrs Cave had pinned her arms and was pushing her towards the Vampyrs.

'Take her!' the old woman shrieked.

'Are you insane?' cried Laura. 'What are you doing?'

The sucker came on, making wide, scything movements with its arm.

'Get your head down!' shouted Phoenix as he sent a bolt thudding into the Vampyr's chest. Laura dug her elbow into Mrs Cave's stomach. Hearing a gasp of pain, she wriggled free and fled across the room. Phoenix, having quickly reloaded, dispatched the final Vampyr, then turned on Mrs Cave. 'You're one of them.'

Mrs Cave just laughed, flaunting her defiance. 'I serve a greater cause.' They were the last words she spoke. Ann Van Helsing turned and shot a bolt into her heart.

'She was a Vampyr?'

Phoenix shook his head. He bent down and pulled down the woman's high, starched collar, revealing a mark like a tattoo. It was in the shape of a bat. 'She was one of the traitors I told you about. This is the Gamesmaster's brand.' He glanced at Bird's Eye. 'Is the attack over?'

Bird's Eye shook his head. 'I see movement in the street. It's barely even started.' Then his eyes widened. 'They're below us. Get away from the middle of the floor!'

Hardly had the words left his mouth when the floor erupted, tiles spinning everywhere. A Wolver was bursting through from the cellar below their feet. Ann and Bird's Eye hit it in the back and throat with bolts. It howled, but it didn't die. Instead, it twisted round and the ferocious jaws snapped at them.

'Here,' said Phoenix. 'Take her. She's one of you.' He kicked Mrs Cave's body at the Wolver. Seeing the creature tearing the corpse to shreds, Ann pumped three shots into the Wolver's face and Phoenix set about it with the hatchet. The beast howled and bellowed with pain. It was shaking its massive shoulders, tossing what was left of Mrs Cave about like a rag doll. In a flurry of silver-grey fur and snapping jaws, it was gone, dragging the body away.

'What now?' asked Laura.

'We can't stay here,' said Phoenix. 'We'll be trapped inside this house. We've got to break out.'

'Which way?' Ann asked her son.

'The back,' said Bird's Eye.

'Sure?' asked Phoenix. 'I mean, you let those things creep up on us. What happened to the famous sight?'

Bird's Eye turned away. Tears were welling in his eyes. 'I don't know. I predicted their coming, but the attack still took me by surprise. I'm sorry.'

'Sorry?' snapped Phoenix. 'You nearly got us killed. And why didn't you know about Mrs Cave?'

Bird's Eye hung his head.

'Stop it!' shouted Ann. 'Why are you doing this? You're not helping.'

Laura backed her up. 'She's right. Why are you being so horrible?'

Phoenix scowled. If any of them had shared one iota of the suspicions that were crowding his mind, they would be acting in exactly the same fashion. 'Seems funny how this sight of yours conveniently failed when the suckers showed up, don't you think?'

Ann turned away. 'We're going out of the back door. With or without you, Phoenix, I don't really care which.' In the event, they emerged from the house together, hurrying along the back alley and into Sevastopol Street, which branched off Inkerman Street to the left.

'Which way?' asked Laura.

Phoenix held up his hand for quiet. 'I don't think it's over yet.' Sure enough, with a hiss, two Vampyrs dropped from a wall, taking Ann down by their weight alone, slamming her face on the pavement.

'Bird's Eye,' Phoenix yelled. 'Get out of the way. I can't get a shot.' The Vampyrs had Ann pinned and helpless. One was wrestling her over on to her back. The other was craning forward, its leering jaws seeking her throat. Still Bird's Eye stood rooted to the spot.

'Move!'

But he was frozen in horror, staring at the struggle in front of him. In the end, Phoenix had no choice but to barge him out of the way. He killed the first Vampyr with a single shot.

'Phoenix!' Laura handed him her bow and he released the trigger. He heard the punching crack of the bolt, but he didn't manage a clean kill. The sucker jolted into the air, and Phoenix saw it coming at him in a rage of pain and hatred. He wanted it slain, wiped out, annihilated, but he was disarmed. The Vampyr struck him a painful blow in the chest, winding him. Phoenix spun round, crumpling under the impact. As he crashed to the ground, the Angel of Death fell from his grip. The demon had him by the collar of his jacket. It was dragging him to his feet. Then he felt a spasm run through its body. Laura had grabbed Ann's gun and pumped two shots into it. Still it didn't let go. Phoenix saw the fangs flash and closed his eyes. He could feel the points bracelet throbbing on his wrist. He knew his score was in free fall. That's when the creature shuddered one last time and finally tumbled to the pavement.

Phoenix turned round to express his gratitude to whoever had come to his aid. 'Bird's Eye!'

It was Robert Van Helsing who had shot the decisive quarrel.

5

It was dawn before they were able to sleep, but when they did it was in spacious rooms, the daylight shut out by heavy, velvet curtains. At last they were safe. Vampyrs stalked the night. Come daybreak, they had to seek the shadows. Sunlight would turn them to ash. Phoenix stretched out on the crisp white sheets and smiled with sheer pleasure in the comfortable bed. Since the attack on Inkerman Street, Ann had given up her thoughts of hiding in another secret location. It was obvious that their every move was known to their enemy. She took them instead to the large town house of Ramsay Foxton, a friend of her late father. He and Ann were the last two survivors of the Committee of Nine. His house had become its headquarters. It was the thought of the Committee of Nine that wiped the smile from Phoenix's face.

Seven dead.

He frowned. Almost the entire leadership of the movement had been wiped out. Resistance to the Legion was hanging by a thread. Phoenix knew that Mrs Cave wasn't operating on her own. The Gamesmaster had to have more pawns working for him. But who were they? Phoenix lay back, allowing the images that had been troubling him to swirl around in his head. Adams was there, the Van Helsings, Mum and Dad and finally a man he had never met, but who may have had the greatest bearing on his destiny . . . Andreas.

Phoenix was woken some six hours later by a knock on the door. 'Yes?'

'There is a hot meal downstairs in the dining room,' said a female voice. 'Given the lateness of the hour, I hesitate to call it breakfast, Sir.'

'Why, what time is it?'

'Just before midday.'

'Thank you.'

Phoenix washed, dressed in the Norfolk jacket and flannels that had been laid out for him, and jogged downstairs, marvelling at the opulent surroundings. The meal was served in a large room with damask curtains. In addition to the long, polished oak table, there were armchairs, a sideboard and a piano. The Van Helsings featured prominently among the photographs that crowded every surface.

'Young Mr Graves,' said a silver-haired, bearded man in a wheelchair. 'I was unable to greet you last night, or should I say earlier this morning? I trust my staff looked after your needs.' Phoenix noticed the people who had admitted them on their arrival.

'Yes, thank you.'

Five minutes later, Laura and the Van Helsings joined them. While the four of them ate toast, bacon, eggs and roast potatoes, Foxton sipped lemon tea.

'Ann tells me you have an interesting story to tell, Mr Graves.'

'Call me Phoenix.'

'You believe the threat of Vampyrism is not confined to this world, Phoenix?'

'The power that threatens us goes far beyond Vampyrs,' said Phoenix, exchanging glances with Laura. 'Our enemy counts as his allies all the nightmares that have ever haunted the human mind.'

'And you believe Mrs Cave was just the tip of the iceberg?' asked a burly man who had been listening from across the room. 'Our society is penetrated by traitors?'

'This is Bradshaw,' said Foxton, 'Without his efforts, none of us would be here today.'

'I know that the Gamesmaster has been a step ahead of you for a long time,' said Phoenix, glancing from Bradshaw to Foxton.

Foxton stroked his beard. 'Given the scale of our losses, that seems plausible. The question is, Phoenix, can you finger our traitors?'

'This is my second day in your world, Mr Foxton. I will need time to understand how it works. In fact, I would be grateful if you would tell me what you know about the Vampyrs.'

Foxton glanced at Ann. 'You have here in front of you, Phoenix, our country's two foremost experts on the creature. I was a friend of Professor Van Helsing. You *are* acquainted with the professor's reputation?'

'He fought vampires.'

'He was *the* Vampyr-hunter. It was in an encounter with the hell-fiends in Transylvania five years ago that I lost the use of my legs, and the companionship of the greatest man I ever met. What do you want to know?'

'Everything.'

'From what you have said already, may I take it that there are Vampyr stories in your world too, Phoenix?'

Phoenix nodded.

'Black capes, garlic, crosses?'

'Yes, that's about it.'

'Then dismiss from your mind all that you have heard. You wish to know about the real Vampyr? It doesn't wear a black cloak. It is not afraid of garlic or running water, nor of crosses or priests of any description. Look in a mirror and you will see its face. Nor is it the tragic figure some popular fiction would have us believe. It doesn't have a conscience and it doesn't mourn past loves. There is nothing about it that is sympathetic or human in the slightest. Its heart is stone cold and utterly devoid of feeling. It is a predator's heart. It ticks like a clock and when your time is up, it kills without sentiment or hesitation. It slaughters its prey by tearing open its victim's throat, or by its bite which injects a sickness that causes a slow, agonizing death. Worst of all, it can transform the poor wretch into one of its own kind.'

Laura shuddered.

'The myth of the Vampyr is common to all cultures. The Babylonians, the ancient Greeks and Romans, the peoples of Africa and central Europe all have their Vampyrs. The Indonesians have the Puntianak, India the Vampir and Ireland the Dearg-dul or red blood sucker. It is, my dear Phoenix, a universal horror. The lord of all Vampyrs is Dracul. From his lair in Transylvania, his evil is beginning to reach out across the globe. He has welded these creatures of the night into a single force, the Vampyr Legion. As a result, the Vampyr we face is not the single, solitary, haunted figure you may have read about in some gothic tale. He is part of a vast army, an unthinking footsoldier of the Legion of the Undead which multiplies every day. As if that were not enough to contend with, Dracul employs a regiment of werewolves. The Wolver is a battering-ram. The moon-born beast can smash through a brick wall, demolish it in a trice. Its jaws are like mantraps. These are our foes, my young friend. They are as lethal and implacable as Fate, and at the moment we are losing the battle against them.'

'You must not be so pessimistic, Ramsay,' said Ann, interrupting. 'It's been this way before. It may take years, but we will prevail. We must.'

'Yes, my dear,' said Foxton, taking her hand. 'You're right.'

Phoenix listened with rapt attention as Foxton ran on, explaining the history of the Vampyr and of its generations of opponents. Finally, a full thirty minutes later, he spoke.

'Thank you, Mr Foxton. Now I have a sense of how my enemy operates in this world. But believe me, you have to forget this talk of a long battle. There isn't time for that. For the sake of your world and mine we have to destroy them, and destroy them now.' He sensed the magnitude of the task. 'If this is, as you say, an army then we have to take their general. We have to behead this Legion.' He thought of the invisible demon-lord behind the scenes. 'And even destroying Dracul is only the first step. The Legion is nothing compared with the evil that is running them.'

6

It was mid-afternoon that same day when Bradshaw burst into the sitting room.

'News?' asked Foxton.

'Oh, I've got news all right,' said Bradshaw. 'We've discovered the nest. A warehouse in Royal India Street, down by the docks.' The moment he made the announcement, something changed in the Foxton House. The air of dejection and pessimism lifted. It didn't have the atmosphere of a beleaguered fortress any longer.

'We must move quickly,' said Foxton, checking his watch. 'We have only two hours of daylight left. Leave a skeleton force here with me and take everyone you can muster. You must destroy the entire brood.'

'We won't fail,' said Bradshaw. 'We have young Robert's gift of sight to guide us.'

Phoenix looked up. He didn't share Bradshaw's confidence.

The Vampyr-hunters filled a car and a delivery van. The legend *Bell's Pies* was painted on the side of the van. By the time they were in position outside the warehouse, there remained less than an hour of daylight for their grisly task.

'Well?' said Bradshaw, looking in Bird's Eye's direction. 'Is our intelligence correct? How many do you see?'

Bird's Eye shook his head. 'You've been misinformed. I don't see anything. It's an empty building.'

Several of the Vampyr-hunters threw down their weapons in disgust.

'You're sure, Robert?' said Bradshaw. 'Absolutely certain?'

'It's an empty building,' Bird's Eye answered.

'Blast it! The man who gave us this information has never been wrong before. Kelly, Hewitt, come with me. We'll take a look around.'

'Mind if I come too?' asked Phoenix.

Bradshaw looked him up and down, then nodded. 'Aye, tag along if you wish, but there will be nothing to see. Young master Robert has always been completely reliable.'

You weren't at Inkerman Street, thought Phoenix, arming the Angel.

'You'll have no need of that,' chuckled Kelly.

Phoenix returned his look without a smile. Laura joined the group as they made their way to the door. The remaining Vampyr-hunters kept their disgruntled vigil outside.

'Ready?' asked Bradshaw in his Yorkshire drawl. 'Then let's go.'

Kelly raised his sledgehammer to dash off the lock, but Bradshaw stopped him and reached for the door handle. 'You never know.' Sure enough, the door was open. It only increased Phoenix's suspicions. The moment the party were inside they were assailed by a foul odour.

'Suckers have been here, all right,' said Bradshaw, pressing a handkerchief to his face. 'That smell of decay, I'd recognize it anywhere.'

Laura gagged. 'I feel sick.'

'It's strong,' said Bradshaw, leading the way down the wooden stairs to the floor below. 'We must have only just missed them.'

'Are you sure we *have* missed them?' asked Phoenix, every fibre of his being alert to the possibility of betrayal. 'I don't like this.' Bradshaw was about to answer when there was a terrible shriek.

'Sucker!' screamed Laura.

Phoenix alone had his weapon cocked. He was first to react, nailing the fiend to the wall with a crossbow bolt. He waved the Angel under Kelly's nose. 'Still think I don't need it?'

'Hewitt.' Bradshaw commanded urgently, 'Get up those

stairs. Warn the main party.' Hewitt was less than halfway up the staircase when a second Vampyr scuttled across the wall. It climbed the vertical surface as if it were running across the floor. Before Hewitt could reach it, the Vampyr had locked and bolted the outside door. Then there was an explosion of fury. A wall had burst apart, showering everyone with dust, plaster and bits of brick.

'Wolver!'

It tensed and hurled itself at the staircase, shattering it with the sheer force of its leap. Hewitt was thrown from the disintegrating structure.

'Back!' yelled Bradshaw. 'Load your weapons.'

Kelly was trying to drag Hewitt out of the Wolver's way, but Hewitt had fallen heavily and cried out in agony. Suddenly the entire building was echoing with inhuman shrieking and howling as Vampyrs and Wolvers spilled from every doorway, climbed from every grating. The appalling chorus was followed by a gargle of blood. The Wolver had claimed its first victim. It had caught Kelly unawares as he tried to help his friend and ripped out his throat.

'What happened to the boy's sight?' cried Bradshaw despairingly, seeing the creatures gathering in the gloom. 'He said it was empty. He didn't mention anything about rippers or suckers.'

'Or about masters,' came a voice achingly familiar to Phoenix. It was Adams. He stepped forward with a strutting arrogance.

'Surprise surprise,' he said. 'Our little home from home isn't so empty after all.'

Phoenix and Laura looked up. The windows were boarded up to keep out the sunset's rays.

'It's a trap,' said Phoenix, 'It always was.'

Phoenix, Bradshaw and Laura backed away pulling the half-conscious Hewitt with them. They were outnumbered and outwitted. In the tense silence they could hear the main party hammering at the outside door.

'Even if they force the door, it's a thirty-foot drop,' Bradshaw said grimly.

'What do we do?' groaned Laura.

'That's simple,' said Adams. 'Three of you die and Phoenix becomes one of us. Do you understand now? You're going to open the gate for us.'

'Open it, but how can I?'

'Believe me,' said Adams. 'You'll find a way.' He turned briskly on his heel and barked a single word:

'Attack!'

7

'Cover me!' yelled Bradshaw, drawing his revolver and turning to aim it at the windows above their heads. Phoenix and Laura shot their bolts into the crowd of demons and started reloading. In the same instant, Bradshaw shot out a window.

'Don't come through the door,' he cried to the hunters outside. 'The staircase is gone.' His warning didn't come a moment too early. The Vampyr-hunters had just sledge-hammered the door and were shooting a volley of quarrels into the demon ranks. 'Get the ropes from the van,' Bradshaw ordered, pumping shots into a Wolver that had come too close. Phoenix finished it with a bolt into the heart. More bolts showered down from the Vampyr-hunters above, thinning the ranks of the demons. As quickly as they emerged the night-terrors melted away into the dark heart of the warehouse.

Phoenix felt the breath shudder through him. 'That was too close for comfort.'

The main party had now joined them. Bird's Eye was pale and trembling. 'I was so sure,' he said. Ann put her arm round him. She looked as shattered as her son.

'There's no time for this now,' said Bradshaw. 'We have to finish the night-crawlers.' There was a low sigh from the darkness.

'They're down here,' said Phoenix, crouching over a grating.

The faces of Laura, Ann and Bird's Eye were as white as salt, their eyes blue points of terror.

'No matter how often I do this,' Ann said. 'I never get used to it.'

'I know,' said Bradshaw. 'Don't let the act fool you. Neither do I.'

Phoenix followed him down the iron ladder that led to the basement below. He would have chosen to be anywhere in the whole world, anywhere but that dank, infested warehouse. 'Anything?' he asked, peering into the gloom.

'Nothing,' Bradshaw replied. 'Just that appalling smell.'

The others followed. Then the Wolvers came, two huge silver forms detonating out of the darkness. There was a split-second between Phoenix and Bradshaw's bolts. Both hit their mark. The crazed howling echoed through the blackness. After that . . . silence.

'Lanterns,' said Ann.

As the flickering, yellow light penetrated the murk, casting vast, dismal shadows on the walls, Bird's Eye saw crates. 'That's where they must sleep,' he said. 'Suckers.'

Bradshaw nodded, and slung his crossbow over his back by a leather loop. He lifted the lid off one of the crates. 'Just as I thought,' he said. 'Nothing. They've all risen.'

'The moon is up outside,' said Bird's Eye. The words weren't out of his mouth before three Vampyrs rose out of the darkness, spitting and snarling. Candlelight cast sinister patterns on the ceiling and walls as the demons sprang from their hiding places, hissing and slashing with their talons.

'Shoot,' ordered Ann, giving the lead. 'Make every bolt count.'

Three quarrels, three kills.

'Don't drop your guard,' she warned. 'It isn't over.'

She was right. Through the half-light came half a dozen more, their red eyes blazing. The onrush of the ghouls claimed another victim.

'No!'

A man by the name of Beck was down, blood gurgling in his throat. Three of the creatures were around him, fangs bared. Bradshaw dispatched one while Bird's Eye took the second. But before Ann could finish the third, Beck was dead.

'They're still coming!'

Suddenly the bows were useless. The lightning-quick suckers were among them, flashing their deadly talons. Thinking quickly, Bradshaw snatched the sledgehammer he had used to smash down the outside door from one of the killing party. 'Everybody behind me,' he bawled. 'Ready with those bows.'

Sweat was glistening on his face and forearms. 'Blasted hell-fiends!' he roared. 'Back.' The swinging sledgehammer drove the Vampyrs back against the wall, where they crouched hissing. 'Bows!' The quarrels sang and the demons fell shrieking and flailing. Then the warehouse was silent, the only sound coming from water gushing from a broken gutter.

'Sweet heaven,' said Ann. 'How many more?'

There was no reply from Bird's Eye, only a hissing coming out of the murk.

'Lanterns,' cried Ann. 'Shine them over here.'

Bradshaw was raising the sledgehammer to break down a door when it burst inwards, flattening him with its weight. Two suckers were at him, their talons slicing through the sleeves of his jacket. They were leaning forward, lurching at him like polecats trying to flush a rabbit out of its warren.

'Get them off me!' It was a command, harsh and angry. Bradshaw wasn't a man who showed fear. Terror seemed to drive him into a savage fury.

The bolts crunched into the Vampyrs' decaying flesh, saving Bradshaw from their fangs, but the battle was still in the balance. The remaining suckers were spilling through the doorway at speed.

'Shoot!' screamed Ann, as a hideous ghoul-face loomed in front of her.

The battle raged on, but at the end of it all the Vampyrs lay dead. A few of the hunters were dabbing gingerly at slash-marks.

'Stake them all,' ordered Bradshaw, producing a flask of whisky. 'I don't want any nasty surprises.'

To the sound of points crunching into bone and flesh, Bradshaw poured alcohol over his mens' wounds. 'Ah, stop your squealing,' he snapped as they cried out in pain. 'It'll stop infection.' He took a swig of the burning liquid and looked around. 'We did it,' he observed. 'In spite of everything.'

Bird's Eye hung his head. He was waiting for Phoenix to add to his shame. But Phoenix had other things on his mind. 'Adams. Where's Adams?'

Bradshaw frowned.

'The Vampyr leader, the broodmaster. His body isn't here.' His words set off a frantic search. The Vampyr-hunters examined every crate, every recess.

'Anything?' asked Bradshaw. He got only shaken heads in reply. 'He's gone, Phoenix.'

Strangely, Phoenix seemed to have lost interest. He was looking at a printed sheet, stapled to one of the crates. It was a bill of lading.

'Where's Constanta?' he asked.

'Constanta,' said Ann. 'Let me see. It's a Black Sea port. That's where my father disembarked on his fatal journey to Csespa.' She folded the bill. 'We'll show this to Foxton.'

8

Back at the Foxton house, there was no sense of euphoria. Two men were dead, another badly injured. Then there was the question of Bird's Eye. But the casualties didn't blunt the group's determination. Rather, there was a renewed sense of purpose. Nobody doubted that they had won an important battle.

'Constanta,' said Foxton, inspecting the bill of lading. 'That's where Van Helsing and I began our ill-fated mission. The Legion is being recalled to Transylvania.' He was thinking of a mist-wreathed castle in the Carpathian foothills. The lair of Dracul. 'He expects us to follow.'

'Then we mustn't disappoint him,' said Phoenix.

'My dear boy,' said Foxton indulgently. 'You can't imagine what we will face there.'

'So tell me.'

Bradshaw and Laura were listening intently, as were the other Vampyr-hunters. Ann was comforting a distraught Bird's Eye in a corner of the room.

'When I close my eyes,' Foxton began, 'I can still see Csespa Castle. That is where Dracul is waiting. I see it as if it is right here in front of me, a monstrous building perched high on top of a rocky outcrop. It is surrounded by spruce and fir trees. The only approach to the castle is a rough track that winds up the steep hill. The walls are set with fortified gatehouses and there are towers at regular intervals all round the circumference. It is quite unlike a castle in our own country, however. The red-roofed buildings that rise from within the grey stone walls are of various designs. Three of them conical. The fourth is in the shape of a bell-tower.' He mopped at his brow with his handkerchief. The very mention of the word Csespa cast a shadow across his heart.

'There is a lime-washed barbican and there are slits here and there all around the fortifications, once used by crossbowmen to fire down at their enemies. Also set into the walls are small leaded windows, dust-grimed and dark like unblinking eyes. The entire building is alive with evil. It watches your approach, then devours you.'

Foxton placed his palms together, as if in prayer and rested his chin on his fingertips. 'That's Csespa.'

'It's decided then,' said Bradshaw. 'We pursue Dracul to his lair.'

Foxton looked into the coal fire and nodded. 'You're right. I only wish there were another way. I lost my greatest friend in that terrible place, the use of my legs too. We fought our way into Csespa, you see, all those years ago. In the depths of the castle we came across and slew a master Vampyr. The battle was long and hard. By the end, we believed we had destroyed Dracul himself. We were elated. We had cleansed the world of a dreadful plague. But just before dawn, as we camped in front of the castle, they came out of the heart of the night. Suckers by the score, rippers too. We lost a dozen men. We hadn't even posted a watch. What was the point? We had destroyed the head. The body would surely wither and die.'

He looked around. 'I had to witness Dracul killing Van Helsing. The creature laughed in my face and taunted me as he slashed my friend's throat.'

Ann looked away.

'Then he came for me. His strength was superhuman. He picked me up like a rag doll and hurled me from the walls of Csespa. He left me for dead on the rocks below.'

'Then we must return for two reasons,' said Bradshaw, 'To destroy this plague and to avenge Van Helsing. This time there will be no mistake. We will destroy him and all his kind.'

Foxton nodded. 'You're right of course. We must return.'

'But are we capable of such a mission?' asked Ann. 'After all, it was only yesterday that we were staring defeat in the face. Now we are preparing a crusade into the Carpathian mountains.'

'I've told you,' said Phoenix impatiently, supporting Bradshaw. 'There is no choice. If we fail . . .'

'Yes,' said Ann. 'I understand the consequences.'

'This project *is* achievable,' said Foxton, interrupting them. 'But it will require the coordination of all our resources. Our frail forces would suffer total annihilation by themselves. The Committee of Nine must be reformed. We will provide the heart of the organization.'

'We?'

'Myself, Ann, of course, and Bradshaw.'

Bradshaw gave Foxton a sideways glance.

'You Phoenix will be number four. Our European contacts will take up the five remaining places.'

'How soon can this be done?' asked Phoenix.

'I will send off the telegrams today,' said Foxton. 'Five of the Committee will be instructed to meet us in Marseille within the month. The remaining, and most important member will meet us at Constanta.'

'And who is he?' asked Bradshaw. 'Who is this final member?'

'His name is Nikolai Dimitrescu,' said Foxton. 'He was our guide to Csespa on that last ill-fated journey. He was also the most cautious and far-sighted of us. We couldn't convince him that the master we had slain was truly Dracul. Had he not left us to search the grounds of the castle for surviving Vampyrs, he might have suffered Professor Van Helsing's fate. He discovered me in the gorge below the castle.'

Foxton ran his fingers through his hair. 'I owe him my life.'

'And he can be trusted?'

'He has fought the Vampyr all his adult life,' said Foxton,

dismissing Phoenix's caution. 'He and his troupe of Szekely horse have resisted the demon plague right at its very heart.'

'It is decided then,' said Phoenix, rising to his feet. 'That leaves us with one piece of unfinished business.' He picked up a knife from the table and advanced on Bird's Eye.

'Phoenix, no!' He found his way blocked by Laura and Bradshaw.

'This isn't the way,' said Bradshaw.

Phoenix stared in bewilderment at their reaction. 'You don't think . . . ?'

He threw his head back and laughed. 'I'm not intending to hurt him. Quite the opposite, I want to save him.' He was met by questioning looks. 'He bears a mark,' Phoenix explained. 'Like the one on Mrs Cave. That's how the Gamesmaster controls minds and plants his own ideas. I have seen it before, in another world. The only thing to do is cut it out.'

'Cut it out?' cried Ann, horrified.

'Either that or the Gamesmaster continues to twist Robert's thoughts. May I?' Bird's Eye submitted to Phoenix's examination. 'Here.' He lifted Bird's Eye's fine blond hair to reveal a tattoo-like mark, no bigger than a finger-nail. It was in the shape of a bat.

'But how?' cried Ann. 'I have never seen this blemish. I would have noticed.'

'Have you been sick recently, or woken up feeling different?' Phoenix asked Bird's Eye.

'Yes,' said Bird's Eye. 'Two months ago. I was down with a fever for several days. It was while I was away at boarding school.'

'Then there was the opportunity,' said Phoenix. He held up the knife. 'Shall I continue?'

'Do what you have to,' said Bird's Eye. 'I won't be used by the fiend another day.'

Later that evening, while the fire was burning low, Bird's Eye dozed, a dressing applied to the back of his neck. Ann was watching over him. Phoenix was about to go up to bed when he noticed Laura slip away. Leaving Foxton and Bradshaw poring over a map of central Europe, he followed her to a large window at the end of the landing.

'Something wrong?'

'It's what Foxton said,' Laura told him. 'We'll be in Marseille within the month. The *month*, Phoenix.'

'You're thinking about home?'

'Of course.'

'I know it probably won't help much,' said Phoenix, 'But if it's like our last adventure, time hasn't changed there. Everything that happens here, whether it is weeks or months, it all goes by in the blink of an eye in our world. Your parents don't even know you've gone.'

Laura nodded. 'I understand that.'

'It doesn't help, does it?' said Phoenix sympathetically.

Laura turned and shook her head. There were tears in her eyes.

A universe away, in a nondescript market town called Brownleigh, John and Christina Graves were living in that blink of an eye, watching their son's progress through a dangerous and frightening world. The time on every clock in the house registered the same moment as when Phoenix had vanished into the computer. The traffic, the trees, the birds in the sky were all caught in freeze-frame. They felt no desire to eat or drink. There was no need to leave the computer screen. Though they could move and watch and talk, they, as much as anything else in the house, were subject to the suspension of time. And as they watched, the picture on the screen faded, crowded out by a snowstorm of threes, sixes and nines.

It was a message.

So it is on to Level Two, the realm of the undead. My domain.

Keep coming, young Legendeer, hurry on into my dark embrace.

How eagerly you race towards me.

Towards your death.

BOOK THREE

The Book of the Undead

1

The new Committee that met a month later in Constanta numbered eight. Dim candlelight lit their unsmiling faces as the brief dusk came and went. The rest of the party, including Laura and Bird's Eye, sat listening from the shadows.

'So where is he?' Phoenix asked rising from his chair and paced the floor. 'Where is Dimitrescu?'

'He will be here,' said Foxton. He waved his hands, palms down, but the calming gesture had precisely the opposite effect.

'Well, I don't like it,' Phoenix snapped. He felt the weight of their undertaking like an unbearable burden. 'This is important. Doesn't he know what's at stake here? He could at least be on time.'

The weeks of waiting had taken its toll on Phoenix. He was at his best when he was able to give himself up to instinct, to fight at the bidding of his ancestry. In those moments, when he responded compulsively, nothing could stop him. It was when he had time to dwell on the enormity of the task ahead that the modern teenager surfaced, sapping his will. Then he would fret and come close to despair. The train journeys, evenings spent kicking his heels in hotel rooms, the endless days at sea had driven him to distraction.

'Well, I say we get started without him,' said Bradshaw who, for all his fifty years, was also champing at the bit.

'No,' said the Swede Andersen. 'The quorum of this Committee is nine. All members must be present before such a crusade is launched. I say we wait.' His words won a murmur of approval. Phoenix, who had barely been persuaded back to his seat, leapt up and stamped to the window. He looked out, taking in the strange sights and smells of the small port. Night had fallen, and here and there in the inky blackness fires flared and candles glowed. What light showed under the central European sky seemed almost apologetic, dwarfed by the endless power of the dark.

'Wait!' Phoenix snarled. 'That's all we ever do. And while we wait, our enemy is gathering his forces. We have to strike, Foxton, and soon.'

'Oh, we will strike,' said Foxton, composed and patient as ever. 'But without Dimitrescu we would be going blind into Dracul's domain. I am not willing to throw this expedition to the wolves.'

Some of the Committee were exchanging anxious glances. They hadn't expected discord so early in the mission. In addition to Phoenix, Foxton, Bradshaw and Ann Van Helsing, seated around the table were Andersen, Schreck from Germany, a Bulgarian by the name of Sakarov and a squat Hungarian, Tibor Puskas. It was Puskas who spoke next. He stood formally, adjusting his waistcoat.

'Gentlemen, and ladies. We are all united in our aims. We have come from every corner of Europe to destroy the demon-lord. Let us have no arguments please. Discord can only blunt our purpose.'

Phoenix scowled.

You're out there somewhere. Dracul.

You, Adams.

And you. Gamesmaster. A trinity of evil.

'Please resume your seat, Phoenix,' said Foxton. 'If Dimitrescu is late, then he has good reason.' The way he said it hinted at some undeclared item of business, something between Foxton and Dimitrescu alone.

'Really?'

'Yes Phoenix,' said Foxton, 'really. There isn't a day that Dimitrescu hasn't faced the Vampyr, or at least felt its shadow fall across his life. He is a Transylvanian. He grew up with the icy breath of the demon on the back of his neck. He will be here.'

Phoenix was about to reply when he heard hoofbeats on the cobbled streets. Half a dozen horsemen were galloping wildly down the streets, as if pursued by all the fiends of Hell, sending passers-by scurrying for safety.

'Now that,' said Foxton with a broad smile, 'sounds like Nikolai. He does like to stage a dramatic entrance. There are those who say he can trace his ancestors back to the Mongol hordes of Genghis Khan.'

Phoenix watched the riders dismount. Three of them immediately took up positions at the front door of the tavern. Two more jogged round the back. His impatience and suspicion began to melt away. The speed and efficiency with which the horsemen inspected and then sealed the exits from the building reassured him. The group's sense of purpose and energy was almost tangible. Giving the street one last look, the sixth man marched into the tavern. He entered without knocking.

He wasn't tall, and his peasant's clothes were rough and ill-fitting. He was quite dark-skinned and had a thick moustache. His cheekbones were high and his features almost Asiatic. Set down on paper, none of this makes him particularly noteworthy, but the reality of the Vampyr-hunger was different. The sum of all those parts, when brought together, added up to one of the most striking men Phoenix had ever seen.

'I,' said the man standing in the doorway, 'am Nikolai Dimitrescu.'

An hour later, agreement had all but been reached.

'Though the roads are not good,' Dimitrescu argued, 'I am convinced that you should come with us, Ramsay. You will be able to complete the journey by carriage. If you were to stay behind in Constanta, you would be vulnerable to the Vampyr's attacks. We will all be exposed out there, but at least there is strength in numbers.'

Foxton laughed. 'I did so hope you would say that, Nikolai. I have spent too many years holed up in my study. It is time I was in action once more. After all, you don't need legs to shoot a crossbow.'

Phoenix was feeling better. Dimitrescu was decisive and committed to an attack on Csespa. 'What about Csespa?' Phoenix asked. 'If Dracul is there, why did you miss him last time?'

'The castle is huge,' Dimitrescu replied, stung by the criticism, especially when it came from a teenage boy. 'It is honeycombed with hundreds of passages and rooms. There are false walls and secret entrances. The entire place is a vast labyrinth.'

Phoenix and Laura exchanged glances. They knew all about labyrinths!

'But the creature we encountered was a murderous opponent. His minions defended him fang and talon, as if he truly were the Father of Darkness. The struggle was long and hard, and many a good man fell. The stubbornness of their resistance convinced us we had slain Dracul. Had you been there, you would have forgiven us our mistake.'

Phoenix nodded. 'I believe you. The one we seek is a master of illusion.'

Dimitrescu looked at Phoenix, as if appraising him, then ran his gaze over the members of the Committee. 'Like the darkness in which the monster lives,' he said, 'Dracul plays tricks on the eye and on the mind.'

'Did you ever return to Csespa?' asked Phoenix. 'Have you ever been back?'

Dimitrescu shook his head. 'To the castle, no, but I recently rode through the district. The darkness is strong there. There are many *moroi*.'

'*Moroi*?' asked Phoenix.

'Yes,' said Dimitrescu, '*moroi*.'

'The *moroi* are the undead,' Foxton explained. 'It is a far more common term in these parts than Vampyr.'

'Only a brave man travels the roads of Csespa in the hours of daylight,' said Dimitrescu. 'And after dark, none at all. The villagers shutter their windows and bolt their doors. There is precious little hospitality in that region.'

'So what you're saying is . . .'

'What I am saying,' Dimitrescu said, 'is that tomorrow we shall be riding into the jaws of Hell.'

2

The Vampyr-hunters left Constanta at the crack of dawn, hoping to slip out of the port unnoticed. By the time they set off, however, scattering the nightbirds by their progress, a substantial crowd had gathered to watch their departure. The four score spectators who had gathered at the tavern watched in silence, but you could almost touch their expectation. The front of the column was made up of Dimitrescu's Szekely cavalry, unsmiling men in grimy jackets and fur caps. The bodyguards who had accompanied Dimitrescu the night before had been supplemented by twenty more. They had spent the night at an inn on the edge of town. One of them was holding the reins of a cart, tightly bound tarpaulins hiding its cargo. Next came the Committee and Bird's Eye. They too were on horseback. Finally, clattering along with outriders to front and rear, was the carriage bearing Ramsay Foxton. Phoenix and Laura had joined Foxton inside, hitching their mounts to the coach. At the final crossroads on the edge of the town, an old man stepped forward, seemingly oblivious to the oncoming horses.

'Is it true what they say?' he asked, planting himself in their way. 'You go to slay the *moroi*?'

'What business is it of yours?' demanded Dimitrescu, reining back his steed.

'Only this,' the old man replied. 'I have just arrived from my home in Csespa. I was driven out by the *moroi*. The undead killed my wife and daughter. There is only one thing I want from my life, and that is to see this land cleansed of the *moroi*.

Take this token. It will convince the people of Csespa that you are serious in your undertaking.' He produced a wooden figurine. It represented a young girl, sleeping with her arms crossed over her breast. The foot of the statuette had been carved into a deadly point, like a stake. 'It is from the wood of the fir tree. You understand its significance, your honour?'

For a moment, the old man stared at Dimitrescu as if he recognized him. Then Dimitrescu nodded and accepted the offering before waving the column on. Phoenix and Foxton looked back, watching the old man disappear into the mist of daybreak.

'Why a fir tree?' Laura asked out loud.

Turning away from the window, Foxton answered her: 'There is a custom in Transylvania of planting a fir tree above a Vampyr's grave. The root is meant to pierce the heart of the undead buried beneath.'

Laura shuddered. 'I wish I hadn't asked.'

'No, my dear, don't try to shut it out. If you are to survive in these parts, you must face the truth, however ugly.'

'Fine,' said Laura. 'So you want me to scare myself silly. Tell me about Csespa then. What are we getting ourselves into?'

'The village lies in a bleak corner of the Carpathian foothills. It abounds with tales of the undead. There are three manifestations of the ghoul.'

Three.

'The *moroi*, the male, you have already heard about,' Foxton continued, unaware of the significance of the number. 'The feminine form of the demon is the *strigoi*. Then there is a creature which changes into animal form, such as a dog or a wolf, the *pricolici*.'

'The Wolver,' said Laura.

Phoenix was preoccupied, still reflecting on the way the three forms of the Vampyr mirrored the number patterns that ran through the myth-world.

'Quite,' said Foxton, smiling at Laura. 'The Wolver. We will find the moon-born waiting like a hellish watchdog, guarding the approaches to Csespa. Towering over the village is the castle itself. It is much more like a stone pile. It is a silent, brooding reminder of the Vampyr's presence. Though the local people hate the ghoulish plague that has blighted their lives for generations they do not take kindly to strangers and refused point blank to cooperate with our last expedition.'

'So we will be on our own?'

'Unfortunately, yes.'

Some hours later they took a winding path through an entangled forest. In the woodland gloom, conversation died. It was only after they had been moving through the woods for over half an hour that Laura spoke.

'How far is it to Csespa?'

'Two days' ride,' said Foxton, 'Given favourable conditions. We will rest overnight at Buzau, then go on into Transylvania tomorrow.'

'The last time you made this journey,' Phoenix asked, 'how long before the demons started taking notice of you?'

'Oh, they've been watching us ever since we disembarked,' said Foxton. 'You can be certain of that. But if you are asking about the attacks, they began the second night, a few hours ride from Csespa.'

'But you fought them off?'

'Yes, we won our skirmishes, both on our way to the castle and within. Looking back, however, I can't help but wonder whether the whole thing wasn't all an elaborate charade, a trick to put us off the scent of Dracul himself.'

'So you expect it to be harder this time?' asked Laura.

'Yes, my dear,' said Foxton candidly. 'I expect our approach to bring a tempest down around our heads. Darkness will strike back with all the fury it has at its disposal. But we have two advantages. First, our young friend, Bird's Eye. We will have need of that sixth sense of his.'

'So you believe Bird's Eye is free of the Gamesmaster's control?' Laura asked.

'Yes, I am quite sure he is.'

'You mentioned *two* advantages,' said Phoenix.

'That's right,' said Foxton, his eyes twinkling. 'The other is your good self.'

'Me!'

'Of course. That is why I still believe young Robert's vision. No false modesty, please. You have added an extra dimension to our cause. At last we have an explanation for the Vampyr's actions. We believed him to be engaged in wanton destructivness and evil. Now we can see more clearly. He has a purpose, the invasion of your world, and that means he has a weakness too. In your own way, you have insights every bit as important as Robert's. Ann and Bradshaw have both remarked on it. You meet the Vampyr's ruthlessness with a determination every bit as pitiless. You anticipate his actions. You were born for this.'

There it was again, the rumour of destiny. Phoenix looked away and stared out through the screen of fir trees towards the distant mountains.

Is that what I am to become, a pitiless hunter?

He watched the sun's progress behind the tall trunks. It was a pale yellow orb, following them. It reminded him of an eye, an unblinking, all-seeing eye. Like the eye of the Gamesmaster.

'Foxton,' he asked, without turning. 'How do you rate our chances?'

Foxton smiled grimly. 'Better than ten to one, worse than evens. Does that answer your question?'

Phoenix felt a tremor go through him.

There is no going back. Your destiny awaits you.

He met Foxton's eyes. 'It isn't the answer I would have liked, but it's an honest one. When the time comes, I will be ready.'

Foxton smiled. 'I never doubted it for a moment.'

3

The innkeeper accepted their custom without question. Not so his patrons. The moment they laid eyes on the Szekelys, they started to point and shift uneasily in their seats. Dimitrescu said something to them in gruff Romanian.

'What was all that about?' asked Laura.

'The words are too coarse for a young lady's ears,' Puskas told her. '*Good night, gentlemen,* would be an adequate translation.'

Ann shook her head while the German Shreck chuckled mischievously.

'How many nights will your honour and his entourage be staying?' asked the innkeeper, trying in vain to disguise his unease.

'Just the one,' said Foxton, taking over from Dimitrescu. He seemed keen not to ruffle the locals' feathers. His bridge-building didn't get very far. It was immediately undone when Dimitrescu set down the figurine given him that morning on the road out of Constanta. The handful of men who had been drinking at the tables got up noisily and left. The innkeeper shrank back, crossing himself.

'You seek the *moroi*?' he gasped.

'That's right,' said Ann. 'We do.'

'Then you must go,' the innkeeper said in a barely audible whisper. 'You will bring the night-plague down on this house.'

Foxton was about to negotiate, but Dimitrescu made his intentions clear by planting himself at a table and putting his feet up.

'I think that means we're staying,' Bradshaw announced, taking a seat opposite Dimitrescu.

'Stay then,' said the innkeeper. 'But you will be alone. After dark, they will come. And, believe me, when they do no sane man would choose to be here. My wife and I will leave you now. Anything you find in my humble inn, you may have. You have the run of the place. It is the privilege of dead souls.'

The speech cut little ice with Ann, Foxton, Bradshaw and the Szekelys, but Bird's Eye and Laura listened wide-eyed.

'We will stay with family until you are gone. I would be grateful if you would pay your board in advance.' He took his money. 'Thank you. And may God have mercy on your soul.' Whipping off his apron, he started barking orders to his wife and staff. Within minutes, the place was virtually empty.

'You will rue the day you passed this way,' hissed the innkeeper, in his broken English. 'I warned the Darkman, but he wouldn't listen. He never returned.'

Dimitrescu and Bradshaw laughed, but Phoenix didn't. He stared after the innkeeper as he hurried away.

'Something wrong?' asked Foxton.

The Darkman. Or a man called Darke?

Phoenix was after him in a split second. 'Wait,' he cried. 'Tell me about the Darkman. I want to know about him.'

'I have nothing to say to you.'

Phoenix drew the Angel of Death. 'Oh, I think you do. Now, the Darkman.'

The innkeeper sighed. 'He was like you, a stranger. English. He came alone. If you are interested he left some of his belongings in his room. They are behind the counter.' He stretched out a hand. 'A few coins and they are yours.'

Phoenix scowled, and offered him nothing. 'I want to know about the Darkman.'

'We warned him of the dangers, but he just laughed. He treated the *moroi* as a joke. It was all a game to him.'

That's right. A game. And it killed him.

'When the Darkman left, he wasn't alone. He was being followed.'

'Followed? Who by?'

'A *moroi* such as I have never seen. One who walks by day.'

Phoenix started.

Adams.

'I wanted to warn the Darkman,' the innkeeper babbled. 'But I feared the consequences. You must understand, I have a family.'

Phoenix waved him on his way with the stock of the Angel. 'Yes, I understand.'

'What was all that about?' asked Foxton, the moment Phoenix walked back in.

'We're not the only ones to come in search of Csespa castle,' said Phoenix. He glanced at Laura. 'A man from our world, Chris Darke, came this way recently.' Laura gasped. Meanwhile, Phoenix stepped behind the counter and pulled out the innkeeper's ledger. 'Yes, here's his name.'

Foxton looked at the signature, then flicked the page back and forward. 'You mean he came alone?'

'That's right.'

'One man?'

'One man.'

'Was he mad?'

'No,' said Laura, 'Not mad. But he didn't have a clue what he was letting himself in for.'

Foxton frowned.

'The computer we told you about,' Phoenix explained. 'The machine that brought us here. This piece of equipment . . .' He showed them the points bracelet. 'He uses them to turn the events here into a game.'

'A game!' roared Bradshaw indignantly. 'A game, you say? Odd sort of game that has murdered so many of my comrades.'

'I promise you,' said Phoenix, 'That's it, a complex, addictive and deadly game. That's how the Gamesmaster is going to open the gateway between the worlds . . .'

'By disguising it as an entertainment?' asked Bradshaw incredulously.

'That's right.'

Phoenix searched for Chris Darke's belongings. He laid them out and gave a low whistle.

'What is it?'

'His notebook. See these numbers?' he indicated a row of threes, sixes and nines.

'This is the language of the game.'

'Ah,' said Foxton. '*Omnia in numeris sita sunt.*'

'I beg your pardon?'

'A phrase from the ancient science of numerology: everything lies veiled in numbers. They say . . .'

Foxton's explanation was cut short. Bird's Eye suddenly stumbled against the counter. 'I see it,' he said. 'I see the gateway between the worlds. It came when you mentioned the numbers.'

'You see it? How?'

'For a moment, I glimpsed how it opens. I saw both you and Laura standing before it. Don't believe me? Then I'll describe it to you. I see a golden portal, multiples of three etched in silvery light around the edge of the gateway. Is that it?'

'Yes,' Phoenix replied. 'That's it exactly. But where?'

'Give me a moment,' said Bird's Eye. 'Yes, I see a room with an exit but no entrance. That's where the gate can be opened.'

'An exit but no entrance,' Laura repeated. 'Now he's started talking in riddles. What's that supposed to mean?'

Bird's Eye shook his head. 'I don't know, but it's up there . . .'

He looked out of the window at the evening mist stealing like smoke up the mountainside. 'It's in Csespa castle!'

4

The Legion came an hour before dawn. Bird's Eye had predicted as much about ninety minutes earlier, starting from his troubled sleep with a cry of terror. The mind-pictures tore through him. He didn't understand at the time why his announcement hadn't generated more excitement. There was a burst of activity around the doors and windows as eyes searched for an invisible enemy, but as the minutes ticked away, most people soon slipped back into an exhausted sleep. Only Phoenix, Bradshaw and the Szekelys remained alert at their posts. When the attack finally came, it was the Wolvers first, smashing their way through the wooden shutters of the tavern as if bursting through a paper screen. Such was the speed of the assault, that Bird's Eye had barely had time to shout a warning before they were inside the building.

'Rippers!'

They roared ferociously, unleashing a din that thundered in his skull until he staggered back from the pain of it. His throat was so dry and tight, he could imagine what it would be like to be strangled from within. He had predicted this. So why had they done so little? Why weren't they better prepared?

'Help me!'

Bird's Eye had edged towards the windows just before the attack. Unwisely, he had neglected to take his crossbow with him.

'Help!'

The nearest of the beasts exploded into the air, snapping and snorting with all the blind savagery of a hurricane. It was upon

Bird's Eye in an instant, pinning him to the floor with a huge paw. The needle points of its fangs began to close over him.

'No!'

Phoenix was coming at the run, bringing down the ripper with a single shot from the Angel. Bird's Eye gratefully scrambled from under its terrible weight. By the time he got to his feet the room was a confusion of clattering bolts, waving torches and snapping Wolvers. The first skirmish barely lasted two minutes and ended with every one of the rippers lying dead.

Ann turned towards her son. 'Is it over?'

Bird's Eye shook his head. 'It has barely even begun. Take a look if you wish. Out there.'

Laura ran to the nearest window. 'Oh no!' she cried.

There in the moonlight were more Wolvers. Twenty of them. Battle-strength. Their baying echoing and re-echoing round the walls of the town square. The Vampyr were following, their eerie, almost featureless faces gleaming in the half-light. Bird's Eye tried to control his galloping heart. He picked up his bow and clutched it hard.

'What happened to Dimitrescu and his men?' he demanded. 'They were all here an hour ago and now they're nowhere to be seen. And where's Bradshaw?'

This time he wasn't sure what he was seeing. There was something, definitely something. A shifting in the darkness. Grey etched against black. But whether it was friend or foe, he just couldn't say.

'Why don't they attack?' asked Laura, staring at the ranks of the demons. Her face was gleaming with a sheen of sweat.

Phoenix smiled and walked behind the counter. 'They're looking for the Szekelys.'

While Laura was still wondering what there was to smile about, Phoenix laid the Angel on the floor and took a longbow from its hiding place behind the counter. 'Now, Bradshaw,' he shouted.

Bradshaw appeared from a side room. He lit the end of the

specially prepared arrow and handed it over. Drawing the bowstring to his ear, Phoenix moved to the window and shot high into the air, tracing an arc of light over the square.

'What are you doing?' demanded Laura.

The rippers and suckers were pushing and jostling, staring at the arrow's fiery path.

'What's going on?'

Phoenix tapped his nose. 'You'll see.'

Which is exactly what Bird's Eye did at that very moment.

He saw.

He saw Dimitrescu and his men emerging from doorways all around the square. He saw the flaming arrows being aimed and fired at the encircled ghouls. He saw a fiery ring of death. 'You knew about this!' he cried.

Phoenix nodded. 'Of course I did.'

'You knew?' Laura repeated. 'You knew, and you didn't say anything!'

Phoenix walked straight past his friends. 'What was there to say? You were dozing off again. We had to make preparations.'

'You could have kept us awake,' Laura retorted. 'We had a right to know what you were doing.'

'I haven't got time to stand here arguing the toss,' said Phoenix. 'A few of us decided to act on the information Bird's Eye gave us. It allowed you to snatch some sleep. Now, we can argue the rights and wrongs of our decision later, if you want. But we've got a fight on our hands. The battle isn't over yet.'

It was true. The monsters in the middle of the square had been destroyed but more were massing in the side streets, hissing and baying, tensing for the final charge. It was beyond the Vampyr-hunters' worst imaginings.

'So many,' murmured Bird's Eye.

Like an ocean of death.

Vampyr fliers were settling on the rooftops, ready to plunge down and feed on the people below. Laura, Bird's Eye and Ann exchanged glances and followed Phoenix outside. Dimitrescu and his men had saddled up and were forming a line, blazing arrows aimed at the advancing monsters. The rest of the Vampyr-hunters took up positions along the wall of the inn, bows trained on the Legion's ranks.

Then it began, the hammer-blow onslaught of the Wolvers and the shrieking, hissing attacks of the Vampyrs. The Szekelys thinned the demon ranks with their death-torches, but their arrows could not halt the Legion's advance. Puskas fell first, screaming hideously as he was carried off by a Wolver. Schreck was taken moments later, caught unawares when a Vampyr burst from a darkened doorway. Within seconds he was overwhelmed by a pack of suckers.

'There are too many!' screamed Andersen.

He was right. The advantage the Vampyr-hunters had won by surprise was being lost because of the overwhelming superiority of the Legion's numbers.

'Get inside!' yelled Dimitrescu, motioning to his men to dismount.

The second phase of the battle had begun. The Szekelys defended the ground floor, everyone else the first floor. The Wolvers were propelling themselves forward in furious waves, crashing into the walls, and though the defenders' bolts and arrows took a heavy toll, the momentum of the attack never slowed. The Vampyrs added their own contribution, spitting and screeching as they swarmed over the roof and upper balconies, trying to gain entry.

'Ann, Bird's Eye, Laura,' yelled Phoenix, running downstairs from the upper floor, 'come with me.'

'You need us now then?' Laura retorted, not yet ready to forget the way he had left her in the dark.

'Are you coming or not?'

Bird's Eye almost dropped his bow as he reached the top of the stairs. In the thirty seconds it had taken Phoenix to summon them, the suckers had broken through, driving Sakarov and Andersen from their positions and onto the landing.

'Get back!' yelled Phoenix.

The men flattened themselves against the wall and the crossbow bolts hissed their lethal message.

'Where's Bradshaw?' shouted Phoenix as he reloaded. 'And Foxton?'

'In here,' shouted Foxton. 'Quick!'

Phoenix and Bird's Eye almost collided with Bradshaw as he backed towards the door. He was engaged in hand-to-hand fighting with two Vampyrs. As Sakarov followed Phoenix into the room, Ann cried out in terror. Over their shoulders she had seen Foxton being dragged towards the window.

'Stop them!'

Phoenix raised the Angel, but his shot was blocked by Bradshaw as he wrestled off one of his assailants and dispatched it with a stake. Ann pushed past the pair of them and shot the Vampyr to Foxton's left. It gave him the chance to get a handhold on the window frame. Bird's Eye and Laura took the remaining ghouls and Foxton fell heavily to the ground.

'Thank you,' he panted, grimacing with pain.

But still the battle raged as more and more suckers swarmed through the windows and down through holes they had torn in the roof.

'We're not holding them!' shrieked Andersen as three suckers surrounded him. 'It's finished.' But nobody else believed they were finished.

Bradshaw was fighting like a madman, with stake and hatchet. Sakarov joined him, and the two stood back to back, taking on the Vampyrs in close combat, while Ann, Bird's Eye and Laura did their best to keep out further Vampyrs with steady volleys of crossbow quarrels. Satisfied that they were holding their own, Phoenix ran to Andersen.

'Get off him!'

The suckers were clinging to him, ripping and tearing at one another in their feeding frenzy. Phoenix shot his bolt into the nearest of them, then hammered a stake into the second. The third came up at him, spitting and snarling. The sheer power of the attack caught him off balance and the boy and fiend tumbled fighting down the stairs. As they hit the floor at the bottom, Phoenix saw the creature above him. Its eyes were like dark stones, its fangs curved and dripping venom.

'No!'

As the Vampyr lunged forward, he smelt the sour death-decay on its breath.

'No!'

Then it shuddered. It threw back its head and shrieked. A flaming arrow was sticking out of its back. It was the work of Dimitrescu. Suddenly the roaring and shrieking was abating, replaced by a strange rustling and crackling.

'What's happening?' Phoenix asked.

'They're retreating,' said Dimitrescu, wiping the sweat from his forehead. 'It's dawn.'

5

By the time the townspeople finally decided it was safe to emerge from their homes, the funeral pyres of Schreck and Puskas were burning fiercely in the town square, sending a plume of grey smoke into the clear morning sky. Bradshaw, always businesslike, had begun the process of purification within minutes of the Legion's forced retreat. The innkeeper was among the first to approach the Vampyr-hunters, eyes bulging and arms windmilling in a show of outrage.

'See the destruction you have brought upon our town,' he cried. 'Look what you've done to my tavern.'

Foxton shook his head wearily and threw something to Dimitrescu to pass on.

'Here,' said Dimitrescu, depositing a fat purse in the innkeeper's hand. 'Now stop whining. There will be enough here to return your wretched tavern to normal. Take it and get on with your miserable, little life. You should be thanking us for what we have done, not ranting on about your precious building. Roofs and windows can easily be mended, but what about broken bodies and shattered lives? Nothing short of bitter struggle will drive the Vampyr from our land.'

'You can't end the horror,' shouted a priest who had been listening from the church doorway opposite. 'We have endured the *moroi* for centuries. Evil never sleeps, my friend. We will have to learn to live with it for many more. Go home. We don't want you here.'

'What?' cried Dimitrescu, 'Endurance, is that all you can offer? Is that the way you want your people to live? Will you really permit the endless slaughter of innocents? No, I will not go away. Our crusade will continue.'

The innkeeper seemed to speak for most of the townspeople. 'Well, we want none of it. All you are going to do is bring worse disaster down about our heads. So the blood-suckers take the odd unfortunate. The rest of us go on living, don't we? We bury our dead and struggle on. Now, clear out and leave us to repair the damage.'

Dimitrescu shook his head. As he passed Phoenix, he spoke sadly. 'Not all my people are such cowards.'

'They're not cowards,' Phoenix replied. 'Just too terrified to fight back. We have to show them the darkness can be defeated.'

Dimitrescu nodded grimly. 'That's just what I have been trying to do for twenty long years, and I'm growing tired.'

'There's a difference,' said Phoenix. 'This time we can finish it.'

'You really believe that?'

Phoenix remembered Bird's Eye's vision of the gateway and the glowing numbers. Csespa castle was only a day's ride away. It was up there amid the dense carpet of pine and spruce and the rolling mist, and it held the promise of a reckoning with the Gamesmaster and the journey home.

'Yes, this time we really can finish it.'

Dimitrescu shoved his way past the hostile townspeople and started inspecting the horses. Phoenix watched the Szekely leader patting his own horse and talking soothingly to it. Then, detaching himself from the complaining innkeeper, he sought out Laura.

'Still mad at me?'

'Not really,' she answered. 'I just felt you were treating me like a kid last night.'

'We didn't want to make too much of a song and dance,' Phoenix explained. 'We could have alerted the Legion to what we were doing. Then . . .' He paused. 'It doesn't bear thinking about.'

Laura turned to look at him. 'You're changing.'

'Am I?'

'You don't talk to me as much as you used to. You hardly act like a teenager any more. You were always serious. Now . . .'

'Yes,' said Phoenix, 'I know what you mean.'

My destiny. It's coming.

Laura spoke again: 'Adams didn't join the fight last night.'

'No,' said Phoenix. 'I've been wondering about that myself. He and Dracul will be at Csespa, at the Gamesmaster's side.'

The trinity of evil.

'So it's true what Ann just told me,' she said.

'What's that?'

'Last night was just the first round. There's worse to come.'

'No doubt about it,' said Phoenix, sensing the darkness coiled and restless beyond the mountain tops. 'The closer we come to Dracul's lair, the more ferociously he is going to defend it.'

Goaded by the none-too-friendly attentions of the townsfolk, Dimitrescu was hurrying along the preparations for the group's departure. Two of his men were lifting Foxton into his carriage. The old man was nursing cuts and bruises from the previous night's fighting. Others were securing the tarpaulins covering the cart's mysterious cargo.

'It looks like we're about to leave,' said Laura, walking towards the carriage. 'Coming?'

Phoenix shook his head. 'I'm going to ride today,' he said. 'I need to think.'

Laura smiled. 'OK.' She was about to climb into the carriage when she saw Andersen lifting himself into the stirrups. His movements were heavy and awkward. He seemed to have fared even worse than Foxton. 'What's the matter with him?'

'He came within an inch of being the third casualty last night,' said Phoenix. 'Three suckers had him pinned down. I killed two of them. Dimitrescu got the other.'

'Lucky man,' said Laura before joining Foxton in the carriage.

But if she had taken a closer look, Laura would have quickly changed her mind. As Andersen spurred his mount forward through the muttering crowds, he scratched at his neck. The irritation came from two raised blisters on his throat, just above the collar bone. They were a mixed black and crimson colour and they were seeping. The bruising around the puncture marks had taken on a familiar shape, that of a bat. Phoenix was wrong. Andersen hadn't come close to being the third casualty of the Vampyr attack.

He *was* the third casualty.

6

As the Vampyr hunters started their climb up the wooded slopes, the weather changed. Driving rain forced the riders to don capes and wide-brimmed hats and bend beneath the lashing storm.

'Welcome to Transylvania,' said Dimitrescu, gesturing towards the cheerless mountainside. The Szekelys didn't betray a flicker of emotion. It was different for the hunters. They blinked against the icy rain, as if trying to make out the shapes of the undead among the trees. They were entering the heart of darkness.

'See anything?' Laura asked Bird's Eye.

'Nothing,' he replied. 'Not the slightest hint of a vision. Maybe it's the fear.'

Yes, thought Phoenix, *maybe it is the fear*. He was feeling it too. It was all coming together.

His destiny.

His fear.

They passed through a hamlet. It was quite deserted, or so it seemed. Every house was shuttered and not a soul walked the dirt track that served as a main street. The hunters rode on, leaving its occupants cowering behind the shutters. As the miles passed, a feeling of gloom and foreboding crept into every heart. Phoenix was no exception. He felt it stealing through him like an icy dart. But he felt something else.

Expectation.

Up ahead, beyond the dark waves of trees, beyond the

glistening, silvery rain, his enemy was waiting. Slowly, imperceptibly Phoenix fell back from his comrades. He was content to bring up the rear, cast adrift among his own thoughts.

It was there, in the trembling darkness, a room with an exit but no entrance. It was a place made equally of horror and of hope; a trap and a gateway.

Soon we will meet.

Phoenix brushed the rain from his eyes and stared ahead. The rider in front of him had slowed and the two of them were becoming separated from the main column. He spurred his horse to a canter.

'Hey,' he said, coming up on the shoulder of the rider. 'We're falling behind.' He saw that it was Andersen, slumped low in the saddle, most of his face buried in his cape. 'Are you all right?' Andersen gave a moan and slid from his saddle, tumbling to the ground like a heavy bundle. 'What's the matter?' Phoenix asked anxiously. 'Are you ill?' He dismounted and rolled Andersen over. 'Andersen.' There was no reply. The Swede's breathing was slow and laboured. 'Andersen!' Phoenix stood up and shouted after the column, but they were already out of earshot. 'Listen Andersen,' he said, bending down to speak directly into the man's ear. 'You've got to give me a hand.'

But Andersen was in no shape to give anyone a hand. Phoenix looked at his pale, waxy skin and found himself in an agony of indecision. He couldn't afford to lose the rest of the column. But equally, he couldn't leave a sick man on this road, in this forest.

'Here.' He tried hauling Andersen to his feet, but the Swede was a big man and Phoenix was tugging uselessly at a dead weight. He knelt beside him in despair. 'There's got to be somebody,' he cried, his words echoing across the treetops, 'Anybody!'

And out there in the woods there was somebody. Somebody known to Phoenix. And he was coming.

'How did this happen?' groaned Phoenix. 'It couldn't have been any worse if it had been planned . . .' His voice trailed off.

Planned?

He looked around at the rain drumming on the webwork of tree roots and leaf-mould, then at the winding, empty forest track. Soon the approaching figure's footfalls would shake these tiny pools and rivulets.

Planned!

'Of course,' he said. 'This *was* planned. It's a trap.' He tugged feverishly at the scarf round Andersen's throat. The moment he saw the bite marks, the bat-shaped bruise, he fell backwards. Slowly, and without registering Phoenix, Andersen sat up. When he opened his mouth to gulp the chill air, there was no disguising the curved fangs.

He was changing, becoming a Vampyr.

'But it's daylight,' said Phoenix. 'You can't . . .'

'Oh, but he can,' came a voice behind him. 'Just as I can.'

'Adams!'

'I'm so glad you remembered me.'

The Vampyr who walked by daylight seemed even taller and more powerful than before.

'You see, Phoenix my old friend,' Adams said sneeringly. 'For very different reasons, both Andersen and I can walk abroad in daylight hours. I, you see, am no real Vampyr. As part of my apprenticeship, I am permitted to adopt the creature's more useful trappings. They are gifts from my master, I have its strength, its talons, its fangs. As for Andersen, blood was exchanged last night. At the moment, this tired, bewildered zombie is half-man, half-Vampyr. He isn't even aware of his part in my little plan. But by tonight he will have completed his transformation. Then he will be a soldier of the Legion, and he will never again feel the sunlight on his skin. There's a certain sadness in it, don't you agree?'

Phoenix was edging backwards, reaching for the Angel, hanging from his mount's saddle.

'Looking for this, Phoenix?' asked Adams, holding up the crossbow. 'Too late, I'm afraid.'

Phoenix felt for the axe in his belt.

'So,' said Adams, 'You feel like chopping some firewood, do you?' He uprooted a sturdy sapling from the roadside and hurled it in Phoenix's direction. 'Then cut away.'

Phoenix stared at the young tree at his feet. It would have taken two full-grown men half an hour to uproot it. Nervous sweat made the axe-handle slippery to hold.

'Scared?' asked Adams, stepping forward. 'Of course you are. But how scared? Scared to death? That's the easy kind of scared; the numbed, hopeless fear that makes the victim just lie down and die. But yours isn't like that, is it Phoenix? You're not like a lamb to the slaughter, at all. You're a fighter. You've still got hope. I know exactly what you're thinking. *Maybe I can get him with the axe. Or the stake. Maybe I can trick him. Maybe there is enough of the human left in Andersen to help me.*'

Phoenix winced. Every one of those thoughts had flashed through his mind.

'It's the hope that makes it worse,' said Adams. 'It makes the victim fight on long after any hope of escape has gone. It makes the kill long, and slow, and so, so painful.'

Phoenix felt the chatter of the points bracelet. His score was nearly down to zero.

'That's right, Phoenix,' said Adams. 'You're in the red zone now. So tell me, Legendeer . . .' He leaned forward, fangs bared.

'Are you ready to die?'

7

Lightning flashed far away, bluish light arcing over the densely packed trees. Phoenix heard thunder too, rolling through his head. Then he understood, it was the pounding of his own blood.

'What now, Phoenix?' asked Adams.

What now? I don't know.

'Do you stand and fight, or do you run?'

Phoenix stood facing Adams, feeling his old enemy towering over him, feeling his own weakness.

This is what I am. Nothing. And that's what his destiny was. Nothingness.

Seeing Phoenix rooted to the spot, the rain streaming over his face, Adams reached forward and picked up the tree trunk he had uprooted.

'This is no sport,' he said. 'All this time I have been waiting to settle accounts with you, and what do you do? Is this it? Is this the way I am to experience my victory? Are you really going to surrender so easily?'

Phoenix watched Adams wielding the tree like a club. 'What's happened to you, Adams?' He gave a bitter laugh. 'Do you know what's funny? Your mother actually thought I might have done something *to you*!'

For a split second he saw the shadow of emotion working in Adams' face, as if what was left of the teenage boy was trying to fight its way to the surface of the demon-apprentice who was advancing on him.

'You want to know what I'm going to do?' Phoenix asked,

shifting backwards. 'Well, I'm not going to lie down and die.'

His decision was made. Without the Angel, he was virtually unarmed. He turned and ran, his feet scrambling over the damp, sliding surface. Behind him, he heard a roar of triumph, then Adams making surprisingly agile progress through the trees. Horror flickered through Phoenix in cold needles. This creature he was facing wasn't the jealous, bullying boy he had encountered in Brownleigh. This was something else entirely, larger than life; stronger, quicker and more savage. Every time he leapt, Adams seemed to leap further, closing the distance between them. Every time he jinked, Adams seemed to do it faster, bringing himself closer to his quarry.

'Having fun, Phoenix? Enjoying our little game of cat and mouse?'

Phoenix plunged forward, branches whipping against his face. He tried to blot out Adams' voice, fixing his attention on the raindrops whispering through the forest canopy. Lightning flickered again through the glistening rain. As he ran, he even found his thoughts turning to his parents. He imagined them at the computer, willing him to run, to escape. But there was no escape, just the rain, the lightning and *him*, the remorseless hunter, never flagging, never tiring.

'This is good, Phoenix,' Adams chuckled. 'Very good.'

Phoenix wanted to turn and ram Adams' words down his throat. But that would be fatal. Flight was his only chance.

Chance. Chance of what?

It was hopeless. He had no weapon, no direction, no plan. All that was left to him was the will to survive.

To win.

But the effort to force himself on was almost more than he could bear. His breathing was coming in shallow, tortured gasps. He paused, clinging to an overhanging branch, and retched. He heard Adams behind him and threw himself forward. His left foot caught in a root and he rolled helplessly down a sudden, steep slope, the breath crashing out of him. As he rolled and somersaulted through the downpour he saw more light.

What Phoenix was seeing, bobbing through the waterlogged murk of the forest, were lanterns. Yes, lanterns and torches! Then he heard voices. Laura's voice. Then Ann's, Bird's Eye's, Bradshaw's.

'I'm here. Over here!'

Behind him, dark and lowering in the gloom, stood Adams. He had his head cocked, listening to the approaching voices.

'You've lost me, Adams,' yelled Phoenix, triumphant. 'Hear that? It's my friends.'

The Vampyr-hunters were running towards him, crossbows primed.

'The next time you see me, I'll be prepared. We're going to destroy you, Adams. You, Dracul and your master.' He was searching for his enemy, but he had lost him in the shadowy heart of the forest. 'Do you hear me? We're coming for you.'

But Adams had gone.

Ten minutes' walk brought them back to Dimitrescu's horsemen.

'You're safe,' said Dimitrescu.

'Yes,' said Bradshaw brightly. 'The lad's safe, all right. You won't believe it. There he was in the middle of a strange forest, hundreds of miles from home, and he was heading right for us.' He threw his arms wide. 'That's right, he found his way in this wilderness.'

'It's as if he had a compass,' said Ann.

'I did,' said Phoenix.

He tapped his forehead. 'It's in here.'

'This is all very interesting,' said Laura, who knew all about Phoenix's instinct. 'But I think we had better get moving.'

All around them night was falling.

8

There was no sunset that evening. Instead, the daylight began to surrender bit by bit, its frail glow gradually engulfed. Upon hearing Phoenix's story, Dimitrescu had hurriedly dispatched two riders to find Andersen, in the hope that his soul might still be rescued. It was something Phoenix was beginning to understand about fighters like Dimitrescu and Bradshaw. Behind their ruthlessness, there was a bond with everyone who took up arms against the undead. Even with somebody who had been bitten, their veins invaded by the contagion of Vampyrism. A few minutes after leaving, Dimitrescu's men returned with the Angel and two loose horses, but without Andersen.

'We have lost valuable time,' Dimitrescu said, devastated by the turn of events. 'This will set all our plans awry.'

'Plans?' Phoenix repeated. 'What plans are these?' He caught Laura's eye. It was his turn to be excluded from the group's decisions.

By way of a reply, Dimitrescu dismounted and wrenched back a corner of the tarpaulin covering the cart.

'Explosives!' cried Phoenix. 'Did you give permission for this, Foxton?'

Foxton nodded. 'It was our plan to deploy them after we reached Csespa. We thought that we would have a few hours of daylight to complete our work.' He glanced fearfully at the oncoming night. 'Now we have lost two hours. The storm slowed us down by well over an hour, and we lost a good thirty minutes looking for you. Young Robert was able to lead us into the general area of the forest, but that was all.'

Phoenix hung his head.

'No no, my boy. I meant to apportion no blame. It is simply a fact. None of us are to blame for the treacherous ways of the Vampyr. Circumstances have conspired to leave us stranded in this infernal forest.' He glanced at his fob watch. How long would it take us to reach Csespa, Nikolai?'

'At least another half hour.'

'Then we had better face facts. We are going to have to confront the demon hordes here, then fight our way through to the village.'

As if to confirm his words, a lone Wolver started to howl, its unearthly cry echoing across the mountains.

'Up there,' said Laura.

The silver beast was perched on top of a gaunt crag. Within seconds its mournful howling had been taken up at points all around them.

'What do you see, Robert?' asked Ann.

Bird's Eye was overwhelmed. 'Shadows,' he said, 'And shadows upon shadows. It's like a tidal wave, mother. So many, so many . . .'

Then the dimming sky was filled with shadowy figures. Dozen of them, Vampyrs on the wing, skimming across the heaped cloud like black kites.

'Get to it,' Bradshaw urged Dimitrescu. 'Unpack the explosives.'

The mountain track became a hotbed of activity as the Vampyr-hunters made their preparations. Sticks of explosive were strapped to arrows, stakes were hammered into the ground, braziers were lit in a circle around them. Then Bird's Eye was shouting, bawling at the top of his voice.

'It's starting. We're under attack!'

As ever, the Wolvers led the way, hurtling out of the darkness, rain spraying from their fur, their eyes flashing red, their mantrap jaws snapping. In response longbow arrow and crossbow bolt hissed and crunched, cutting a swathe through the attacking ranks. But, no matter how many fell, still more came on, roaring and howling, splintering the six-foot stakes like matchwood. In response the Szekelys thundered forward setting off explosions right at the heart of the Wolver charge. The night itself seemed on fire, the huge bodies of the demons lifted into the blazing sky.

'Retrieve what arrows you can from the bodies,' Dimitrescu ordered. 'The moment we slacken our fire, they will have us.'

Even as the defenders within the burning circle kept up their withering hail of fire, the noose was tightening. Vampyrs fell out of the sky, hideous shrieks bursting from their throats.

'Ramsay,' Ann asked, 'Did you ever see so many?'

Foxton shook his head. Fear had strangled the words right out of him. Shattering explosions continued to rip the darkness apart, but such was the mass of suckers and rippers swarming through the woods that the defensive positions were already being overrun. The night became a symphony of terror. The hiss of arrows mingled with the whipcrack of explosives and the hoarse shouts of the Szekelys, the shrieking of the Vampyrs, the howling of the Wolvers.

'Phoenix!' cried Laura. 'Behind you.'

Phoenix spun round but too late. A Vampyr was upon him, its talons shredding his jacket and raking his back. Only three thick layers of clothing saved him from a mortal wound. As he struggled against the vice-like grip of the sucker, Phoenix heard Adams' voice behind and above him. It was crackling with menace.

'Why fight?' he asked. 'Why torment yourselves?'

As Phoenix strained to hold off the gleaming fangs, he saw his enemy, standing on the very crag where he had seen the first Wolver.

'Why labour so to delay the inevitable?'

If he hadn't been in such a precarious state, barely holding the Vampyr three inches from his throat, Phoenix might have found Adams' words laughable. The inarticulate bully he had met only months before would never have spoken in this way. Transformation indeed!

'It's hopeless. The night is my domain.'

Your domain! But you're nothing.

Phoenix found his voice. 'You're just the Gamesmaster's lackey!'

'Lackey?' said Adams. 'Is that what you think? How wrong you are, Phoenix. I am the disciple. That makes me head of his Legions, heir to his power.'

Phoenix's senses reeled. Heir to his power. It couldn't be!

Rage gave him new strength and he grappled with the sucker, feeling in his belt for a stake. The terrible struggle resulted in the pair of them, youth and creature, falling heavily to the ground and rolling through the trees. As he tumbled through the downpour, jolting agonizingly over the rough ground, Phoenix glimpsed brief freeze-frames of the battle. He saw Sakarov wielding his bow like a club, desperate to hold off the onslaught of the demon that had been Andersen. He saw Foxton shooting bolts from his chair, flanked by Ann and Bird's Eye. He could just make out Bradshaw and the Szekelys trying to give some kind of shape and purpose to the madness of battle.

With a roar, Phoenix yanked the stake from his belt and plunged it into the ghoul's back, penetrating the heart from behind. The thrill of triumph only lasted a second. Barely had he felt the creature's hold slacken than he realized with horror that they were teetering on the edge of a steep rock face. The Vampyr was either dead or dying, but it was still clinging to him, its weight pulling him forward. Just as he felt his feet finally slip off the rock, he heard Laura's voice.

'Phoenix, no!'

Then he was falling, wind rushing up at him, towards the jagged boulders far below.

And all was blackness.

9

Craning forward as far as she dared, Laura gazed down into the gorge. She could make something out, a dark star against the bleached paleness of the rocks. That had to be them, or at least one of them. She wanted to shout down, to call to Phoenix that she was coming. But that would have been foolhardy . . . or useless. She stole a glance at Adams, who had been watching the course of the battle from his vantage point high on the exposed crag. He followed Phoenix's fall, then vanished from the spur.

I've got to reach him first, thought Laura, unnerved by Adams' disappearance.

She started to edge down the cliff. Once over the shelf of rock on which she had been crouching, she found to her relief that it wasn't as steep as she had at first thought. Still looking around for some sign of Adams, she scrambled down, bringing herself closer to the dark star below. She could still hear the sounds of the battle, but they were becoming muffled. Where there had been nothing but savagery and explosions, there was now only the dripping darkness. Laura felt guilty abandoning the fight, but she couldn't leave Phoenix down there, hurt . . . or worse.

'That's right,' she said under her breath, 'Steady does it. No risks.'

She felt every step of the way through the thin soles of her boots. But even this wary descent was not without its danger. Once she dislodged a chip of rock, sending it bouncing down the slope. She held her breath, but the dark star didn't move.

Down and down she climbed, barely daring to breathe, barely daring to look as the dark star came closer.

'Just a few more steps. Just a few more.'

Eventually she reached the bottom. The rain had stopped and the mood glided from behind the clouds, illuminating the ground at the bottom of the cliff. She saw the dark star close up. It was the Vampyr with which Phoenix had been fighting. It was lying spreadeagled over a boulder, and quite, quite dead.

But where was Phoenix?

All of a sudden, from a thicket to her left, there was movement. The shaking of the branches set off a flush of gladness in her chest. She was tempted to rush forward. An instant later, she was thankful she hadn't. Red eyes raked the night.

Wolver!

She heard the snuffling, snarling approach. No doubt about it. There was a ripper among the small fir saplings not ten yards away.

Please, no!

She flattened herself against the ground, feeling the damp and cold strike up through her dress. Her breath was being shaken out of her by the relentless banging of her heart. Then she saw it. Not the whole creature, not tail, legs, head, fangs. Just a silver-grey blur. A scrap of wolf-demon shifting across the edge of her vision. The thought flared fire-bright in her brain:

It's seen me! She pressed her face into the mossy earth, as if trying to bury herself. What was it doing? She found herself making a list of really stupid instructions: Stay still. Don't breathe. And if you have to . . . do it quietly! The silence weighed heavily. It began to crush her. She wanted to look up from the sodden ground, but she didn't dare. Then she heard it shifting.

Can you see me?

But the beast didn't need to see. It smelt girl and it smelt fear. It knew who she was and what she was feeling.

So why don't you strike? Trying to suck the breath deep down inside her she turned her eyes towards it. Then she understood. Midway between the spot where she was lying and the Wolver lay Phoenix.

You're guarding him.

Lifting her head, Laura saw Adams making his way down the cliff. He was coming to retrieve his trophy. She wanted to rush over and shake Phoenix awake and warn him, but the Wolver gave a low, throaty growl, a kind of rumble that drummed over the chilly gooseflesh on her arms.

He's alive, she thought, looking at Phoenix lying face down. He has to be. Why guard a dead boy?

She had to act, but how? She could feel the weight of her crossbow, slung over her back. There was a single quarrel primed in the slot. It posed an agonizing dilemma.

Two demons, one shot.

She could taste her own fear, thick and pungent in her throat. And the low, inhuman rumble came again, rising steadily into a nerve-shredding whine and finally the eerie, moon-born howl of the Wolver.

'Get away from him!'

Laura was on her feet, crossbow in her hands, pointing it first at the ripper than at Adams.

'What the matter, Laura?' he asked. 'Spoilt for choice?'

Then the silver-grey fur and the snakk-snakk-snakking mantrap jaws were fused together in a terrifying primal rage. Laura squeezed the crossbow trigger. The ripping never came. Instead there was a scream, half-animal, half-human and the silver-grey killing machine kicking, yelping . . . and dying.

'Excellent shot,' said Adams, as he reached the floor of the gorge. 'But now what?' He drew the bolt from the Wolver's body and snapped it in pieces. 'A successful kill, but it has left you completely unarmed.' He started to walk towards her. 'At long last,' he said. 'I have you both. You've led my master a merry dance. Now I do believe the game is over.'

'Get back . . . Don't you dare come near me . . . Keep

away.' Her words were coming out in gasps; angry, frightened sobs of helpless rage.

'It's all over, Laura,' said Adams, reaching out.

But it wasn't. Just as his talons were brushing her cheeks, he stiffened. Then his hands began to tremble wildly. One hand flew to his shoulder blades. A moment later, he was staring down in disbelief at the crossbow bolt he had drawn out.

'Oh, it's over all right,' said Phoenix. 'But not the way you thought.'

As Adams sank to the ground, Phoenix reloaded and aimed. Laura was about to protest. Not like this, not in cold blood. But it never came to negotiation with Phoenix. She was about to speak when she saw something swooping, kite-black and hissing.

'Phoenix, behind you!'

He dropped to one knee, turned and shot. The swoop of the Vampyr ended with the airy song of the Angel. The moment's respite was all Adams needed. The sucker had given him a way out. Staggering from his wound, he plunged into the black depths of the woods. Phoenix made as if to set off in pursuit, but Laura grabbed his sleeve.

'We'll never find him in there,' she said.

'We've got to. This will never be over while he lives.'

'If you go in after him, you'll be killed. Imagine how many demons are in there. Besides, you've seen his powers of recovery.'

Phoenix hesitated.

'Is that what you want? To throw your life away?'

Phoenix consulted the points bracelet. His score was healthy. The hesitation became resolve. 'No,' said Phoenix. 'Let's climb back up and see how the battle went.'

So they started to climb, every step full of hope, and dread.

10

Laura looked around the mountain track. 'Where is everybody?'

There was evidence enough of a struggle. The earth was gouged by the hooves of the horses and pitted by dynamite blasts. Bolts and arrows stuck up out of the ground and from the trunks of the trees, like pins from a cushion. The braziers had burned low but still cast an eerie glow over the battle-ground. But of Wolvers and Vampyrs and their beleaguered opponents there was no sign. Not a single body lay on the churned earth.

'Phoenix,' Laura asked anxiously. 'Is this good news, or bad?'

Phoenix shook his head, willing the ploughed ground to give up its secrets. 'I don't know what to think.'

Another inspection of the area yielded a find. Phoenix picked up the wooden effigy Dimitrescu had been given at Constanta.

'A lot of good this did us,' he said.

Laura cupped her hands, and was about to call out.

'What do you think you're doing?' snapped Phoenix.

'I was going to call for help.'

'And what if our people lost?' Phoenix said. 'What if they're all gone? You would be bringing the demons down on our heads.'

'Sorry.'

After a moment or two his tense face relaxed, and he smiled. 'It's all right. I know you're scared. So am I. But we have to think. We've got to get to Csespa Castle. It's the key to everything.'

'But what can we do, just the two of us?'

Phoenix shrugged. 'Whatever we can.' He spent a few minutes retrieving crossbow bolts, then walked along the track a way. 'Laura,' he hissed, 'Come here.' He pointed ahead, indicating hoofprints and the twin furrows cut by the wheels of a cart or a carriage.

'They're alive!' Laura exclaimed.

'Either that,' said Phoenix cautiously, 'or the demons took the horses and transport.'

'I wish you hadn't said that.'

A great, unnatural silence had settled over the forest. The only sound came from the raindrops tapping off the branches.

'Keep to the side of the track,' said Phoenix, 'Out of the moonlight.'

There was a shiver in the mountain breeze, a nervous, unsettling cold that had the pair of them starting out of their skins at the slightest movement in the woods. After a few minutes Phoenix felt Laura close by him. She linked her arm through his and they walked on, huddled together. After over half an hour Phoenix was almost sleep-walking, trudging along like a robot, his eyes half-closed with exhaustion. For some reason, tired as he was, he couldn't bring himself to put down the wooden effigy. It was a link with their comrades.

All of a sudden Laura pulled her arm from his.

'What is it?'

'Up there!'

She was slightly ahead of him, pointing excitedly. 'The castle.'

It was just as Foxton had described it, jutting abruptly out of the mountain top on which it perched. The huge stone pile was marked by walled outworks, into which there were carved tiny slits of windows. The entire dizzily rising edifice was topped by red-tiled turrets and towers. Any entrance was hidden by the tangle of fir and spruce that seemed to claw half way up the sheet walls.

'Journey's end,' said Phoenix.

'So what do we do now?' asked Laura.

'I know what we don't do,' Phoenix answered. 'We don't go near the castle while it's still dark.'

Laura smiled. 'Who's arguing?'

It was another fifteen or twenty minutes before their lonely trek ended. They found a rough, wooden hut. There was no furniture and it was barely possible for even one person to lie down. It hardly mattered. Phoenix was so tired he used the effigy, wrapped up in his coat, as a kind of pillow. Even sitting up in their damp clothes, they were soon fast asleep.

Phoenix was being shaken awake. Through barely parted eyelids he saw the pinched, bearded face of a man in his late sixties or early seventies looking down at him. A stream of incomprehensible words came from his lips.

'I'm sorry,' said Phoenix. 'I don't understand.'

Laura was also awake. 'Maybe he thinks we're trespassing.'

Another torrent of gruff Romanian followed.

'It's no good,' said Phoenix, holding out both hands, 'We don't understand.' He stood up to make his point. 'We come from England.' As he rose to his feet, the effigy slipped from behind him. The peasant's eyes widened. One word Phoenix recognized:

'Moroi.'

'Yes,' he said, keen to reassure the man. 'We're Vampyr-hunters.' He realized how stupid that must sound coming from two teenagers, but the peasant wasn't interested in what they looked like, only the strange, wooden carving.

'Moroi.'

'That's right,' said Phoenix, sounding like something from a 1950s farce. 'Here. Lots of *moroi*.' Then the man was backing away, ashen-faced.

'You don't need to go,' said Laura soothingly. 'We come to

help.' But the peasant had seen enough. Retreating into the thin morning sunlight, he started to run.

'Come back,' shouted Phoenix. 'Please.' But he was gone, snapping twigs and trembling branches the only clue to his path.

'Whatever that thing is,' Laura said, remembering the tavern at Buzau, 'it scares the hell out of the locals.'

Phoenix picked it up and stared through the trees at the walls of the castle. 'Let's just hope it does the same to Vampyrs.'

'You mean we're going up there?'

'That's right.'

'But shouldn't we find the others?'

Phoenix stared at the ground. 'What others? You saw his face. We're the first strangers he'd seen. That seals it for me. They didn't get through.'

'Oh no.' Laura sank to the ground.

'And where's Adams?' said Phoenix. 'You can be sure he's up to something. Maybe he's up there right now, preparing our reception party.'

Laura hugged herself, as if suddenly chilled to the bone.

'From here on in,' said Phoenix. 'We're all on our own.'

11

The castle wasn't approached by a drawbridge, but by a narrow, paved walkway, cut out of the rock on which it stood. To either side, over the low walls, Phoenix and Laura could gaze down the dizzying drop.

'That's where Dracul threw Foxton,' said Phoenix.

They didn't look down too often, preferring to keep their eyes straight ahead. Neither of them was over-fond of heights. From their raised vantage point they could see the hamlet of Csespa itself, nestling among the spruce trees. At this distance it seemed impossibly pretty, a picture-postcard view of central Europe. But they both knew what the picturesque vista hid – a history stained in blood and a population living in terror.

'Do you think this is wise?' Laura asked as they approached the thick, iron-plated wooden door at the end of the walkway. It stood ajar like the half-open jaws of a sleeping reptile. Phoenix rested the Angel in the crook of his arm.

'No,' he said, 'I'm sure it isn't, but wisdom and caution don't really come into it. We're all that's left of our mission. We've got no choice.' They eased their way through the gateway, looking up at the huge barbican. 'At least nobody is pouring boiling oil down on us.'

Laura crouched protectively. 'That isn't funny.'

Once through the gateway, they found themselves in a huge square, confronting the irregular jumble of buildings that made up the central complex of the castle. The dirt-grimed panes of glass set deep into the stone were hardly like windows. They gave the outsider no view into the building and would afford precious little to anyone on the inside trying to look out. The paint on the window frames was peeling and yellowish. Phoenix stepped back, raising his eyes to the upper storeys.

'He's in there somewhere,' he said.

Laura nodded. 'That's what I'm afraid of.'

Phoenix gave a half-smile. 'Come on, we've work to do. You know what we're looking for: a room with an exit, but no entrance.'

Laura followed him up to the front door of what must once have been living quarters. As Phoenix turned the handle, she started to wish it was locked, but with a creaking noise the door gave and yawned open. 'Ugh, that smell.' They recognized it immediately, the stench of decay. The perfume of the living dead. 'This is his lair, all right.'

The high ceilings were a lattice-work of cracks and many of the walls sported brown damp patches, while the patterned carpet beneath their feet had faded almost beyond recognition. The furniture too sported the patina of age. The whole place, in short, reeked of neglect. Phoenix took a few steps inside, then paused, looking down one of the murky galleries that ran to left and right. When Laura followed him, she took the precaution of slipping a bolt into her crossbow. Phoenix had been about to remark on the quiet inside the house, but the words didn't come. The door had slammed shut behind them.

From then on it wasn't the silence, but the amount of noise that began to strike him. There was nothing loud, just a slow, stealing chorus creeping through the dank air. Woodwork snapped and clicked, floorboards creaked, window frames rattled and somewhere deep within the maze of passages the wind whistled. There was something else too. The daylight itself seemed lost in the great gloom of the castle. It was like a guttering candle on the brink of extinction.

'What a foul place!' said Laura.

'Did you expect anything else?' asked Phoenix. They moved forward uncertainly.

'Which way?' asked Laura, 'And don't you dare say we're going to split up. I never know why they do that in the movies.'

'We're going to search the place room by room,' said Phoenix. 'Stay close and only speak when it's really necessary.'

They took one of the long galleries, inspecting every room, alcove and recess. In some of the rooms they found oil lamps or candlesticks, but not one was ever lit. The entire collection of rooms was a temple of half-light. After an hour of exploring the oak-panelled corridors, they found themselves back in the main hall, facing the great staircase.

'I suppose that means it's upstairs next,' said Laura.

Phoenix led the way, listening to each stair creak protestingly as he climbed. At the top of the staircase there was a huge oil-painting. The figure it depicted was wearing battle-dress, possibly late Middle Ages. He wore his hair long. But what distinguished him were his piercing eyes, very dark and very hard.

'That's him, isn't it?'

'Dracul. Yes, it could well be.'

The eyes were fiery and there was a definite reddish hue to the long hair. While they looked at it a deep moan seemed to steal through the house. Now they could put a face to Dracul, but what of the menace lurking behind, the Gamesmaster himself?

'Did you hear a voice?' asked Phoenix.

'I heard *something*.' Though it wasn't yet noon, they were speaking in hushed tones as if it were blackest night.

'Which way now?'

The green-tinted passageways to left and right looked identical, but Phoenix was determined not to show indecision. He struck out to the left, and all the way he heard the sounds of the castle's macabre inner life. What Phoenix had mistakenly taken for silence when they had first entered was something else entirely. There were a whole range of barely audible noises. Though muffled, they were definitely there, the sounds of scratching and scraping, a dull thud almost like a heartbeat, the grinding of something being dragged along a floor above their heads.

'Do you hear that?' asked Laura. 'The whole place is alive.' Like a maggoty corpse, the corruption seething just beneath the skin.

'I know.'

Again and again they looked into rooms, but every time they were empty. What's more, they all had entrances and exits, doors and windows.

'This is hopeless,' said Laura.

'We keep going,' insisted Phoenix. 'It's here somewhere. It's got to be.'

So on they went, from one room to the next, the belief growing that they were chasing shadows. It was halfway down yet another identical passageway that Laura stopped suddenly. 'Did you hear something?'

'I've been hearing things ever since we entered.'

'No, this is different. Not a little sound,' said Laura. 'Something else.' The words were hardly out of her mouth, when there was a crash, like a pane of glass being smashed in.

'You're right,' said Phoenix. 'We're not alone in here.'

12

He stood rooted to the spot listening.

'Adams?' Laura asked.

'He's the only demon who walks by daylight,' said Phoenix. His arms and legs felt heavy, his body a patchwork of tiredness and pain. For the first time he remembered that he hadn't eaten and became aware of the gnawing at his stomach. He feared the demon he didn't know, the waiting Dracul. But one thing more than any other added to the aching tiredness, and that was the knowledge that Adams was close by. And he was stronger, quicker, more completely ruthless than Phoenix would ever be.

I don't want to fight him again.

'Phoenix, are you all right?'

'Don't worry about me, I'm . . .' His voice choked off. A split-second after he had started speaking, he had heard somebody moving somewhere in the depths of the castle. The sound was more distinct this time, the regular beat of footfalls on the stairs. The expression on Laura's face confirmed that she had heard it too. 'It's closer,' said Phoenix, lowering his voice to a whisper.

They edged towards the stairwell, darting nervous glances at each other. Laura caught sight of movement below them and shrank back, flattening herself against the wall.

'Who is it? *What* is it?'

Phoenix craned over the wooden rail, trying to see. 'Aim for the top of the stairs,' he hissed, scurrying over to a wooden chest, which he used for cover.

Through the larger windows that lit the galleries on the east side of the castle, Phoenix could see the wind-swept mountainside and the blanket of fir and spruce. For a moment he thought he saw shadowy movement. Maybe it was people moving up towards them, but a moment later there was no sign of them at all.

Now I'm seeing things.

He waved gently to Laura, signalling the best he could that she should hang fire. Laura gave a nervous thumbs up and looked down the stock of the crossbow, taking careful aim. At last the cause of their anxiety came into view. Phoenix's finger had been stroking the crossbow trigger, itching to shoot. It didn't come to that. With an overwhelming sense of relief, he took his hand away.

'Bird's Eye!'

'You're alive!' cried Laura. 'What about the others? Where are they?'

Bird's Eye sat down heavily on a window-seat. 'I thought I would never catch up with you.'

'How did you get away? Where have you been?'

Bird's Eye took a deep breath, then started to tell his story: 'We were being overrun. I don't know exactly when you two vanished into the night, but the fight was chaos. The demons were in amongst us. We couldn't use bows for fear of hitting one another. It was terrifying. I'm not sure how I got separated from the others. One minute Bradshaw and my mother were right beside me, the next I had two Wolvers on my heels. They chased me into the woods. I was fleeing for my life, when one of Dimitrescu's men appeared out of nowhere. He slew one of the Wolvers, but the second was too quick. He gave his life saving mine. I recovered myself enough to kill the second Wolver, but by the time I got back to the track, everyone had gone.'

'Any idea where they are?'

'I don't know. At least some of them are alive. I see their shadows, but faintly. I can't make out faces. I've been on my own for hours.'

'So how did you get here?'

'I don't really know. I must have walked most of the night. I probably went round and round in circles. In the end I couldn't walk any more and got what sleep I could at the roadside. I just huddled under my cape and lay there. I've never been so cold, or so alone. Shortly after dawn I started following the most obvious landmark, hoping to find survivors.'

'You headed for the castle?'

Bird's Eye nodded. 'I had a vision. It led me up here. That's when I saw the two of you. You were a good distance ahead of me, making your way across the walkway into the castle. I followed you, of course. The door was locked. I had to smash a window to get in.'

'The door was locked, you say?'

'That's right.'

Phoenix and Laura exchanged glances.

So who locked it?

'When I got inside I couldn't find you. I didn't dare call to you. I didn't know what else might be moving about in here. I'd just about given up hope of finding you.'

'It's good to see you too,' said Laura. 'You must have been so scared.' Bird's Eye was close to tears.

'We've been looking for the room you told us about,' Phoenix told him. 'The one with an exit but no entrance. We've drawn a blank so far.'

'It won't be in this part of the castle,' said Bird's Eye. 'It can't be. The sight came to me again on my way up here. The room I saw is high up, *really* high. In my vision I could make out the ground a long way below. It wasn't even a room to be honest, more of a large recess in the castle wall.'

'Higher up?' said Laura. 'Then it's got to be one of the towers.'

They were about to head for the front door when they became aware of a change in the brooding house. All the small creaking, scuttering sounds seemed to be coming together in one ominous rush of noise. It was like a tidal wave breaking, and it was coming towards them.

'What is that?' Phoenix couldn't place the sound, but it was rising in volume. It reminded him of rainfall, but it crackled with menace. He imagined a blizzard of autumn leaves, but it was infinitely more threatening. 'Bird's Eye?'

'I see a brown tide. It's on the ceiling and on the walls.' Laura ran to the top of the stairs, and screamed.

Bird's Eye put his hand to his mouth, as if he was about to be sick. 'Cockroaches. I see a flood of vermin.' Which was exactly what was sweeping towards them.

'This way.' Phoenix led them into a gallery they had not explored, but it was the same story there. They could see the brown carapaces of thousands of insects coating the floor, walls and ceilings, turning the passageway into a heaving, chattering tunnel.

'What do we do?' cried Phoenix.

Laura was tearing at her face. 'Get me out of here,' she pleaded. 'I can't bear the things. Not on my skin, not touching me.' The noise was now deafening, drilling into their brains.

'It's no good,' said Phoenix. 'I can't think.'

Nor could Bird's Eye, but he could see. 'Here.' He was pointing to a small recess in the shadows. 'This is our way out.'

Phoenix pulled a flashlight from his belt and trained the beam into the recess. He highlighted a wooden panel. 'Stand back.'

Laura was holding her ears, trying to blot out the rustling approach of the insects. 'Hurry.'

Phoenix used the stock of the Angel like a hammer. The panel started to splinter. 'It's giving.'

'Hurry!'

Phoenix kicked in the remainder of the panel. 'What's down there?' he asked Bird's Eye.

'I can't help you,' came the worrying reply. 'All I see is darkness.' The carpet of insects had almost reached them.

'We've no choice anyway,' said Phoenix, 'Follow me down.'

With that, he dived into the void. At the end of the dizzying drop he found himself crawling across a stone-tiled floor. 'Laura, Bird's Eye.' For several agonizing moments, there was no answer. Then he heard Laura's voice somewhere to his left.

'Where Bird's Eye?'

'I'm over here. I think I've found the way out.'

13

They emerged through a small hatch, low down in the castle wall. Outside, the sky was beginning to grow darker, flakes of snow swirling in the gusting wind. The air had become bitterly cold, slicing through clothing and snipping at skin.

'I'm not sure this is any better than indoors,' said Laura, shuddering.

'Don't worry,' said Phoenix, gazing up at the tallest of the castle's towers. 'We'll be inside again soon enough.'

Bird's Eye was walking slowly backwards, never looking away from the tower. 'This is the one,' he said, 'I can feel it.' Then it was as if he were up there, shivering against the wind's blasts, and looking down at the ground below. He cried out and staggered, clinging to Phoenix for support.

'What is it?'

'I was up there,' Bird's Eye replied. 'I was looking down at you.'

'Where from?' Phoenix demanded. 'Which window?'

Still hanging onto Phoenix, Bird's Eye pointed upwards, at an opening just below the top of the tower. 'There.' What Bird's Eye had indicated was a windowless opening in the rock. Strangely, it reminded him of an old man's mouth.

'I'm going up. Who's with me?'

'Not me,' said Bird's Eye. 'Not up there.'

Phoenix smiled. 'That's all right. We need you down here to point it out.'

'I suppose that means I'm coming with you,' said Laura.

'You must. I need somebody to cover me.'

Phoenix led the way to the rotten wooden door at the foot of the tower. Pausing for a moment to look at the dark mass of drifting snow-cloud, he stepped into the gloom. He pulled a torch from his belt and started up the winding stone steps. They had been climbing for a few minutes when Laura yelped.

'Sorry,' she said when Phoenix looked round, 'Cobwebs.'

'Honestly,' he said, 'You and creepy-crawlies.'

She wasn't going to take that. 'Those roaches freaked you out too, remember.' A few more minutes into their climb, and they came to a door.

'Do you think it's the one?' asked Laura.

'Hardly. We can't be more than half-way up. I just want to get my bearings.' Phoenix crossed the straw-littered floor to the window. It was barred. 'Won't open,' he grumbled. 'I can't get Bird's Eye's attention.'

Behind him, Laura was wondering out loud: 'What was this place for, do you think?'

Phoenix jerked a thumb at a dark recess. 'See for yourself.'

Laura registered the skeleton and the manacles hanging loosely from its fleshless wrists. 'Ugh, let's get out of here.'

The higher they went the more aware they became of the howling wind. At this height, the storm was raging with unimaginable ferocity like a colossus tearing at the stone walls. They examined several rooms before they reached one whose window they could open.

'Bird's Eye,' Phoenix yelled. 'How far?'

But Bird's Eye couldn't hear him. Phoenix's voice was being swallowed up by the roaring wind. He leaned further out, where the hailstones stabbed at his face.

'Bird's Eye!' Again there was no response.

'I know.' Phoenix pointed his torch at Bird's Eye. Bird's Eye immediately started skipping up and down and gesturing towards a point somewhere above his head. He was holding up two fingers.

'It's the second window up,' Phoenix declared triumphantly. 'Come on.' But they were in for a disappointment. From the tower's uppermost window they could look down on the opening. When they went down to the door below the opening was above them. 'So that's what Bird's Eye meant,' said Phoenix. 'The room has been walled up. Maybe it never had a door at all.'

'How could that be?' asked Laura.

Phoenix shook his head. 'All I know is this,' he said. 'We've got to find a way in.' But no matter how they searched, there was no sign of a secret door, or of loosened stones, nothing that might give them access to the room. Phoenix pounded a couple of steel tent pegs into the masonry, but it had little effect. 'At least we've marked the spot,' he said. Utterly discouraged, they started the long climb down to the ground. When they eventually opened the door and stepped back out into the strengthening wind, they couldn't see Bird's Eye.

'Where is he? Bird's Eye?' Fear knotted Phoenix's insides. 'Bird's Eye!'

'Phoenix, Laura, over here.'

They ran towards his voice. For once, it was good news.

'Dimitrescu! Bradshaw!'

Bird's Eye saved his greeting for somebody far more important. 'Mother!'

Led by Dimitrescu's horseman, the column were making their way up the hillside.

'Robert, thank goodness you're all right.'

'Does this mean you won the battle?' Phoenix asked.

'Aye,' Bradshaw replied. 'We won. But at a cost.'

'Six of my men,' said Dimitrescu sadly. 'And Sakarov. All dead.'

'But where have you been?'

'Down there,' said Bradshaw. 'In those endless woods. We were searching for you three. In the end we gave up hope and sought shelter in the village. We never dreamed you would be foolhardy enough to come up here. Not on your own.'

'Then my father spotted a light shining from the great tower,' said Dimitrescu.

'Your father?' An old man appeared from the back of the group. It was the peasant they had met in the hut that morning. 'You mean?'

'This is my village,' said Dimitrescu. 'I left as a young man, disgusted by their lack of fight. I returned twice, once to fight alongside Foxton and Van Helsing, once last year when my mother died.'

'But how did you know we were up here?' asked Laura.

Bradshaw answered that one. 'It was when old Dimitrescu told us about the youngsters he had disturbed this morning that we realized who was up here. Did you find anything?'

Bird's Eye pointed to the opening. 'That's the room, but there is no door. We searched high and low.'

'So the only way in is from the outside?' asked Ann. Phoenix nodded.

'Well, there will be no scaling the tower in this storm,' said Bradshaw, squinting against the blizzard. 'We will defend our position in the village and return tomorrow.'

Phoenix took one last look at the tower.

Until tomorrow.

14

It was during the late afternoon of that day, as the snow fell heavily and the wind clawed at the walls, that Phoenix found himself thinking. Sitting by the fireside in the Dimitrescu household, dipping small pieces of bread in his bowl of soup, he thought of his parents. He thought of them as Laura had so often thought of her own mother and father. He had seen the look on her face. The longing to be home. But at least Laura's parents were spared knowing what was happening in this other world. Frozen in a single moment in time, they didn't have to watch their daughter fighting for her life. For Christina and John Graves it was different. They were spectators at an electronic Colosseum. He knew they were there at that very moment, watching. Always watching.

'Are you all right, Phoenix?' asked Ann, seeing the faraway look.

'Yes, just thinking.' He caught Laura's eye. There was a flash of understanding.

'It's almost dark,' said Ann. 'We'll have to go.'

With a sigh, Phoenix got up from his stool and put his bowl on the bare wooden table. It wasn't just Mum and Dad. There were other thoughts spinning in his mind, of the room with an exit but no entrance, of the gateway, and of the trinity of evil that stood in their way. If the battle was won tonight and the weather was kind tomorrow, it might be just a matter of hours before he finally came one step closer to defeating *him*, the owner of eyes that burned through the worlds.

The Gamesmaster.

'I'm ready,' he said.

As he trudged through the deep snow after Laura and the Van Helsings, Phoenix saw the stream of villagers heading for the church, responding to the urgent tolling of its bell. It was Dimitrescu's plan, to gather the entire population and defend a building which could hold them all.

'Look,' said Laura. 'You wouldn't think it was a church, would you?' She was right. The building had the appearance of a small fortress. Every window had been boarded up and crossbowmen were posted in the bell tower. The walls and the surrounding snowdrifts were stained by a crimson sunset.

As if with blood.

They had almost reached the low stone wall around the church, when Bird's Eye drew back sharply.

'What's the matter, Robert?' asked Ann.

'The suckers,' he gasped. 'They're already here.'

'Here?' They stood, peering into the Transylvanian dusk. They were being buffeted by the crowds of villagers, desperate to be inside.

'Bird's Eye,' Phoenix asked, 'What do you mean *here*?'

'I can see them, in the darkness.' He raised his face to the sky where the moon would soon be rising. 'They're moving, reaching up towards the moonlight.'

Phoenix frowned.

Reaching up. But from where? Then he saw it.

'The graveyard. Of course, they're in the graveyard. That's why the castle was so empty. They're *here.'*

A few families were making their way past the gravestones, glancing fearfully at the encroaching darkness. They obviously understood better than any outsider that this was a place of the undead.

'Get away from there!' Phoenix yelled. Then the words came, the only words he knew that they would understand: '*Moroi, strigoi.*'

But one man had taken a step too close to the graves.

Phoenix saw the earth erupting beneath his feet and a taloned hand reach up out of the soil and grasp his ankle.

'I'm coming. Laura, Ann, get those people into the church. Quick!' He ran to the stone wall, hurdling it with ease, and raced up the path to where the unfortunate man was already buried up to the waist. Two pairs of clawed hands were clinging to him, tearing at him, while unearthly shrieks bubbled up out of the earth.

'Give me your hand.' There was a look of confusion on the man's face. Phoenix reached out. 'Your hand. Now!' Gripping the man's wrist with one hand, Phoenix shot a bolt with the other. Then he was hacking at the exploding earth with the hatchet. Suddenly the man catapulted out of the demons' grasp and half-ran, half-crawled towards the relative safety of the church.

'Phoenix,' came Laura's voice. 'Run!' Soil-grimed Vampyrs were bursting from every grave, squealing like enraged beasts. From the bell tower and from slits in the boarded-up windows came a hail of crossbow quarrels, thudding into the suckers as they rose. Ducking under the flight of the arrows, Phoenix raced for the church. He was almost there when a Wolver came careering round the back of the church. He heard shouts of *pricolici*! Phoenix instinctively pressed the Angel's trigger but it clicked uselessly. He hadn't had a chance to reload. Only Ann's reactions saved him. She dashed forward, rested the stock of her bow on Phoenix's shoulder and shot into the creature's heart.

'Get inside,' Foxton was shouting from the church doorway. 'Hurry.' No sooner was the door locked, bolted and barred than a hurricane of fangs and claws fell upon the church. Above the din, a pounding could be heard from the roof.

'The bell tower,' said Bradshaw. 'Get those men down.' The bowmen were out of arrows and came spilling down the ladder, before turning and securing the hatch through which they had come. Phoenix heard them shouting breathless reports. He didn't understand the words, but he got the drift. The Legion was attacking in force.

'Why weren't people told to go to the village hall?' Phoenix asked angrily. 'Surely Dimitrescu knew the danger, the church being so close to the graveyard.' He looked around. 'Where is he, anyway? Where are the Szekelys?' He remembered the inn at Buzau and sought out Bradshaw. 'There's a plan, isn't there?'

Bradshaw lowered his crossbow and gestured to Laura to take his place at the window. 'Come with me.' He led Phoenix up to a pulpit. 'Look through here.'

Phoenix pressed his eye to a hole drilled through the heavy boarding. A force of fifty horsemen was flooding out of the village hall, launching fiery arrows into the night.

'But where did all those men come from?' asked Phoenix.

'Where do you think?' Bradshaw growled. 'Nikolai finally persuaded the villagers to fight. It's not a minute too soon, either.'

The Wolvers were cannoning repeatedly into the church's west wall. Already cracks were appearing and plaster was falling in lumps, showering people with dust. Phoenix and Bradshaw ran to reinforce the bowmen at the windows. The demons had ripped away most of the boarding by now and were reaching through the windows. Everybody, even the children, were striking back with anything to hand. They fought with spades, pitchforks, scythes, anything to keep the ghoulish tide at bay.

'Why don't they use the explosive again?' asked Phoenix, shooting into the throat of a bleach-faced sucker.

'We've got plans for it,' said Bradshaw. 'There isn't a stick to spare.'

Phoenix gave him a quizzical look, but it was no time for a question-and-answer session. Two Vampyrs had overwhelmed the defenders at a window just above the altar and were inside the building. Ann and Phoenix were the first to respond, bringing them down with quick, accurate shots.

Suddenly, the shrieking and howling outside reached fever pitch.

'It's the Szekelys,' said Bradshaw. He reached down the aisle, recruiting anybody who looked capable of fighting, putting together a force to go out and help Dimitrescu's commando. Phoenix elbowed his way to the front.

'Open the doors . . . now!' The moment Bradshaw's group was out, the great door slammed shut behind them. Out in the rush of the wind, Phoenix could see the size of the task facing them. There were still dozens of rippers and suckers pounding the outer walls of the church. But the odds were no longer impossible. Ghouls had stopped swarming up out of the graveyard and the skies were clear of Vampyrs.

The tide was turning.

15

The Legion came twice more before dawn broke over Csespa, but neither attack had the titanic force of that first onslaught.

'We've done it,' said Ann, as the demon tide receded into the lightening sky just before daybreak. 'We've fought them off.'

Foxton wiped the dust and sweat from his face, and turned his wheelchair in her direction. 'Yes, we've won this round. Get some sleep. We'll be on the move again later today.'

'So soon?' asked Ann.

Phoenix cut in: 'It's the castle, isn't it? We're going back to the castle.'

Foxton smiled wearily. 'Of course it's the castle. It's the fount of terror, and your path home. There we will find both the dark and the light sides of our world. We're going to burn Dracul out of his lair. This time he must perish.'

By the time Phoenix woke from his restless sleep, the first party had already been dispatched to the castle. Bradshaw and Dimitrescu were its leaders. Phoenix joined Foxton in his carriage.

'What are they doing up there?' he asked. 'I think I've a right to know.'

Foxton smiled at Laura climbing up after Phoenix, then addressed him: 'We're going to burn out the nest for good and all,' he explained. 'They're laying dynamite in as many rooms as they can. What they can't blow up, they plan to burn. Never in my sixty years have I been so close to victory.'

Panic took hold of Phoenix.

'Blow it up! But why wasn't this discussed? There should have been a meeting of the Committee.'

'There is no Committee,' said Foxton. 'Half our number are dead. All decisions have been taken by Bradshaw and Dimitrescu and myself. There can be no delay. Even now, after everything we have done, Dracul's power isn't broken. He is up there, waiting for us. We have to destroy his lair before night falls. But don't worry, my young friend, the fuse will not be lit until you have been given the chance to unlock the secret of the room. As you have made it clear many times, this is more than just a Vampyr plague.'

It was Laura's turn to be anxious. 'But what if we don't unlock its secret? You can't just go ahead regardless. Don't you understand, Mr Foxton? It's our only way home. We could be trapped here forever.'

'I'm sorry,' said Foxton as the carriage started to roll, 'You must understand our situation. We have broken the back of Vampyr power, but they can make more of the dead, an endless multiplication of terror. A single Vampyr can be the germ from which a new epidemic flourishes. We cannot allow them to recover, and spread their contagion anew. This has to be the death-blow. You will be given your chance to return home.' He consulted his fob watch. 'It is two o'clock. Darkness falls in two and a half hours. The remaining hours of daylight are your time. But, no matter what the result of your efforts, by nightfall this day Csespa castle must be destroyed.'

As the shuddering carriage moved out of the village, the inhabitants lined the route. They stood grim-faced and unsmiling, watching the second group of Vampyr-hunters depart.

'You'd think we'd lost,' Laura said. 'Just look at their faces.'

'These people have witnessed many false dawns,' Foxton told her. 'They have paid a terrible price for living in the shadow of the Vampyr. There will be no rejoicing until every one of the hell-fiends is destroyed.'

Phoenix looked out of the window, craning to catch a

glimpse of the castle. His destiny awaited him up there in that dark tower. The blood was pounding in his ears, every inch of his skin prickling with a mixture of fright and expectation. Why hadn't the Gamesmaster done more to stop them? Where was Adams? It could only mean one thing. The tower was their greatest challenge yet.

There's more to come, isn't there?

It was a bright day, crisp and still. The snowfall of the previous night lay banked to either side of the mountain track. Conditions for reaching the opening in the tower were as good as they were going to get. There was a window of fine weather before the storms closed in again. He followed the winding road, watching it curve upwards towards the menacing jumble of the castle.

'Are you ready?' asked Laura.

Phoenix shook his head slowly. Doubts were clawing at him. 'I could tell you better if I had any idea what's waiting for me up there.' He looked round at her. 'What if he's too strong? What if I don't know what to do?' And somewhere, from far away, came the secret voice.

You must. You must know what to do. He felt a light breeze skipping over the blanket of glistening snow. *It is your destiny.*

'What did you say?' Laura asked.

Phoenix started. Her words stabbed into his mind. He had been in a trance, repeating the words in his head. 'A voice,' he said. 'I hear a voice.' He tapped his forehead. 'It's in here. That instinct of mine, I know where it's coming from. I suppose I always did.'

Laura frowned. 'I don't understand.'

'It's Andreas. He's our guide.'

'Andreas! But he's . . .'

'Dead? Yes, I know. But he's speaking to me. The Vampyr can rise again, why not a mortal man?'

Foxton listened to their conversation for a while, then leaned forward. 'You really believe you are being guided by a spirit?'

'No,' Phoenix retorted. 'Andreas is inside me. I am meant to complete his destiny. It isn't a matter of believing. I *know*.'

Foxton met his eyes. 'I admire the certainty of youth. Now you have the chance to put your theory to the test. We're there.' He offered each of them a hand. 'Let me wish you well, young friends. If Robert is right about the room, then we shall not meet again. Good luck.'

Phoenix and Laura shook hands and climbed down from the carriage. The Szekelys had laid most of the explosive and were now clearing the snow from the squares and courtyards around the castle buildings. Bradshaw greeted Phoenix with a smile:

'We've been waiting for you. We have planned your way in. I hope you have a head for heights.' Phoenix lifted his gaze towards the roof of the tower. There was a trembling in his stomach and an unsteadiness about his legs. 'We're going to lower you from the topmost window.'

Phoenix heard Laura suck in her breath. 'And I've got to be lowered down the same way?'

Bradshaw gave another mischievous grin. 'If you want to go home, and your route truly lies in that room, then I'm afraid it's the only way.'

Phoenix could almost feel the fear eddying from her, reinforcing his own. 'Bird's Eye, you're sure we will find the gateway up there?'

Bird's Eye nodded. 'That's what I've seen. You and Laura standing before the gate.'

Phoenix sensed the truth of the image and set his jaw. 'Then up we go.'

What had appeared a frightening and dizzying prospect from below looked utterly terrifying from the heights of the tower. Dimitrescu's men had torn out the window in the top room and hammered away several stone blocks, leaving a large opening. Still as the day had appeared at ground level, at the summit of the tower a gale was blowing. Phoenix inspected the impromptu pulley system.

'You're sure this is safe?'

'As safe as we can make it,' Bradshaw replied. Phoenix's breath shuddered through him. 'Sorry I can't be more reassuring, lad.'

'Don't worry,' said Phoenix, fighting down his fears. 'I'm ready.' With that, he stepped into the makeshift harness and took a few tentative steps towards the opening. As he looked down his senses reeled. The whole earth seemed to pitch and sway beneath him. 'I'm not sure I can do this,' he stammered, the icy wind cutting into him.

'You have to,' said Ann, 'if you want to go home.' Then Phoenix could see the whole picture, the Vampyr-hunters ringing the castle, the explosives primed and ready, the gateway waiting just below his feet.

'You're right,' he said, his voice shaking. 'Lower me down.'

Bradshaw rested a hand on his shoulder. 'Once you're in line with the opening, you have to swing out to take you inside. Tug twice on the rope when you're out of the harness.'

Phoenix nodded, and confided in those nearest him: 'I can't swallow.'

Bradshaw smiled sympathetically. 'Just think what's at stake. It will carry you through.'

Phoenix looked around, at Bradshaw and Dimitrescu, Ann and Robert Van Helsing. 'How will you know if we've made it through the gate?'

'When we lower Laura down after you,' said Bradshaw, 'Hang on to the rope. Three tugs will mean you have opened the gate. Then we will set about burning this hideous place to the ground.'

The time was past for farewells, or for doubts. Gripping the rope for all he was worth, squeezing it until his knuckles went white, Phoenix stepped into the buffeting gale. As the Szekelys took the strain, he felt himself being lowered in sickening, jerking stages. The Szekelys had done what they could to give him some control over his progress. The rope ran underneath his thighs and he was able to steady himself by placing a foot in a loop at the bottom. Nothing however could prevent him swinging wildly in the swirling wind. And, no matter how he tried not to look down, nothing could stop the world below from spinning and lurching as he turned.

I really can't do this. Get me out of here. Take me back up! He was pleading inside, desperate to be hauled back to safety. He looked up. They wouldn't hear him in this wind, but he only had to tug on the rope to abandon his mission. He clung to the rope, feeling the rough fibres digging into his palms and fingers.

Please. But the descent continued until he was facing the opening. The snow had begun again, thickening and stinging his eyes. It was impossible to see what was inside. Expectation started to wear away the fright.

I'm almost there. Jut got to swing out. But the very idea of adding to the swaying movement of the rope tortured his insides. He hung there miserably, refusing to give up, but lacking the courage to go on.

What now?

Then he had his answer. The opening was gaping in front of him. It was now or never. Closing his eyes, Phoenix swung himself out. Three times he clawed at the stonework, fingernails splintering, and three times he was torn away. But the fourth time he secured a handhold and dragged himself inside. As he disentangled himself from the harness, his eyes widened in fright. There was no sign of the gateway, but there was a familiar and terrifying object. In the far corner of the bare room, on a bed of filthy straw lay a roughly constructed box, some seven feet long. It didn't resemble the smooth, elaborately fashioned sarcophagus of popular imagination, but there was no disguising its purpose.

It was a coffin.

16

Unaware of Phoenix's discovery in the room below, Laura stepped into space with a frightened yelp.

'You'll be fine,' Bradshaw reassured her. 'Just don't . . .'

'Look down,' panted Laura, completing his sentence. 'Yes, I know.' So there she hung, just for a moment, squinting at her comrades through the driving snow. She smiled thinly, not knowing if they could see her face through the dizzy white maelstrom. 'I'm ready,' she shouted against the roar of the wind. 'Lower away.' And lower they did, the rope grinding and creaking disconcertingly above her head. 'At least I can't see the ground,' she said to herself through chattering teeth.

It was true. When she did dare to glance down she could see little but her own feet kicking helplessly against the chill air, keen to feel something solid beneath her. Then she could see it, the large, gashed opening in the side of the tower.

'Phoenix?' There was no reply, but what did she expect through the hollering wind? For a moment, the briefest of moments, she thought she saw movement. Curiously, it looked like two shadowy figures circling each other, but how could that be? 'This is it, Laura girl,' she told herself. 'Swing out.' But as she started to thrust her feet forward and her body back, she felt a hard tug on the rope. Thrown into a spin by its force, she looked up through the blizzard. Something was wrong.

'What is it? What's the matter?' She could just make out Bradshaw's face peering down at her. His mouth was open wide, his eyes staring. He was shouting something. A warning.

Clinging to the rope with one hand, Laura cupped the other theatrically to her ear. 'I can't hear you.' Then, straining hard, she started to make out snatches of what he was saying.

'Bird's Eye . . . the sight . . .'

She shook her head, and Bradshaw shouted louder.

'Someone in there . . . not safe.' Then the shouted plea: 'Come back up!' The two circling figures. The shadowy combat. It hadn't been an illusion. Somebody was in there with Phoenix. It was him. It had to be.

Dracul.

Feeling the upward movement of the rope, Laura screamed in protest. 'No. NO!'

Then, for all her fear of falling, she began to twist and turn, struggling for all she was worth against the direction of the rope. 'Please, you can't make me come back.' She glimpsed the puzzled look on Bradshaw's face. 'I have to be with him.'

'No,' he bawled back. 'It's a trap.'

'Please!'

Then she was hauling herself up out of the harness. 'I'll jump.'

'Don't be stupid, girl.'

'I will. I'm going home. I'd rather die than stay here.' That did the trick. Bradshaw gave a nod of resignation and she sat back down in the harness.

I'm coming, Phoenix.

She swung herself several times, twice cannoning into the stone wall, but eventually she found herself standing precariously on the edge of the opening. She was standing on the border between two worlds, the fading light of day behind her, the gloom of the mysterious chamber ahead. What she saw next filled her with despair. Phoenix was lying sprawled against the far wall. Blood was spilling from his mouth and nose. Between the fallen boy and Laura stood the figure from the portrait.

Dracul.

Laura eased herself out of the harness, careful not to make any more noise than was necessary. Meanwhile, Dracul advanced on Phoenix. Laura slipped her crossbow off her back, then looked around for the Angel. Phoenix's weapon lay smashed to smithereens by the coffin. She gulped, but her throat was dry and painful. That's when Phoenix saw her. He tried to control his expression, but hope registered in the widening of his eyes. Dracul turned.

'Welcome,' he said, speaking for the first time.

Laura pointed the bow at his heart, and released the trigger. The bleached face of Dracul registered contempt. He caught the quarrel in his taloned hand.

'Is that all you can do, child? I expected better.'

Laura felt icy fingers closing round her heart. In desperate fury, she lashed out with her crossbow. Strangely, Dracul snarled but he didn't retaliate. Then she understood. She was standing in a pool of watery winter sunlight at the entrance to the chamber.

'Phoenix, get him into the light.'

Dracul spun round, but Phoenix was already up. Armed with a mallet and steel pin, he hammered the spike into Dracul's shoulder, only prevented from penetrating the heart by a sweep of the creature's arm.

Csss! Dracul reeled, taking a step backwards towards the light before steadying himself and slashing with his talons.

'Hurt, does it?' asked Phoenix. 'Then try this.' He tried to hammer in a second pin, but the Vampyr was too quick, sending the mallet spinning from his hand. His reflexes were too fast for Laura too. In spite of the wound to his shoulder, he parried a second bolt.

'Your efforts are useless,' he snarled. He loomed over the boy, mouth widening to reveal his dripping fangs. But Phoenix wasn't finished yet. He scrabbled among the splintered wreckage of the Angel and yanked loose the steel bowstring. Just as Dracul was reaching to stop him, Laura swung her bow and cracked him across the skull.

'It will take more than that to stop the Lord of the Vampyrs,' sneered Dracul.

What it took was Phoenix. Hurling himself at the distracted Vampyr, he wrapped the wire round the creature's throat.

Css! Dracul reacted wildly, twisting and writhing as the makeshift noose bit into his cold flesh. The wild squirming pulled Phoenix off his feet. Twice he was dashed into the stone walls, the impact shuddering right through him. His hands were streaming with blood where the steel bowstring had bitten into his palms. But still he hung on.

'Don't let go!' Laura yelled, arming her crossbow a third time.

This time Dracul was unable to fend off the bolt and it crunched into his chest. Black blood spilled foaming from his mouth.

'Get out of the way,' Phoenix roared, releasing the wire. Laura did as she was told and Phoenix hurled himself at the staggering Vampyr, propelling him forward towards the opening. The moment the creature stumbled into the light, he started to scream. Phoenix was about to finish his grim task by hammering his hatchet between Dracul's shoulder blades, when he saw that there was no need. The last rays of the sun did their work. Flames leapt around him and started eating at his body, searing through to the bone. The white skin flaked away, peeling back from skull and skeleton, then from deep inside the disintegrating Vampyr came a death-shriek that echoed hellishly into the gathering dusk. In just a few instants Dracul had crumbled to dust.

17

'Is that it?' Laura asked, her face flushed. 'Have we won?'

'No,' said a voice behind her. 'You haven't.'

The speaker was Adams. He was standing in the doorway, his large frame set against the dimming winter light.

'Tell her, Phoenix,' he said. 'Explain that our fanged friend was expendable. He was a puppet, no more.' Adams glanced in mock sadness at the pile of dust on the floor.

'Did you really think it would be this easy, Laura? You can stake a Vampyr, but how do you destroy my master? What is he: a haunting, a phantom, a spirit who roams the world? You are trying to kill a vapour.'

Laura looked at Phoenix.

'That's not the whole truth though, is it Adams?' Phoenix retorted. 'He is not a spirit by choice, is he? Why else would he fight so hard and so long to enter our world?' He saw Adams' expression change and knew he was on the right track. 'In some way I don't yet understand the Gamesmaster suffered a defeat. He became a ghost, or something like. Well Adams, how am I doing?'

Adams snorted. 'It's true. My master longs to be free, to take on physical form. Believe me, when he does, he will choose a perfect vehicle for his power. Sadly, you will not be there to witness it.' He looked around the chamber. 'So this is your goal,' he said. 'The room with an exit and no entrance.' He shook his head. 'Did you really trust Bird's Eye? Bird Brain is more like it.'

'But the gateway . . .' said Laura.

'Gateway,' sneered Adams. 'Do you see any gateway? All is illusion. This room is a dead-end street, the final cul-de-sac.'

Laura snapped a bolt into the groove of her crossbow. 'There *is* a gateway,' she said. 'There has to be.' She pointed the bow at Adams' heart.

'Oh, put it down,' said Adams. 'You won't shoot.'

'Don't push me,' said Laura.

But Adams did just that. Stretching out an arm, he pushed her shoulder, shoving her back towards the opening. 'I know you Laura. I know the softness inside you, the weakness. When you look at me, all you can see is the boy I was. Why kid yourself? You can't kill.'

'Stop it!' She gripped the stock of the crossbow. 'Get back.'

Phoenix leapt at Adams but was hurled across the room, crashing painfully into the far wall.

'And if I don't?' asked Adams, shoving her again.

'I'll shoot.'

'No,' said Adams reaching for her again. 'No, you won't.'

'I will,' she tried, her finger squeezing the trigger.

'And cut me down in cold blood. I don't think so.' Then he pushed her again, right to the edge of the opening. Laura's feet scrambled on the stone floor. A split second later she lost her footing and tumbled backwards.

'No!'

Phoenix picked himself up, and launched himself forward. He made a despairing lunge for Laura, but he was too late. Or so he thought. Just as Laura was falling backwards, a blurred figure hit her from behind, blasting the breath from her body and jettisoning her forward across the room. As she sprawled on the straw-covered floor, Laura felt the crossbow go spinning from her hands.

'Dimitrescu!'

The Szekely leader used the rope to continue his forward momentum. Having swept Laura to safety he twisted round and threw himself at Adams.

'Your contagion dies here, broodmaster,' he yelled, clinging to Adams.

But Adams wasn't to be overcome so easily. Crashing his elbows into Dimitrescu's ribs, he smashed his fist into the Vampyr-hunter's body, propelling him back out into the storm where the Szekely fighter hung winded and one-handed, spinning helplessly on the end of the rope.

'Nikolai!'

'Save your breath,' snarled Adams. 'Within the hour night will have fallen. The dark angels will flaunt the skies and you will all be dead.' He stroked Laura's cheek. 'Or maybe I will have them turn you into a pretty little attraction for the undead. Ever wondered how you'd look with fangs?'

Laura recoiled at his touch. Out of the corner of her eye, she could see Dimitrescu still hanging, his legs pedalling as he hung precariously.

'Take your hands off her!' yelled Phoenix.

In reply, Adams slapped him to the floor. Laura ran to Phoenix and helped him up into a sitting position. Their backs were pressed against the wall, their eyes searching frantically for a way out, the way out Bird's Eye had promised them. But there was no escape.

Adams came on, framed against the storm. Behind him, Dimitrescu was straining to hang on, his muscles screaming. Adams' talons, his fangs, his dark eyes flashed, his leering face glistened in the dying light.

'Say your prayers, Legendeer. Cry out to whatever gods you believe in.' He was towering above them, death-fire in his eyes.

It was in that moment that Laura spotted her bow. She caught Phoenix's eye and saw the look of recognition. He knew what he had to do. Instantly he threw himself on Adams and Laura dived for the bow. Adams shook Phoenix off with ease and lunged with such heart-stopping speed that Laura's bolt was touching his body by the time she had it in her hand. This time there was no hesitation. She shot the quarrel. Adams fell back, squirming and writhing on the bolt, a savage shriek bursting from his throat. But, while Laura fumbled with the second bolt, Adams was already starting to draw out the first.

'Hurry it up, will you!' Phoenix cried, still wracked with pain from Adams' attacks. He could see his nemesis easing the point of the bolt from his punctured flesh.

'I'm trying!'

Then the bolt was in the groove. Leaning back, Laura took aim. But there was no respite. Adams was still coming, his taloned hand slashing at her face and throat. Phoenix was swinging desperately with the hatchet he had drawn from his belt, barely fending off the frenzied attack.

'Reload. Reload!' He saw Adams' fangs dripping venom over his face. 'Please!'

But Adams was too fast, too powerful. He dashed the crossbow from Laura's hand. Phoenix closed his eyes. All hope gone, he awaited the death-blow.

18

The death-blow never came. A new struggle had exploded about him.

'Nikolai!'

Dimitrescu must have succeeded in steadying himself and now had his arms and legs wrapped round the astonished Adams. Hauling Adams away from the two teenagers, Dimitrescu threw the pair of them back out into the storm. In an instant they were clinging together, high above the ground. They were like condemned twins, dancing from the gallows.

'We've got to do something,' screamed Laura, searching for the crossbow.

Phoenix reached the weapon first. He snatched it up and raced to the opening. 'It's no good,' he groaned despairingly. 'I can't get a clear shot.'

The two figures were spinning ever more wildly, clinging to one another and wrestling for supremacy at the same time, becoming a single dark shape in the confusion of the storm, and the murky uncertainty of the growing dusk. Phoenix heard the sounds of the castle. The creaking, the rustling, the hissing. The Vampyr Legion was coming to life.

'Do something,' cried Laura. 'We've got to help Nikolai.'

Phoenix could hear the dark menace of the awakening ghouls. In a matter of minutes they would be swarming over the walls. He aimed the bow, but he didn't dare shoot. 'I can't. I could hit Nikolai.'

'Phoenix, you have to take a chance. Shoot.'

Phoenix stared at that threshing figures. He trained the crossbow on the twisting pair and felt despair like an ache gnawing at him. 'It's no good.' He closed his eyes and felt the tears coming. He heard the Szekely leader's cries of pain as Adams proved the more powerful. 'Nikolai, I'm so sorry.' That's when it came. A voice flooded his mind, like joy.

Do it. Phoenix eyes flickered.

No! Don't even open your eyes. Trust what you know within.

Instinct took over, and Phoenix shot. Then, as quickly as it started, it was over. There was a piercing cry and one of the fighters fell, arms flailing into the depths of the blizzard.

Laura turned round, her face flushed with joy: 'Phoenix, you did it. Nikolai is all right.' Then her voice changed. 'We have to open the gate. It's almost dark. They're going to blow the castle before the Vampyrs can rise.'

Phoenix nodded. At last he knew what to do. For a moment he watched Dimitrescu climbing up the rope, then turned to the wall. He placed the tips of his fingers against the stonework.

Trust yourself, came the silent speaker. *The gateway is where you wish it to be.* There they were, the numbers from the computer game, the silver and golden numerals that had flashed in the portal of light. **333 666 999**.

Do as before. Feel with your mind. He saw the numbers glowing in the darkness. *Guide me, Andreas. Show me.*

He pressed his fingers into the stone, gouged them in, and suddenly something was happening. The ungiving stone yielded, becoming molten and plastic. His fingers were moulding it, carving the gateway out of molten rock.

'Phoenix,' cried Laura, 'You've done it! We're going home.' Outside, the storm was beginning to abate and the moon was drifting lazily from behind the clouds. 'It's time,' said Laura. 'The charges are laid.'

Phoenix nodded. 'The Vampyr perishes this night,' he said. 'Let's go.'

'Listen,' said Laura as they approached the gate. The first

explosions were ripping through the castle's great hall. 'We did it.'

Without another word, they stepped together through the gate.

Victorious.

EPILOGUE

Make or Break

It is the way of life that after 'The End' there is always something else.

Christmas came and went that year. *Vampyr Legion* duly appeared and topped the computer games sales chart on both sides of the Atlantic. But it was what didn't happen that mattered to Phoenix and Laura.

The Parallel Reality suit didn't materialize. The game's players didn't *get into* that game in any physical sense. The gateway between the worlds didn't open. The Gamesmaster didn't appear.

It was the end.

Or was it? Day after day, Phoenix found himself asking the same question. What if there was something *after* the end?

'Seen this?' Laura asked on the bus into school.

Phoenix took the label from her, saw the miniature photograph printed on it, and gasped. 'Where did you get it?'

'It was on a milk carton in the supermarket.'

Phoenix stared at the photograph. It was Adams, but not as they had seen him in the myth-world. This was Adams as he had been once upon a time in another life, a human being with at least a suspicion of innocence, a smiling schoolboy. Before *The Legendeer*. Before the darkness.

'Hard to believe he was ever like that, isn't it?' asked Laura.

'I know.'

Phoenix read the appeal:

Missing

Can you help?

Steven Adams is fourteen and has been missing for four months. He vanished from his home without warning and hasn't been seen since. He is dark-haired, of slim build and tall for his age.

There were more physical details and finally a number to call.

'I can't believe it's the same person,' said Laura.

'He is in a different world,' said Phoenix, 'and living by different laws.'

'You think he survived the fall, then?'

'I *know* he did.'

'How?'

'He flew up to the chamber, didn't he? He could also fly down again. Besides, I have this feeling.'

'You almost sound as if you want him to be alive.'

You don't know how much. 'Maybe I do.'

Laura stared at him in disbelief. 'But how could you? He's insane. He almost killed us both.'

Phoenix looked out of the window of the bus. 'But when he's alive, I'm alive.' Laura's shocked expression demanded an explanation.

'You mustn't ever tell my parents,' said Phoenix, 'But I don't feel as if I belong here any more. Everything is so small, so trivial, so tedious. I am the Legendeer. My destiny is out there with the demons. I belong to the myth-world. They are the dark half of me.'

'That's crazy talk.'

'Is it?' said Phoenix. 'Is it really? Why?'

'It just is.'

'Listen,' Phoenix told her. 'Ever since I returned I've been desperate to go back.'

'To Csespa?'

'No, it's all over there. I need to be wherever the Gamesmaster is.'

'Is something wrong at home?' asked Laura. 'Are your parents giving you a hard time?'

'Far from it,' said Phoenix, 'They could have been a lot worse. They're actually letting me out again by myself, as long as I take my keep-in-touch kit with me.' He held up a bleeper and a mobile phone.

'Don't believe in half-measures, do they?' said Laura.

'No, but it isn't them anyway. It's me. Remember the entry I read you from Andreas' diary? The way he felt like a stranger in his own world. That's me too. It's the way it's always been, I suppose.'

'But look what happened to him!'

'Oh, I know exactly what happened to him. It didn't mean he was wrong though, did it? It isn't over, Laura, I know that. In your heart of hearts, I think you do too.'

Laura nudged Phoenix. 'It's our stop.' Phoenix followed her off the bus. He knew she was glad of a break from that particular conversation. But there was no respite, not from *The Legendeer*.

'Have you played it yet?' asked a first year in front of them.

'*Vampyr Legion*?' said his friend. 'Yes, it's cool.'

'Could have been better though, couldn't it? They were supposed to have those Parallel Reality suits. That was a let-down.'

'There'll be no let-down this time.' Phoenix and Laura exchanged glances.

'How do you mean?'

'It's in here.' He produced a copy of *Gamestation* magazine.

'Could I see that?' asked Phoenix, looking over the boy's shoulder.

'Get your own.'

'I will. I mean, I have. I've got a subscription. It'll be on the mat when I get home.' He saw the hesitation in the boy's face. 'Look, I'm not going to steal it. Here, you can even keep hold of it while I read.' The boy agreed and Phoenix and Laura read the piece that headlined the news section:

Make or break-time for Magna-com

It is make or break time for Magna-com's highly-successful *Legendeer* series. Despite more than healthy sales figures this autumn and winter, the company's flagship game will be judged ultimately on its promise to come up with a: 'feel-around, fear-around experience'. That means delivery of the long-awaited Parallel Reality suit that will transform computer games from something you watch to something you take part in. A third failure to deliver the technology would be sure to disappoint the series' millions of fans. And disappointed fans quite simply stop buying. *The Legendeer, Part Three* is currently under development.

Word has it, the game's designers are planning a final, conclusive battle between good and evil.

Let's hope Magna-com don't come out of it as big-time losers.

'Thanks,' said Phoenix, walking away.

'That's it then,' said Laura, hurrying after him. 'You've got your way.'

Phoenix met her eyes. 'It doesn't matter what I want,' he told her. 'It's what has to be. This is my destiny, just as it was Andreas'.'

At that very moment, in John Graves' study, destiny was on somebody else's mind. The as-yet undeciphered sequence of numbers was flashing across the computer screen. It was the voice of the Gamesmaster:

Have you read it, Legendeer? Such perceptive work. **Make or break** *it is.*

But believe me, young hero, it is not I who will be broken on the wheel of Fate. Your victories have been won over my disciples, not over me. I have had to watch while they failed me. Soon I will pay you and all your kind back in blood and terror. My strength is growing. I have planted a seed, and it is growing sturdy and tall. Soon I will have no need of others to do my bidding. I will tread the stars again, and burn out your senses with my fury. Enjoy your victory while it lasts, boy.

For the first time in so long, I can smell the rising wind, I can feel the beat of my blood, the buzzing of my nerves, the snaking tug of my muscles. I can hear the groaning of the worlds, the miserable pleading of my enemies. I can smell their funeral pyres. There is no peace for you, young hero. You are about to reap the whirlwind.

The game is not over until it is won, Legendeer.

Game on.

WARRIORS OF THE RAVEN

PROLOGUE

The Mischief-Maker

He could feel them boring into him. They were like diamonds, brilliant but sparkling with malice, the Mischief-Maker's eyes flashing in the far shadows of the firelit hall.

He hates me.

It hardly mattered. The boy thought he was invincible.

Nothing can harm me.

Legend made it so.

He was the bright prince, favourite of the gods of Asgard. No sword could cut him, no axe lay him low, no spear pierce his flesh. This was the great gift Fate had given him. He could feel his strength coursing through his veins like a stream of molten iron.

Nothing can hurt me.

He met the Mischief-Maker's eyes, yellow and unblinking, like a wolf's.

Not even you.

'Ready for your test?' said a gruff voice.

He looked in the direction of Odin, greatest of the gods, read encouragement in the All-father's one eye, and nodded.

Do your worst.

And they did. Every warrior of Asgard took his turn. They launched a hail of javelins but they bounced off the boy like raindrops. Some flung stones but they fell to the ground harmlessly, like dust. Others set about him with their swords, yet he was still not injured. The deadliest weapons came within hair's-breadth of him then glanced off, or simply clattered uselessly to the stone floor. It was as if he were protected by an invisible outer skin. He looked around proudly and smiled as the applause of god and hero alike echoed round the walls of Valhalla.

'Brave Balder,' said Odin. 'Because you are pure in heart neither javelin, nor stone, nor sword can hurt you.'

That's me, Balder the hero. I can't be harmed.

He smiled again, revelling in the praise, but something troubled him. It was yellow-eyed Loki, the Mischief-Maker. Where had he gone? It wasn't long before the boy discovered him whispering in a corner.

What are you talking about?

He was aware of Loki's nature. Wily, cunning, born to make mischief. He felt its hostile power in the marrow of his bones.

Nothing good or decent, that's for certain.

But there was no way of finding out what Loki was up to. He was too far away, and he had covered his mouth with his hand in order to hide his words.

I am invincible, so why am I afraid of you?

What trick have you got up your sleeve?

Odin's son Thor, the god of thunder, marched across the hall and handed the boy a huge drinking horn, filled to the brim.

'Drain it in one, young Balder,' he roared.

The boy looked around and saw the gods cheering him on. He looked into the horn of mead and grinned.

'All right, I will.'

And he raised the horn to his lips and started to drink.

'Drink, drink, drink,' chanted the gods of Asgard.

He could feel the intoxicating mead spilling down his chin and onto the front of his tunic.

'Drink, drink, drink.'

His senses started to swim but he was determined to finish it. In this hall the boy could become a man. At last he had drained it right to the bottom. His cheeks were on fire, and the walls seemed to spin. A rich, comforting heat swept through him, making him want to laugh out loud.

'This mead is strong stuff,' he said.

His words brought a roar of approval.

'Hear that? The lad likes his honeyed drink.'

'It is strong indeed,' said Thor. 'But not as strong as our young prince. He stands up to our weapons as if they were mere toys.'

'That's what they are,' he agreed. 'Toys.'

The thunderer clapped him on the shoulder.

'Listen to him, he calls our weapons toys. Will nobody else try his hand against Balder the invincible?'

The boy was laughing, both at the words and at the effects of the mead, but the smile faded as his eyes fell once more on the lean, prowling form of Loki. The Evil One had sidled up to blind Hodur and was whispering in his ear.

I recognize this.

It was foretold in the legends. Hodur has a role in Balder's downfall.

***My** downfall.*

But what was the prophecy? What danger could sightless Hodur pose?

I am charmed against injury.

What can a blind man do to me?

They had played the game of weapons and he had won against all comers. But life is never without risk.

Every game has that one unsettling rule that can turn the whole thing on its head, the trick, the twist, just like the joker in a pack of cards. How did the prophecy go? By neither metal nor stone can Balder be injured. But there was more to the prophecy.

I have to remember.

But the drink was dulling his senses.

There's more. What's the joker in the pack? How does it go?

He could see Loki whispering in Hodur's ear, encouraging him to do something. He saw the narrow, wolfish eyes and wondered what the Evil One had in store. Then Hodur was stringing his bow.

That's it.

I've discovered the joker.

I know what it is!

Mistletoe.

Balder was invincible against all things. All but one.

All things save the mistletoe!

Suddenly the drink was a curse. The thrill of its taste, the warmth it had spread through his body, he couldn't enjoy them any more. It was its other effects he felt. His movements were slow, his legs were unsteady, his words were slurred. He wanted to shout out, to yell a warning.

It isn't a game any more.

He's going to kill me.

The boy saw Loki's murderous eyes and he opened his mouth. But the words wouldn't come.

'What's that, Balder?' asked Thor.

'Speak slowly,' said Odin. 'I can't understand you.'

But he could do nothing. He saw Hodur's arrow nocked on the bowstring and at last he understood. That's what Loki had been planning. Poor, blind Hodur. The only one present who would be unable to see Loki's trickery. The Evil One had handed him a mistletoe twig shaped like an arrow, the deadly arrow of pain.

'All part of the game,' Loki hissed, no longer caring to hide his words.

The boy's lips formed a protest.

'N-no.'

It's no game.

But his words came out in a slurred mumble.

'What's that?' asked Thor. 'Speak up, brave Balder.'

He couldn't speak up. He couldn't explain himself and he couldn't defend himself. Encouraged by Loki, Hodur had drawn the bowstring back to his ear. In his ignorance, the blind man thought it was mere sport, all part of the game, one more harmless attack like the javelins, the stones and the swords. Amid the carousing and laughter, Hodur allowed his aim to be guided by Loki. A cunning smile filled the Evil One's face.

'No.'

The string stretched back and even amid the noise in the hall, he could hear the creak of the bow. The deadly shaft was aimed straight at his heart. At last terror wrenched a cry from his lips.

'NO!'

Jon Jonsson flew across the room, propelling himself away from the arrow, a hand flung across his chest in a protective gesture.

'What's got into you?' said an anxious voice. 'It's only a game.'

Jon didn't answer. He was too busy tearing off the mask and gloves and yanking leads out of computer sockets. He saw his father and he felt like crying out for sheer joy. He was back in the real world. The sense of relief was overwhelming.

'Jon?'

Jon. Not Balder. Jon. He was no longer playing a part, no longer caught up in the crazy game. This was his real self. He shook his head. He was beginning to recover from the fright the game had given him.

'It's OK,' he said. '*I*'m OK.'

He started giggling fit to burst. Though his senses were clearing, he was still feeling the effects of the mead. Besides, he was on the edge of hysteria.

'It's a game. That's all it is, a game.'

'Of course it's a game,' his father said. 'I'm the one who designed it, remember?'

Dad was staring at him, the clear-blue eyes riveted to his. But the stern look didn't bother Jon. Nothing could faze him now, not after Loki's evil glare.

'It's unbelievable,' said Jon. 'So real. It was as though I was actually there. I wasn't me in there. I wasn't *playing* Balder. I was him.'

His father's expression relaxed.

'Now *that*'s something I'm pleased to hear,' he said. 'It's got to be a totally convincing experience. You really like it?'

Jon hesitated.

'Well?'

'I'm not sure like is quite the right word,' he replied. 'I was scared witless. But it blew me away. What a rush!'

'Go on,' Dad said. 'Tell me what you mean by that. Exactly. This game has got to work. Our future depends on it.'

Jon nodded. He remembered the day Dad got the job working for Magna-com. He had danced round the living room like a madman, waving the letter in triumph.

'The most successful, innovative computer-game company in the world,' he had cried. 'And they want me to help design their new game.'

Jon knew all about Magna-com, of course. What teenage boy didn't? He had the first two parts of the *Legendeer* series, *Shadow of the Minotaur* and *Vampyr Legion*.

They'd been his Christmas and birthday presents. He'd marvelled at the graphics, shuddered at the realism of the monsters. Now here was Dad, *his* dad, given the responsibility of taking *The Legendeer* forward to new heights. The next game was going to use all this Virtual Reality stuff. Magna-com had postponed its introduction twice. Production difficulties, they said. Jon picked up the mask and gloves, then ran his hands over the skintight black suit he was wearing. The ultimate accessories for the ultimate game. What was the advertising angle? Yes: *The Game You Really Get Into*. These were the things that were going to blow away the opposition and make *Legendeer 3: Warriors of the Raven* the hottest computer game ever.

'Virtual Reality,' Jon murmured, still able to taste the mead on his lips. 'The ultimate game.'

'Parallel Reality,' his father said, correcting him.

'I beg your pardon?'

'Parallel Reality, that's what Magna-com calls it. It's a step beyond Virtual Reality. You're not just seeing your surroundings. This is a complete multisensory experience. You touch your surroundings, smell them, taste them. This thing you're wearing is a PR suit. It makes the illusion possible.'

Jon didn't care what it was called. The sensation was amazing. Once he was inside the suit, the world of the Norse gods had come alive. He had smelt the logs burning in the great hall of Valhalla, he had heard the hiss of the warriors' swords leaving their scabbards, he had felt the fire's heat, most of all he had tasted the mead. For the first time in his life he had actually been drunk! And all with his parents' permission too. The one sobering thought occurred to him when he looked down at his wrist. He was wearing a gizmo rather like a watch. It was his points bracelet, and it registered a big, fat zero. He'd entered the red zone. Red for failure, red for blood. The price of being the target of a mistletoe arrow.

'I lost,' he said.

'You lost,' his father told him, 'because you panicked. You allowed yourself to believe the illusion. The secret of winning is to keep cool, to know the limits of the game.'

Jon glanced at the monitor screen. The screen-save had kicked in, a flurry of numbers, threes, sixes and nines.

'You'd have panicked too,' he said. 'That arrow of mistletoe.

It's in the rules. It's the one thing that can hurt me. And Loki, what a villain. Those eyes. How did you get them like that? The way he looked at me, it made my flesh creep.'

'That's the general idea,' said his father. 'Magna-com want you spooked right down to the tips of your toes. That's the buzz. It's like a horror film. If it doesn't take you to the edge of your seat, you feel cheated. Their games promise a white-knuckle ride. That's the big selling point. You feel you're there. We daren't disappoint our audience. It's not all down to me, of course. Magna-com have a whole team of programmers and designers working on the game. I'm not sure who came up with the eyes.'

'You mean you haven't met the rest of the team?'

'I haven't even spoken to them.'

'You're kidding!'

'No, that's how Magna-com works. Each of its designers and programmers has been working alone on one tiny part of the whole game. I got level eight: *Balder and the Arrow*, and the last two levels, *Warriors of the Raven* and *Ragnarok*. At least, I collaborated on them. Working this way is like painting one piece of a jigsaw without seeing the whole picture. Top-secret stuff. I suppose that's how they stop their competitors catching up with them.'

Jon peeled off the PR suit.

'There is one drawback though.'

His father's face fell. The game was about to hit the shops.

'What's that?'

'I'm not sure I want another go. My stomach is turning over at the thought of it. That's how scary it was.'

He remembered the arrow pointing at his heart, the one thing that could kill the hero Balder, and he felt the rush again, an adrenaline burst of horror.

'It gets a lot scarier,' said his father. 'The Balder episode comes just before the big finale. Level nine is when the forces of good and evil line up. But just you wait till you get to level ten. That's Ragnarok, the final battle. The Norse gods, led by Odin, descend from Asgard to battle the forces of darkness. It's got demons, dragons, zombies, streams of fire, earthquakes, mass slaughter. End-of-the-world stuff. We're talking Armageddon.'

'Not sure how I'll handle that,' said Jon. 'Scarier than the Balder level, you say?'

'Much scarier. Balder is dead, or at least living on as a ghost, so the player becomes Heimdall, the watchman of the gods and arch-enemy of the evil Loki. You have to warn them of the coming evil and summon them from Asgard to fight the final battle.'

The promise of excitement got the better of Jon.

'Can I have a go at it?' he asked, just about overcoming his fear of the game. 'This Ragnarok level?'

'You'll have to wait a while before you can get onto the final levels,' Dad replied. 'You have to complete this one first.'

Jon looked disappointed.

'You will play again though, won't you? I'm relying on you for the teen angle. You're my guinea pig.'

Jon remembered the feeling of invincibility, the forbidden sensation of being drunk. No way would he get that feeling any other time. His parents were strict about that sort of thing. No doubt about it, he was already itching to go again. Maybe if he continued to trial it, he'd get a shot at the other levels. *Warriors of the Raven* was certainly addictive. The fright he had felt as Hodur aimed his arrow was already fading. He winked at his father.

'Just you try and stop me.'

BOOK ONE

The Book of the Legendeer

1

That same evening, many miles away, another teenage boy was making his way through the trembling, drizzly darkness of a mid-February evening. Watching him, you might be forgiven for thinking he was being followed, pursued even, such was his haste. Phoenix Graves was heading home from a friend's house. At fourteen, he was the same age as Jon Jonsson, as dark and sallow as the other boy was pale and blond. Phoenix owed his looks to his Greek ancestry, on his mother's side. His family had only been in England for three generations. Up to this point, however, though there were many similarities in their lives, Phoenix didn't even know of Jon's existence. But that was about to change. He had played *The Legendeer* just as Jon had. He had been the very first player in fact, a guinea pig for his own father, the first man to work on the game. Like Jon, he had seen the threes, sixes and nines spiralling on the screen, and wondered what they meant. He had worn the PR suit and been hooked up to the computer. He had been sucked into its terrifying worlds, forced to face its demons. But there was a difference. Jon still thought *The Legendeer* was entertainment, fun. Phoenix knew better. He knew what lay behind the marketing and the graphics, and it haunted his dreams. You didn't play this game. It played you. Here, on this lonely street, he was already bracing himself for the night. With night came dreams, and with those dreams came terror. Soon he and Jon would meet, and at that crossroads in time and place their lives would be turned upside down.

The trill of a mobile phone rippled through the damp air.

'Hello?' said Phoenix, pulling it from his blazer pocket. 'Oh, hi, Mum. Something wrong?'

'Only a son who was meant to be home over an hour ago,' she replied frostily. 'Where have you been till this time – Laura's?'

'That's right, I phoned Dad to ask if I could go round to hers after school. Didn't he pass on the message?'

Mum's impatience fairly crackled through the air.

'We're talking about your dad. He's out. No note though.'

'I did tell him. Honest.'

The voice at the other end softened.

'I know. It's not your fault, Phoenix. Where are you, by the way?'

'By the bank in the High Street. I'll be with you in ten minutes.'

'See you then.'

Phoenix slipped the mobile back in his pocket and shook his head.

'Dad! Can't you get anything right?'

At that moment he glimpsed his reflection in a shop window. Seeing himself rendered faint and ghostly by the darkness, he was overwhelmed by memories. Phoenix was a boy who had his demons. They perched on the cusp of his memory, waded through the murky backwaters of his dreams. They had their claws in him and they were never going to let go. Just a little further on, he came face to face with one of those demons. A poster was displayed on a notice board outside Brownleigh police station.

STEVEN ADAMS, 14.
DO YOU KNOW THE WHEREABOUTS
OF THIS BOY?

Phoenix read the details. Steve Adams. He was the boy who'd been his tormentor at school and had followed him into the terrifying world of the game. He had not returned. Missing since the autumn, the poster said. If only they knew. Phoenix read right to the end. Not that he was going to learn anything new. He knew the whole thing by heart. What's more, he knew exactly where Adams was. But it wasn't the kind of information he could share with the police. Their jurisdiction didn't stretch that far.

Five minutes later, Phoenix was home.

'Mum?'

She emerged from the living room.

'Is he . . . ?'

'If you're after Dad, he walked in the moment I put the phone down. Not a word of apology for forgetting to tell me where you were, of course.'

Phoenix rolled his eyes. That was the old man. Only one thing on his mind. A game called *The Legendeer*. Mind you, with the stakes as high as they were, he could hardly be blamed for being obsessed.

'And yes, before you ask, he is in the study.'

Phoenix dropped his bag in the hallway and joined his father in the cramped, cluttered room. There had to be order in the chaotic piles of books and notepads, but it defeated Phoenix. The latest stack was all about the Viking legends. A torrent of publicity had announced that the new *Legendeer* would be based on them. It was called *Warriors of the Raven*. After the Greek myths and the gothic world of vampires and werewolves, it was a logical choice. Phoenix flicked through one volume, pausing at an illustration of the evil Loki. The Norse myths had been unfamiliar to him, but he was rapidly becoming an expert. The gods of Asgard on the one hand, Loki and his legions of hell on the other.

'Anything?'

'Give me a moment.'

Phoenix had asked the question more in hope than expectation. He wasn't surprised when John Graves gave a shake of the head.

'A couple of accidental hits on our website. Just random surfers mostly, and a couple of boys looking for the official Magna-com website. Nothing to help us though. I don't know what to do next.'

He shoved his chair back on its castors and eased into the headrest, closing his eyes. He'd been chasing shadows for weeks and it showed.

'I had high hopes of the website. I thought it would stir up a little interest from somebody. Looks like it's just another dead end. It will be a disaster if the game goes on sale but there doesn't seem to be any way to stop it happening.'

'We can't give up,' Phoenix protested, hearing the resignation in Dad's voice.

'I don't intend to,' said Dad. 'I was the first programmer to work on it, I kind of started all this. So don't you worry, I intend to finish it. But I will admit I'm starting to feel discouraged. I've been trying to find out who they got to take over my old job for months now.'

John Graves had been as delighted as Jon Jonsson's father when he was asked to develop *The Legendeer*. But delight had soon turned to horror. Now he was a thorn in Magna-com's side.

'I've tried every contact I know . . . *twice*. I tell you, whoever Magna-com got to finish *The Legendeer* this time, they're not in this country.'

'What makes you say that?'

'Because I must have talked to every single programmer and designer based here. Want to see our phone bill? The company must have moved the project abroad, out of our reach.'

Phoenix glanced at the PC.

'So what do we do?'

Dad shook his head.

'I've read everything on the Norse legends and every computer game and website you can imagine. Nothing. The launch date is just round the corner. Let me sleep on it, son. I'm all out of ideas. I need time to think.'

Phoenix sighed. Time was just what they didn't have. Did he have to remind Dad what came to him every night? Demons, hundreds of them, all knocking on a virtual door. Demanding entry to this world.

'Have you forgotten what we're dealing with?'

Their eyes fell on the computer games in the corner, then on the Parallel Reality suits. Finally, there were the folders full of cuttings, the fragments of a tale of menace.

They had been the first to understand what *The Legendeer* was all about. Not illusion, but a different, menacing reality. Not entertainment, but horror.

'It's more than a game, Dad. It's a plague. We've got to find a way to stop it.'

'Phoenix,' said Dad wearily, 'I haven't forgotten anything. I want to put an end to this as much as you do. I just don't know how to. For the first time I actually feel like I'm on the losing side.'

Seeing the expression of defeat in his father's eyes, Phoenix lowered his voice.

'Sorry, I'm frustrated because we don't seem to be getting anywhere.'

Dad smiled.

'You and me both.'

Phoenix looked out at the yew trees in the back garden. For a fleeting instant he thought he saw somebody watching from the lane. But he'd felt that way ever since he first played *The Legendeer*. If he could look into their nightmare world, they were quite capable of looking out at him. Phoenix couldn't turn his back without sensing the terror at his shoulder.

'What are you looking at?' Dad asked.

Phoenix continued to stare, as if trying to peel away the darkness, layer by layer.

'I beg your pardon? Oh, nothing. Just my mind playing tricks.'

But it was more than that. It was the shadow of his demons.

Phoenix was in a room. There were brilliant white walls – so white it was hard to keep his eyes open – and a black carpet and curtains. Against the far wall somebody was sitting with his back to Phoenix, working on a computer.

'Who are you?' Phoenix asked.

'Don't you know?' came the reply.

Phoenix recognized the voice immediately and retreated to the door.

'No,' he said. 'It can't be.'

The chair swivelled round and a familiar pair of eyes met his.

'Surprise surprise.'

Phoenix saw a teenage boy, the boy from the police-station poster. At least the face was that of a fourteen-year-old boy. The body was muscular and powerful beyond his years.

'Adams!'

Steve Adams grinned. He held up a copy of *The Legendeer, Part Three*. Phoenix focused on the new title *Warriors of the Raven*. It was only then, as he stared at the illustrations on the case, that Phoenix became aware of a second presence, barely visible at all. Adams was threatening enough, but this second presence, the one that pulled his strings, was pure evil. He was there all right, the force behind *The Legendeer*, the Gamesmaster. He was playing Adams the way a puppeteer plays his marionette.

'Coming out to play?' asked Adams, rising to his feet.

The hands that reached out towards Phoenix seemed to be dissolving and disintegrating as they came closer. The flesh bubbled and cracked open, scraps of greying skin peeling away and dropping to the floor. A new face was taking shape beneath the old. Serpents were sprouting from the head, writhing and twisting above grotesque eyes and mouth.

In an instant, the image had changed. A vampire's fangs flashed and dripped venom. Finally there was a new face, framed by hair as red as flame and wicked eyes that flashed yellow. They were burning into him with a hatred beyond human imagining.

'No!' yelled Phoenix, shrinking back. 'No, no, no.'

He woke up, dripping with sweat. His demons were coming out of the darkness.

2

Jon tracked his father down to the bottom of the garden. He walked gingerly on the frozen ground. Dad was wielding a huge, long-handled hammer, smashing away at the wall of a crumbling brick outhouse.

'It's time for the game,' said Jon, clapping his gloveless hands together against the cold.

Dad consulted his watch.

'That time already. This is taking longer than I'd expected. The condition it was in, I thought it might fall down by itself.'

'What are you going to do with it?'

'If I can manage to demolish it, I'm going to have a self-contained study room built out here, using the old foundations. No phone, no distractions.'

He wiped his face with a handkerchief and leaned the hammer against the wall. Jon seized on it immediately, swinging it round his head.

'Hey, watch that thing,' said Dad.

'Don't you see?' said Jon. 'I'm Thor the mighty thunder god and this is Mjollnir my magic hammer.'

'There's a safer way to be a Viking hero,' said Dad. 'Let's play the game. You're a lucky lad. Everybody else has got a few more days to wait.'

Jon nodded eagerly. He had been waiting for this moment all day. What if he could complete the whole thing before anybody in school even had the chance to buy a copy? He led the way indoors. As he stepped into the PR suit and pulled it up, feeling the material clinging to him, he had mixed emotions. The thrill of expectation was combined with a sense of horror.

'Are you OK, Jon?' his father asked, handing him the mask and gloves, already hooked up to the PC.

'Fine.'

But there was no disguising the shake in his voice.

'That scary, huh?'

Jon nodded. His throat was dry. A question popped into his head:

What next after death?

'Dad?' he asked, feeling the mask snap over his jawline. 'How does this Balder story turn out, anyway?'

'In the old Viking legend, do you mean, or in the computer game?'

'Both.'

'Well, in the legend, Balder dies. It's the incident that leads to the final conflict between good and evil.'

'*He dies?*'

'Uh huh. The evil Loki tricks blind Hodur into slaying him. It is the event which leads to the day of reckoning, Ragnarok. Some call it the twilight of the gods. That's what the whole game is leading up to, a massive showdown between the gods of Asgard and the forces of darkness.'

'But that spoils the whole game. How am I supposed to win if I'm dead? That's stupid.'

'I think you're missing the point about computer games, Jon. It's up to the player. The story on which it is based is just a starting point. You rewrite the legend yourself. Computer games take all sorts of liberties with the original stories. Within the rules of the game, anything's possible. It's my job to make kids believe they can conquer huge monsters. Look, if you want a crack at the top levels, you've got to stop putting it off and get past this one.'

Jon nodded, but he still didn't like the sound of it: Balder dies!

He listened to the reassuring purr of the PC and strapped on the last piece of Legendeer apparatus, the points bracelet.

'Ready or not,' he said defiantly, 'here I come.'

The credits rolled and three ancient women appeared, cloaked in grey robes. They acted as guides through *Warriors of the Raven*.

'Welcome to the world of *The Legendeer*,' they chorused. 'We three sisters are the Norns. We are creatures of the past, the present and the future. We spin the fates of men and women. We pave the path you tread through life, to Asgard on high . . . or to foul Hel below.'

Jon felt his breath catch as the sisters beckoned him on.

'Our story begins in glorious Asgard itself, home of the gods. You will play the part of young Balder, noblest and greatest in spirit of those who dwell within its impenetrable walls. He is loved by man and god alike. As a result of his fame, he is hated by the Mischief-Maker, that most evil of spirits, wily Loki.'

Jon gritted his teeth. As bad guys went, this Loki was *bad*. The Norns led him to a jutting horn of rock, from which he could see the whole of the strange world of the Norse gods. Stretching out beneath the white sky was a plain ringed by bare, rugged hills. The snow lay in thick drifts below him. But hanging motionless before him was the most curious feature of the entire vista, a frozen rainbow that arched glistening into the sky. He had set foot on it before, the first time he had played, but he still marvelled at it. It was unlike any rainbow he had ever seen, opaque and sparkling like frost. Even that wasn't all. In the glittering light, as if through a window, he could see the vastness of space.

Prepare to have your mind blown, he thought.

'Behold,' the Norns continued, 'the path called Bifrost. On the other side of this rainbow bridge you will find Asgard, and within its walls Valhalla where the fallen heroes carouse for all eternity.'

Milky wreaths of stars, planets and blazing comets flashed in the brightness of the rainbow. But, as still and monumental as it stood, Jon could almost feel the tension in the sparkling arch. It was like a groaning giant, desperate to unburden itself and crash to earth. In the furthest distance, half-lost in the snow-glare of the distant hills, he could see something else. The palace of Asgard. He remembered the huge, studded doors, soaring turrets and glistening roofs from his first go on the game.

'In this journey through the Northland,' the Norns went on, 'you will relive the fate of Balder, then of Heimdall, watchman of the gods. To win, you must blow the Gjall horn and summon them for their final battle with the Evil One and his demon army. As Heimdall you have an awesome responsibility. You are the one who must slay the demon-master Loki himself. Are you ready to begin?'

'Ready,' said Jon.

And so his second game began. He crossed the rainbow bridge and entered Asgard. He was hailed as Balder and accepted the challenge of the weapons. He felt his own invincibility, the sensation of the mead inflaming his senses, the terror as Loki guided blind Hodur's aim with the bow. He glanced at his points bracelet. He had a healthy score.

This time I won't panic.

He could feel the effect of the mead, but he kept his concentration. The score on his points bracelet climbed.

This time I'm going to win.

I'm going on to the next level.

He saw Loki whispering in Hodur's ear. Then, ever so slowly, and with murderous intent, the bow was aimed at his chest. The effect of the mead was becoming stronger.

Got to think, to stay alert.

Easier said than done. His mind was getting fogged. He could feel the vibration of the points bracelet as his score started to fall.

I won't shout out.

I won't ask for help.

I'll just jump out of the way.

But he was unable to move, never mind jump. He was rooted to the spot, paralysed by the effects of the mead. The bowstring went taut, then the arrow was loosed.

There was a sickening thud, an impact that threatened to rearrange his insides, and he was falling, falling, the room spinning and darkening around him. He could hear his father's voice, as if from far away.

'Jon, what's wrong?'

He could feel his father's fingers on his face. He was going to remove the mask and break the game's spell.

'No,' he said. 'Don't.'

The words came back to him, the ones that had come to mind earlier.

What next after death?

But he wasn't dead at all, not really. He could see and hear. There was more to learn from the game.

'I'm all right,' he said stubbornly. 'I don't need any help.'

Then his father's voice and touch drew away, as if fading into the far distance, and Jon was once more part of the game.

What's happening to me?

What kind of game is this?

'Ready to continue your journey?' said a voice. 'Ready to take the final step, to go beyond illusion into another world?'

He found himself standing on the deck of a ship.

'Where am I?'

On the prow of the ship stood the Norns, the three dark-veiled sisters. Around them the sea appeared to be on fire. Flaming arrows filled the sky above them.

'Why, this is your funeral ship, Balder.'

'Funeral ship? Am I dead?'

'For the purposes of the game, yes. But the game goes on. The game is without end. You are not just one hero, intrepid player. You are *all* heroes. Remember, if you take up the challenge, you will play the part of Heimdall. You will blow the Gjall horn and summon the gods to the final battle. Do you dare?'

Jon's mind was working overtime. You die and you can still win? This was the weirdest game he had ever played.

'Behold,' said the Norns. 'The gods of Asgard bid Balder farewell. But their anger turns against Loki. They see his tearless eyes and they know he is the guilty one.'

The ship began to sail, drifting through banks of thick fog. Then the mists started to clear.

'Behold,' said the Norns, pointing the way. 'This is the Mischief-Maker's fate, his punishment for the death of Balder.'

Loki was being dragged down steep stairs in an underground cavern. All the way he was shouting and cursing his captors.

'Unhand me,' he shrieked. 'It wasn't me. Hodur did it.'

'Yes,' said Thor. 'Hodur shot the arrow, but you guided his hand. Yours is the crime, Loki.'

'This is the gulf of Black Grief,' the Norns explained. 'Here the Evil One will lie bound in chains on three sharp-edged rocks. Above him is fastened a giant serpent. Venom drips from its jaws and will fall for all time upon Loki's face. This is the punishment for the Mischief-Maker's crime.'

Jon watched fascinated yet horrified as Loki twisted and writhed, struggling to avoid the poison. He witnessed the Mischief-Maker's torment, heard his screams.

'His anger will grow. It will fester and turn against all

mankind. Every moment of every day he lies tormented here, he will plot his revenge. Above all he will blame you. One day those chains will break and the Evil One will walk free once more. Make yourself ready for that day of vengeance, player, for on that day of Ragnarok you will surely have to face him again.'

Jon saw Loki's head turn and the yellow eyes fixed him with a look of utter hatred, a loathing that seemed to set the air alight. He recoiled, horror piercing his heart more effectively than any arrow. Ahead of him he saw something golden, a kind of portal of shimmering light.

'Step through,' said the Norns. 'Cross the threshold and you will no longer be playing, but *living* the game. That's right, enter the game's embrace. We are offering you a world beyond your wildest imagining.'

Jon looked into the light and felt his heart lurch. He could see shadows, the hidden shapes of strange creatures. There was a pain in his chest and his mind was haunted by Loki's yellow eyes. No, he wouldn't go into the light. He wished he had let Dad remove the mask. Something was wrong.

Very wrong.

'That's it,' he said, pulling at the mask of the PR suit. 'This is just too weird. I've had enough.'

But the game wasn't ready to let him go just yet. The mask clung to him, tugging at his face as if it was going to peel away his skin. He clawed at the skintight mask, but still it wouldn't budge.

'Dad, help me!'

Two pairs of hands were tugging at it now. For a moment, Jon could actually feel his skin beginning to tear from his face. Thousands of fragile strings seemed on the verge of snapping inside his flesh.

There was only one thought in his mind now. To escape from the game.

To be free of it.

'I don't want to be Balder,' he cried. 'I don't want to be Heimdall either. And I don't want your stupid challenge. Game over. Game over NOW!'

3

Phoenix turned his key in the lock. Laura Osibona followed him to the living room, giving the study a quick glance. She was his best friend. She knew his secret. She was always aware of it, the unremarkable boxroom where it had all started, where something as seemingly harmless as a computer game had turned into a nightmare. She thought of the menace that buzzed through the computer's hard drive and the monitor screen that had been transformed into a window onto horror.

'So what's the next move?' she asked.

'Good question,' Phoenix replied, dropping his school bag on the floor by the couch. 'Dad's completely stumped. Me too. The game is about to go on sale and we can't get anyone to listen to us. Still no news on the designer either. We know nothing about it except that it's about to hit the shops.'

'And that it's evil,' said Laura.

Laura had been part of it from the very beginning. Phoenix's partner in a two-player game. She had worn the PR suit and entered it alongside him. She had become aware of the malicious power that, unknown to either of them, was stealing into Jon Jonsson's life.

'I'm sure we'll get a lead somehow,' said Laura. 'After all, he's only . . .'

Her voice trailed off.

'Only human, is that what you were going to say? That's just it, Laura, Gamesmaster is simply a name we've given him. We don't know what he is. Come on,' said Phoenix. 'I'm going to see if our website has attracted any interest.'

'Legendeer.co.uk,' said Laura, reading the directory. 'Sounds like an official website.'

'That's the general idea,' said Phoenix.

They sat side by side at the work station, eyes fixed on the screen.

'Nothing,' Phoenix said disgustedly.

He shoved the mouse away.

'You'll find a way back into the game,' said Laura.

'You think so?'

'No,' said Laura. 'I *know* so. You will find a way back because you're not just another player. You're *the* player. That's what everything we have been through has taught us. You are the Legendeer.'

She was right. He was the one who had been at home there, among the demons and monsters. The same creatures that inhabited *The Legendeer* had haunted his dreams since early childhood. His whole life had been one long preparation for the game. Entering its world had been like coming home.

'For months I've felt like it was my destiny,' he said. 'But now . . . I have my doubts. Look, there's no connection any more. *Warriors of the Raven* is the hottest thing since colour tv, but we're still being kept at arm's length. We've no access to the new software.'

'But what about the numbers?' said Laura. 'To everybody else they were a mystery, just random figures on the screen. But you understood their importance. You knew they were the language of the game, its secret code.'

'That's just it, Laura. The numbers are the way in, but we don't even get them coming up on the screen any more. The Gamesmaster has shut us out. It's like nothing ever happened.'

'But it did happen,' Laura replied. 'It happened *to us*. We're not mad and we didn't make it up.'

She reached into a cardboard box next to her, and held up one of the Parallel Reality suits Phoenix's dad kept packed away.

'Remember this?'

'Of course I remember it,' said Phoenix.

The suit was how it had all begun. He remembered the skintight material pinching his flesh, the macabre sensation as it started binding with its skin, growing into it. He remembered the points bracelet blinking away, recording his score. Finally he remembered the shimmering golden portal, the gateway between the worlds.

'It's no accident that you were chosen to play,' said Laura. 'Your dad was the first to work on the game. Then there's Andreas . . .'

Phoenix closed his eyes. Andreas. He was the final part of the jigsaw, the reason that Phoenix was different from anyone else who had played the game. Andreas was his great-uncle. He was a man who had died years before Phoenix was born. Yet he was always in Phoenix's thoughts. And his dreams. It was the one thing that saved him from madness through all his adventures. No matter how terrible the menace that crouched in Phoenix's dreamworld, there was always Andreas in the distance, a comforting, ghostly presence, a secret speaker, a voice to guide him.

'It's like he's still alive sometimes,' Phoenix murmured. 'I hear him, here, in my mind.'

Andreas had been the first to enter the jaws of the nightmare. As a country schoolteacher in Greece, he had discovered that the demon world existed, the same world Phoenix had revisited in *The Legendeer*. He had given his life trying to warn people of the danger.

'You don't have to remind me of my destiny,' Phoenix said. 'I live with it every day. I know I have to beat the Gamesmaster. I know the terror that's waiting if I don't. But how do I get to him?'

Laura shrugged her shoulders.

'I only wish I knew. Anyway, show me this website of yours. I haven't seen it yet, remember?'

Phoenix brought it up on the screen, and Laura leaned forward.

'Well, those graphics ought to catch somebody's eye,' she said, mainly for Phoenix's benefit.

She watched the images from *Legendeer* Parts 1 and 2 crowding the screen: the Minotaur lumbering through the labyrinth, Medusa haunting the depths of her cave, Vampyrs lurking in the darkness. It was the stuff of fantasy to any surfer who came across the page, but it was memories to Phoenix and Laura. They'd been there. They'd faced those demons. It was real.

'I can't wait to see what you've put in it,' Laura said. 'What on earth did you say?'

Phoenix scrolled down.

'It wasn't easy. We didn't want to put anyone off by sounding like cranks. In the end, we decided to do it by asking questions.'

Laura's eyes roved over the page.

'What do you think?'

'I think it's very clever,' Laura replied. 'I just hope it's being read by the person that matters.'

The person that mattered was sitting on the floor of a room hundreds of miles away, kicking away the PR suit, and unfastening the points bracelet. He just wanted to get away.

'What happened?' asked Jon's father.

'That's it,' said Jon, his breath coming in sobs. 'I'm finished. I've had it with that stupid game.'

'But what's got you so upset?'

'What do you mean, what's got me upset? You were tugging at the mask, same as me. I thought I'd never get it off. I felt like I was going to be trapped in there. Besides . . .'

'Yes?'

'Dad, it's sick. I mean, *really* sick. What are you doing, getting involved in something like that?'

'Jon,' his father said patiently, 'just calm down and explain exactly what it is that's got you so spooked.'

'In a normal computer game,' Jon said, 'if you get killed you just go back to the start and begin again.'

'That's right,' said his father. 'And?'

'It's your game,' said Jon. 'You tell me. What's all this about the funeral ship, and Loki being tortured by poison? I mean, the look on his face. When he breaks free, I'm not going to be around to face him. It's like I'm being set up. The bad guy's going to come back and rip me to shreds.'

'Tell me about the funeral ship,' said his father.

'You know,' said Jon impatiently.

'No, Jon, I don't. It's completely new to me.'

'You mean you didn't write it into the game?'

'No.'

'Well, it's like this, I got hit by the arrow. Here.'

He touched his chest and winced. It actually hurt.

'Then it's like I'm a ghost. The Norns say I'm going to play again, I'm going to be some character called Heimdall.'

'That's right, Heimdall the watchman of the gods. He's the hero of level nine.'

'But they take me to this cave and show me what's happening to Loki. It's a torture chamber. You can hear him screaming. Then he looks at me and the Norns tell me that he'll break free one day. And guess what? When he does, he's going to come looking for me. Well, forget it. I'm not sticking around. Not the way he was looking at me.'

'Jon,' his father said, 'we are talking about a game, you know. OK, so somebody else on the team has added a new episode . . .'

'We're not just talking about an episode,' Jon protested

angrily. 'It's really sinister. I was standing there watching somebody getting tortured. I could see what the poison was doing to him. It just went on and on. You should have heard the screams. It was awful. And Loki's blaming *me* for it. If I go through the gateway, I won't ever come out.'

Jon had had enough. He wasn't even going to stay in the same room as the game. He started to get to his feet. A stabbing pain in his chest made him blow out his cheeks.

'Ow!'

The stabbing pain was now a dull ache, gnawing away inside his ribcage.

'What's the matter?'

'Are you sure the electrical equipment's safe?' Jon asked, clutching his shirt. 'It's done something to me.'

His father helped him over to a chair.

'Where does it hurt?'

'Well, my face is still burning from that stupid mask,' said Jon, remembering how it had clung to his skin. 'But it's my chest mostly.'

'Where?'

'About here.'

Jon touched his chest and winced.

'Jon,' said Dad, 'I think I can see a spot of blood.'

'Ow. I wouldn't be surprised. It really does hurt. This shouldn't happen, should it? I mean, I feel like I've been kicked by a horse.'

'I think we'd better take a look. Just unbutton your shirt.'

Jon did as he was told. As he gingerly unfastened the last button and pulled open his shirt, he heard his father gasp.

'What is it?'

He looked down. Covering the entire middle of his chest was a band of ugly, blue-black bruising, and right over his heart there was an ugly weal.

'This is impossible,' his father said.

Jon ran a finger gingerly over the raised ridge of flesh.
'I don't believe it.'
But it was true. The skin was actually broken.
'It's as if I really was shot by an arrow.'

4

The following afternoon Phoenix heard footsteps behind him.

'Hey, hold up.'

'I thought you had netball practice.'

'Cancelled.'

'Weird, isn't it?' said Phoenix. 'In a few days they're going to start selling a game that's about as safe as enriched plutonium, and here we are talking about netball practice. I wonder what we'll be doing come the end of the world, playing snakes and ladders?'

Laura gave him a sideways look.

'Life goes on,' she said. 'Until we find out who's developing the next part.'

'So you're ready to play again?'

'Try to stop me.'

'Good. I'd be lost without you.'

Laura was looking at Phoenix, wondering quite what to say next, when a red, single-decker bus swept past.

'Oh no!' she groaned. 'That's ours.'

'Forget it,' said Phoenix. 'It'll only take us twenty minutes to get home. Besides, I wouldn't mind a walk. Blow out the cobwebs.'

As they set off down the road, Laura nudged him. He seemed distracted.

'Some cobwebs. You're miles away.'

Phoenix chewed at the high collar of his coat.

'There's something else, isn't there? Go on, you can tell me.'

'It's Grandpa, he's dying.'

'But that's been going on for months. You already knew how ill he was.'

'No, I mean really dying. Mum got a phone call last night. They don't think he'll last the week.'

Laura squeezed his arm.

'I'm so sorry.'

Grandpa's death would see the snapping of a connection to the past, to Greece, to his twin brother, Andreas. The man who walked with Phoenix in his dreams.

Andreas.

'I wish I could have talked to Grandpa about Andreas. Really talk, I mean. Thirty years apart, Andreas and I each became aware of the myth-worlds. Maybe Grandpa could have helped me understand. Now there's no chance.'

'So what's happening?'

'Mum's going down to London tomorrow. We'll probably follow her at the weekend.'

'But what if somebody gets in touch about the game?'

'Not much I can do. He's my grandfather.'

Laura squeezed his arm again.

'I could look in on the house for you. Check your e-mails. I did it when you were away in Greece that time.'

'Do you want to come back now?' asked Phoenix. 'We'll ask Mum and Dad.'

Laura stopped and unzipped her bag.

'Hang on a minute. I'll phone Mum.'

She rummaged around inside.

'Where's that stupid mobile?'

While Laura was speaking to her mother, Phoenix watched the wind in the trees. He thought of Grandpa dying, and of Andreas, his twin brother who had died thirty years earlier, locked away in a madhouse. The first man to see the demons.

And the first to pay the price.

Half an hour later, in Phoenix's room, Laura interrupted his daydreams.

'A penny for your thoughts,' she said.

'Just thinking about Grandpa,' said Phoenix, 'and Andreas.'

'Imagine dying the way he did,' said Laura. 'Completely alone. A sane man shut up in an asylum.'

Phoenix didn't answer. He was staring intently at the carpet, remembering the story. How his great-uncle Andreas had been plagued by waking nightmares and been locked away for it. Those nightmares had come back to life in a computer game called *The Legendeer*. It was as if Andreas was actually there, in the room with them, prompting him, telling him where to look to unravel the mystery. Words came to him, like a spell, an incantation.

Everything lies veiled in numbers.

He saw them in his mind's eye. The sequences of threes, sixes and nines that filled the monitor screen and were printed on the gateway of light that opened to admit you deeper into the game.

'Right now somebody else is playing *The Legendeer*,' he said.

The words came again.

Everything lies veiled in numbers.

'But how do we find them, Laura? How do we warn them?'

5

Maybe Phoenix wouldn't have to warn anybody. Jon Jonsson had had his warning. It had taken three stitches at the hospital to close the wound.

'But how could this happen?' his mother demanded in the car on the way home.

'I've no idea,' Dad replied. 'I've examined the suit, gone over it with a fine-tooth comb in fact. There is nothing sharp in it, nothing that could inflict an injury like that. I don't understand it at all.'

'But what else could have caused it?'

'Nothing. I was standing right there beside him when it happened. He didn't hit anything. It's like he was struck by an invisible fist. It's a complete mystery.'

'Well, he's not playing it again,' Mum said firmly.

'I don't want to,' said Jon. 'It's evil.'

His mother looked round.

'What an odd thing to say. Don't you mean dangerous?'

No, he meant *evil*. Evil the way the Minotaur was evil. Evil the way Medusa was evil. Evil the way the vampyrs were evil. Evil. That's what held *The Legendeer* together.

'Evil, Mum, I mean evil.'

'Jon, you're worrying me.'

'You don't know what happened to me in that game. You can't even begin to imagine.'

His parents exchanged glances.

'I hope you're not going to take this lying down,' said his mother. 'This is our son's safety we're talking about. And he's completely terrified. What's that company of yours done to him?'

Jon sensed his father's irritation.

'It's not *my* company. I agreed to work for them in good faith. I didn't expect anything like this.'

Mum looked away.

'I'm sorry. I didn't mean to raise my voice. Look, don't you think I'm concerned? I've e-mailed Magna-com demanding an immediate explanation.'

'Why didn't you phone them? I'd want to speak to somebody in person about something this serious. For goodness' sake, it goes on sale in a few days.'

Jon watched his father shifting uneasily in the driving seat.

'I don't have a phone number.'

'I beg your pardon?'

'No telephone number. It was one of their rules from the very beginning, communication by e-mail only.'

'Are you telling me a major company like Magna-com doesn't even have a switchboard?'

'That's exactly what I'm saying. My salary is paid by computer and all messages come the same way. Come to think of it, I haven't dealt with a single flesh-and-blood human being once since I took the job.'

'What about at the interview?' Jon asked, suddenly more than interested. 'You must have met somebody then. Who took you on?'

'No interview,' Dad replied. 'I sent a cv by e-mail. Everything has been done by computer. I was impressed at first, the technology of the future and all that, but on second thoughts it does seem a bit odd.'

'A bit!' exclaimed Mum. 'I'd say it was downright sinister.'

They pulled up at the side of the house and stepped out onto the pavement, sprinkled with a fresh dusting of snow.

The discussion continued indoors.

'So you've never met a single person from Magna-com?'

'Never.'

'And never spoken to any of their people face to face?'

'Never.'

'I do wish you'd told me. Didn't it seem a bit strange?'

Jon soon tired of the argument. It wasn't getting anywhere. Leaving his parents to it, he headed for his room. Dad's workroom was now securely locked. Jon wouldn't be able to play *Warriors of the Raven* even if he wanted to. He undid a shirt button and touched his bandage gingerly. And he certainly didn't want to play, not if this was what it did to you. Buttoning up his shirt, he sat on his bed.

This is crazy.

Impossible.

But it had happened. He had the proof right there on his body.

'I've been wounded by a virtual arrow.'

It sounded even crazier said out loud. But the thump as it struck him, the stabbing pain through his heart, the hatred in Loki's yellow eyes, they were too real to be a mere game.

'What have we got ourselves into?'

He switched on his tv and channel-surfed for a few moments. He happened on a commercial for *Warriors of the Raven*. He watched it to the end then sat, hands on knees, facing his own PC.

There were no PR suits in his room and no disc for *Warriors of the Raven*. No danger, in other words. Yet he couldn't take his eyes off the screen.

I'm becoming completely paranoid.

But it wasn't paranoia. A game called *The Legendeer* had

brought fear into his predictable, cosy life. He thought about what Mum had said.

You're not going to take this lying down.

'So let's see what I can find out about you,' he said.

He sat down and typed in his password: *JJ*. He waited for a few moments for the Internet to connect then typed in the address of his favourite website.

www.ask arthur.com

He used it for his homework. You just typed in your question and it came up with a list of websites where you could get the information.

'Question: where do I find out about *The Legendeer*?'

Then he waited. He was offered twenty sites in all. *Legends of the world, Greek and Roman legends, Norse mythology.*

Then he saw what he was looking for.

www.legendeer.co.uk

He leaned forward and inspected the graphics on the opening page. The Minotaur, Medusa, werewolves, vampires, the images from the first two games.

'So what am I looking at, an unofficial fanzine?'

He scrolled down and started reading.

Have you played yet? Felt the Minotaur's breath on your neck? Heard the hiss of Medusa, the Vampyr's shriek?

That's exactly what it was, an electronic fanzine.

'Yeah, yeah,' he said. 'Been there, done that.'

Hooked on The Legendeer, Parts One and Two? the computer asked. **Can't wait to play the next one?**

'I've played it,' Jon said out loud. 'And I wish I hadn't.'

Counting the hours until it's out? The big one that Magna-com has been promising, the one with the Parallel Reality suits. Can you imagine it? Being transported body and soul into an alien world. Where you can see, hear, touch, even smell and taste your surroundings.

Now Jon *was* interested. The website had captured his

unsettling experience perfectly. But as he progressed through the questions, enthusiasm was replaced by something else. His blood ran cold. Excitement turned to horror. Suddenly every question seemed to be directed at him personally.

Have you looked into the face of terror, been impaled on eyes of pure evil? Said to yourself: this is real, this is real, this is real.

Too real.

His pulse quickened. But it was the final question that set it racing and made the back of his neck prickle.

Have you wondered about the mystery of the numbers, been drawn into their patterns, the power of three, the magic of nine, the trinity of trinities?

He remembered the snowstorm of numbers that came up every time Dad worked on *Warriors of the Raven*. They had wondered about them often.

The numbers. Yes, of course I've seen them.

Then the screen glowed with an elaborate pattern.

Threes . . .

. . . sixes . . .

. . . nines.

'That's right, that's what comes up.'

Have you noticed the connection between the world's mythologies? How so many things come in multiples of three? Whether it is ancient Greece or the Viking north, the pattern is the same. The nine rivers of Hades, the nine worlds of the Norse myths, the three Muses, the three Furies, the three Norns.

'Three Norns,' murmured Jon.

What about three-headed Cerberus, the three Gorgons, the three years of Fimbulwinter, the three rocks on which Loki's body is bound? The connections go on and on. That's what holds it all together. You have to understand— the myth-code rests on a base of three.

Jon pushed back the chair and stood up. Three Norns, three

rocks. He didn't know about the other stuff, but that certainly rang a bell.

'You do know something. Who are you? How could you . . . ?'

There was one final item at the bottom of the last page, an e-mail address.

Do you recognize the things we have mentioned? Have you been there? Have you been tempted by the golden portal of light, the gateway between the worlds? Want to share the experience with somebody? Then contact us.

Jon stared at the words, wondering whether he should trust them:

Contact us.

6

The phone call came on Friday night. Phoenix took it. Mum was in tears at the other end of the line.

'Phoenix, it's me. It's happened.'

'You mean he's . . . ?'

'Your grandfather passed away this afternoon.'

'I'm sorry, Mum.'

'At least his suffering is over. Put your dad on, will you?'

'Dad,' he called. 'You'd better take this. Mum's calling from London.'

'Coming.'

Dad mouthed a question:

Grandpa?

Phoenix nodded and stepped back. Grandpa dead. As he retreated to the study doorway, Phoenix saw the computer screen and felt a pang of anxiety. The funeral. They would be going down to London sometime soon. He would have to let Laura know. Just in case.

'Stupid,' he murmured. 'Nobody's been in touch for weeks. Why should it change now?'

But nothing would make the nagging doubt go away. However the odds were stacked against it, he couldn't quite accept that the game was over. He had an unfulfilled destiny. It had begun with Andreas and lived again through him. There was a chance, always a chance.

Dad hung up and turned round.

'The funeral is on Thursday. You'll have to take the day off school.'

As Phoenix made his way upstairs, he was acutely aware of the secret menace that had stolen into his life through the circuitry of the computer. Time was ticking away towards the deadline.

The launch of the game was approaching fast, and with it the unleashing of the demon threat. He hesitated at the top of the stairs. Hearing Dad behind him, he glanced back.

'Thinking about the game?'

Phoenix nodded.

'Aren't you?'

'I can't get it out of my mind,' said Dad. 'You know what comes out loud and clear from my reading of the Norse myths, what makes them stand out? It's this: Evil is predestined to win. That's what makes the Viking legends so different. The gods are so vulnerable, almost like ordinary men and women. Thor, Balder and the rest, they can all die and the forces of darkness can win. Even Odin, the king of the gods, loses an eye. The Gamesmaster couldn't have picked a better battle-ground than the Norse myths. In a world where Evil has the upper hand, the odds will be stacked against us.'

Phoenix stared at Dad. It all made sense. The Gamesmaster had chosen well. A land where Evil deals the cards.

'Anyway,' said Dad, 'I'm taking a shower.'

Phoenix watched Dad walking away along the landing. He had read the same books and now he was coming to the same conclusion. That's why the Gamesmaster had chosen the Viking world. It was to be the final victory of Evil.

Five minutes later, on his way back from the bathroom, Dad found Phoenix sitting on the bed.

'What's that you're reading?'

'Andreas' journal.'

'It's a wonder you don't know it off by heart by now.'

'I keep thinking that I'll find something in it,' said Phoenix.

Dad glanced at Phoenix sideways.

'There has to be something more we can do, something we've forgotten.'

'If there is, then I can't think of it.'

Phoenix rose to his feet.

'There has to be something *I* can do. Remember when Laura and I came back the last time, *I* did that.'

He remembered the second game, the final fight in the Vampyr's crypt. He had conjured the numbers. Not the computer, *him*. He remembered the way his fingers had prickled with a raw, elemental force. In a way, *he* had become the computer.

'It wasn't technology that brought us back. It was . . . a power. The same power Andreas felt when he saw *his* demons. I've inherited it from him, I just know it. I can't explain it, but it's got something to do with the numbers. I could read them. I made the gateway open.'

He couldn't work out Dad's expression. Was he really interested or was he just humouring him?

'Go on.'

'The question is: why can't I do it again? Why can't I find my way to wherever the Gamesmaster is?'

'I don't know,' said Dad. 'Have you tried?'

'Have I tried! I've done nothing but try. I just can't call up the numbers in the right order. I have a theory.'

He didn't tell Dad how it had come to him, the night before. In a dream, of course.

'You want to hear it?'

'Fire away.'

'There's a different sequence to each of the myth-worlds. It's like the combination to a safe. Get the combination right and the tumblers fall into place. Open sesame, you're entering a different world.'

'But you can't get the right combination?'

Phoenix raised his eyebrows.

'Can you imagine just how many permutations of three, six and nine there can be? I don't even know how many numbers there are in the sequence. There could be three. There could be ten. There could be thirty. It's harder than winning the National Lottery!'

Dad set off down the landing.

'The Gamesmaster won't win,' he said. 'We will stop him, you know.'

Phoenix followed.

'How?'

He caught up with Dad and looked him in the eye.

'There's just over a week left before *Warriors of the Raven* comes out. We're going to stop him, are we? Go on, tell me how?'

Dad wished he'd kept quiet. Finally he was forced to admit:

'I don't know.'

7

If Jon Jonsson brought up the *Legendeer* website once in the next few days, he must have done it a hundred times. He was like a non-swimmer diving in at the deep end. He stood all ready to go, trembling with anticipation, but he could never quite bring himself to take the plunge.

'I just wish I knew what to do.'

Dad was no use. He'd been dithering too. Stay with Magnacom, or just make a clean break and resign? He had sent his e-mails, loads of them. He had demanded a meeting with the company, but all that had come back was a message thanking him for his work on the game, and a fat cheque by way of a bonus.

'It's a bribe,' Dad had said when he opened the envelope. 'They want me to keep my mouth shut.'

Other than that there was nothing. No apology, no explanation for the accident, no hint that they were taking him seriously. But instead of coming to a decision, he would just wander outside and smash at the outhouse with his hammer. As if he were smashing away at an unknown enemy. Jon shut his computer down and wandered downstairs. Mum was at her evening class. As for Dad, no prizes for guessing where he would be.

'Dad, are you in the workroom?'

'Yes. Do you need me?'

Jon hovered in the doorway. He hadn't entered the room since playing the game the second time.

'No, I just wondered what you were going to do?'

Dad was packing the PR suit in a cardboard box.

'I've made my mind up. Magna-com have fobbed me off long enough. They're taking me for an idiot. This is their last chance. I've been in touch with that consumer programme on the television, the one your mother likes. If I don't get a satisfactory explanation from the company, I'm going to send them the game and all the equipment. There is something seriously wrong with it. It can't go on sale, not like this.'

He taped up the box, addressed a sticky label and pressed it down.

'I've e-mailed Magna-com, telling them what I intend to do. I'm giving them a few days to provide me with a proper explanation, then all this goes to the reporter I've been speaking to.'

'Wow, you have thought it through, haven't you?'

Dad smiled grimly.

'Jon, what happened to you was really serious. I can't have any other youngsters hurt by this company's negligence.'

Dad joined Jon in the hallway and locked the workroom door from outside.

'That's where the game and the PR suits are going to stay until I hear from Magna-com, or until I am forced to go to the media.'

Jon nodded. Dad had finally made his mind up.

Fair enough. Now I'm going to do the same.

He went back to his room and typed in the website address:

www.legendeer.co.uk

He scrolled down and copied the e-mail address.

'Let's see what you've got to say for yourselves.'

Phoenix wasn't part of Grandpa's funeral. He was there, but he didn't want to talk to anyone. His mind was elsewhere, with the twin brother nobody mentioned.

He hovered at the edge of the funeral party and watched Great-aunt Sophia. She must have been remembering Andreas too at that moment, almost as much as she was remembering Grandpa, but she didn't mention him. Not once the whole day. He remained a kind of ghost, a darkness at the edge of the family's lives. He drifted over to the sideboard and looked at the collection of family photographs. No Andreas.

'I know what you're thinking.'

Phoenix turned round.

'Aunt Sophia.'

'We did Andreas a terrible wrong.'

It was a shock to hear her even mention him. Phoenix was about to mumble a reply, but she held up her hand.

'No, you don't need to be polite. You don't need to forgive. I am an old woman. I can do without such pleasantries. We let the villagers get away with a terrible crime. All because they closed their eyes to the nightmare world. Andreas was telling the truth. There is horror all around us. There *is* a nightmare world.'

'Then you know Andreas wasn't crazy?'

'Of course. I always knew, but I was afraid, afraid to be different like Andreas. I didn't have his courage. I didn't dare walk alone.'

There was a moment's silence, then she spoke in a hushed voice.

'It's happening again, isn't it? Your mother told me.'

Phoenix returned her stare.

'Yes, it's happening again.'

'Then you must not be afraid as we were. You must face the darkness. You must fulfil my brother's destiny.'

And that was it. Pressing a small, black and white photograph into Phoenix's hand, she walked away. Phoenix examined it, a photo of the brothers standing in front of a whitewashed house in Greece. He wondered exactly how, with just two days left before the game's launch, he could fulfil his destiny, when his mobile phone rang.

'Phoenix, it's come.'

'Laura?'

'I've just checked your computer. You've got an e-mail from Iceland.'

'Iceland! Why Iceland?'

'It's a boy called Jon. His father is the one. He's been working on *Warriors of the Raven* and it's all going wrong. Phoenix, it's just like you and your dad all over again. I've already e-mailed Jon back. He can send us a copy of the game, Phoenix. It's the breakthrough we've been looking for.'

Phoenix looked down at Andreas' face and smiled. So Dad was right. They had moved it abroad.

'Thanks, Laura. I'll tell Dad. We'll be home tonight.'

8

Jon's parents were still at work when he got home from school. He glanced at the hallway clock. They should be home any time. Just a few minutes until he told Dad about the website. He took the latest e-mail from his pocket. The print-out was tattered with repeated reading. He almost knew it off by heart. It didn't prevent him reading it again:

Jon,

You're right. There is something wrong with the game. What you saw wasn't just graphics. It's a real world. That's right, every bit as real as this one. I have been there. I've been in the position you are now, but I went through the gateway and became part of its world. The first two games were just like the one you entered, but we got in the way of the Gamesmaster's plans. What Magna-com put on the market was just a pale imitation of the real thing. Now it's starting all over again. Through this game the barrier between the worlds can be broken down. We can enter the nightmare world of the ancient myths. And the creatures from that world can break into ours. Do you understand what I'm telling you? Monsters could walk among us.

That's what your father has been paid to do. He wasn't helping to write a computer game. He was bringing the two worlds into line. He was making it possible for the demons you have seen to break through. Imagine what that would be like. Your worst imaginings come true. And it's tomorrow, Jon.

Tomorrow!

But it isn't too late. There is something you must do. Send me the game, or at least a copy. It is the only way I can stop the nightmare from happening.

If you have been inside the game, you know what I'm talking about.

Send it, Jon. Send me the game.

Phoenix.

Jon looked at the locked workroom door. The sealed package was inside. For a moment he actually thought about smashing his way in. But he rejected the idea just as quickly.

I'll get the game to you.

But how do I convince Dad?

He knew that what Phoenix had told him was true. Anyone who had entered the world of the game would be convinced. But would Dad be so sure? Jon returned to the living room and drew back the blinds to look up the road for his father. Just as he was moving away from the window, he caught a glimpse of something. It flickered across his field of vision, sending a shudder through him. But there was no doubt about it. Somebody was inside the house with him.

'Who's there?' he asked.

There was no reply, but he hadn't been imagining things. There was definitely a noise, and it was coming from the workroom.

But how?

It was locked.

'Mum, Dad, is that you?'

But he knew it wasn't them. Jon edged to the door, peering up the hallway. His heart missed a beat. Whoever was moving around the flat had left a trail of paper clips on the floor. It was no accident, either. It was a deliberate act, meant to unnerve him. The intruder was putting on a show. The trail of clips was to let him know he wasn't alone. The plastic pot that had held them was still rocking outside the kitchen.

Worse still, the intruder was between Jon and escape. Panic took hold, coiling round his windpipe, choking off his breath.

Got to think.

But he couldn't think. He looked around the room for something to defend himself, but immediately snapped back to attention. The empty pot had changed direction and was starting to roll towards him. It hadn't shifted by itself. Somebody was making it roll.

'Who are you?' he called, his voice sounding feebler and fainter than ever.

Discovering a burglar had always been one of his worst fears. Now he would have given anything for it to be a burglar. He remembered what it said on tv. If you disturb someone breaking and entering they usually run. But this intruder wasn't running.

'Who's there?'

There was no reply, just another pot rolling into the hallway. Then another and another. Six plastic pots in all, spilling pencils, erasers, drawing pins. The intruder was teasing, mischievous.

'Please stop it,' Jon said.

Immediately, he regretted saying it. That's what the intruder wanted, to have him begging and pleading. That's what the pots were all about. Cat and mouse. A power game. He wasn't doing it because he had to. He was doing it because *he liked it.*

Belatedly, Jon changed tack:

'I'm not afraid of you.'

Even that was counterproductive.

The intruder spoke for the first time, in a sing-song voice tinged with malice.

'Poor little Jon, all alone. Not afraid, you say?'

He stepped out into the corridor. Jon gasped.

'Then you should be.'

It was *him*, the owner of the yellow eyes.

'Please don't hurt me.'

Jon was trying to make sense of the evidence of his eyes. Facing him was a puzzle rather than a human being. He had the face of a teenage boy, but the muscular frame of a grown man. Then there were those eyes, Loki's eyes.

'Oh, I'm not going to hurt you,' the intruder told him. 'Not that I couldn't if I felt like it. There's no need. I just came to get this.'

He was holding up the computer equipment from the study, the *Warriors of the Raven* disc, a PR suit and a points bracelet.

Jon shook his head.

'You can't have it. It doesn't belong to you.'

The intruder took a step forward, a look of bored amusement on his face.

'And who is going to take it from me? You?'

He shoved the PR suit and points bracelet back in their box.

'Your father had a job to do. He shouldn't have interfered.'

Jon thought of Phoenix waiting for the disc.

It's the only way to stop the nightmare.

'You've got to give them back.'

'I don't *have* to do anything. That's the beauty of serving the Gamesmaster. It gives you total freedom.'

The intruder smiled.

'How can I explain it to you? How can I make you understand how stupid it is for you to give me orders? The Gamesmaster isn't a man, you see. He is a power. For many years he has been a power trapped in another world, a ghost, a phantom. Now he is about to rise. He is a power that will make the worlds tremble. And I serve that power. I am its hands and eyes. Now do you see why you shouldn't tell me what to do?'

Jon was wondering what to say when he heard a key scraping in the lock.

'Dad.'

'Well, fun over,' said the intruder, picking up the box. 'I've got what I came for. Time for me to go.'

He walked straight past Jon and into the workroom. Jon followed him with his eyes, then turned to greet his father.

'Jon, who were you talking to? Who's in there with you?'

Not knowing what to say, Jon gave the only answer he could.

'Somebody is in the workroom. He's got all the game gear.'

Dad pushed past him and stared for a moment at the splintered doorframe, the broken lock. It had clearly been smashed open from the inside.

'What the . . . ?'

He walked into the workroom.

'Dad, be careful.'

But Dad turned round.

'Jon, there's nobody here.'

9

Phoenix and Laura sat side by side at the computer. John Graves stood behind them, looking over their shoulders. The e-mail from Jon Jonsson made grim reading.

Phoenix,

I've let you down. I know this sounds crazy, but it was him. Loki. We've been robbed by a character in a computer game! There really is no other explanation. The workroom window was locked. He came out of the PC and took everything. I've blown it.

Jon.

'He's got the game!' Laura exclaimed. 'Now what do we do?'

Phoenix closed his eyes.

'Give me a moment to think.'

'But without the game, we can't follow Adams. We can't do anything. It was Adams, wasn't it?'

'Oh, it was him all right. He's the only one of the Gamesmaster's disciples who can pass through the gateway. From what Jon tells us, he's obviously taken the part of Loki in the game. The Mischief-Maker, most cunning and evil of the Norse gods. Suits him, don't you think?'

Phoenix fingered the photo of Andreas and stared at the screen.

'Well?'

'I'm still thinking.'

He lowered his head, as if turning in on himself. After a few moments he looked up.

'I have to play in Jon's place. I'm the only one who can end this nightmare. I'm the Legendeer. I've got to go in after Adams, take the part of Heimdall, Loki's arch-enemy. I will be the hero.'

The screen-save clicked on, planets, stars and comets. Phoenix frowned.

'What is it?' Dad asked. 'Speak to us, Phoenix.'

'I wonder.'

'What? Tell us what you're thinking about.'

Phoenix stared at the screen-save for a few more moments, then brought up E-mail Express again. He clicked Compose Message.

'What are you doing?'

'Trying a long shot. Dad, do you remember what I told you? About the numbers, I mean?'

'That they're the language of the game and you think you can manipulate them? Of course I remember.'

'Now's the time to test my theory,' said Phoenix.

Fulfil Andreas' destiny, Great-aunt Sophia had told him. Maybe he still could. He typed in his message:

Jon,

You've no need to feel guilty. There's nothing you could do. The person you saw is called Steve Adams. He entered the game about the same time I did, but when it came to taking sides, he chose darkness. He does the dirty work for the one who controls the game, the Gamesmaster. You recognized him because he plays a part in it. We play the hero, he plays the villain. That's right, in a way it *was* Loki you saw in your flat. Now think. We've got one chance left. The game works on a computer language, something completely different to most information technology. The base number is three. Do those numbers appear on your father's PC? Does it mean anything to you? You have to look for them. I repeat: multiples of three.

This is urgent.

Phoenix.

He hit Send and drummed his fingers impatiently on the computer table.

'This is crazy,' said Dad. 'We're relying on a fourteen-year-old boy.'

'Dad,' Phoenix said coolly, '*I*'m a fourteen-year-old boy.'

The reply came a few moments later:

Phoenix,

Yes, I've seen the numbers you mean. They're flashing on the screen right now. What do you want me to do?

Jon

Phoenix looked at Dad and Laura, then wrote a new message:

Jon,

You've got to act immediately.

Go to the computer and look for any strings of numbers you can recognize. I know it's hard. You will see hundreds of numbers, maybe thousands, but they are not random. There *are* patterns. You've got to look for clear combinations. Hurry. Our enemy could be reading this message.

Phoenix.

Laura read the e-mail. As Phoenix hit Send, she asked him the obvious question:

'Will this work?'

Phoenix glanced over his shoulder, as if for support. Dad shrugged his shoulders:

'You're the Legendeer, son. You tell us.'

'I've no idea, but I've got to try.'

10

Jon glanced out of the window. Mum and Dad were standing on the pavement, talking to the policeman. He had come to take a statement while Jon was exchanging e-mails with Phoenix. For a frustrating quarter of an hour, while his mind raced with thoughts of magic numbers and other worlds, Jon had had to tell his story over and over again. He had wisely omitted any mention of the intruder being a character out of a computer game. Finally, the policeman had enough information and Jon could run to the computer. It was still blinking away, the way it had been when the intruder came.

Jon sat down in front of the monitor screen and there they were, the confusion of numbers.

The language of the game.

The language of other worlds.

*There **is** a way.*

He gave another quick glance out of the window. His parents were still talking to the policeman.

'A sequence,' he murmured. 'Look for a sequence.'

It was easier said than done. What confronted him was a snowstorm of seemingly unrelated numerals.

'This is hopeless.'

He remembered the optical illusions some of his friends had brought into school and the advice that helped you find the hidden picture.

*Fix your attention on one spot and look **through** the pattern.*

It was easier said than done.

'Oh, come on, Jon, you can do it. Now focus.'

Then, suddenly, amid what had appeared an impenetrable maze of numbers, he was able to make out a sequence.

For a moment he couldn't believe his eyes, but there it was.

3–3–3 3–6–9 3–3–3

A definite string of numerals. It seemed to detach itself, take on solid form and present itself to him, a single distinct combination. He scribbled down the numbers and stood up.

'Got it.'

That's when it happened. The screen began to clear. In place of the numbers there was a fiery background, and in place of the sequence was a familiar face. The hard, cheerless features. The yellow, hateful eyes.

'You!'

'Surprise surprise.'

Then a golden light was filling the room. Jon retreated to the door. The numerals that had so recently been racing on the monitor screen were pulsating in the portal of light.

It's the gateway.

He's coming through.

Thinking quickly, Jon yanked the plug from the wall.

'No power, no entry,' he said.

To his horror, it made no difference. The PC continued to purr, powered by something stronger than electricity. The gateway continued to shimmer. The intruder was coming back. It was him, Adams.

'The numbers. Of course, you want the numbers.'

Jon turned and ran to his room where his own PC was on, the prepared e-mail ready to go. All it needed was the numbers. Jon started typing:

3–3–3

'I wouldn't do that.'

The back of Jon's neck prickled.

Adams was in the doorway. He was standing right behind him.

3–6–9

Jon felt strong fingers closing round his arms.

'I said: I wouldn't do that.'

Before Jon could struggle or protest, he was flung bodily across the room. He picked himself up to see Adams leaning over the keyboard.

'No, get away from it.'

Just as the words were leaving Jon's lips, the front door slammed.

'Dad, Mum, up here!'

Adams turned.

'You'll regret you ever said that.'

Dad was already on the landing outside the room.

'Jon, what's wrong?'

Then Dad saw Adams and the blood drained from his face.

'Where did you come from? Get away from my son.'

He threw himself at Adams, propelling him against the wall. It was a brief struggle. Adams possessed the power of the myth-world. He easily shrugged Dad off and sent him crashing into the doorframe. But it gave Jon the time he needed. He scrambled to the keyboard and typed in the last three digits:

3–3–3

As Adams turned and saw what he had done, Jon smiled triumphantly and guided the mouse across the pad.

'You won't win,' he shouted defiantly.

For the first time, the superior sneer vanished from Adams' face.

Delighted at the reaction, Jon left-clicked the mouse to dispatch the e-mail.

Send.

11

'You know what I've got to do, don't you? If Jon finds the numbers, I mean.'

'Yes,' said Dad. 'We've been here before, remember. Your mother and I both understand. You're the Legendeer. You have to fulfil your destiny.'

He tapped the monitor screen.

'We'll be watching your every move, just like the other times.'

Phoenix smiled grimly.

'*If* we get the numbers.'

Then, as the words left his lips, a single digit registered in the Inbox:

(1)

'Open it,' Dad said excitedly.

It was exactly what they'd been waiting for:

3–3–3 3–6–9 3–3–3

Phoenix scribbled down the numbers, then looked at Laura.

'There's no time to lose.'

She nodded.

He turned to his father.

'It's all right, Phoenix,' he said. 'There's nothing more to say. Finish it.'

Phoenix smiled and reread the string of numerals. He picked up a points bracelet and snapped it onto his wrist. Then he did what he had done in the Vampyr's crypt. He started to trace the numbers, sketching them in the air with his finger.

If I really am the Legendeer, this is going to work.

He traced the numbers again:

3–3–3 3–6–9 3–3–3

It was an electronic Open Sesame.

Within moments the screen had begun to clear. There in front of his eyes was a wintry landscape. Amid a howling blizzard he could make out a rocky outcrop, and beyond that he could just about distinguish seven bands of glittering colour.

'Bifrost,' he said, recognizing it from his reading of the Norse myths. 'The rainbow bridge.'

Phoenix laid his hands flat on the screen, as if reaching out to it, and a magical transformation occurred. It became liquid, malleable to the touch. He was able to prise it open, just like molten plastic. He was tearing a hole in reality.

I can do it.

I really can!

'Dad,' he cried, thrilled by what he had done. 'Dad!'

But the transformation was accelerating. A shimmering golden oval had appeared, imprinted with silver numbers, the combination he had traced on the monitor screen. Phoenix held out his hand to Laura, and she took it.

'There's no going back,' he said.

'Good,' she replied. 'Because I don't want to go back.'

They both turned and waved to John Graves, but he was already a barely distinct, blurred figure. Phoenix and Laura stepped into the portal of light, passing through the gateway and closing the door to their old world behind them.

BOOK TWO

The Book of the Gamesmaster

THE LEVELS

Level Nine

Warriors of the Raven

1

Phoenix was spiralling through time and place, spinning and tumbling out of control, and when the spinning stopped he found himself lying sprawled on a blanket of snow. What confronted him on the other side of the gateway was a high-ridged landscape whipped by bitter north-easterly winds. For a moment, flashing against the grey sky he saw a menu, as if lit in neon. Only one option was highlighted:

Level 9. Warriors of the Raven.

As the flashing menu faded, Phoenix turned away. His thoughts were directed at the Gamesmaster:

Still going through the motions, are you?

Still pretending it's all a game.

But everything around him reminded Phoenix that this was much more than that. He was standing on a bare hillside, some hundred metres from the summit of a claw-shaped crag, overlooking the waters of a frozen inlet. Half a dozen longships were beached on the shore. The peak was awhirl with a furious blizzard and the bitter cold sank its teeth right into the marrow of his bones. He knew that back in Dad's study there was no Phoenix and no Laura. They had entered another world entirely.

I'm back.

He looked around for Laura.

'Where is she?' he wondered, peering into the storm.

Then he noticed something. Half-lost in the swirling mass of flakes there was a building. What was it, a stone cairn, a derelict chapel?

'Laura, are you in there?'

He continued up the hill in silence and stopped at the wall of the stone pile before them.

'What is this place?' he murmured, inspecting the carved symbols that covered the stonework.

The wind was howling and whipping against his face as if trying to cast him out.

'Laura?'

He was about to make his way inside the mysterious structure, when he heard her voice.

'Laura?' he asked.

'In here.'

There were more carvings inside, grotesque images of giants and elves, witches and dragons.

'What is all this?' she asked.

'This,' said Phoenix, touching the roughly scored lettering beneath the pictures, 'is the runic alphabet. The Vikings carved these letters on wood or stone. Each letter is meant to possess magic powers.'

'Can you read them?'

Phoenix shook his head.

'But look at this. The episodes are laid out in levels. I think this one's the death of Balder, the level Jon played in the game. This is where we are now, see the outline of the building and this . . .'

His voice trailed off. He had become aware of Laura staring at something behind him.

'What's wrong?'

Her dark eyes flicked in the direction of three hooded women. They seemed to have appeared from nowhere.

'You are welcome back, player,' they said. 'So you changed your mind? You wish to enter our world.'

'You mistake me for somebody else,' said Phoenix.

At the sound of his voice, the women appeared startled and confused. They huddled together, discussing the turn of events in hushed voices.

'We did not read this in the runes,' said one in a dismayed voice. 'This was not meant to be.'

'You must leave,' cried another. 'Your presence upsets the balance of the world. You cannot go against Fate.'

'Get away,' shrieked the third, waving Phoenix away. 'The runes forbid your presence.'

'Then consult them again,' he retorted. 'I'm not leaving.'

Once again the three women turned away, whispering and gesturing.

'We are the Norns,' they told him finally. 'Our power is as ancient as the stones. The fate of men is in our hands. Who are you to command us?'

'You know who I am,' said Phoenix. 'I am Heimdall.'

'No, you are not the one.'

'I am Heimdall,' Phoenix repeated in a strong, defiant voice. 'I belong here. Now do as I say. Consult the runes.'

'You crave your destiny,' said one of the Norns. 'And we have no power to deny you. You claim the name of Heimdall. So be it.'

'But know this,' said another. 'It is a dangerous hunger you have in your belly.'

The third detached herself from the others and rattled half a dozen stones in her bony hand before tossing them to the ground. Five lay on their faces. She crouched down and examined the single upturned stone. It was etched with a symbol.

'I am Verdande,' said the Norn, picking up the stone. 'I represent the past. This rune is called Mannaz. It stands for Man. You will champion the cause of Man.'

Phoenix nodded. 'Mankind is threatened. I am here to defend it.'

His words set off much muttering among the Norns. The second of the sisters stepped forward to throw the runes. Again just one lay face up.

'I am Urd. I represent the present. This rune is called Ansuz. It stands for Odin and the other gods of Asgard, the Aesir.'

'I am here to fight at the side of the Aesir against the forces of darkness.'

The Norns exchanged glances. The third of the Norns cast her runes.

'I am Skuld. I represent the future. This rune is called Raido, the rune of journeying. Your path will be long and dangerous. I see the shadow of death falling across it. Look about you – we've had three years of Fimbulwinter, heavy snow everywhere, no sign of blessed summer. Ill-doing surrounds us like a sour mist. The forces of darkness gather and life hangs by a slender thread. It is Heimdall's destiny to be a beacon in the darkness.'

Laura looked at Phoenix. He was unmoved.

'Tell me something I don't know. Now, we'd be grateful if you would set us on our way.'

The Norns gathered together whispering to each other. Finally they turned to face Phoenix and Laura.

'You have come this far, so we must guide you, but your destiny awaits you in this frozen Northland. It may not be the one you wished for. Great Odin gave one of his eyes to gain wisdom. It is a quality you would do well to prize. You have time to reconsider. You were not meant to come. The Northland rebels against your presence. You may still turn back.'

'There's no turning back,' said Phoenix. 'Show us the way.'

'The past you know,' said Verdande. 'Loki has used trickery to slay brave Balder. For his crime the Mischief-Maker is bound in chains at the end of the world. His blood beats with rage against the gods of Asgard.'

'So here you stand,' said Urd. 'Men will look upon you and know you a Heimdall, watchman of the gods. If you go on you will draw the ire of Loki and all his legions. Do you still want Heimdall's destiny?'

'If it's the part I have to play,' said Phoenix. 'Fine, I'm Heimdall.'

Urd scowled. She didn't appreciate his flippant answer.

'The future is yours to make,' said Skuld. 'The world shivers under endless winter. Men wait in vain for the coming of summer. The Age of Evil has come upon earth. The world is hard and cruel. Brothers slay brothers. Daughters betray mothers. The wicked fall upon the innocent and the good, while their protectors cower behind locked doors. Soon Loki will break his chains and lead them. On the fateful day of Ragnarok you must raise an army of men and gods. At Vigrid plain you must fight the Mischief-Maker and his legions. It will fall to you to meet yellow-eyed Loki in fearful battle. Do you still crave Heimdall's fate?'

'It's why I came,' said Phoenix.

'Then the die is cast,' said Skuld. 'Men will know you as Heimdall, watchman of Asgard. Fulfil your destiny.'

The wind roared, hail stung Phoenix and Laura's eyes. When they were able to look again, the Norns had gone.

2

'We still don't know which way to go,' said Laura, crossing the floor of the stone building. 'In fact they didn't tell us anything.'

Phoenix nodded.

'I don't think it matters. Something will show us the way.'

He awaited the secret speaker who had guided him before. He awaited the voice of Andreas.

'Or someone.'

Laura walked outside onto the misty hillside.

Phoenix was following her when she recoiled, bumping into him.

'What is it?'

She turned round. Her eyes were hard points of horror. Phoenix saw what had startled her. Hanging by a noose from a single, twisted oak tree was a corpse. It was turning slowly like a compass needle from north to east, then from east to south, the rope round its neck creaking under the weight. Phoenix stared. The corpse filled him with unease.

'Phoenix,' called Laura. 'Why don't you come away?'

'Something isn't right,' he told her.

Then he realized. One finger on its right hand was moving. Ever so slightly it's true, but there was definite movement.

It was alive.

A moment later two, no three, fingers were twitching compulsively. Then all five fingers were flexing. Before Phoenix knew it, the right arm was bending slowly at the elbow. He could see muscles and tendons moving through the rotting flesh. Then the creature was reaching up towards the rope.

The left arm followed suit and both hands started to grip the branch of the ancient oak. Hand over hand, the corpse began to haul itself up. There was immense power in its arms and they lifted the body until the rope went slack around its neck. With a couple of tugs followed by a macabre shrug of the shoulders, the head was free.

'I know this,' said Phoenix. 'This thing is a dead-walker. A man who dies as a hero in battle ascends to Valhalla. A man who dies any other way, like this one hanging from a noose, joins the unhappy dead and dwells with the queen of the Underworld, Hela. This is one of her creatures, a zombie.'

The creature dropped to earth and turned in their direction. Was this the kind of monster the Gamesmaster planned to release into his world?

'Laura,' Phoenix yelled. 'Run!'

'Run where?' cried Laura.

'Who cares?' Phoenix snapped, fleeing himself. 'Just run!'

They'd put fifty metres between themselves and the lonely building before Laura ventured her first glance back.

'Is it there?'

'Don't ask,' he panted. 'Don't talk. Don't even think.'

He was unarmed and unsure what he was dealing with.

'Just run.'

The creature was marching on, half-hidden by the swirling haze of snow.

'How do we stop that thing?' he said.

'Keep going,' cried Laura. 'There's something ahead, at the bottom of the hill.'

In the hollow there was another building, made of wood this time. A plume of smoke rose from a hole in the roof.

'Look, see the smoke? That means there are people in there.'

'I wish I knew exactly who was in there,' said Phoenix, hesitating.

'With that thing following us,' Laura panted, 'I think it's worth taking the chance. If they're sitting around a fire, at least they are flesh and blood.'

She forced the pace.

'Well, what do you say? Anything is better than our zombie friend.'

They were standing in front of the door of the building that was their destination. Phoenix reached for the finely wrought handle.

'Now *I*'m having second thoughts,' said Laura. 'I hope we're doing the right thing.'

Phoenix pulled open the door.

'I don't think we've got much choice.'

The moment he opened the door, Phoenix wondered whether Laura hadn't been right after all. They had stepped into a wild feast, a riotous affair lit by torches and a huge log fire. In a hall hung with rows of decorated shields, pelts and battle-axes, dozens of burly, bearded men were gathered around a long table. A huge banner emblazoned with a giant black bird hung over their heads.

'A raven,' hissed Phoenix. 'The symbol of Odin. Father of the gods.'

Laura accepted the information but looked around aghast.

'Phoenix, I think we've made a mistake.'

The diners were shouting and laughing, and noisily draining their ale from drinking horns. The air was heavy with wood-smoke and the spit and hiss of roasting meat. But the entry of the two teenagers brought everything to an abrupt halt.

'Ye gods,' said a great ox of a man as he rose from his seat. 'What have we here?'

He inspected Laura and Phoenix from head to toe.

'They're not Northmen,' barked a second man, his blue eyes cold with hostility. 'That's for sure.'

Phoenix and Laura edged closer together for support. They had their hands on the door jamb and were probably turning the same difficult decision over in their minds. Stay and face the rough justice of this rowdy, drunken gathering or flee and risk running into the dead-walker out in the storm. It was Phoenix who made the decision. Shoving the door closed behind him, he took a step forward.

'My name is . . .'

He'd chosen to put on a bold front, but it backfired. Before he could name himself as Heimdall, the man who had spoken first dashed his drinking horn down on the table.

'Who told you to speak, boy!'

Laura's fingers tightened on Phoenix's arm, her nails digging into him.

'No man – no, nor unshaven boy, either – enters the mead-hall of Halfdan Forkbeard uninvited and presumes to speak without my bidding.'

'I didn't . . .'

The man who had announced himself as Halfdan Forkbeard threw his arms wide and thundered out his words to the entire gathering.

'Will you listen to him? There he goes again. Have you ever heard the like of it? This pimply cub thinks he can just walk into the hall of the Berserkers and presume to speak. He needs to be taught a lesson.'

'Yes,' came a voice from the back of the hall. 'And you're the man to give it to him, Halfdan Forkbeard.'

The speaker was greeted with a roar of approval.

'Have you heard of me, lad?' demanded Halfdan, planting his fists on his hips. 'I am the sword-wielder, the wolf-wrestler and dragon-master. I march beneath the raven banner of the All-father. My ships have combed the bright sea-tresses from here to the edge of the poisoned sea. Do you know this name that makes the mountains shiver?'

Phoenix weighed up his options. In the end, he thought it better to say nothing.

'I am Halfdan Forkbeard, Jarl of Skaldheim, Lord of Berserkers. I am defender of the gods of Asgard, ring-giver of heroes, ice-strider, slayer of the dead-walkers and all demons of the night. Kneel, boy.'

Phoenix was all too ready to bow his head, if only under the weight of the chieftain's many titles. In fact, at that moment Phoenix would have readily flattened himself before Halfdan and kissed his boots. What stopped him was the silent speaker, a voice from far away that only he heard.

No, face this man.

Phoenix nodded grimly. There was certainty in the voice. He had to do as he was told. He had to act like an envoy of the gods. Phoenix gave Halfdan Forkbeard his answer in a quavering voice:

'I am afraid I can't kneel to you, Halfdan Forkbeard.'

His reply was met with a loud gasp.

Laura dug her nails into the back of his hand. This time she almost drew blood.

'What are you doing?'

'I'm not exactly sure.'

Halfdan strode forward until he was standing, feet planted apart, inches from Phoenix. Phoenix was tall and well-built for his fourteen years, but Halfdan easily eclipsed him both in height and bulk.

'By the beard of Odin,' roared the huge figure, his own grease-stiffened beard wagging menacingly. 'Do you know who you're speaking to? I've ground the skulls of men bigger than you, and picked my teeth with their bones.'

Phoenix heard the voice again.

Courage.

He had to make a show of boldness.

'I am speaking to Halfdan Forkbeard,' said Phoenix, barely able to stop his legs giving way beneath him. 'The man who *claims* to slay the dead-walkers.'

This time the hall was stunned to silence.

'But my companion and I have just encountered one of the undead.'

A murmur ran through the gathering.

'That's right,' said Phoenix, finding his voice. 'There it was, large as death, and within spitting distance of this hall. Not too scared of you, was it? Where were you when you were needed, Jarl of Skaldheim?'

Halfdan gestured to two of his warriors.

'Take a look outside.'

But Phoenix had become intoxicated by the danger of his words, and was letting his tongue run just a little too far:

'Hiding in your drinking horn, were you, Lord Halfdan?'

There were no gasps of astonishment this time. The entire crowd were leaning forward, their interest in the impudent stranger intense. What gave this sapling the gall to insult a great oak like Halfdan Forkbeard?

'Nothing,' Halfdan's men reported on their return, the blizzard's blast following them into the hall.

'What do you say to that, boy?' demanded Halfdan. 'I hope you have a good answer. Bloodletter here knows how to deal with those who cross me.'

He ran a finger down the edge of his battle-axe.

'I say,' Phoenix told him, 'that I am here on a mission to raise an army.'

'An army, eh?' chuckled Halfdan. 'And who sent you on this mission?'

'I do the will of the gods,' said Phoenix.

A murmur went round the hall.

'I am Heimdall, watchman of Asgard.'

The claim provoked outrage.

'Blasphemy,' cried some.

Halfdan held up his hand for silence.

'Heimdall, are you?' asked Halfdan. 'The far-seer, the watchman of the gods?'

'I am.'

'He's no god,' protested a warrior at the back. 'Send him back out into the storm, ring-giver.'

Halfdan strode around the hall, raising his arms.

'No, my brothers,' he said. 'We dare not risk the wrath of the gods.'

Halfdan eyed Phoenix warily.

'Odin, lord of Asgard,' he roared. 'Thor, the thunderer, I appeal to you. If this is indeed your watchman, send me a sign.'

His speech brought renewed protests and demands for Phoenix's head. Other voices counselled caution.

'Do it, Halfdan, call upon the gods.'

The quarrel looked like getting out of hand but the hubbub subsided as quickly as it had begun. There was a loud knock at the door. In the hushed silence that followed, fearful glances were exchanged.

'It can't be.'

The knock came again, so loud and forceful it almost smashed the door.

'Who will answer it?' asked Halfdan.

Nobody stirred.

'What's the matter, zombie-slayer?' asked Phoenix, his confidence growing. 'Afraid of who is on the other side of the door?'

Halfdan spun round, confusion written on his broad face.

'No, it's a trick. It has to be.'

'Then answer it, Halfdan,' came a shout from the right side of the hall.

'What if the lad's a demon in disguise?' said another. 'What if Loki sent him? Beware of his trickery.'

'What's trickery compared to the gods?' snarled Halfdan. 'If this is Odin's watchman, then there will be a sign.'

The warriors waited. When nothing happened the shouting started again.

'Throw the boy out.'

'Send him on his way.'

But the chorus of shouts was interrupted by another loud crash and a huge, long-handled hammer flew across the hall, landing on the table.

'Mjollnir?' gasped Halfdan. 'The thunderer's hammer. Do my eyes deceive me?'

He stared questioningly at Phoenix.

'Is it true? Can you really be the one you claim? Are you Heimdall?'

Phoenix stared at the hammer with almost as much amazement as Halfdan, but finally managed a reply.

'I am Heimdall.'

'Don't believe him, Forkbeard,' protested one man seated at the far end of the table. 'He has an accomplice. That's all, an accomplice lurking outside.'

Halfdan marched to the shattered door and looked out.

'Then the accomplice is fleet of foot. There is nobody here. And there are no footprints in the snow.'

A murmur ran round the hall.

'Leave the lad be,' cried one brave warrior. 'He has been sent by the gods.'

'Yes,' said another. 'It would be blasphemy not to welcome him into our hall.'

Halfdan looked down at the hammer as if in awe of it.

'Is that the verdict of you all?' he asked. 'To leave the boy be?'

Halfdan's question was answered with thunderous acclaim.

'Then take your place at the table, lad,' said the chieftain. 'You're the first representative of the gods to come our way.'

'I'll be happy to accept your hospitality,' said Phoenix. 'One small favour, though. Could my friend join us?'

He indicated Laura, who appeared to be trying to shrink into the floor.

'Very well. You have the blessing of Thor and Odin. She can join us.'

Laura sat down next to Phoenix. The pair of them glanced from the hammer to the shattered door, already being patched with rough planks by two of Halfdan's men. So who *had* thrown the hammer?

3

'So,' said a voice by Phoenix's left shoulder, 'you tell Lord Halfdan that you are Heimdall, watchman of Asgard. The gods have not forsaken us then?'

For all the man's suspicious tone, Phoenix looked up from his plate with some gratitude. He didn't need much of an excuse to stop eating. The gristly meat was swimming in a pool of fat that was congealing into a brown and white swirl. As for the black bread that went with it, the stuff was as tasteless as cardboard and hard enough to file metal.

'This bread,' Phoenix asked. 'What's it made of?'

'Pine-bark,' came the unappetising answer.

'And the meat?'

'Walrus belly.'

Phoenix grimaced.

'Don't turn your nose up. In these dark times that amounts to a feast. Or do you still dine on succulent meats in high Asgard?'

The man who had addressed him with such sarcasm and rescued him from a meal worse than death had been sitting to the right of Halfdan Forkbeard when they first entered the hall.

'Before I tell you anything,' Phoenix replied cautiously, 'may I know who is asking?'

'I am the Jarl's chief counsel. I go by the name of Eirik Bluetooth . . .'

He pulled back his upper lip.

'Though, as you will see, this useless fang is grey rather than blue, the result of a lucky punch by a bruiser of a Night Elf.'

He leaned forward to confide in his listeners.

'That Elf now lies headless in five fathoms of icy water. A rascal's reward.'

He drew a dagger and drove its point into the wood of the table.

'So die all enemies of Skaldheim.'

Laura turned away, but it wasn't in fear of the dagger. Eirik Badbreath might have been a better title for Halfdan's gnarled adviser.

'Well, Eirik Bluetooth,' said Phoenix, ignoring the menacing introduction. 'You know who I am. This is Laura.'

Eirik gave Laura the briefest of glances then fixed Phoenix with his fierce, blue eyes. They glinted with suspicion.

'And what business does the watchman of Asgard have with the men of Skaldheim?'

'The forces of evil are rising,' said Phoenix. 'Loki is about to shake off his chains and lead his legions against Asgard. On the day of Ragnarok, man and god must stand together against him. I am here to summon you to arms.'

Those who overheard stopped what they were doing and stared. One even gathered himself up in his cloak and retreated outside. Phoenix could scarcely have caused more consternation if he had lobbed a grenade into the gathering. For the second time, he had brought silence to the hall of Skaldheim. Eirik waved away the listeners' attention. As the conversation and banter resumed, he leaned closer. His breath was a heady mix of ale, ox-meat, onions and rotting teeth.

'Lower your voice,' he advised. 'The Mischief-Maker strikes no note of terror in my heart. These other souls, however, their horizons are narrow. They give Halfdan Forkbeard unquestioning obedience and live and die in his service to protect Skaldheim from the forces of evil. Don't ask these men to look too high towards the heavens or too far down into the underworld. The Berserkers are simple men. Ale, a fully belly, a warm bed and a good fight. That's all they need to be happy with their lot. As to matters of heaven and hell and the fate of the gods, they're best forgotten.'

'But if they don't fight,' Phoenix replied, 'this whole world will be destroyed. You will be overwhelmed by creatures like the one we encountered.'

'And you come to save us?'

'I come to save your world.'

'You ran into a dead-walker, you say?' Eirik asked, the same expression of suspicion in his eyes.

'Yes,' said Laura. 'Do you see them often?'

'They are the undead, the spawn of Hela, creatures of the Underworld. With the onset of this Age of Evil they swarm across the earth. By now they probably outnumber the living. They serve the Evil One.'

Phoenix felt his stomach clench. He remembered the menace that lay in the circuit boards of the computer.

The Evil One.

A fitting ally for the Gamesmaster.

'Then you will fight?'

'Fight?' Eirik repeated. 'I don't know if there is much fight left in the men of Skaldheim.'

'But you must,' said Phoenix. 'Didn't you hear me? The Evil One is about to rise. He's the one I came to destroy.'

Eirik cut him short, pressing a finger to his lips. He took Phoenix by the sleeve and led him to a corner. Halfdan was watching with interest. Giving his lord a glance, Eirik whispered into Phoenix's ear:

'Loki has spies everywhere. Not all who shelter in the hall of Skaldheim owe allegiance to Forkbeard. So don't go wagging that tongue so freely in future.'

He peered into Phoenix's face.

'A boy who declares to the world that he will kill Loki! Do you not understand his power, the greatness of his malice? You are either very brave or very foolish . . .'

He paused before finishing.

'. . . or in the service of the Evil One.'

'I am neither brave nor foolish,' said Phoenix. 'And I will never serve Loki. You saw the hammer. Surely you know the truth when you see it. I have a mission. I can only complete my quest by cutting out this evil.'

'By the beard of Odin, your trick with the hammer may have convinced these simple souls, but I have witnessed mysteries in my time. I have seen the Valkyries ride, I have seen the unburied dead dance on the storm-tide. I need more proof than this.'

Eirik's eyes shifted from Laura to Phoenix. He picked up the hammer from where it lay on the table.

'Do you expect me to believe that this is truly Mjollnir, the hammer wielded by the thunderer himself?'

'No,' said Phoenix. 'But it is his sign.'

'A sign?'

He scratched his matted beard.

'Maybe it is. I would like nothing better than to believe you. It would be good to take a stand against the Evil One.'

He seemed to put aside his suspicions for a moment.

'What you say has been foretold. The Evil One will rise. Soon giant and demon, wolf and serpent will issue forth and engage in battle on Vigrid Plain. The gods will ride out from great Asgard and join the battle. Then the sun will darken at noon, and heaven and earth will turn red with blood. Good and evil will perish alike in the slaughter and the stars shall vanish from the skies. Now do you understand why I do not want you speaking of such things in the company of these men? It is their grim present . . .'

He cast his arms wide, indicating the raging blizzard.

'. . . their grimmer future too. What man of woman born wishes to face his destiny if it means only blood and fire?'

'But if you know all this, why do you hesitate to fight? What have you got to lose?'

Eirik shook his head.

'Why, because for three winters every soul in Midgard has been shivering behind barred doors. Farmers have broken their ploughshares on the frost-hardened ground. Babes have frozen in their cribs for want of warmth. Everywhere there is greed, law-breaking and the corruption of all faith. How can we trust anyone? Who is to say you were not sent by the Mischief-Maker?'

'Then I will speak to Halfdan Forkbeard.'

'I have fought at Halfdan's side for twenty years. Who do you think he will listen to?'

'So you will hide yourself away here?' asked Phoenix bitterly. 'Like cowards.'

'Skaldheim is a sanctuary. A sacred grove amid the wasting of the Northland. We take our stand against Evil. You cannot shame me with your words, stranger. Prove beyond a shadow of doubt that you serve the cause of the gods. Then and only then will we follow you.'

The fires in the great hall had burned low. Some of the men had gone to their beds, while others slumbered fitfully on their folded arms.

'My liege is about to retire,' said Eirik Bluetooth. 'We will speak again in the morning.'

'But where will we sleep?' asked Laura, casting a suspicious glance at the feasters who were lying sprawled all round the room.

'Where you can,' said Eirik, tossing a pile of rough coverings.

He tugged at an iron ring attached to a wooden hatch.

'You may find some comfort in Lord Halfdan's ale-cellar, though there must be no interfering with his mead casks.'

He leaned forward, leaving them with another sour warning:

'And you will be watched. I will leave you your sword in case you are telling the truth. But one of Halfdan's bodyguard, Ragnar, will keep watch to see that you do not use it for foul means. No treachery, or you will die this very night.'

4

If it was possible, the wind became even stronger in the small hours, booming dismally over the thatched roof and making the timbers grate, while the many draughts that invaded the hall clawed at the sleeping men and made the fire's dying embers glow faintly beneath the grinding rafters. The wind even penetrated to the cellar where Laura and Phoenix lay among the casks of mead and ale. Laura woke from an uneasy sleep, troubled by images of the undead. She was shivering.

'Phoenix,' she whispered, imagining dead-walkers in every shadow. 'Are you awake?'

'Of course I am.'

She threw off her beaver-hide blanket.

'Do you trust that man?'

'Eirik Bluetooth? Yes, I think so.'

'Well, I don't. There is something about him.'

Phoenix laughed.

'Because he mistrusts us, or because he smells?'

'He does reek a bit.'

'I knew it. That's the twenty-first-century girl talking.'

Laura scowled. He wasn't taking her seriously. She changed the subject.

'Is it safe to talk?'

'I don't think anyone is listening.'

'There's one thing I don't understand. Where *did* the hammer come from? It's not like we're used to getting help when we play the game. It couldn't have really been from Thor, could it?'

Phoenix shook his head.

'I just don't know. There is one possibility.'

Laura waited.

'Andreas.'

'Are you telling me we were saved by a dead man?'

'I hear his voice.'

Laura shook her head.

'But this wasn't a voice. Voices don't throw hammers.'

She brought her arm down to illustrate her point.

'This was an enormous sledgehammer and somebody threw it. Believe me, Phoenix, we're not the only players in the game.'

Some time later Phoenix was woken, first by a dull thud then by a scraping noise. It was coming from above. He wasn't imagining it, somebody was opening the hatch of the mead-cellar. He heard the wooden staircase creak. Somebody was coming down. His skin began to prickle.

Why now, in the dead of night?

Reassuring himself that Laura was asleep, he closed his hand round the hilt of the longsword and waited. Another creak. Whoever it was, they were descending slowly.

What do they want?

Phoenix had been sleeping on his right side with his back to the staircase. Holding his breath and shifting his weight bit by bit, he eased himself over, until he could see the dark figure out of the corner of his eye. The fires in the hall had burned down low and it was impossible to make out any details. Phoenix watched the man's approach and his heartbeat quickened. There was no innocent explanation for this furtive movement. It was at that moment that Laura woke up.

She too saw the dark figure and cried out. The intruder

reacted by jumping the rest of the way down the staircase and drawing a dagger. It was time to act. Phoenix threw back the pelt under which he had been sleeping and brandished his longsword. Blade struck blade and a desperate struggle began, boy and man crashing about in near total darkness, slashing at one another. Phoenix was hard-pressed to hold off his assailant and the points bracelet clicked away at his wrist.

'Phoenix!' cried Laura as he rolled away from one slashing thrust.

His attacker drove a boot into Phoenix's ribs. Phoenix felt the breath knocked out of him and clutched his side. He looked up in pain as his opponent's dagger flashed. He just succeeded in locking the hilt of his sword against the blade.

'Who sent you?' he panted.

He already knew the answer. This had to be Loki's man, and he was slashing and hacking with a fury that had Phoenix on the back foot. Seeing Phoenix hurt and falling back, Laura rolled a mead barrel into the attacker's path. It earned Phoenix a brief respite and he threw himself forward, sword swinging. For the first time, he was fighting on equal terms.

'Now you are going to tell me who sent you,' said Phoenix.

But the fight ended as quickly as it had begun, the attacker slumping to his knees with a groan.

'What happened?' asked Laura. 'Did you . . . ?'

Phoenix shook his head.

'I wanted him alive.'

He examined the body.

'I don't understand. I didn't touch him.'

'No,' came a voice. 'I did.'

It was Halfdan, holding a firebrand in his left hand.

'Somebody woke me up. I don't know who it was, he was gone back into the shadows before I could open my eyes. But believe me, you have a friend here, watchman.'

Laura and Phoenix exchanged glances. Meanwhile Halfdan

shone the firebrand over the dead man and pulled the great axe Bloodletter from between his shoulder blades.

'A traveller,' he said, 'to whom we had given shelter. He slew Ragnar, my faithful bodyguard, to get at you. So this is how he repays my hospitality.'

Eirik appeared and examined the body.

'Maybe you were telling the truth all along. Do you have any idea why he would want to kill you?'

Phoenix examined the man.

'Here.'

There was a mark like a tattoo on the man's neck. It was in the shape of a wolf. Halfdan frowned.

'What's wrong?'

'The assassin bears the mark of the Evil One. This is the brand of Loki. These are evil days indeed.'

'I've seen something like this before,' said Phoenix. 'It is worn by our enemy's disciples. It gives him power over their thoughts and actions.'

'Loki?'

Phoenix had meant the Gamesmaster, but he wasn't about to contradict Halfdan. For the purposes of the game, it amounted to the same thing.

'The Evil One knows we're here,' said Phoenix. 'He will do anything to destroy us. You have to act, Lord Halfdan.'

Eirik inspected the wolf tattoo and whispered something in Halfdan's ear.

'If Loki sent this assassin,' said Halfdan, 'then maybe you were right about the dead-walker. This may well be the second attempt on your lives. In the morning we will climb the hill and take a look at the shrine. Try to get some sleep.'

But he was asking too much. Neither Phoenix nor Laura closed their eyes again that night.

5

By the white light of early morning, Phoenix and Laura led Halfdan Forkbeard and his men up the windswept hillside to the shrine. In the dawnlight, Phoenix could see clearly the runes and the creatures of the Northland: serpents, wolves, bears, and the sacred raven, the bird of Odin. The warriors' beards and hair were matted with grease and their tunics were heavily stained where the ale had spilled down their chests. Most were nursing ferocious hangovers.

'And this is where you saw your dead-walker?' asked Eirik Bluetooth as they reached the squat, grey building.

'There,' said Laura, 'on the other side of the wall. It was hanging from the tree.'

By speaking out so freely, she set off much sullen muttering among Halfdan's followers. The Berserkers weren't used to such boldness in a female.

'Asgard must be a stranger place than I had ever believed,' said Eirik, addressing Phoenix. 'Where boys keep vigil and womenfolk talk out of turn.'

Laura's eyes flashed angrily. There was something about this man with his reeking breath and his discoloured tooth. She thought of the would-be assassin from the night before and wondered how many more traitors there were in Skaldheim. How she would have liked to really talk out of turn! But she knew better than to provoke the Berserkers to anger, and said no more.

'Why, it wouldn't surprise me if you didn't set infants up as kings!' bellowed Halfdan, blissfully unaware of Laura's thoughts.

'What Laura says is true,' Phoenix insisted. 'There *was* a body hanging from that tree. It came alive and . . .'

'A body,' scoffed one sceptical soul. 'Now we know the boy is lying. Sacrifice occurs every ninth year, and it is barely a twelvemonth since the last festival.'

'You allow human sacrifice!' gasped Laura, horrified.

'The rites have not been practised for many years,' Halfdan explained. 'In better times they fell into disuse. But when the time of cold and want fell upon our land, the demand for blood became irresistible.'

'But how could you?' Laura demanded, oblivious to the angry looks of the men.

'Stop this talk,' Halfdan commanded. 'This shrine was standing when the world was new, and I will not have its traditions dishonoured. Those who died here were obeying the will of the gods.'

He glared at Phoenix.

'Either you control the wench's mouth, or you will find our goodwill towards you has gone too, watchman of Asgard.'

Phoenix glanced at Laura wondering how exactly to persuade her, but there was no need. She nodded briefly. They were in no position to argue. Meanwhile, Eirik Bluetooth was leading the way into the shrine. In the light of day it looked harmless enough.

'There is no sign of your dead-walker,' he said, examining the ancient oak. 'And as for it hanging from this branch . . .' He ran his fingers over the bark. 'Why, there is no rope and no sign of chafing on the bark.'

His suspicions of the night before returned.

'Maybe it *was* all invention,' said Eirik, darkness clouding his face. 'A tall tale to wheedle your way into our company.'

The suggestion raised a growl of hostility among the warriors.

'Can it be possible?' mused Halfdan Forkbeard. 'Did you make it all up?'

'You mean the same way I made up the assassin?' asked Phoenix. 'Or the way I made up the hammer?'

He was facing the men, waving his arms to reinforce the point, when Laura screamed.

'Laura?'

'Phoenix. Look!'

Phoenix turned to see something that made his heart miss a beat. The oak had been transformed into a giant, malformed hand. It reminded him of the hands of the undead. Fleshless, the last remains of skin were peeling back to expose earth-blackened bone. More importantly, it was moving, and the branches that had been so hideously transformed into fingers were pinning Halfdan's Berserkers against the stone walls. Horror was printed on their faces.

'Very well then, watchman,' said Halfdan. 'We believe your tale. Now tell me, what are we to make of this witchcraft?'

'I don't know, Halfdan. I . . .'

But his admission of ignorance had a dramatic effect on the tree. Or at least, his voice did. All five of its finger-branches turned towards him. They seemed to be reaching for him.

'It wants you, boy,' said Halfdan.

The finger pointed to the north.

'What's going on?' asked Eirik.

The palm flattened. For a moments nothing happened. The onlookers exchanged glances. Some fell back in terror.

'What are we meant to make of that?' asked Halfdan once more.

But the hand hadn't finished. A tongue of flame sprang from the palm. Something moved within, a serpent's scales.

'By the All-father!' cried Halfdan.

Then, in the heart of the flame, a figure appeared. Tall and lean, he had a gaunt face, framed by hair as red as flame. And the eyes were sharp and alive, like fires. Phoenix recognized him immediately. Adams. But the Berserkers' reaction surprised him. It wasn't a boy from another world they saw.

'Do you know him?' asked Phoenix.

Eirik met his gaze, but it was Halfdan who spoke:

'The one you see is known throughout the Northland. His features are carved into every rune-stone for miles around. We are looking upon the Father of Lies. That is the Evil One, Loki himself.'

Then the flame seemed to collapse in on itself and disintegrated into a mass of black shapes. Dozens of crows were rising into the sky in a swirling black mist.

'Crows,' snarled Halfdan. 'It is three long years since we saw the raven take wing. Odin is besieged in Asgard and his holy bird is missing from our skies. Bad times indeed.'

'Loki is risen,' said Eirik, wrapping himself in his cloak and walking off down the hill.

In muttering groups, the Berserkers retreated to the security and shelter of their longhouse. For a few minutes Phoenix and Laura remained behind, staring at the oak tree which had returned to its original form.

'These men are terrified,' said Phoenix. 'I don't know how we'll ever raise them to fight. I don't like the way things are going.'

'We've faced danger before,' said Laura. 'You're not telling me this is worse, are you?'

'Maybe.'

'But how?'

'It's Adams. In *The Legendeer, Part One* he was a bit player. By *Part Two* he had become part-monster. Now he takes the role of the Evil One himself. What's happening?'

Laura didn't even attempt an answer.

'Listen,' she said.

They could hear the sound of raised voices. By the time Phoenix and Laura reached the doorway, a furious row had engulfed the hall of Halfdan Forkbeard.

'It's him, the unshaven boy who claims to represent the gods,' argued one man. 'He has brought evil upon Skaldheim.'

This was immediately rebutted by another:

'And did he bring three fatal winters on the land? Did he make our crops lie barren in the ground? Did he set brother against brother, father against son? Don't blame the boy. Blame the Father of Lies.'

'I agree,' said another. 'The lad claims to be Heimdall. What if he is? Will we go against the will of Asgard?'

'Heimdall?' scoffed another. 'This whelp?'

'Does it matter?' asked the second speaker. 'Loki is behind all that is sick in this land. I say we smash the Evil One's followers before his power grows.'

'Enough,' cried Halfdan, raising his arms to quell the furious debate. Phoenix and Laura looked hopefully in his direction. He would know what to do.

'We will not fall out among ourselves,' he thundered.

Then he dashed Phoenix and Laura's hopes.

'What we saw at the shrine was an omen. We will not be tempted into rash decisions. We hold fast in our stronghold of Skaldheim. We will not retreat, nor will we run headlong into his clutches. But let the Mischief-Maker come knocking at our door then, believe me, he will have his battle.'

Laura glanced at Phoenix. He was horrified. This was it, the endgame, the time of reckoning, and all Halfdan could say was: *sit tight*.

'Is this what your Berserkers stand for?' he cried indignantly. 'Skulking in their hall?'

'Watch your tongue, boy,' snarled Eirik. 'You strain our hospitality.'

He and his men had all assumed the same sullen pose, hunched over the great table, heads sunk into their massive shoulders.

'No!' cried Phoenix. 'Knock me down if you wish, but I'll say my piece first. You boast about your exploits, men of Skaldheim, how many dead-walkers you have slain, how many blades you have broken on the skulls of your foes. But I don't see fighters. You may sing of great deeds, but when was the last time you rode into battle?'

Laura watched him striding the length of the hall, darting accusing glances at the frowning warriors. He had shrugged off all thoughts of defeat. The boy was growing into a man before her eyes.

'Look at you.'

He picked up a drinking horn and flung it against the wall.

'What are you good for, men of Skaldheim?'

'Take care, lad,' warned Eirik. 'You go too far.'

'Yes,' agreed a tall, lean wolf of a man who wore a patch over his left eye. 'Treat us with respect, or I'll come over there and stop that runaway mouth of yours.'

'Do it then,' shouted Phoenix. 'Don't just talk about it. Do it!'

Andvar reacted by reaching for his weapon.

'No,' said Halfdan. 'There will be no fighting in this hall.'

He stepped between them.

'Save your courage for our enemies.'

He turned to Phoenix.

'When this boy demanded that we bear arms against Loki, Father of Lies, we turned our backs on him. It was too soon for battle, we said.'

He indicated the giant cloth that hung at the end of the hall.

'But when will we rally to the raven banner? When will we fight, warrior brothers? *When?*'

He took his place at Phoenix's side.

'Do we want to live forever?' he demanded. 'In a draughty hall, sheltering from the wind's blast. Do we want to grow old hiding ourselves in Skaldheim?' He forced them to look at themselves. 'Like this?'

A murmur of agreement ran through the ranks of the Berserkers.

He turned to Phoenix.

'If we follow you, watchman,' he asked. 'Can you lead us to Vigrid where good and evil must contend?'

Phoenix heard the whispered voice in his head.

The way is straight for the Legendeer.

He nodded.

'Yes, I can find the way.'

Halfdan immediately sprang onto the table, ripping the raven banner from the wall and waving it over his head.

'Will we cower beneath this roof like craven curs? Will we accept this living death?'

The eyes of Halfdan Forkbeard blazed fiercely through the feeble dawnlight, bright with indignation.

'Or will we fight?'

He got his answer in the form of a thunderous roar that shook the rafters of the hall. But not all joined in. Watching suspiciously from the back was the one-eyed man, Andvar.

6

A world away, Christina Graves was standing behind her husband, looking over his shoulder. Her eyes were fixed on the computer screen. Time was frozen around them. Clocks didn't tick, the tv screen was in freeze-frame, advertising the game that was due in the shops in a matter of hours. Even dust motes were caught motionless. The only time that moved was the time of the game.

'My poor Phoenix,' Mum murmured. 'Isn't there anything we can do?'

'Nothing,' said John Graves. 'You know that, Christina. Now that they've entered the world of the game, they are beyond our reach. It is all up to Phoenix now.'

'But he's just a boy.'

The mother in her was talking.

'No,' Dad replied. 'That's where you're wrong. You of all people should know. He has a destiny, like Andreas before him. You have stood here beside me twice before, witnessing his adventures. Worlds that would drive any normal person insane are like a second home to him. If anybody can end this madness, it is Phoenix.'

'You really believe that?'

John Graves remembered his son's previous desperate struggles. Burying his doubts, he turned to his wife with a reassuring smile.

'I know it.'

*

'Is it true what Eirik Bluetooth says?' asked Andvar, reining in his grey stallion beside Phoenix and Laura. 'You are leading us to sacred Vigrid. You take us to the land that lies beneath the home of the gods?'

Andvar wasn't asking, he was *interrogating*.

'Yes,' said Phoenix, hunching forward in his saddle. 'That's where the final battle will take place. Vigrid plain.'

Laura saw Andvar's eyes burning into Phoenix. Something about his expression unsettled her.

'I wonder,' said Andvar slowly. 'Are you truly sent by the gods, or by the Evil One?'

'What?' cried Phoenix. 'You still mistrust us?'

Andvar's hand moved to the jewelled dagger that was hanging from his belt.

'Somehow you have pulled the wool over Halfdan's eyes, convinced him you were sent by the gods, but I can see through you. Ours is a harsh and brutal land. Betrayal is our bread and treachery our wine. I trust nobody but my comrades in arms.'

A fight was only prevented by the arrival of Eirik Bluetooth.

'What is this?' he asked. 'Sheathe your weapons. We're only half a day's ride out of Skaldheim and already you are at each other's throats.'

'How do we know this isn't a trap?' snarled Andvar. 'We follow him to Vigrid, to face who knows what odds.'

'We know nothing,' Eirik replied. 'Only that the Mischief-Maker is about to rise and Odin's warriors must stand and be counted.'

With a scowl, Andvar spurred his horse to a canter and left them behind.

'We are in your debt, Eirik,' said Phoenix.

'Andvar is quick to anger,' said Eirik shortly. 'Try not to give him cause.'

With that he rode ahead, leaving them to consider what had just happened.

'Doesn't anybody trust us?' said Laura.

'Not wholeheartedly,' Phoenix replied. 'Would you?'

'If these are our friends,' said Laura, 'what are our enemies going to be like?'

Phoenix smiled.

'They're all we've got. If we are to win, we will need their help.'

Laura was about to say something in reply when suddenly her horse reared.

'Phoenix, help me!'

Her mount was kicking up clouds of powdery snow with its hooves. For a few moments the snow-cloud hit the ground around them and the rest of the Berserker column. Then Phoenix saw the reason for the horse's panic. A few steps ahead of them, the ground was cracking. A huge, scaly shape twisted in the fissure.

'Dead-Biter!' cried Halfdan Forkbeard.

Eirik rode back and helped Phoenix gain control of Laura's terrified mount.

'Dead-Biter?' asked Phoenix.

'Aye,' Eirik replied. 'The foul serpent that gnaws endlessly on the Tree of Life, the creature of emptiness and forever night. It brings the walkers.'

As if to confirm his words, the undead began to rise from the broken ground, first in dozens then in scores.

'Draw swords,' bellowed Halfdan. 'Defend yourselves.'

But the dead-walkers made no move forward. They seemed content to form up in foul, flesh-creeping ranks.

'What are they doing?' asked Laura.

'I don't know,' Eirik answered, surveying their grisly lines, 'but I don't like it.'

'There's your answer,' said Phoenix, pointing to a high ridge.

A tall, flame-haired figure was standing on a rocky peak, looking down at them. A pack of wolves prowled round him.

'Do you know me, Halfdan Forkbeard?' he asked.

'Aye, I know you, Loki, Father of Mischief.'

He pointed at the dead-walkers.

'And I know your evil spawn.'

Loki smiled.

'Is this your army, Halfdan? Is it with this motley crew that you intend to stop me?'

Phoenix watched the blazing eyes roving over the Berserkers, counting the warriors.

'There are no gods to help you, Forkbeard. Even now an army of giants is laying siege to the walls of Asgard. The great wolf Fenris howls before its battlements. Surt the flamer unleashes his fire-demons on the Asa-gods. And who is there to relieve great Odin and his sky-lords? Why, boozy Halfdan and his pot-bellied Berserkers!'

He chuckled at the thought.

'Do you really expect to reach Vigrid with this ragged band? And what will you do there, a few hundred mortals against my demon army? Return home, Halfdan, to where the ale is strong and the meat is tender. This isn't your fight.'

Halfdan took a step forward and gave his reply:

'A long time ago a boy was taken to the holy ground of Vigrid. He stood proudly beneath the raven banner of Odin and he was shown the rainbow bridge, Bifrost. His father foretold the fall of heaven and he grieved. To comfort him in the darkest moment of his childhood, he was given a golden ring and told to wear it until the day that mortal men would take their stand against the legions of Evil. I am that boy, Lord Loki.'

He raised his fist, flaunting the ring in defiance.

'And I wear the ring today. I will not turn back from my destiny.'

Loki grinned, gesturing to his demon supporters to hold their ground.

'A pretty speech, Jarl of Skaldheim, but it will take more than your raggle-taggle band to thwart me. Let's see if you sing such a brave tune when the time comes to fight.'

He looked at Phoenix for the first time.

'And you're the one they follow. What's the name you go by now, Legendeer? Heimdall, is it? The one who must face me on the day of judgement. The game is in its closing stages. Are you ready for the last throw of the dice?'

Phoenix thought of hundreds of thousands, maybe millions of copies of *Warriors of the Raven*, just waiting to be bought, and imagined the havoc they would wreak. He roared his reply.

'I'm ready.'

Then he glanced at Halfdan.

'We all are.'

7

It was close to nightfall when Halfdan gave the order to set up camp. The Berserkers had ridden all day into the teeth of a piercing Arctic wind and men and horses were exhausted. Many were wondering why Loki hadn't attacked. His sinister game of cat and mouse made them nervous.

'Get those tents up!' barked Eirik, relaying his chief's curt command. 'I don't care how tired you are, you can't rest without shelter. Half of us could perish on a night like this.'

The Berserkers set about their task in silence; dark, sullen men labouring in the winter twilight. Laura had her eye on Eirik. She was thinking of the assassin who had attacked them in Halfdan's hall, a man with a wolf tattoo.

'I still don't trust him.'

Phoenix shook his head.

'It's Andvar we have to watch. If anyone serves the Gamesmaster, it's him.'

Then the crows came back.

Nobody noticed them at first, dark scraps flickering against the greying sky. Laura was the one to realize.

'Phoenix. Something's happening.'

She answered his questioning look by pointing to the north. There, wheeling lazily over a ridge, were a few score of the shrilly cawing birds. Phoenix shuddered despite himself.

'Dark,' he said, 'like death.'

Laura stared at the crows.

'What made you say that?' she asked, trembling. She wasn't sure what caused the gust of fright, the massing birds or Phoenix's words.

'The crow belongs to the dark places,' Phoenix replied, watching the birds gathering. 'It is an omen. A harbinger of ill fortune.'

Within moments the few dozen crows had grown to several hundred, some clustered on the wind-blasted pines that clung uneasily to the thin soil, others on the wing above the sprouting encampment.

'Phoenix, there's definitely something wrong here.'

'I know.'

He was speaking in a monotone, as if bewitched. He and Laura weren't alone in sensing the menace. The Berserkers had stopped pulling on their guy ropes. All eyes turned towards the growing mass of birds.

'Heimdall,' murmured Eirik. 'What is this?'

Phoenix turned slowly in a circle, following the line of settling birds. The creeping twilight went on forever and it was all birds. The sky, the land, the air itself was growing crow-dark. The points bracelet started to click. Phoenix's score was falling.

'I know what's happening here,' he said in a voice muffled with fear. 'We're being surrounded.'

'What?'

Surrounded!

The secret speaker was whispering a warning.

'Stop them,' yelled Phoenix, suddenly alive to the danger. 'We can't afford to let them form a circle.'

'Why not?'

'Believe me, it would be bad for us.'

Eirik didn't need any more convincing.

'To horse!' he ordered. 'Stop the birds from forming a circle.'

Andvar was the first into the saddle, galloping forward and swinging his Skull-crusher at the carpet of crows.

'Yaagh!'

His voice raked the dusk, hoarse and brave.

'Yaagh!'

Then the entire troop of horse was thundering across the frosty ground, scattering the birds to flight. It wasn't a moment too soon. To the north, where the crows were at their thickest, the air was choked with the fluttering of thousands of wings. It was a strange sound, an irregular snapping and clattering. But amidst the shifting, rippling chatter of bone and feather there was another beat. Something deep and repetitive, a distinct and recognizable pounding.

'What is that?' asked Laura, her heart skipping inside her chest. 'It sounds familiar. Like . . .'

The low, concealed beat continued, often completely swallowed up in the roaring of the Berserkers and the tide of wingbeats. But still Laura listened, trying to distinguish what she'd heard.

'Phoenix,' she asked. 'What did you mean? Why do we have to break the circle?'

'It's Andreas. He's warning us.'

Laura stared at him for a moment, then turned towards the main flock.

'What *is* that sound?'

She almost shouted the question. She was angry with herself. Why couldn't she put a name to it?

The Berserkers were riding up and down the frozen ground, roaring and waving their arms, scattering the crows wherever they landed. Eirik led the way. He was doing anything he could to prevent the birds settling. Andvar was just as keen and loud. The remaining warriors did their bit, but with less enthusiasm.

They were keeping the circle open, but their efforts fell short of shifting the main flock to their north. It was forming a solid mass, a swelling mound of birds. No, not a single mound. Ten, a dozen, twenty black shapes.

Like . . .

Like the forms of men.

'Of course,' cried Phoenix as the crow-blackness became legs, arms, hands, a head. 'Halfdan, Eirik. The crows. They're not just birds. They are part of the darkness. If we allow them to settle they will make dead-walkers.'

'Hear that?' bellowed Halfdan. 'It's a trick. Dead-walkers. The Mischief-Maker thought to encircle us with dead-walkers.'

Until then the Berserkers had been following Eirik and Andvar's example only half-heartedly. Now that they understood their enemy, they set about their winged tormentors with renewed fury, slashing and hacking at the dark shapes. But if they were beginning to disperse the birds to the south and east, to the north an unbroken phalanx was forming. A regiment of dead-walkers. Suddenly, in the sky above, Loki appeared riding a great eagle.

'My power is growing, Legendeer. Surprise, surprise!'

A Berserker's arrow just missed him, but the eagle swooped low.

'The dark power is rising,' he said. 'Soon you will meet the one you fear.'

The Gamesmaster.

The undead legions continued to advance. Laura glimpsed the points bracelet and its falling score.

'We have to fight this,' cried Phoenix, 'without delay.'

'To arms!' bawled Halfdan, throwing back his heavy cloak to reveal a chain-mail jacket. 'This is something we know, something we can fight. Archers, draw up your lines.'

At the first volley of arrows the as yet unformed dead-walkers exploded in a deafening tumult of sound. The air was filled with the shrieking of thousands, tens of thousands of the creatures.

'That's it,' cried Phoenix jubilantly. 'The transformation isn't complete. Hit the dead-walkers before they're fully formed.'

Then the shafts sang, and each time their arrowheads thudded into a mound of crows the tattered black shapes spiralled into the thickening gloom.

'Strain your arms, lads,' shouted Halfdan encouragingly. 'Keep your aim true and win the fight.'

With a final volley, the archers dispersed the last of the dead-walkers and roared their triumph at the blizzard of crows. Phoenix and Laura joined their celebrations. But their victory shout had barely left their throats when another voice crackled through the night.

'Think you've won, do you, Halfdan?'

It was Loki himself.

'Surely you know better?'

'Where is he?' asked Laura.

Phoenix could just make out an eerie glare in an oak grove. It was a violent and destructive flame, leaping and licking at the tree-tops, sending showers of sparks into the night sky. Loki's voice came from the heart of the blaze.

'You want a *real* fight?'

He paused as the earth began to shake.

'Then fight this.'

The muffled heartbeat which had worried Laura so much was now deafening. While the fiery light flared and the frozen ground cracked, a huge serpent body could be seen arching through the gaping earth. It was the monster's heart she'd heard.

Dead-Biter.

Moments later armies of the undead began to spill in countless thousands from the gap.

'By the gods of Asgard!' gasped Halfdan. 'There are hundreds, thousands. Never have I seen so many.'

As the words left his lips Loki added his comment.

'Worried, Legendeer? Surprise, surprise.'

The sky above was black with crows, the hills around them a grey carpet of dead-walkers. The noose was closing.

8

'Don't let them complete the circle!' cried Phoenix instinctively. 'We've got to break out.'

The Berserkers rode at breakneck pace. After a furious fight, they smashed through the dead-walkers' ranks, but there was to be no respite for Halfdan's battered army. Just minutes after the break-out, Andvar had returned from a scouting mission to the top of the nearest peak with ominous news.

'I saw them, Halfdan, down in the valley.'

'How far?'

'A league. Maybe less. I could sense their fury even from such a distance. Their numbers are growing all the time. And they have dragons now, and other creatures of the night such as I have never seen before.'

A murmur of dismay ran through the ranks. It was indeed the rising of the dark powers.

Ragnarok was at hand.

'Enough,' barked Halfdan, feeling the spirit draining out of his men. 'We may have been badly mauled, but we won't go to our graves moaning like cattle.'

It was only then, as Halfdan marshalled his fearful warriors, that Eirik Bluetooth noticed the change that had come over Phoenix.

'What ails you, watchman?'

Phoenix was slumped in his saddle, his head hanging to one side, his eyes half closed.

'He's hurt,' said Laura.

This time nobody turned to stare at her. The arrogance of the Berserkers had been shattered by their near-defeat at the hands of the dead-walkers.

'We have to get him down.'

As if confirming Laura's words, Phoenix started to slip from his horse. It was only Andvar's strong right hand that prevented him falling.

'Lift him down,' Halfdan ordered. 'Gently does it. Mind his head.'

While Laura knelt anxiously beside the half-conscious Phoenix, Halfdan dispatched more scouts.

'No fires,' he ordered. 'We snatch what rest we can and trust our sentries to alert us to any attack. Don't unbuckle your weapons, or even take off your boots.'

'What's that, Halfdan?' asked Andvar. 'Do you really think we could sleep after what we have seen this day?'

Ignoring Andvar, Halfdan continued; 'We will ride at first light. We must reach Vigrid and open a way for the gods to ride out of Asgard. It is our only hope, and theirs too. But if the Evil One moves before then we must too. We cannot fight him alone. The gods need us, but we need them more.'

'What is your plan?' asked Eirik.

Halfdan took his adviser to one side.

'To live to see the morning,' he replied grimly. 'Why, do you have anything to add?'

'Nothing, ring-giver,' said Eirik flatly.

Overhearing their gloomy exchange, Laura felt her heart go cold. Nobody spoke after that. Andvar made Phoenix as comfortable as he could, and Laura lay next to him, watching as he tossed and turned in his trance-like sleep. She couldn't take her eyes off the points bracelet. The score was ominously low. The game was almost lost.

'You're going to be all right,' she said: 'You've got to be.'

She tried to stay awake, but weariness soon overcame her. To begin with she dozed a little, before snapping to attention, then grew heavy-lidded once more.

Eventually she was unable to keep her eyes open and slipped into a fitful sleep. This time, it was her turn to dream. She saw the crows circling, then gather into hideous, misshapen statues. She ran round and round the circle begging to be allowed out, but the statues turned their eyeless faces on her, closing in on her, tightening the circle like a noose.

'No!'

She sat bolt upright and saw Andvar and Halfdan looking at her.

'Sorry,' she said. 'I had a bad dream.'

Andvar simply snorted and rolled over, but Halfdan gave a sympathetic smile.

'There will be many bad dreams before daybreak,' he said. 'We have never seen the dead-walkers in such numbers before. The tramp of evil shakes the earth. The Mischief-Maker's time has come.'

'We're beaten, aren't we?' asked Laura.

Just a day before, her question would have been dismissed scornfully by the proud Viking lord. But Halfdan didn't reply at all. He buried his face in his jacket and clapped his gloved hands together against the bitter cold of the night.

'Halfdan,' Laura began. 'Is there . . . ?'

Her question was cut short by a shout in the darkness.

The Berserkers were on their feet in seconds, drawing their swords and battle-axes.

'Who goes there?' cried Halfdan.

One of the sentries replied, 'It's riders, my lord.'

All eyes turned towards the thud of hooves. Moments later two riders galloped into view.

'Lord Halfdan,' shouted one, his voice a mixture of excitement and despair. 'There is something you must see.'

Halfdan mounted his horse.

'Eirik,' said Laura, 'will you watch Phoenix? I want to go with them.'

'Yes, I'll watch the lad. You go.'

She smiled. How wrong she had been about him. She joined Halfdan's party. They followed the scouts into the darkness with a growing sense of dread. As they rode up the slope and through a screen of pines, Laura became aware of hundreds of lights flickering in the lowlands around them, their gleam penetrating through the dense woods like searchlight beams.

'What's that glow?' she asked.

She was answered as they rode out onto open ground and looked down from the brow of the hill.

'By the beard of Odin!'

'We're surrounded,' cried Andvar. 'And this time there's no breaking the circle.'

Laura gazed in dismay at the enemy hordes camped at the foot of the hill. Many of the ghoulish figures were completely enveloped in flame.

'But how did they surround us without our hearing?'

'We are dealing with the undead here,' Halfdan said. 'They do not speak to give orders, or to reassure one another as mortal men do. They are soulless. They simply obey their master's orders.'

'But why the fires?' asked Laura. 'If they're the undead, why do they need warmth?'

'They don't,' said Halfdan. 'The fires are for our benefit. The Mischief-Maker wishes to break our sleep and plant the seed of terror. They have set their fires to tell us that we will die in the morning.'

'And will we?' asked Laura.

Halfdan gestured at the ocean of firelight.

'Nothing,' he replied, 'is so certain.'

THE LEVELS

Level Ten
Ragnarok

1

John and Christina Graves watched transfixed as their son lay semiconscious, his head pillowed on the coarse material of a warrior's jacket.

'Surely it can't end like this,' said Mum, pressing her fingers against Phoenix's image on the computer screen.

For once, there were no reassuring words from her husband.

'John?'

'Christina, I'm afraid,' he said finally. 'Not once in either of the other games were the odds so heavily stacked against him. The game seems different this time. This is a world where even gods can die.'

No sooner were the words out of his mouth than the computer screen started to fill with a myriad of numbers, the familiar maelstrom of threes, sixes and nines. Then, from out of the jumble of numerals, came a message, direct and chilling:

This is the endgame. The time of my victory. In a matter of hours the wall between my world and yours will be destroyed and we shall meet.

Phoenix's parents looked into the numbers. For the first time, they saw them decoded.

'It's the Gamesmaster,' said Dad. 'He thinks he's won.'

It was always going to be this way. I chose my terrain well. The Norse myths. Where man and god are both mortal. Where the power of Evil can triumph. Ragnarok the final battle is about to dawn. All my enemies will be slain on Vigrid plain, the Legendeer among them. The gateway between the worlds will open and I will be made whole, no longer a phantom but a living, vengeful being. I have my vessel, the means by which I will live again. Soon the Gamesmaster will stride the universe, master of the many worlds.

With that, the numbers cleared. Phoenix's parents looked on, not speaking, paralysed by the knowledge that the Gamesmaster had won. Then came new terror. A shadow fell over Phoenix as he lay unprotected.

'Wake up,' cried Mum, 'Phoenix, before it's too late.'

2

Phoenix was gradually coming to his senses. His body ached, but he was more concerned with the figure standing over him. He could see somebody, silhouetted against the first rays of the rising sun, looking down at him. At first Phoenix was unable to speak. He was struggling to throw off a crushing weariness. Finally he uttered a few words:

'Who's there? Laura?'

But the blurred shape was too big to be a teenage girl. Phoenix strained to focus his eyes. He saw a beard, smelt the reek of rancid breath.

'Eirik?'

There was no reply.

'Eirik Bluetooth, is that you?'

Thank goodness. A friend.

But there didn't seem anything in the least friendly about this presence. Phoenix hauled himself into a sitting position. He was starting to see clearly. Eirik was leaning over, scratching distractedly at his neck. Icy currents rippled through Phoenix's veins.

'What are you doing?'

Then he saw the dagger in the Northman's hand, and the scratching took on a sinister meaning. He realized with horror that he had been a fool to trust Eirik. He had been warned and now he was lying defenceless at Eirik's feet.

'Laura was right!'

Eirik spoke for the first time.

'The girl asked me to watch over you.'

He chuckled, seeming to see the funny side.

'I, the demon-lord's man, watching over the watchman!'

Phoenix tried to cry out, the Eirik clamped a rough hand over his mouth.

'Our brave Berserkers are too preoccupied with the Evil One's legions to listen to you.'

Phoenix could feel a dull ache gnawing into his back and legs. He was hurt and exhausted. He couldn't fight back.

'This won't be hard to explain,' hissed Eirik. 'Few of the men ever really trusted you. It won't be difficult to convince them that you were an assassin and a traitor all along. Now Halfdan's trusted adviser has exposed you.'

He raised the dagger to strike. Phoenix closed his eyes, expecting the blow. A moment later, instead of the dagger's thrust, he was flung backwards by Eirik's body falling heavily on him. He screamed and tried in vain to fight off the clumsy attack. But Eirik wasn't doing anything. In fact, he was a dead weight. What *was* he doing?

'Are you all right?' said a boy's voice. 'He didn't hurt you, did he?'

Phoenix finally crawled free. He pulled back the Berserker's long hair and saw the wolf tattoo. Eirik had been Loki's man all along. Tears of relief streamed down Phoenix's cheeks. Above him stood a boy about his own age, blond and blue-eyed, the sledgehammer that had felled the traitor clenched in his fists.

'Who are you?' asked Phoenix.

He recognized the sledgehammer.

'You're the one,' he said. 'The one who came to our aid in Halfdan's hall.'

'I threw the hammer. I couldn't think of anything else to do. It was me that woke Halfdan too. I saw the assassin kill the guard. I came back for the hammer after you'd left Skald-heim.'

Then the scales fell from Phoenix's eyes.

'Of course! You must be Jon.'

The newcomer nodded and held out a hand to Phoenix.

'Jon Jonsson.'

'But how?'

'Dad didn't pack everything to send away. He couldn't bring himself to do it. He decided he needed to keep some insurance, hang onto proof that what he said was true. Your friend Adams should have checked the box properly. I came across the PR suit and the back-up disc by accident. The moment I found out there was a way back into the game, I knew I had to help you.'

Phoenix wiped away his tears.

'But why didn't you let on? Why be so secretive?'

'I didn't plan to keep you in the dark. It just happened that way. I found the stuff that Dad had stashed away. I used them secretly on my own PC. But I had to choose my moments carefully, or my parents would find out. They were scared enough without me adding to their worries. And I couldn't stay long or they would know.'

Phoenix chuckled.

'You needn't have worried about the time,' he said. 'When you enter the game, time freezes in our world. If they weren't in the same room as the computer when you entered they would be frozen too. They would never know you were gone.'

'Is this true?'

Phoenix nodded.

'I should know. This is the third of the myth games I have played.'

'So I didn't need to go back?'

Phoenix shook his head. 'No. But how could you pass back

and forth between the worlds? Once you're inside you're trapped. That's the way it has always been before.'

Jon shrugged.

'Nobody told me that. I just came and went as I pleased.'

Phoenix frowned again.

'Unless . . . Of course, the Gamesmaster can't hold you here the way he has me and Laura because *he doesn't even know you've entered*. You're an unknown player. You've got a freedom I never had.'

Jon leaned on the hammer.

'Then we hold the advantage.'

'Not for long,' said Phoenix. 'He'll soon discover you're here.'

He pointed at Eirik.

'That'll give him a clue.'

'Then we have to act quickly,' said Jon. 'It will soon be time for the final battle. Ragnarok.'

'It's time already,' said Phoenix, pointing.

Jon gasped in wonder. Until that moment the morning mist had cloaked the plain, concealing its majesty. Now, in the dawn light, his senses reeled at the scale of the stark landscape. He saw the great rainbow in the sky.

'Bifrost,' said Phoenix. 'The rainbow bridge of the gods.'

Jon stared at the ice rainbow. Bifrost arched right across the wintry sky, curving over the heads of Loki's army. Thousands of crows took flight and swept overhead.

'But how do we win?' asked Jon. 'Against that?'

'I don't know,' said Phoenix. 'The Gamesmaster has chosen this world for the final battle. These Northern myths are the gloomiest of all. The good are predestined to fall, the evil fated to destroy. All things will be put to the torch. Listen, Jon. Go back through the gate. While you're able to, while there's still time. Run the game, question your dad. Try to find something, anything we can use.'

'You can trust me,' said Jon. 'I'll find something.'

'I hope so,' said Phoenix. 'This time there are no second chances. It is the day of destiny. *This* is Ragnarok.'

3

By mid-morning the defensive preparations were made and the Berserkers were standing in anxious knots waiting for the order to take up their posts.

'I can hardly believe it,' said Halfdan, blinking away the driving sleet. 'Eirik, my most trusted comrade.'

'That wasn't Eirik,' said Phoenix. 'It was the Evil One's spirit in his body. Our enemy poisons the minds of those he seeks to control. Remember the assassin in the cellar? He had the same tattoo.'

Halfdan nodded.

'At least we have discovered the traitor. Now the lines are clearly drawn. Us against them.'

Laura viewed the hideous group at the head of the demon army. Flanking Loki were the giant wolf Fenris and Hela, goddess of the Underworld. The left side of her body was that of a young woman, pale and fair, but her right side was a rotting corpse. Behind them stood Surt the fire demon, all flame.

'Everyone is here,' said Phoenix. 'All the monsters of legend.'

Laura shook her head.

'Everyone but the gods.'

She gestured in the direction of the distant sky palace, a cluster of roofs almost hidden by the swarms of crows.

'It will be their turn soon,' said Phoenix. 'First the dark

hordes destroy the forces of Man, then they storm Asgard itself.'

'You talk as if we're beaten already,' said Laura.

Phoenix pressed his hands to his temples.

'Just look at them,' he said. 'Their ranks go on and on like an ocean. I don't know how to get us out of this one.'

'Maybe Jon will find something,' said Laura.

'Maybe,' said Phoenix.

But his voice was flat. He didn't seem to hold out much hope. What was Jon against these legions? As if to press home the huge odds against Halfdan's army, a great, nerve-shredding roar went up in the valley below. Braying horns immediately began to sound around the hilltop, calling the Berserkers to arms.

'This is it,' said Phoenix, his voice shaking.

'But what's the plan?' asked Laura.

'At this moment in time,' Phoenix answered, 'there isn't one.'

Laura was about to say something else when she screamed in terror.

'What is it?'

The ground in front of Laura had given way suddenly, leaving a huge fissure.

'Halfdan!' Phoenix roared. 'Give me some of your men. Dead-walkers. Coming from below.'

Andvar and a dozen warriors hurried to Phoenix's side and peered into the hole.

'Steady,' Andvar ordered. 'Aim your arrows into the darkness. Don't shoot until I give the command.'

They could hear the start of the assault on the Berserkers' positions, the dragons bombarding the hillside with jets of flame.

'Come on, you hell-fiends,' snarled Andvar, desperate to get back to the front line.

'I see something,' hissed Laura.

Andvar's archers drew their bowstrings.

'Steady,' said Andvar.

The word had hardly left his lips when shards of rock started flying from the hole. One of the archers, impatient for a fight, loosed his arrow.

No, came the secret speaker. *This is not your enemy.*

'Stop!' yelled Phoenix. 'Don't shoot.'

'Why?'

'I don't know. Just trust me.'

There was another shower of rocks, then a blond head appeared. Jon.

'I told you I'd find a way,' he said. 'I remembered this mountain from level eight. It stands above the gulf of Black Grief. Where Loki was held.'

'Who is this?' demanded Andvar.

Just in time, Phoenix remembered the rules of the game.

'Are you telling me you don't recognize Balder the good?'

Andvar stared.

'Not just one representative of Asgard, but two. And this second one risen from the grave!'

Jon jumped out of the hole.

'There's no time for introductions,' he said. 'By now my presence will be known. We have to act quickly. Let's go.'

He was cut off by a warning shout from Halfdan.

'Down!'

They scrambled for cover behind a row of boulders just in time to avoid a searing blast of fire from a dragon's nostrils.

'Let's get out of here,' said Laura.

'But we can't run away,' cried Phoenix. 'This is my destiny. Shouldn't I stay and fight?'

Then the secret speaker came again.

No, it told him. *Not here. Vigrid is the place where you will face your destiny.*

'So I should flee, scurry away like a coward?'

What you must do could not be achieved by a coward. Your task is to open a way for the armies of Asgard.

'I don't know if I can.'

This is my last word, young Legendeer. My time has passed. I have done everything that is in my power. The rest is up to you.

'Andreas?' said Phoenix.

But the secret speaker had fallen silent. Phoenix knew he wouldn't hear the voice again.

The rest is up to me.

'We must retreat,' he announced.

Andvar bristled.

'The Berserker does not run away,' he retorted.

'Then the Berserker is a blithering idiot!' cried Laura.

'Maybe this will wake you up,' said Phoenix. 'Just look about you, Andvar. The enemy are overrunning your defences. Is that what you want, a noble death? Noble, but quite, quite useless. You will be called on to make your sacrifice soon enough, but do it for a purpose.'

He was right about the defences. The Berserkers' hastily built fortifications were on fire, set ablaze by the swooping dragons. Through the intense heat, oblivious to the licking flames, came the dead-walkers and the fire-demons. Phoenix could see the warriors wilting under the assault, unsure whether to tackle the threat first from the front, the rear, or overhead.

'Well,' he said. 'What's it to be, Northmen?'

He was suddenly sure of himself.

'Will you choose a hero's retreat or a fool's death? Don't just stand there, Andvar. Tell me, do you trust me or not?'

The Berserkers were engaged in fierce hand-to-hand fighting. Andvar cast a glance in their direction.

'Well?' Jon demanded, standing on the edge of the hole.

'We've got to follow him,' cried Laura.

'Not without my lord Halfdan,' said Andvar stubbornly.

Phoenix grabbed his sword and raced to Halfdan's side, dashing a dead-walker out of the way with the hilt.

'There's one way out,' he panted, pointing to the hole.

Halfdan stared for a moment, then nodded as he dispatched a fire-demon with his axe.

'Fall back,' he cried. 'Archers, cover the retreat.'

As the Berserkers fled under the cover of a hail of arrows, he had a question.

'What's to stop them pursuing us into the mountain?'

'Me,' said Andvar. 'I trust you now, watchman. I'll hold them off until you get away. Who will be at my side?'

Volunteers joined him immediately.

'I was wrong about you,' said Phoenix.

'And I about you,' said Andvar.

As the last of the Berserkers tumbled past him, Phoenix smiled at Andvar.

'Into the mountain,' shouted Andvar. 'Live to fight again.'

'You!' came a voice from above.

It was Loki, sitting astride his eagle. He was snarling at Phoenix.

'You've got away many times but this will be your last!'

Phoenix searched Loki's face for the boy Adams, but he was quite transformed. A dragon appeared beside him belching a raging stream of fire. The livid mass of flame started to roll towards the hole.

'Go!' yelled Andvar, shielding himself from the flames and loosing an arrow in the direction of the hovering dragon.

Phoenix could feel every nerve and muscle shuddering with the effort. With a last look back, he followed Jon and the rest of Halfdan's band into the darkness of the mountain's tunnels. By the time the first fire-demon had penetrated them, Halfdan's army was gone.

4

Halfdan's men were defeated. They sat alone, or in silent groups. Some looked furtively into the murky passages that led from the huge cavern in which they were sitting. Phoenix glanced down at his points bracelet, a further reminder of their plight. It registered barely above zero.

'What now?' asked Laura.

Phoenix didn't meet her eyes.

'I don't know.'

He wished he could hear Andreas' voice, but it was silent. As Phoenix's knowledge and power had grown, Andreas' had faded.

I'm alone now.

The thought weighed heavily on Phoenix.

Any decisions I make are my own.

'We can't just sit here,' said Laura, nettled by his silence. 'They'll find us eventually.'

She couldn't stand still. The thought of the hell-creatures massing above made her insides crawl.

'You're right,' said Phoenix, without turning his head. 'They will.'

'Then we get them,' said Jon, eyes sparkling with enthusiasm. 'Before they get us.'

'Oh, great plan!!' cried Laura. 'In case you hadn't noticed, there are thousands of them, tens of thousands.'

Jon coloured. He suddenly felt very foolish.

Get them, thought Phoenix.

Or get him.

'No,' said Phoenix. 'Jon might have something.'

Laura threw up her arms.

'Oh, I give up! You're the one who's supposed to have the answers; you're the Legendeer. Do you remember how many of them there are?'

'How could I forget? But I'm not talking about the whole army.'

'Then what are you talking about?'

'Think about it,' said Phoenix. 'Ever since we entered the game, who have we been fighting? Demons, Northmen, Loki. That's the problem. We're fighting the monsters, not the one who's behind them. Find *him*, find the Gamesmaster, and we behead the enemy.'

'And how do we do that?' demanded Laura. 'We've played the game three times, in three different myth-worlds, but not once have we got close to him. I sometimes wonder whether he exists at all.'

'Oh, I know he exists. But you're right. So long as he is a disembodied spirit, hunting the Gamesmaster is like chasing shadows. And yet . . . I have a feeling that this time it's different. Don't you see? Look what's happening: Ragnarok, the end of days, the Evil One's triumph. It's different to the other games. Why did he choose this particular myth-world? There's a pattern to it. It's telling us something. It's the endgame. We're going to meet the Gamesmaster.'

After several moments Laura spoke.

'Are you sure?'

Phoenix nodded.

'Sure as I can be. None of this is happening by chance. The Gamesmaster lives through these worlds. The other two games told us what kind of creature he was, one that feeds off terror. They told us what his plans are. To enter our world. This game tells us *when* he is going to do it. You do understand, don't you? He has existed only as a presence, in the computer, in the game. Until now he has been a watcher, a phantom, waiting to rise. But his power has grown. Unless I'm completely mistaken his time is close. He is ready to take on physical form.'

'But how do we find him?' said Jon. 'If that's all he is, a ghostly presence, he could be anywhere.'

'Think about it,' said Phoenix. 'What's the one thing that runs through all three games? Monsters come and go, Medusa, the Minotaur, vampires, werewolves, we beat them all but we didn't win the game. Who's always there?'

Laura stated the obvious.

'Well, we are.'

'And?'

'I don't know . . . Yes, I do, Adams.'

Phoenix gave a grim smile.

'Exactly. Adams. The real terror isn't the monster at all. It's the monster inside ordinary people. Look at Adams. He began as a bullying schoolboy and was gradually taken over by the evil in the game. He's gone from being an unthinking disciple to being something utterly unfeeling and monstrous. Each time we have met him, there has been less of Adams and more of the demon. I know what's happening to him.'

Jon and Laura exchanged glances.

'We just didn't see it, Laura. All this time we've been looking for the Gamesmaster, thinking he was going to appear as himself. We missed the obvious. He must have been searching for a human vehicle. Well, he's found him. He has been growing inside Adams, slowly taking him over. It's perfect. For the Gamesmaster to come to life what does he need?'

'A body.'

'That's right. A body . . . and a mind that is easy to influence. Adams is the perfect candidate. Turning him to the dark side must have been like shaping clay. Bit by bit, the

Gamesmaster has modelled him in his own image. Now the takeover is nearly complete. We've got our final trinity. Three evil spirits in one: Adams, Loki, the Gamesmaster.'

'So he's the one we have to find,' said Jon. 'Adams, Loki, whichever you want to call him.'

Phoenix's mind was working overtime, rerunning everything that had happened in the game. He walked over to one of the passages and peered into the darkness.

'Jon, remind me how you found these tunnels.'

Jon frowned.

'You said they were near something.'

'Oh that. Yes, I recognized them from level eight. Loki was imprisoned close to here.'

'That's it,' said Phoenix. 'That was his dungeon, his place of torment. It's somewhere he has to return to, the myth demands it. Can you lead us to it?'

'I think so.'

'But surely you don't expect to find him just waiting for us?' Laura protested.

'Maybe not,' Phoenix replied. 'But it's as good a place to start as any.'

'I think this is crazy,' said Laura. 'He must be long gone.'

'Then you're not coming?'

Laura armed herself with a longbow and a quiver of arrows.

'What do you think?'

5

Phoenix followed Jon into the darkness. Laura walked beside him. She didn't speak. They had left Halfdan bemused and unsure about his next step. But he had allowed them to go without protest. They had earned his trust. For an hour, maybe longer, they trudged through the chilly gloom. It was Jon who finally broke the silence.

'Listen.'

Phoenix gave him a questioning look.

'I can hear water dripping.'

He was right. Somewhere at the end of the darkness, water was dripping. It echoed eerily.

'That has to be it. The cavern where Loki was bound in chains.'

'There's light up ahead. We've found it.'

He stepped into a vast cave. High above light filtered down through an opening, casting dappled shadows across the floor.

'See,' said Jon. 'The chains are still here. This is where he was bound. Up here . . .'

He pointed to a shelf of rock.

'This is where the serpent lay, dripping poison on his face.'

He was about to continue when a new voice echoed round the cave:

'Loki's torment obviously made a great impression on you.'

It was a female voice. Jon was the first to see her as she emerged from the shadows. He gasped out loud.

'Do I offend you, boy?' she asked.

One side of her face and body was that of a young woman, the other that of a rotting corpse. Jon turned away.

'Are you revolted by somebody who is life and death in one?' said Hela. 'Go on boy, look at me, look at my children.'

At the sound of her voice, fleshless fingers started to push up through the gaps between the stones in the floor of the cavern. Hands followed, claws of mouldering flesh. Bloodshot eyes, some dislodged from their sockets, hanging on cheeks, fixed them menacingly. Several dead-walkers were emerging out of the ground.

'Get back!' Jon warned. 'It's a trap.'

'It is indeed,' said Hela. 'And you are caught in it. Listen.'

From the passage behind them, Phoenix and Laura heard a crackling noise.

'That is the sound of Surt's fire-demons, come to see who disturbs the cave of Loki's torment. Such remarkable creatures. They are made all of flame, but they are never consumed. Only their enemies suffer the fate of immolation. Dead-walker ahead, death-maker behind. Which will you choose?'

'We came for Loki,' said Phoenix. 'Not for you.'

'But I am of his kind, flesh of his flesh,' said Hela. 'If you take a stand against him, then you make me your enemy. Besides, the Mischief-Maker has other things on his mind.'

She glanced upwards, towards the light.

'Above, on Vigrid plain.'

Instinctively Phoenix, Laura and Jon followed her gaze up towards the opening above their heads.

'That's right. Even now our legions are flushing Halfdan's Berserkers out of their hiding place. The final battle is about to begin. Maybe you can hear them whimpering and begging for mercy. You pitted yourself against the Wily One, the wolf-lord, the earth-shaker, and you have lost.'

Phoenix consulted the points bracelet. It was touching zero.

He drew his longsword and joined Jon. Laura strung the bow and made it three against the undead.

'A touching display,' said Hela. 'But quite hopeless. I must take my place on Vigrid plain. I leave you to the tender mercies of my dead-walkers. Your mission is over. I advise you to lay down your arms and accept a quick and relatively painless death.'

With that she was gone. Behind them, the three teenagers could hear the fire-demons moving closer, their blazing bodies flaring in the tunnels.

'We have to act,' said Phoenix. 'And fast.'

He held up the points bracelet for Jon and Laura to see.

'We mustn't let ourselves get caught between two enemies.'

'Meaning . . . ?'

'We know the dead-walkers. We've encountered them before. They are the lesser evil. We fight our way through them.'

Before anyone could argue, he had leapt forward and beheaded the first dead-walker with a downward slash of his sword-blade. Laura immediately loosed an arrow into a second. Jon joined them, swinging the sledgehammer. At first they seemed to be cutting a swath through the dead-walkers. Triumph showed on Jon's face.

'Just like the computer game!' he cried, his face flushed.

Gradually however the press of the undead started to force them back. The demons felt no pain, no fear. His smile vanished.

'Listen,' cried Laura. 'The fire-demons, I can hear them. They're close.'

So close she could smell them as well. Brimstone filled the air.

Jon swung his hammer in desperation but the dead-walker that had been his target clung to it and wrestled him to the ground.

'Jon!'

The creatures were pressing forward, keen to devour him. He flinched at their slimy embrace. Phoenix hacked at the closest of the creatures, then stood over Jon protectively, swinging his sword.

'Laura, use your arrows against the fire-demons. Try to hold them off.'

She loosed her arrows one after another at the shapes blazing in the darkness, but nothing stopped their advance. Her shafts merely fell to the floor as so much grey ash.

'Phoenix,' she cried, 'the quiver is almost empty, and they're still coming. I don't know how to stop them.'

Jon got to his knees and felt for his hammer. An oily, skinless hand seized his and started tugging at it. Phoenix was only just able to fend off the attacker.

'It's over, isn't it?' Jon croaked. 'We're finished.'

Phoenix shook his head furiously, but in his heart of hearts he knew it was true.

6

'Phoenix!'

The fire-demons were spilling from the tunnel behind him. Laura shot an arrow but it burned away the moment it struck its target.

'What do I do?'

'Fall back.'

Phoenix, Jon and Laura instinctively stood back to back, facing the enemies that encircled them. Their predicament had reduced them to what they were, three scared teenagers surrounded by creatures from their worst nightmares.

'Phoenix,' said Laura, 'do something.'

He glared at her.

'There's nothing I can do. What do you want, a miracle?'

And miracle is exactly what he got. As the fire-demons crouched ready to pounce, there was a shout from above.

'Take the rope!'

'Andvar!'

The giant warrior was bloodied but alive.

'How?'

'Enough questions, watchman. Take the rope.'

A knotted rope was dangling from the shelf of rock several metres above their heads. Jon and Laura seized it eagerly, while Phoenix took up the rear swinging his sword at the advancing demons.

'Now you,' cried Andvar. He was standing, feet planted apart, with the rope wrapped round his back and shoulders.

Phoenix gripped the rope and allowed himself to be hauled out of the reach of the roaring demons. Moments later he was clawing himself up onto the shelf of rock.

'How did you find us?'

'Later,' said Andvar.

Close up, his battle scars were more evident. He bore a wound which ran the length of his face and part of his left ear had been cut off.

'Are you all right?' asked Phoenix.

'I'll live to slay my share of monsters,' said Andvar. 'Follow me.'

He plunged into a tunnel. Once inside the cramped space, Jon and Laura were coughing and squinting. The smell of brimstone was overpowering. The fire-demons were coming.

'We must move fast,' said Andvar. 'Don't let me out of your sight.'

That was easier said than done. Even the faintest speck of light had disappeared. They could scarcely distinguish Andvar in the surrounding darkness. They were following a black shape in the blackness.

'Andvar?'

'I'm still here. Now, get ahead of me. The way is straight.'

'What are you going to do?' asked Laura.

'Don't worry about me, I'm not ready to sacrifice myself quite yet. I'll be with you presently.'

As they moved forward, they could hear him grunting and straining.

'What do you think he's doing?'

Then the answer was clear. There was a harsh, grating sound. He was blocking the tunnel with large rocks.

'That will hold them for a few minutes,' he said, catching up. 'Now, we are nearly free.'

Laura turned the next corner and squealed with delight. Light flooded into the tunnel.

'I never thought I'd be so glad to see snow,' she exclaimed as she stepped into the winter sunshine.

'Keep going,' said Andvar. 'Once we find a vantage point we can defend, we will rest.'

Their climb led them to an exposed peak, from which they could see Loki's army.

'Well,' Phoenix demanded, 'so how *did* you escape?'

'The dragon saved me,' said Andvar.

'You found a friendly dragon?' gasped Laura.

'Hardly,' chuckled Andvar. 'Its fiery breath killed most of my companions, but the blast hurled me down a deep shaft. I found myself falling. The only other survivor somehow evaded the demons and found me clinging to an outcrop of rock. He used this rope to save me, just as I used it to rescue you.'

'So where is he now?'

'Dead,' said Andvar with a sigh. 'The fire-demons slew him. He gave his life to save mine.'

He stared at the milling demons.

'I reached Halfdan.'

'And where is he now?'

'Still in the cavern, surrounded by Loki's fighters.'

Andvar looked into Phoenix's eyes.

'He asked me to go after you. He says you can summon the gods.'

'It's in the legend,' said Phoenix. 'I blow the Gjall horn.'

'That's it,' said Andvar. 'That's it. We must call down the gods from lofty Asgard. The seeds of this world's end were sown at its birth. Beyond the clamour of Ragnorak, Evil plans to rise.'

Phoenix looked at his friends. They knew more than Andvar how true that was. The Gamesmaster was about to take on human form. Soon he would be able to use the game to travel the worlds. He too would make the numbers dance. Nowhere would be safe from the madness that was already engulfing the nine worlds of the Northmen. The world they had left, and in which they had grown up, would be wasted just like this one.

'But what can we do to stop him?'

'Loki has eluded us,' said Phoenix. 'That bit of unfinished business will have to wait. We must return to the Berserkers. If I am to blow the Gjall horn, then we have to reach the foot of the rainbow bridge. There we will summon the gods to battle.'

Laura felt her insides lurch.

'And how do we do that?'

Phoenix turned his face to the wind. In the absence of Andreas' voice in his own head, he had to find the answer in himself.

'I will discover a way. I've got to. My whole life has been leading up to this moment.'

He stretched out his arm to indicate the battlefield.

'Ragnarok is more than a battle: it's my destiny.'

7

Finding Halfdan's Berserkers wasn't much of a challenge. As they descended the mountain, the warriors poured from a cave-mouth with a shattering roar. Phoenix's attention was drawn to the huge barrels slung between some of the horsemen's saddles. They had been carrying them ever since Skaldheim. Water barrels, he had assumed.

'Andvar found you,' said Halfdan.

'Andvar saved our lives,' said Laura.

'That was my intention,' Halfdan replied. 'Did you discover the Evil One?'

'No,' said Phoenix. 'He is too well protected. To reach him, we need the help of the gods.'

'The Gjall horn,' said Halfdan.

'Yes.'

'It lies yonder,' said Halfdan. 'There where Bifrost begins. There is a cave beneath the snow.'

'But how do we reach it?'

'We attack Loki's army. If we can draw them off, you will be able to reach the horn and summon the gods.'

'The odds are too great,' said Phoenix. 'You'll be cut to pieces.'

'There is no other way.'

'But it's such a waste,' said Laura.

'She's right,' said Phoenix.

Halfdan smiled grimly.

'It is written in the runes that out of the ashes of Ragnarok there will rise a new world, more beautiful, more hopeful, more precious than this one. If it costs our lifeblood to bring it about then the sacrifice will have been worthwhile.'

Phoenix thought of his parents watching on the computer back home. He thought of the millions of unsuspecting buyers of the game.

The sacrifice is worthwhile.

'Wait until you hear our battle-cries,' said Halfdan, 'then move quickly. Skirt their ranks and don't look for a fight.'

He looked back and waved farewell, before vanishing into the snow-glare. Phoenix noticed that Jon was trembling.

'What's wrong?'

'I don't know. It all seems so hopeless.'

'Nothing is ever hopeless,' said Phoenix. 'You heard what Halfdan said.'

The words came from part of him that had been gradually coming to life for months, ever since he first played the game.

'Ragnarok is not annihilation, but death before rebirth. The great cycle of life will turn again. The Berserkers' struggle will not have been in vain. The many worlds will be made safe. This I promise as watchman and Legendeer.'

A hoarse roar rose into the still air.

'That's Halfdan's attack,' said Phoenix.

He set off up the slope.

'He won't be fighting for nothing. I'm going to summon the gods. Who's with me?'

Jon and Laura exchanged tired looks, then trudged after him. While Phoenix, Jon and Laura struggled up the frozen mountainside, Loki's army massed in front of the Berserkers, readying themselves for the impact of the Northmen's charge. As the outnumbered warriors closed on the demon army, Loki barked his threats:

'A hundred miles this plain stretches in length and a hundred miles in width. Before this day is out, Halfdan, blood will stain every inch of it.'

A dismal roar greeted Loki's words, causing the earth to quake beneath the Berserkers' feet. When the battle cries finally subsided Halfdan's voice could be heard again, hoarse and almost breaking, but defiant.

'We are not afraid to die, Evil One, and know this, every one of my men who gives his life this day will take ten, a dozen – aye – even more of your odious brood with him.'

Loki raised his sword and laughed out loud.

'Look upon my demon army, Northman,' he roared, indicating the ocean of ghoulish creatures. 'You could each slay many thousands and there would be enough left to overwhelm you. My ferocious, unthinking disciples stretch to the furthest horizon.'

Halfdan knew the truth of Loki's words. A shaft of despair pierced his heart. But the Jarl of the Berserkers didn't speak again. Casting aside any concern for pain or survival, he collided with the front row of the demon army and allowed his great battle-axe Bloodletter do his talking. Andvar was at his right hand and laid about him with a terrible power, reaping the heads of the dead-walkers like corn.

'Surt,' Loki commanded. 'Let loose your fiery legions.'

The fire-demons swept towards the Berserkers. Seeing the dead-walkers stepping back to let them through, Halfdan raised a gloved hand.

'Now!'

At his command, twenty pairs of horsemen rode forward. Between them they were carrying huge barrels.

'Have you worked it out yet, Mischief-Maker?' Halfdan cried. 'Have you guessed what we have for you?'

The horsemen swept in a broad arc to the top of a rise and released the barrels which came rolling towards the fire-demons. The flaming ghouls were without fear, driven only by a soulless hatred for mortal men. But their very heartlessness and fearless battle-rage were their undoing. The moment the barrels hit the rocks that jutted everywhere out of the blanket of snow they burst open, showering the demons with icy water.

'Water,' spluttered Loki, seeing his regiment of fire extinguished in one daring movement. 'Where . . . ?'

'Why, we used what lay all around us, demon-lord,' chuckled Andvar. 'We simply melted the snow.'

The water worked like salt on slug, making the fire-demons wither and perish.

'You will pay for that,' cried Surt, their master. 'I will return with the rest of my army and destroy you.'

He jabbed a flaring hand in Halfdan's direction.

'No trick will save you then. I will tear your flesh from your bones with my own hands.'

So began a furious fight on the frozen ground: demons, goblins, dragons and Hela's living corpses swarming around the Berserkers' positions. Crows fell from the sky to peck and harry them. But Halfdan's men held their ground, his archers thinning the enemy ranks and his swordsmen and axemen hacking down wave after wave of the demon army.

'Help us, Odin!' roared the Berserkers as they steeled themselves against yet another maelstrom of screaming, clawing demons.

But their weapons were no longer scything down the enemy with the same concentrated fury and the crows' beaks left them bloodied and weary. And as they tired Loki's masses poured forward in ever-increasing numbers.

'How long can we hold them?' panted Andvar, taking a swipe at a flapping crow.

Halfdan tore open a screeching goblin with his battle-axe.

'I don't know,' he said grimly. 'May destiny grant us a little more time. We must stand our ground until the Gjall horn sounds.'

It was only then, as the Berserkers struggled to hold back the press of hideous bodies, that Loki spoke.

'Where is he, Halfdan? Where is the Legendeer, the one you call Heimdall?'

Halfdan drove his sword through yet another dead-walker.

'You'd love to know, wouldn't you, Evil One? Well, this is one Northman who will not tell you.'

Loki turned his eyes towards Bifrost.

'You've no need to, Lord of Skaldheim. I see through your ruse.'

Without another word, he sprang onto the back of his eagle. Accompanied by a flight of cawing crows, he headed for the foot of the rainbow bridge.

8

In his haste to reach the Gjall horn, Phoenix had outpaced Jon and Laura. He was far ahead of them when Laura called to him.

'Not so fast. We can't keep up.'

'You must,' Phoenix shouted back against the gusting wind. 'The battle is almost lost. There's no time to lose.'

He paused to look down at the plain below. He could just make out Halfdan's men. He admired their courage, but he had no doubt about the battle's outcome. The Berserkers were being pressed back on three sides and only Halfdan's archers were preventing them being totally surrounded. The moment their quivers were empty Loki's horde would engulf them.

'Hurry!' Phoenix yelled.

He scrambled up the slope, fighting with all his strength against the sliding snow and the driving wind. Sometimes he had to go on all fours, sometimes he sank waist-deep in the drifts

This is my destiny.

To fight him to a standstill.

'Hurry!'

He looked back to check on their progress. He was about to speak when he saw a grey-white object detach itself from the demon army and begin speeding towards him.

'What's that?'

Laura and Jon stopped to look. Phoenix set off again towards the cave. He knew what it was.

'It's him.'

'Adams?'

'Adams, Loki, whatever you want to call him now. I'm not sure there is even a trace of his human self left. They are part of the Gamesmaster now.'

The three of them drove forward, hearts hammering, their breath catching in their throats.

'Phoenix,' cried Laura. 'He's almost here.'

Phoenix didn't even glance back. He fixed his eyes on the mouth of the cave where the Gjall horn was kept.

My destiny.

With one final effort he stumbled inside. Almost immediately he felt a rush of air above his head.

'So,' said Loki from his perch on the eagle's back. 'You thought to outwit me. A mortal with the temerity to compare himself to my dark power. You have failed, Legendeer. The victory is mine.'

Phoenix saw the Gjall horn hanging from the wall.

'You will never reach it,' said Loki.

Phoenix slashed with his longsword but the eagle carried Loki out of harm's way.

'I expected better,' Loki sneered, 'from one who has thwarted me twice before.'

Phoenix's blood ran cold.

Thwarted ***me***.

He had been right about the spirit seeking a body. This wasn't Loki, not even Adams playing a part. This was the Gamesmaster himself.

The Gamesmaster ran his hands over his chest and arms.

'I live at last. Can you imagine how long I have waited for this moment? I am *free*.'

'And Adams? What's happened to him?'

'What do you think, Legendeer? He thought he was my disciple, but I don't need anyone. His body was merely the chrysalis within which I could grow, steal through the pathways of his mind, take on life.'

Phoenix saw Laura and Jon arriving at the cave mouth.

'He welcomed me,' the Gamesmaster said, 'rejoiced as my spirit took root within every fibre of his being. He thought he was the chosen one.'

'Steve,' cried Phoenix. 'Can you still hear me? Fight back against him.'

The Gamesmaster shook his head.

'A teenage boy,' he said, 'fight me? I am the Gamesmaster, the demon-lord. Week after week I trained Adams, taught him how to think, to fight, to be. He thought I was preparing him for something great, to become my disciple. But what is greater than giving birth to your master?'

Phoenix stared into the eyes of the Evil One. They were points of cold anger. He could see nothing of Adams in them, but he had to try.

'Steve, you've got to resist. For him to come to life, you have to die. Do you understand? He is killing you. Fight him!'

His pleading was useless.

'Do you know the term "pyrrhic victory", Legendeer? One gained at too great a cost. That is all you have ever won. In the Minotaur's lair, Medusa's cave, the Vampyr's lair. What you thought were triumphs were but stepping stones to defeat. Now that I have physical form, all is possible.'

Phoenix saw Jon stealing closer until he was standing immediately beneath the hovering eagle.

'Do you understand now, Legendeer? The game is won. We are two sides of the same coin. We share a power. I too can make the numbers dance. But while I was trapped in spirit form, I was unable to use my powers. Now that I am reborn I can open the gateway between the worlds. My time has come at last.'

Phoenix was paralysed, but one person sprang into action, undeterred by the Gamesmaster's boasts. Jon seized the opportunity to hurl his sledgehammer at the underside of his mount. Startled, the eagle pitched and almost dislodged its passenger.

'You were right,' Jon cried, thrilled by the effects of his throw. 'You did make everything possible. But you're no longer a phantom.'

Phoenix stared.

What does he think he's doing?

Jon rushed forward and drove his sword into the great bird's wing. Bright blood spurted and stained the feathers. Its shriek was terrible to hear. The Gamesmaster looked startled, strangely vulnerable even. While he was fighting to regain control of the threshing eagle, Phoenix raced for the Gjall horn and sounded a blast that echoed across the frozen plain.

He had summoned the gods.

9

'I will see your blood stain the ground,' yelled the Gamesmaster.

'Blood there will be, Gamesmaster, but it will not be ours alone. Look at the sky.'

The clouds above began to boil and the Valkyries, warrior-maidens from Valhalla, raced across the sky, their battle-shields flashing blue and black, the colour of storm and raincloud. In their wake came the Asa-gods thundering down the rainbow bridge, Bifrost. A flight of ravens led the way. Thunder bellowed as Asgard emptied its garrison, and when the armies met the crash threatened to burst the eardrums.

'It's begun,' said Phoenix. 'The final struggle.'

Then something marvellous happened. As Odin led the charge over Bifrost, the crows that had plagued the Berserkers, pecking and stabbing with their beaks, lifted their siege and wheeled away to the north.

'It's Odin,' said Phoenix. 'He has sent his ravens to reclaim the sky.'

And there were the giant birds, driving away the crows. At the sight, the Berserkers gave a roar of defiance and raced to meet the Asa-gods. Their joint charge carved a deep wedge into the ranks of the demon army and, for a brief moment, it looked as if they would carry the day with one magnificent attack. But as they hacked their way through, their onslaught slowed, bogged down in hand-to-hand fighting with the numberless enemy.

'Phoenix,' Laura began, her voice full of horror. 'Can they win?'

'I don't know,' said Phoenix.

He saw Odin, his golden helmet flashing, cutting his way towards the Fenris wolf, and Thor wielding his hammer Mjollnir. He glimpsed blind Hodur, the unwitting killer of his brother Balder, lashing out with his axe, and right beside him the giant Andvar striking at the demons.

Halfdan wiped his brow, exhausted by the effort of beating back the march of Evil that was unstoppable.

'But who cares?' said Phoenix, drawing his sword. 'We've got to help. We have to join Halfdan.'

That's when Phoenix saw the Berserkers' leader go down, crumpling beneath a mass of dead-walkers.

'No,' he cried.

But Halfdan was up, hauled to his feet by Andvar. As Phoenix, Laura and Jon struggled through the snowdrifts the clash continued.

'Rally to the raven banner,' roared Halfdan, daring any among his comrades to disagree. Seeing even the gods mired in the bloody stalemate, he was fighting a battle with his own despair, but he could hear the great banner snapping in the gale and drew strength from the sound. His cause was a worthy one.

'Make your shield-wall, warriors, stand fast and lay about the foe with sword and battle-axe,' he urged. He could feel the presence of Andvar, yet there was a great sadness in the air. Something was wrong.

'I sense that your hearts are heavy with grief, brother.'

'Our archers have fallen,' said Andvar, 'torn apart by wolves. There is no cover for our front-fighters. Our ranks are thinning, and we are completely surrounded.'

Halfdan cursed loudly and forced himself to fight even more stubbornly. He was everywhere, shoring up his faltering line. He towered above his men, helmet blazing, axe flashing. He was their inspiration.

'What keeps you going, ring-giver?' asked Andvar admiringly. 'Even the gods grow weary of the slaughter.'

'The watchman has fulfilled his destiny,' said Halfdan. 'The gods fight at our side. Hope for the future strengthens my arm.'

'There is no hope for us,' said Andvar, shearing off the head of a dead-walker. 'The odds are overwhelming.'

'Are these truly the words of my bravest comrade?' Halfdan asked. 'Look into your heart, Andvar. Destiny is a cruel master. We knew the outcome of this day before we began. None of us will live to see the good we do. But does it matter, old friend, so long as we take our stand against the enemy?'

Still the furious onslaught continued, swords and axes clashing, wolves baying and the fiery breath of the dragons hissing on the wind.

'Put aside your doubts,' said Halfdan. 'You have taken your stand against Evil. Don't give in now.'

Andvar clasped his hand.

'We die for the future,' he said.

'Never surrender,' roared Halfdan to his men, cracking the skull of a pouncing wolf. 'Fight to the last man.'

He looked around and managed a smile. His allies were true as steel. But hide it as he tried, he was plagued by doubts. Was the watchman, this Legendeer, strong enough to face the demon-lord? He wondered how the boy was faring.

Hope and apprehension filled him at the thought of the Evil One.

'Halfdan,' cried Andvar. 'Dead-Biter.'

Halfdan felt the earth pitch and roll beneath his feet like a vessel at sea.

'Where?'

'To our right.'

He heard the serpent's hiss and the thunder of Thor's hammer. An ancient prophecy was being fulfilled. God and serpent met in a furious fight. Thor finally split Dead-Biter's skull with his hammer Mjollnir. But in the moment of his victory, as Thor slew the serpent, its poisonous breath overwhelmed him.

The thunder god staggered back nine paces and died, and upon his fall a tremendous groan resonated through the defenders' ranks.

'No slackening,' yelled Halfdan, his voice hoarse. 'Arm yourselves against the horror. Fight on, for Asgard, for the future.'

He held up the raven banner so that it could be seen by all, snapping in the bitter wind. The war-god Tyr struggled against the wolf-dog Garm until both fell from their wounds. The bloody fight was resulting in the destruction of both sides.

'Are you sure your young watchman can fulfil his destiny?' panted Andvar.

'He will,' Halfdan answered, refusing to listen to his own doubts. 'He will because he must. Out of this slaughter will come renewal, a future cleansed of Evil.'

But even before the words had left his lips, the fortunes of his beleaguered men suffered another reverse. The Gamesmaster was cutting his way through the Berserkers' ranks bellowing his death-lust.

'Who will face me?' he raged, hacking at the shield-wall.

'I'll go up against you, Mischief-Maker,' said Halfdan. 'For Asgard and for the future of all.'

'Future,' snarled the Gamesmaster. 'And what future is that, Forkbeard? Look about you, your ranks are stretched to breaking point while my demon army teems about you like an ocean.'

His eyes were staring, his gaunt features streaked with blood, his hair wound into stiff horns.

'Before long you will lie at my feet, begging for your life.'

'I shall not beg, Evil One. If die I must, then I do it with a glad heart. I will rejoice to have died a hero's death.'

'Then fight,' said the Gamesmaster.

Halfdan hurled himself forward, swinging his battle-axe Bloodletter in a great arc about his head. Such was the ferocity of his attack that the Gamesmaster fell back, shaken to his core. But he soon rallied, hacking with his murderous longsword. It was Halfdan's turn to give ground, deep cuts oozing blood, weakening him. Andvar made as if to take the wounded Halfdan's place, but his war-chief pushed him aside.

'Give way, Andvar,' he said. 'This is my fight.'

Halfdan raised Bloodletter and strode forward swinging the great battle-axe.

'Do your worst, Jarl of Skaldheim,' said the Gamesmaster.

'I need no urging,' yelled Halfdan. 'I wield this weapon to seek vengeance for all my fallen brothers.'

The Gamesmaster swung his longsword but the blade clashed against Halfdan's axe-head.

'Yield,' said the Gamesmaster, 'and I will make your death a quick one.'

'Make it as slow as you like,' retorted Halfdan. 'Victory in arms will be yours, much good that it may do you.'

Halfdan smashed the battle-axe into the Gamesmaster's shield. As the axe started to fall, the Gamesmaster thrust upwards with a thin dagger he had concealed in his sleeve. The blackness of death came upon Halfdan.

'No!' cried Andvar.

With tears streaming down his cheeks he looked around the battlefield. Only a handful of Berserkers and gods were left standing, surrounded by the monstrous tide of the demon army. He saw the black dragon Nidhog, master of his kind, soaring through the air with rustling, night-black wings, blasting the earth with fire.

'The day is lost,' he murmured. 'All that is left is to die sword in hand.'

He rested a hand briefly on another warrior's shoulder.

'Afraid?' he asked.

His comrade shrugged.

'We die together in the hope of a brighter future,' the exhausted Berserker said. 'Comrades united beneath the raven banner.'

Andvar smiled, then draped the raven banner round his own shoulders and plunged into the fray. The warriors who were left followed him into the most bitter fighting.

10

Phoenix slumped to his knees. With Jon and Laura he was high above the battle. A sheer face of rock stood between them and the triumphant demon army. What could he do now that Halfdan's army was destroyed and the gods were defeated?

'What's gone wrong?' asked Jon. 'This can't be true. The Gamesmaster has won.'

'No,' said Phoenix, plunging his fists into the snow. 'It can't be true.'

'Just look down there,' cried Laura. 'Look at that carnage. We've lost. Now that the Gamesmaster has taken physical form, he can do anything.'

Phoenix stared at her.

'What did you say?'

Laura looked puzzled.

'You mean that he can do anything.'

'No,' said Phoenix. 'The other part.'

He remembered the look on the Gamesmaster's face when Jon attacked the eagle. How vulnerable he looked, how *human*.

'That's it! When he took Adams' body he took the part of Loki. You must have felt it, Jon. He can hurt, he can kill, but he can also be hurt. Now that he is flesh and blood *he can be killed*. We can destroy him.'

Laura pounced on his words.

'You mean it? There's still a chance.'

'More than a chance. If I'm right, the Gamesmaster can use the legends, but he can't break their basic rules. If he takes Loki's form, then he accepts Loki's destiny. One part of the legend remains to be fulfilled. Loki is meant to be destroyed by Heimdall. By me. But I don't know how to reach him.'

'Listen,' said Laura.

It was obvious from a deafening roar that the last warrior had fallen. Phoenix knew immediately what it meant. It was as if his heart had stopped beating.

Goodbye, men of the raven banner.

Laura seized Phoenix's wrist and looked at the points bracelet: 'This isn't right. The battle is lost, but the score is rising!'

Phoenix was about to offer an explanation when he heard a familiar voice.

'You've lost, Legendeer,' came a familiar voice. 'Soon the gateway will open and your world will lie defenceless at my feet. My demon army will pour from every computer-screen.'

It was the Gamesmaster. He had arrived fresh from the battle, surrounded by dead-walkers. He had outflanked Phoenix by climbing the slope above them before descending. The three teenagers turned with their backs to the cliff's edge. They were trapped.

'The warriors of the raven are no more,' said the Gamesmaster. 'They lie annihilated on Vigrid Plain. Soon dark Surt will unleash a sea of flame and this land will be razed. You have lost, Legendeer. The final victory is mine.'

'Is it true?' asked Laura.

Phoenix didn't answer.

'It is pointless to resist,' said the Gamesmaster. 'Your allies all lie dead. Your powers are as nought compared to mine. It is time to face facts, Legendeer. All your efforts have been futile. It's over, Legendeer.'

The Gamesmaster turned to go.

'Finish them,' he said to his monstrous followers.

'Finish me yourself,' said Phoenix.

'What?'

'You heard me,' said Phoenix. 'Don't leave it to them. Do it yourself. Or are you afraid of the legends? Do you still wonder whether Heimdall might defeat Loki after all?'

That the Legendeer might defeat the Gamesmaster.

'Well?'

Phoenix drew his sword.

'You're nothing,' said the Gamesmaster.

'I am the one you are destined to fight at the end of the world,' Phoenix reminded him. 'What's wrong? Afraid?'

'Of you? You have a sense of humour, Legendeer.'

The Gamesmaster drew his own sword and charged at Phoenix. Instinct jerked him back and he narrowly escaped the Evil One's sword-thrust.

'Not so easy, is it?' Phoenix taunted.

But the Gamesmaster's blade flashed again, lightning-quick, and Phoenix felt the rush of air as the killing edge narrowly missed him.

'Not so difficult either,' retorted the Gamesmaster.

He thrust downward as Phoenix's knees buckled.

'Phoenix!' cried Laura.

The Gamesmaster came on slashing with his bloodstained sword. His savage power smashed all the strength out of Phoenix's limbs. Phoenix could only raise his blade, doing his best to fend off the muscle-wasting blows. Three times the Gamesmaster's sword was held over him. Three times Phoenix squirmed out of the way. But the fourth blow hit its mark, slicing through the flesh of his underarm. He winced with pain and dropped his sword.

'And you thought I was afraid,' sneered the Gamesmaster, holding Phoenix's hair with one hand and pressing the sword's edge to his throat. 'Of *you*.'

Phoenix's fingers were clawing at the snow, trying to reach his sword.

'Say goodbye to your friends.'

But Phoenix wasn't ready for goodbyes. He remembered what Jon had said.

By taking physical form, you've made yourself vulnerable.

I can hurt you.

At long last I can hurt you.

Phoenix felt the sharp edge of the sword under his hand. There was no time to feel for the hilt. Instead he gripped the blade itself, crying out as blood spilled through his fingers.

'You're forgetting something,' he yelled, almost choking on the pain. 'This is the myth-world. We are all playing a part. You are Loki . . .'

He drove the sword into Loki's boot. He felt the electric shock of his enemy's agony.

'. . . and I am Heimdall . . .'

He threw his arms round the Gamesmaster, pulled him to the ground.

'It is my destiny to destroy you.'

Both bleeding from their wounds, they rolled down the slope to the cliff's edge.

'Phoenix,' warned Laura, 'you're too close.'

But the warning went unheeded. For a moment boy and demon fought on the very brink of disaster. Then when everything seemed frozen in time, they pitched forward and fell.

11

With Phoenix gone there was no longer a threat from the dead-walkers. The moment the Gamesmaster disappeared from sight, they became little more than statues. For several minutes Jon and Laura stood side by side staring down the sheer precipice. Their pinched faces were a mixture of horror and bewilderment. Where was Phoenix? Was he . . . ? They were both too shocked to put the question into words. In the distance they could see the demon army celebrating their victory. In their midst stood the fire-demon Surt. The two youngsters remembered the prophecy of Ragnarok.

'We've got to move,' said Laura. 'Fire. The Northland will be cleansed by fire.'

There was little time. They half-climbed, half-slid down an icy slope to the plain. Looking around cautiously, they started to pick their way gingerly through the ranks of the dead. They found the torn and broken body of Halfdan Forkbeard first. Andvar was away to their right.

'What a waste,' said Laura. Then she called out, 'Phoenix.'

There was no reply.

'You have to be here,' she said.

She looked at the precipice from which Phoenix and the Gamesmaster had plunged.

'You've got to be.'

She searched ever more feverishly and impatiently, stepping

over the corpses of men and demons alike. She moved in circular sweeps, but still there was no sign.

'Where are you?'

He should be here, either standing waiting for them, or broken under the raven sky.

'Phoenix!'

In the distance, the burning had begun. A sea of red flame was sweeping across the battlefield. Jon turned to look.

'The dusk of the gods,' he murmured.

Everything felt so final. Were they going to perish here too? Were there no winners on this terrible plain?

'Phoenix, please.'

She could hear the roar of the great fire, the crackle of the bodies as they were consumed. Every instinct was telling her to get away, to flee for her life. Then she saw it, the body of the Gamesmaster. She looked down at his face. The features were softer now. She could see Adams in them.

'But where's Phoenix?'

She searched frantically, but there was no body.

'Laura,' Jon yelled, his voice flying up on the wind. 'We've got to go.'

'I can't leave without him,' Laura said tearfully.

'There's nothing more we can do,' said Jon. 'We've just got to hope Phoenix made it. The game is won. Somewhere the gateway must be open, I just know it. Do you understand? We can go home. We've just got to find it. If we stay here we'll be killed.'

The fire was coming closer.

'We have to go now. We've got to run.'

'Run, run, run,' echoed the hills.

The prophecy had come true. The sun was darkening at high noon, the heavens and the earth had turned red with blood. The moon was lost in darkness and the stars had vanished from the sky. Fire was enveloping the land, black smoke wreathing the mountain tops.

'The gateway, Laura,' said Jon. 'We have to find it.'

'The end has come,' Laura murmured. 'Ragnarok.'

But it was the end only of this world.

'Look,' cried Jon. 'There, the gateway is open.'

There it was, a golden portal of light imprinted with silver numerals.

'We've done it, Laura. We can go home.'

Laura looked at the gateway, then at the tidal wave of roaring fire. She examined the footprints on the snow in front of the gateway. Did they belong to Phoenix? Had he opened it for her? And if so, where was he now?

'What about Phoenix?'

'We have to go,' said Jon. 'If he's alive he'll find us.'

The fire was almost upon them. Acrid smoke was stinging Laura's eyes and clogging he throat. She cast one more desperate glance over the carnage of the battlefield, then her mind was made up.

'Let's go home,' she said.

12

Two weeks later Laura Osibona was crossing the road when she saw a familiar figure. Her heart missed a beat.

'Phoenix, is that you?'

She hurried to the kerb, hesitated for a moment, then rushed to him, throwing her arms round him and clinging to him.

'Phoenix, you're alive!'

She could hardly believe her eyes. So much had happened in the last fortnight: her parents' endless questions, the police investigation, the publicity. Everybody was talking about Phoenix's disappearance, and linking it to that of Steve Adams. Each day that had passed had made her more certain he was dead.

'Does this mean you're back?'

Phoenix smiled thinly.

'For good? No.'

'Then why are you here?'

'I want you to do something for me.'

'Of course, anything.'

'I want you to call on Mum and Dad, to tell them you've seen me and that I'm all right.'

Laura frowned.

'But why not tell them yourself?'

Phoenix shook his head.

'I'm not putting them or myself through it. They'd only beg

me to stay. It would be too upsetting for us all. No, it's better this way.'

'But Phoenix, it's crazy. What's stopping you from coming home?'

'The Gamesmaster.'

They walked together through the trees.

'The Gamesmaster? But he's dead. I saw his body. We won, didn't we?'

Phoenix watched a sheet of newspaper skipping down the path, blown by the wind.

'Did we?'

'Of course we did. Magna-com has gone out of business, completely bankrupt. It's caused quite a scandal. *Warriors of the Raven* never made it to the market. *The Legendeer* trilogy has been withdrawn from the shelves. It's over, Phoenix, it really is.'

Phoenix stopped and turned towards her. He shook his head.

'No, it isn't over.'

'What do you mean?'

'Just that. The body you saw was Adams. Remember what the Gamesmaster said. Steve was a vehicle, something he used. All I did was destroy the body. The spirit lives.'

'I don't believe it. I won't. He died in that fall.'

'Who are you trying to convince?' asked Phoenix. 'Yourself?'

Laura held his hands.

'You can't throw your life away on a wild goose chase. I tell you, he's gone. Phoenix, you've won.'

His face was hard, impenetrable. She knew immediately that her words were falling on deaf ears.

'No, he's out there somewhere, preparing.'

He was already looking past her, as if fixing his attention on a world beyond her.

'But where, Phoenix, where have you been?'

'You should see it, Laura. So many worlds, they just go on and on. Every myth, every legend, every strange story that has haunted the human imagination, they exist. Anything can happen, any dream can come true. It isn't just nightmares any more. It's so wonderful.'

He leaned his forehead against hers for a moment.

'You could come with me. I could show you.'

Laura smiled:

'This isn't about the Gamesmaster, is it? It's about you as well. You don't *want* to come home.'

She gave him a look that cut through him like a knife, then gently withdrew her hands.

'You've made your choice, Phoenix. I think we always knew what it would be. But I belong here. This is my world.'

Phoenix lowered his eyes.

'It's not mine, Laura. It never was. For me and Andreas there was only ever one choice, one destiny. I was always going to leave it one day. For the first time in my life, I feel like I belong.'

'So you've made up your mind then, you're not coming back?'

'No, Laura, I'm not coming back. I know Mum and Dad are upset, but deep down I think they knew all along. It was my destiny.'

There seemed to be a great distance between them. The old familiarity was gone, replaced by a curious awkwardness, as if they were strangers.

'Has it been hard?' Phoenix asked. 'Trying to explain what happened?'

'The police have asked a lot of questions about your disappearance. But they can't prove foul play. They're completely baffled by the whole thing.'

'That's all I needed to know,' said Phoenix. 'So long as everybody is safe.'

'Yes, Phoenix, we're safe.'

There was an uncomfortable silence, then Laura spoke again.

'When you say you're not coming back, does that mean ever?'

Phoenix took a few steps back from her.

'Surely you know the answer to that. If I'm right, and the Gamesmaster is still alive I have to find him and put an end to him for good and all.'

Laura nodded.

'So this is the last time I will ever see you?'

'That's right. The last time.'

'Be happy then, Phoenix, and don't forget me.'

Phoenix laughed.

'After what we went through together, how could I? Listen, I have to go. You will see my parents, won't you?'

'Of course I will.'

'Thanks, it means a lot to me.'

He conjured the numbers in the air and stood in front of the gateway.

'You're sure you can't come?'

Laura shook her head.

'I'm sure.'

'Then it's goodbye.'

Without another word, he stepped into the golden portal and was gone.

'Goodbye, Phoenix,' said Laura. 'Goodbye, Legendeer.'